BAD FRIENDS

Bor                                        Seeber
began her career as an actress. Soon deciding        pull
strings safely behind the scenes, Claire forged a successful career
in documentary television, enabling her to travel the world,
glimpsing into lives otherwise unseen. Also a feature-writer for
newspapers such as the *Guardian*, *Independent on Sunday* and
the *Telegraph*, Claire now combines (furious) scribbling with
keeping a beady eye on her two young children. This is Claire's
second book. Her first, *Lullaby*, was hailed by the *Guardian* as,
'A powerful and sensitive treatment of every parent's worst nightmare'.

For further information about Claire please go to
www.claireseeber.com and visit www.AuthorTracker.co.uk for
exclusive updates.

By the same author:

*Lullaby*

# CLAIRE SEEBER

## *Bad Friends*

**AVON**

AVON

A division of HarperCollins*Publishers*
77–85 Fulham Palace Road,
London W6 8JB

www.harpercollins.co.uk

A Paperback Original 2008

1

Copyright © Claire Seeber 2008

Claire Seeber asserts the moral right to
be identified as the author of this work

A catalogue record for this book is
available from the British Library

ISBN 978-1-84756-048-3

Set in Minion by Palimpsest Book Production Limited,
Grangemouth, Stirlingshire

Printed and bound in Great Britain by Clays Ltd, St Ives plc

**Mixed Sources**
Product group from well-managed
forests and other controlled sources
www.fsc.org  Cert no. SW-COC-1806
© 1996 Forest Stewardship Council

FSC is a non-profit international organisation established to promote the
responsible management of the world's forests. Products carrying the FSC
label are independently certified to assure consumers that they come
from forests that are managed to meet the social, economic and
ecological needs of present and future generations.

Find out more about HarperCollins and the environment at
**www.harpercollins.co.uk/green**

# ACKNOWLEDGMENTS

I couldn't have finished *Bad Friends* without the love and support of some truly good friends and family. I'm lucky to have them – unlike poor Maggie.

Special thanks to lovely Bethy for reading the first draft so keenly, especially Chapter 37; and to the inimitable Flic Everett who made me strong coffee, always listened, and guessed first time around. Thanks also to the rest of the Goldsmiths 4 – Guy, Phyllice and Judy (I promise I'll get that extra chair soon).

Sincere thanks to the multi-skilled Neil White for finding the time (I don't know how!) to fill me in on police procedure; to Roberto Savoia for the Italian; to Louisa Aldridge for her superior musical knowledge, and to my great friend Becca Toms for being such a jet-setter that she knows where the stars shine and the flowers fall. Thanks to Auntie Sue for the gardening tips. (I still don't like chrysanthemums though.)

A *massive* thank you to my fantastic agent Teresa Chris who always spurs me on. To everyone at Avon, in particular my most marvellous editor, Maxine Hitchcock, and Keshini Naidoo – both of whom I'm fortunate enough, I hope, to count as friends as well as colleagues. (Kesh, I will always remember Lewisham!) Many thanks to Sara Foster and Linda Joyce for their eagle-eyed talents, and thanks also to everyone at Midas, particularly Jess Gulliver. Thank you to my father for my website. And finally to Liz Claridge, I really appreciate you being there.

Lastly, to the many friends I've made over the years in television – don't be cross. You're all great really.

For all my parents
and
in memory of my beloved Granny.
I'm running towards you (though it might take me a while).

# BAD FRIENDS

'If love is judged by most of its effects,
it resembles hate more than friendship.'

François de La Rochefoucauld – *Les Maximes*

## AFTER: DECEMBER

I am running for my life, I know that now.

The moon slips behind the clouds. Perhaps the darkness is a boon, but the shadows that fall beside me seem to mock me as I flee, as I fly down the drive from the house. Desperately my hand closes round the bunch of metal; my little finger catches on a jagged edge, I feel my flesh tear slightly, but I ignore the pain. I slide dangerously in the mud but I will not fall, will not allow it; I right myself, though my leaden legs suck me into the stony ground; they scream with every step that I should stop but I can't, I daren't. I push myself on, stumbling on and on, because they are nearer now . . . closing on me for sure . . .

I am off the gravel drive and tracking across the great wild lawn towards the wooden bridge; towards the pub where there is life. I have no time to look around; worse, I can't bear to see how long I've got.

Running for my life. I cannot get my breath; I fight for it until it sobs up through my chest like a dead man's rattle. I was fast once, really fast as a child, running for joy and for gold – but I am out of practice now, I haven't run properly for years and my bad foot hampers me. Terror drives me, terror that drips down and smothers me.

If I can just reach the pub, slam myself inside, I might be safe.

Saved. But God, why was I mad enough to think I *was* safe to come here alone?

It is too late. The car is stopping, skidding behind me, and it's like I am fastened to the house by its beam. I swing round. I have to face my hunter; I cannot stand unseeing, so exposed. The car door opens smoothly as an oily disc of moonshine slides out from behind fingers of cloud. Everything is illuminated so perfectly and I start towards the car in relief – until that smile meets me, and I actually gasp. I reel in shock like I've been punched, gut-punched where it most hurts.

'You?' I say numbly. 'It *can't* be you.'

A small and measured step towards me. 'But it is, Maggie.' And that smile, it is a flat smile. A traitor's smile. 'Weren't you expecting me?'

## BEFORE: JUNE

I breathe hard onto the coach window and watch the fug slowly spread before me. Tracing the small cloud with my finger, I write my name across the middle like a schoolgirl. My name slants; a single tear tracks downwards from the M. I make a fist and vigorously rub myself out again. My hand is damp now; I wipe it dry. Cocooned in this muggy warmth, safe for the moment from the damp, dark night, I'm struggling to stay awake. Far off in the drizzle a tiny house twinkles with beguiling light, nestled into the old church beside it like a trusting child. I gaze wistfully after the enticing image, but we are truly hurtling down the motorway now, a sleek capsule slicing the M4's black, and the house has vanished already.

I hold my breath as the teenage boy beside me bobs his head shyly, uncurls his awkward new height from beside me, scuttling with an odd spider's gait to talk to his mates up-front. Now he's gone there is some space here for my sadness, some room to acknowledge the pain of what I've just left behind. I feel utterly raw; like I've been flayed alive. I bite my lip against the grief. The truth is we've gone too far this time, I can't see a return. We said it all; we let the floodgates down and we got truly drenched.

An abandoned can of Strongbow rolls under my feet. I let the can rattle until it annoys me, hitting my heel over and over. I retrieve it, stick it firmly into the net on the seat-back in front, fighting the urge to lick my wet fingers, drying them instead on the knobbly cloth on the seat beside me. I wish I'd had the foresight to find something to kill the ache before embarking. I wish I had some wine, my iPod, a cookery book – any means, in fact, of forgetting. I wish I wasn't travelling alone. I wish I'd known I would be.

My eyelids droop inexorably until my head bangs against the thick, cool glass.

'Ouch.' I jerk up, feeling foolish, forcing myself upright again. I don't want to sleep here, don't want to surrender to the inevitable nightmares surrounded by these strangers. So I watch the little woman across the aisle, a mousey hobbit who mouths each word of *Northanger Abbey* aloud, scanning each page fervently, her pale lips oddly stiff despite their constant movement. I wish that I'd never read the book myself so that I could have that pleasure again for the first time. The couple in front lean into each other, the tops of their heads touching, their hair almost entwined as he whispers something he wants only her to hear. Right now, I think tragically, it's unlikely I'll ever feel any first pleasure again; that anyone will ever want to whisper anything to me again. I almost smile at my self-indulgence. Almost – but not quite.

Eventually I succumb to sleep, rocked by the lullaby of voices that murmur through the dim coach. I don't notice the dark-haired girl as she passes by to use the poky loo, though later the girl swears blind that she saw me in my seat – she liked my hair, the girl says (God knows, it's hard to miss). Says she knew I was a kindred spirit. But I do notice the tall man who drops his bag as he stumbles past, jolting me uncomfortably back into wakefulness. I am startled again as I glance up, befuddled. My heart stops; I think it's Alex. My heart flames with pain; my belly corkscrews.

I won't catch the man's eye, although I can sense he wants to speak. I can't bear to look at him. He might see what I'm trying so hard to hide, so I turn away again. I find my fists are clenched, nails dug deep into my palms. I twist my hair into a nervous rope, tucking it behind one shoulder. Even in my shadowy reflection I can see the red of it, the flame I can't escape and –

I see something else, something beyond the window, out there in the dark. I hold my breath in shock.

What I see is fear. Pure and undistilled, the face I gaze into is mad with it, big eyes rolling back into the brain until they are all white; a nightmare vision that is in fact quite real. The nostrils flare in panic, the huge teeth bared in a grin of frothing terror, the mane flying in the wind. For one small second snatched in old time, the time that will soon become the time before – the safe time – I find I'm not scared. I want to stretch my hand through the window and smooth the trembling flank; soothe this rearing beast. But then my own terror crashes in around me and I feel very tiny. The horse's great flailing hooves will surely pierce the coach's metal side. Frantic, I press back into my seat, trying to flatten myself against the blow.

The chance to find my voice, to shout a futile warning, has already passed. The lullaby is building to a shriek. The passengers are screaming, have begun to scream as one, because the coach is tilting, tilting on its axis until it cannot right itself again, until finally it topples. It skids across the road in hideous scraping chaos, on its side now – and still the coach keeps moving. I am level with the road; blue sparks fly up from the concrete before me as if a welder were torching the ground. Then I roll, slam hard into a body so all the wind goes out of me.

I cannot see. My hands flail at the blackness. Panting with terror, I am thrown against some metallic edge. A flash of agonising pain fills my left shoulder as I crack it on what must be the ceiling. A child cries piteously. Someone's foot grinds into my gut, a fist pummels my mouth in fear. I claw at my face as something oddly intimate drapes itself across me, a mouthful of hair that chokes and sickens me. I struggle to breathe, to let some air in. Any air. I panic that I am blind. We are still moving. Why the hell haven't we stopped moving?

A huge whump: the central reservation crumples as the coach crashes through, on its back now. It's slowing, and someone near me is screaming, they won't stop screaming, on and on –

A terrible metallic crack ends the voice. The coach is jerked by force into the fast lane. My head whips forward, then snaps back again. There's a crunch as the first van hits us head on, and folds: then the next vehicle, then the next. A hot flash up my left leg. Finally there is silence – almost silence. Just a single horn blaring into the complete darkness, then, soon after, another: a petulant electronic chorus. Closer to me, a whimpering that spreads like wildfire. We have finally stopped moving and now there is nothing. Just darkness. Just the sob of my own breath as I clasp myself and wonder: *Is this death?*

# Chapter One

'Maggie Warren?'

*I am not ready for this.*

I was about to change my mind when the girl came to get me.

I smiled. Such a false smile, it nearly cracked my face.

She was a new girl; she must have started after the –

Since I'd been away. She was confident. Supremely so. More confident than I had ever been at her age. At her stage. She was young and blonde and she walked with a swish of paper-straight hair and an empty click of the long leather boots that promised – something, I wasn't quite sure what. Exactly Charlie's type.

'I'm Daisy,' she threw over an immaculate shoulder as I tried to keep up. I was already unsettled, and her swagger unnerved me more. Did she know something I didn't? Painfully I followed her down corridors, trying to keep up, banging awkwardly through the doors, my crutches unwieldy beneath my arms. Waiting all the time for her to speak. She didn't. I searched for something to say. I contemplated myself in her position, remembering all the inanities I'd spouted since I'd started, the yards and yards of crap I'd sparkled with. The punters have earned it, I always thought. In Daisy's book, though, apparently, I hadn't. But I was different, perhaps.

I needed to fill the silence – the silence aside from the click of her dominatrix boots. She awarded me a thin smile as she pulled open the next set of doors, as she waited for me, not quite tapping her toes, with a smile that said, 'I am leading you like a lamb to your slaughter.'

I said, 'Have you worked for Double-decker before?'

She shook her sleek head. 'Came from the Beeb.'

I loathed people who said 'the Beeb'.

'Graduate trainee.'

Didn't like them much either. The graduate trainee who invariably thought they knew it all. She was remarkably flat-chested for one of Charlie's girls, I noted, as I squeezed past her.

'Oxford, you know.' Had she actually sniffed as she said it?

'Ah, Oxford.' I nodded sagely. That would explain it. Charlie had a penchant for posh.

Before I could struggle any further to be her 'friend', just like all those punters in the past had tried to be mine, we were there. *Pull yourself together, Maggie*, I told myself firmly. But my hands were actually shaking. It was so odd to be here on the other side. The green room was alive with people and light, the buzz and hum of adrenaline and apprehension. The buzz of attention, of being 'the one', the vital one. Everyone was bathed in the horrible neon light that yellowed the skin and made the eyes look dead. The banks of croissants and egg-and-cress sandwiches were already dry and curling; the orange juice was spilt in brilliant pools on the white linen. What was I doing here? Would they see inside me; know I'd sold my soul? I looked for Sally, then for the wine – but Charlie found me first.

'Maggie, darling.' The emphasis was on *darling* as he kissed me on both cheeks, his face lingering a little too long next to mine, his Ralph Lauren jumper tied in that silly knot over his breast-bone. His aftershave was as noxious as ever.

'I could murder a drink.' I was just a little too bright. I contemplated him for a moment. Then I leaned forward and asked, quietly, 'You *are* sure about this, Charlie? I'm struggling a bit with my –'

He clasped my hand, a little too hard, his hooded eyes veiled. 'Not going to back out now, are you, *darling*?'

I winced. It wasn't a question.

'Daisy, get Maggie a drink, would you? A wine.'

Kinky-boots smiled at him, tossing her hair becomingly, and fetched me a drink. Begrudgingly. She'd go far.

'What?' Now Charlie leaned in to catch my words, his hair-oil glinting in the light. Had I spoken aloud? 'Don't freak out on me, Maggie, please.'

'I'm really nervous. This is very –'

'Exciting? I knew you'd see it my way in the end.'

Did I have a choice? 'I was going to say . . . I'm really not sure that –'

'Don't be silly.' He looked impatient. 'We've been through all this. It's going to make the show.'

'What is?'

He leaned forward so only I could hear. 'And, of course, it's your absolute last chance. Don't fuck up. Again.'

'But –' I began, as Sally peered round the door. I was so glad to see her that I cried her name much too loudly. Her jolly broad face was uncharacteristically tense. She smiled back, but even her dimples were subdued. Stress was definitely winning the day.

'Babe.' Her eyes flicked round the room. 'Daisy,' she said as she found her target, gesturing frantically, 'has the anti turned up yet?'

'What anti?' I frowned.

'Oh, don't worry. They're not for you.'

I didn't believe her. My job had lost its allure some time ago, from years of deceiving those we relied on to provide the entertainment. With a nasty lurch, I realised *I* was the entertainment now. Oh God. I shook my head.

'Sal, I really don't need a row on air, Charlie promised. He called it a – a "healing" show'. Who was I kidding?

I lost Sally's attention as Renee swept into the room, pausing by the door for maximum effect. She knew exactly how to work it. There was a brief lull as heads turned, a visible wave of excitement over by the croissants. Renee didn't always bother with the guests these days, but this was a big one. A real ratings winner, if it went right: this year's greatest tragedy – just in time for BAFTA nominations. I shuddered. Sally was off again.

'Sal,' I hissed after her, 'I'm not going to have a row with anyone. Really. Charlie did promise.'

A shadow flitted across Sally's face. 'Bear with me, all right, Maggie? Daisy, get the rostrum tape of the headlines into the gallery. Now, please.' Then she was gone.

I downed my drink in one huge gulp. The headlines. That overwrought outpouring of horrified, voyeuristic – what? Delight? A glut of hysterical sympathy for our terrible misfortune on that coach. Blame, shame and sorrow. I'd managed to avoid most of them the first time. Only occasionally, when a nurse had forgotten to bin –

I skidded the memory to a necessary halt. My head was aching and I wanted a cigarette badly. I wanted to get the hell out of here even more. I must have been mad to agree to this, and right now I couldn't quite remember why I had. I inched toward the door as surreptitiously as my bad leg would let me; then Daisy was by my side.

'Okay?' She smiled that horrible thin smile again.

'I need a fag,' I tried to smile back. Someone stopped Daisy to ask where they could change and that was it; I was off down the corridor as fast as my crutches would carry me. But I wasn't going to make it outside in time so I veered off to the loo. Perhaps they wouldn't look here (they always looked here – I was hardly the first guest to hide behind a locked door). The end cubicle was free. I stood against the door and fumbled for my cigarettes. My skeletons weren't so much rattling the closet, they were smashing down the walls. My hands were trembling so much I dropped my lighter and cursed myself. Two women were discussing Renee over the divide between their cubicles. 'Such pretty hair,' one cooed. If only they knew. Normally I would have smiled, but right now I felt more like crying. Everything was out of kilter. Worst of all, I despised myself. I hadn't realised quite how hard I was going to find this. Oh God. I didn't know if I was more scared about being on the other side for the first time in my life, or of talking about – it. Digging up the past. Would they manage to mine my depths for secrets long untold? I inhaled deeply, reckoning I'd got about five more puffs before the smoke alarm went off. The women clattered out, tutting about passive smoking. My leg throbbed. Holding my fag between my teeth I searched my bag for yet more pills.

'Maggie?' The deep tones of Amanda, the floor manager. 'You in here?'

Daisy had rallied the whole bloody troupe. I held my breath but then the smoke curled up into my eyes, up my nose, and I coughed.

'Maggie? Is that you?' The relief in Amanda's voice was tangible. I held my breath.

'Ten minutes, darling.'

It was useless. 'Just coming,' I whispered miserably.

'I'll wait for you.'

'Great.' I took a last deep drag and dropped the fag into the toilet-bowl, where it died with a tiny fizz. Wiping my sweating hands on my jeans, I opened the door, awkwardly leaning round on one crutch to come out.

'Darling!' Amanda hugged me, sniffing the air. 'Smoking, you naughty girl? How are you, you poor old thing?' I felt like her pet Labrador.

'Oh, you know.'

'Look, do you want to come through now? Take the weight off your poor foot. Is it very sore?' She glanced down at my leg like it might snap. Like it might fall off. My crutch got caught on the sink, and I stumbled, just a little, wincing as Amanda grabbed my arm.

'It's okay,' I said, and I heard my own voice ringing outside my own ears. 'It's just the wine.'

She frowned.

'I'm not pissed.' Actually, that wasn't entirely true. I hadn't eaten anything apart from painkillers since God knew when. 'Don't be silly. True professional, me. But I might just have a quick top-up before –'

Amanda took my arm, gliding me swiftly through the door toward the studio. She was like a little wiry foxhound; I was clenched between her teeth and she was not going to let me get away again. I debated bashing her over the head with a crutch and making a run for it. A stumble for it.

'No time, darling.' Her headset cackled. 'In the break, maybe.' She assessed me with speed. 'You should have been to make-up.'

Daisy appeared in the corridor, checking her mobile with overwhelming indolence, and Amanda glared at her.

'That phone should be off, young lady. You're very pale, you know, Maggie.'

'Pale and uninteresting,' I joked. But nobody laughed. Anxiety set in again.

'Amanda.' This was the point of no return. I took a deep breath, pulled her to one side. 'I'm really not sure – I really don't think I can do this, actually.'

'Course you can, darling. Gosh, if I had a pound for everyone who nearly changed their minds before we started, I'd be a millionaire! And they all come off loving it. All wanting more.'

'This is me, Amanda, remember?' I muttered. The old platitudes would not wash, of that I was quite sure. Pissed or not.

She had the grace to flush slightly. 'Look, I'm going to get Kay up here with some blusher for you. And you,' she poked Daisy with her clipboard, 'get Maggie another drink for her nerves.

Stick some wine in a water-bottle. Just don't let any of the other guests see, for Christ's sake.'

We were at the studio door. We were in the studio. It was so hot in here already. Sally had taken the floor now to do her bit. The audience was laughing at some feeble joke. They loved it, lapped it up. Charlie rushed in, rushed to my side. 'All right, Mags?' No one ever called me Mags, least of all Charlie. Unless . . .

'Oh, you know,' I grimaced. 'Fine and dandy.' I imagined slapping my thigh like a principal boy.

Charlie smiled, his teeth shining brilliantly white under the bright lights. 'Just remember, darling, you're going to get closure now. And that's what you need.'

'Closure,' I repeated like a well-schooled parrot. 'What I need.'

Headlines from the days after the accident suddenly flashed up on the studio monitors. My heart began to race as I was forced to read them. The *Sun* screamed '*CRASH COACH CARNAGE*'; the *Express* enquired politely '*HORSES ON THE MOTORWAY: WHO IS TO BLAME?*'; the *Mail* screeched '*GOVERNMENT'S ROADS CAUSE TRAGEDY*'.

I tore my eyes away just as Daisy arrived with the water-bottle. I took a huge swig. Now Kay was here in a fug of sweet scent and a cloud of powder that always made me think of my mother.

'You all right, ducks?' I loved Kay. I wished she *was* my mum.

'Just a bit of blush to brighten you up, a dab of powder to stop the shine, okay? You can manage without mascara, you lucky girl.'

Pete the soundman rolled up to check my mike. He adjusted it slightly with his hairy little hands, taking pantomime care not to delve too deeply down my V-neck. He winked at me. 'Funny to see you on this side. Break a leg.' Then he backed into my plaster cast and went puce.

And now Renee arrived. She sauntered onto set like the true diva she was; and the audience went mad. They always did. They had no idea of the blood and sweat we poured out for Renee, of the tears (ours) and the tantrums (hers) and, and –

She held her hands up for quiet. Silence dropped like a blanket across the studio. Now Renee was talking. Oh, I knew exactly why she was so captivating. She drew them in – she was every man's friend, every woman's confidante, as she cast her bountiful eye upon them. Like flapping fish on a line she reeled them closer, until they were prone with ecstasy. She dropped her voice, inviting them to lean in, to share her world.

And in this trice, as I listened, as her words washed over me, I began to relax a little. I still felt the surge of adrenaline, but I could play Renee at her own game; I knew exactly how to do it. God knew I'd been in this business long enough. Once I was as naïve as our audience; a true innocent believing everything we revealed on television was for the greater good. Now I was hardened and desperate to escape this trap, so I'd done my deal with Charlie. I'd let Charlie use what he had on me, what happened before the accident, when my world had finally caved in, because I was still too weak to fight when he first came to me. I just didn't know any more if it was the right decision to have made.

But this morning I did at least know what they wanted from me and I had to give it to them. For me, it was a one-time, only-time thing, to be on this side with my make-up done and my mike tucked down my top, under my blue armchair the drink no one in the audience knew was there. I took a final swig and pushed it back with my good foot. I took a deep breath, and remembered Charlie's promise. I remembered Charlie's threats. I just had to ensure I didn't reveal too much. I thought of being on the running track at school and my dad shouting on the touchline, 'Keep going, Maggie, keep on', as I drove myself forward, and I was ready. Whatever Renee threw at me, I was ready.

Renee was delivering her final droplets of wisdom and waving her final fickle wave before she left the floor. Kay gave my hand a final squeeze and Charlie stood behind the curtain and sleeked

16

back his thick and greying hair before giving me an obsequious thumbs-up. Amanda was counting us down, the titles were up on the monitors and the tension that is a live show was zinging in the air, as palpable as the sweat that had started to run down my back. And then Renee was back on the floor, waving, the audience cheering and clapping and whistling until she snapped on the gravitas this subject would take, and hush fell.

And it was then that I noticed the girl for the first time. She was sitting two chairs away from me, on the other side of the eminent trauma psychologist Sally had wheeled on. She was stunning. A cloud of dark hair framed a little heart face and she held her arm, her plaster-casted arm, gingerly in her other hand. As if she felt my stare, she turned and blinked and smiled at me, a smile that filled those big violet eyes, eyes like bottomless buckets of emotion, and I felt very odd. Like – what do they say? Like a ghost had walked over my grave.

# Chapter Two

Fortunately for the show, Sally's anti turned up just in time to go on air. Unfortunately for him, though. The poor man never had a hope in hell. He was just fodder, pure gladiatorial bait – thrown to the hungry audience who were ready for a mauling. Simeon Fernandez, his name was. He was some kind of new-age cognitive therapist wanting to expound his theories on post-traumatic stress being purely in the mind. More to the point, he had a new book to promote. And it was he who brought Fay and me together.

Renee gave Fernandez the floor very early. His fleshy face was flushed with self-importance as he waffled on a bit about this theory and that, Renee pacing lightly behind him, her deadly stance disguised in casual lilac batwings. Lilac mohair. I tried to concentrate, staring hard at Fernandez's chins that wobbled as he spoke. I wondered if Renee's jumper was as scratchy as it looked. My leg was really aching, and my little toe had just begun to itch inside the cast when my name resounded like a whip-crack round the studio.

My head snapped up; apparently Renee was introducing me. There was really no escape now as 'Victim Maggie Warren' bounced off the walls to the sympathy of those devils in the audience. I forced a smile (though I knew Charlie would have much preferred a sob) and then Renee was on me. She came right up and took the chair beside me, perching on the very edge so she could really get to me. I tried not to lean away. Our knees were actually touching and I could smell her cloying scent, so sweet and sickly that my stomach churned – or perhaps that was the booze. I realised too late I couldn't back up in my seat without my crutch clattering loudly to the ground. I was stranded there; so near that I could count the open pores round her nose. She held my hand, and looked deep into my eyes. Her coloured contact lenses were unnaturally bright in the hideous studio light, and I stifled the urge to laugh hysterically.

'Mr Fernandez has written a book on stress,' Renee breathed at me, her Welsh lilt so soft and caring. 'He thinks it's in the mind, and we must fight to overcome it,' – Mr Fernandez nodded smugly, his chins juddering like Sunday custard in a jug – 'but, Maggie, you're testament to the fact that a terrible accident *can* utterly change your life, aren't you?'

Was I?

'Am I?'

I blinked. The muscle in my cheek twitched with an influx of adrenaline.

Renee frowned. Her pancake cracked a little. Charlie coughed most unsubtly from the sidelines. Utter silence fell; the audience leaned forward as one. They waited. I waited. Renee covered my hand kindly (she hadn't so much as shaken it in the past two years) with both of hers – and then I pulled it back quickly, suppressing an exclamation. I was sure she'd pinched me; just a tiny pinch, so tiny that no one else would know, but a pinch nevertheless. I absorbed Charlie's scowl; remembered his words the other night. I breathed deeply. Auto-drive clicked on.

'Sorry. Yes.' How alien Renee's eyes looked. Other-worldly. 'Of course it did. Has. It's turned everything on its head. I –' I paused for what must have seemed like effect, searching desperately for something sensible to say. Anything to say. 'I don't think my life will ever be the same again.'

Renee sat up in triumph. I'd come up trumps. I slumped in

my seat. God, it was hot in here. Fernandez immediately weighed in, uninvited, with how I should overcome my trauma. I was still a young woman, I mustn't give in to my weaknesses. I must believe in positive thought.

'Come on, Maggie. Stress is all in the mind, I promise you.' He looked at the audience hopefully. I looked at him mournfully. I tapped my bad leg sadly. And then I wasn't acting any longer; I was transported briefly into the heart of my own pain.

'This, though, Mr Fernandez, my damaged leg, I mean, this isn't in the mind – is it?' A bubble of misery, like an astronaut's helmet, sealed snug around my head. I must shake it off. Showing real emotion on live TV was not my intention. 'I might never walk properly again,' I murmured. 'I used to run, you know.'

The audience went wild in their seats. They were sure of Mr Fernandez's role now. He was the Wolf to my Red Riding Hood, the absolute villain on the floor, and they could rip into him as they'd been primed. I swallowed hard and milked it like I knew I must.

'I can't work. I need to have help at home,' (sort of true) 'I have nightmares.' (Painfully true. I couldn't continue on that tack.) I twisted the tissue that Renee had pressed into my hand; recovered myself just enough to go on. I cleared my throat.

'I have a bad limp, I've had to have my foot put back in plaster again because –'

A little voice chimed in. 'It's changed my life utterly too.'

Renee turned to the voice, the epitome of eager concern. 'Fay Carter, you too were on the coach that crashed that terrible night. Can you tell us exactly what happened? We can see Maggie is struggling to give us the painful facts.'

A matronly woman in the front row actually said 'Ah.' I smiled weakly, the last lot of painkillers finally kicking in. But Fay was only too glad to join the fray – like a sleek little greyhound tensed against the starting-gate, she was off. I slumped with relief. Surely I'd done enough?

I thought desperately of the drink tucked beneath my chair. I could see Amanda with her stopwatch. We must be nearing the break now, please God. I could feel myself beginning to sweat again as I flicked in and out of Fay's words. The truth was – and how Renee would have loved this, should I have cared to share it with her – the truth was, the accident was too agonising to recall.

'And I was travelling back to London to see my boyfriend, really excited, you know how it is when you haven't seen them for a while.' The audience ah-ed again. They loved a love story – though they definitely preferred a fistfight, given the choice.

'I'd just walked up and down the coach to use the loo, too much tea, you know.' She smiled up at the audience, the audience smiled fondly back. This girl knew how to work it. 'I saw Maggie there when I passed, she was asleep.' She turned her head-lamp eyes on me. 'Sleeping like a baby, you know.'

My skin prickled. I didn't remember ever having seen this girl before. But I suppose I had been – absorbed. I looked down at my hands.

'And I kind of knew then that she was my future.'

My head snapped up in horror. What?

'Call it intuition, if you like. Then I heard this woman scream, and we swerved violently. We – the coach, well, it started to tip, straight away, to go right over, you know. And that – that was it, really.' There was a tiny catch in her sweet voice. I looked down, my stomach rolling with the memory. My tissue was in tiny bits over my good knee.

'The coach just, you know, flipped, onto its back, you see, right into the other lane, you know, right into the oncoming traffic. And it wasn't till – till after that we knew three horses had got out of a field next to the motorway, somehow the fence had come down and they were on the road, poor things.'

The audience clucked with admiration at her benevolence. A little tear escaped from one thick-lashed eye and trickled slowly

21

down her porcelain skin. 'The coach-driver didn't have a chance, poor man.'

Renee asked, very quietly, 'Did he –'

Fay shook her head mournfully. 'No. He didn't make it.'

Renee clasped her hands together across that magnificent bosom. 'Sadly Fay is quite right, ladies and gentlemen. Tragic Stan Quentin didn't survive the horrific accident, along with eleven other poor souls that awful night. I'm sure I speak for all of us when I say', big pause, sad smile, small dip of head, 'each and every one of them is in our prayers.'

Frantic nodding from the audience. A few loud sniffs. Renee neatly changed angles for her close-up in Camera One.

'But does every accident have to end in doom and gloom? Well, no, because as we are about to demonstrate, even accidents can bring folk closer together.' Smooth camera change as One pulled out. 'As these young ladies will bear testament to.'

I peered into the wings to see who was about to be brought in. 'That's right,' Renee continued. 'Fay has something to say to someone very special. Daisy!' If Renee's smile became any wider, her face would explode.

Daisy flounced on now, gurning at the cameras, holding an enormous bunch of flowers. Lilies. My heart started to beat faster. Slowly Daisy handed them to Fay, milking the time she was on-camera. But Fay would be upstaged by no one; she swept up the bouquet and stepped towards my chair. I glanced behind me again as Daisy finally admitted defeat and slunk off.

'Maggie, I just want to say – you saved my life.' I stared at the glistening trail of her tears. 'I can never thank you enough.'

'Maggie.' Renee was beside me now, forcing me to stand. I dragged myself to my feet. 'What do you want to say to Fay, babes?'

'I'm really so – sorry,' I stuttered. 'But I don't know what you –'

'You saved me, Maggie. I was choking on my own blood . . . '

There was an enormous gasp of horror from the audience. Two

over-made-up teenagers in the front row looked like they were going to be sick. That would be a first on live television.

'And you reacted so quickly, you saved my life.'

Had I? Charlie had never mentioned this. 'I'm sorry, I just don't remember anything –'

Fay thrust the flowers at Renee and enveloped me in a huge hug as best she could with a plaster-casted arm, almost knocking me off my good foot. From behind the bouquet, Renee glowered at me. I'd obviously ruined the big moment. Bored of not being the centre of attention, she walked in front of us now as I tried to gently disentangle myself from a sobbing Fay. I wished fervently they'd take the lilies away. They reminded me of things I only wanted to forget.

'Isn't that marvellous, ladies and gents, doesn't it just warm the heart? And so, while we leave these lovely ladies to reminisce,' – *about nearly dying?* – 'coming up in Part Three, the woman who wowed the scientists when she returned from the dead. Not only is she a walking miracle – she's got a whole new face. Yes, Leonora Herbert is one of the very first successful face-transplant patients ever.' Gasps all round. 'But first, right after this break, we'll meet the lady who says there's light at the end of the tunnel – she knows because she met her partner through a bereavement group for trauma victims. Don't go away, folks.'

She shoved the flowers at me; I put them behind my chair. We had exactly one and a half minutes to relax and breathe. I had one and a half minutes to drain my 'water-bottle'. I did so with gusto, then looked hopefully around for Daisy. Charlie crossed to Renee, dropping his voice. I squinted at them, trying to lip-read. I heard the word 'flat' more than once.

Renee tossed her hair as Kay padded up with the powder-puff. Daisy brought Renee a drink that she snatched as rudely as I'd known she would. I tried to attract Daisy's attention, but she was too busy making eyes at Charlie. I tried to attract his attention, but he was now being harangued by Renee. I couldn't believe he'd let Fay do that to me without warning. Actually, no – I could believe it. Fay smiled at me over the eminent psychologist who hadn't got much of a word in yet (too erudite and sensible, probably). A carrot-haired man who'd arrived in the break was being miked-up. I saw him check his watch and frown. Fay's eyes were still drilling into me. I smiled back at her, more than a little uncomfortable. Perhaps she did look familiar . . .

Simeon Fernandez was beginning to bluster to anyone who'd listen. He'd obviously sensed he wasn't there just to promote his great work. Sally had popped in from the gallery to appease him a bit. She patted my hand quickly as she passed. 'Nearly there, Maggie. We just need a little more of the personal stuff if you can bear it. Then we'll bring the copper in.' She indicated Carrot-top. He didn't look like a policeman, I thought hazily. His suit was too untidy.

Renee smacked her lips together as Kay finished applying the gloss. She headed straight to Fay; she'd sensed she had a real ally sitting right there.

'You're fantastic, darling,' she purred. 'I'm going to push you a bit on how the accident has affected your relationships, etc. Okay?' Without waiting for an answer, Renee generously extended her explanation to all now. One happy media family. 'Then we can hear from Mr Fernandez again, and, of course, the wonderful Doctor Draper.'

Doctor Draper looked slightly mollified. He smoothed his lurid tie down over his portly belly. Did all men of science enjoy their food too much? I wondered vaguely. Fish and micro-chips. I grinned. Finally, Renee crossed to me.

'And, Maggie,' she dropped down to my level, dropping her voice accordingly, 'get your head out of your arse, all right?'

I stopped grinning and flushed, feeling the stain burning my skin. Before I could retaliate, she was back with Kay for a final tweak. 'And the set looks bloody drab, Amanda,' Renee snapped. 'Put those gorgeous lilies behind Maggie in the vase.'

I winced as Amanda complied wordlessly then rushed out onto the floor again. 'Okay, guys. Thirty seconds and counting. Settle down, please, though do keep up the great energy. You're a fantastic audience, aren't they, Renee?'

Renee was centre-stage again, extending her scarlet talons before her to give the audience a little clap. The lilies stank. I shrank down in my chair.

'Darlings,' she dropped her voice subtly, then spread her arms wide to include each and every one of them, 'I'm going to let you into a little secret, all right?'

Oh yes, it was more than all right. They actually craned forward. Infinitesimal pause. Wait, wait, wait . . .

'You're my best audience of the year so far. And', they craned a little further, 'it's not far off Christmas – so what does that say?!'

They whooped with joy. They had no idea she said this every show. And if they did know, if they were old regulars, why would they care? They were Renee's special audience, today, here and now – and that was all that mattered.

'And we're back in five, four, three, two –' Amanda finished her count. The title music blared. Renee composed herself, flung on her tragedian robe so grandly.

Fernandez and Draper had a row. Charlie looked a little happier. Fay talked about how terrified her parents had been when they turned on the news and saw the accident before they'd heard from her. The plant in the audience tried to stir things up even more by asking me whether I thought trauma was to be expected if we all led such adventurous lives and didn't just stay at home and mind the kids. I pointed out as coolly as I could that I didn't have kids and travelling down the motorway to get home in a National Express coach because my car had broken down outside Bristol (they didn't need to know the truth) hardly constituted adventure.

Then Renee started on the relationships. I licked my dry lips anxiously, but the wine was going a little way in protecting my poor aching heart. Only a little way, though. Fay, on the other hand, was basking in it all. Warhol's 'fifteen-minute fame game' had truly taken hold; the fluffy rabbit of celebrity was tantalising the quivering greyhound.

'You know,' she blinked up at Renee, her voice all small and wounded again, 'I've found it very hard with Troy since the accident.'

*Troy!*

'Darling.' Renee crossed the floor in a grand swirling gesture, the batwings flapping. Fay looked tiny beside her. 'Can you share, babes? Can you tell us why?'

My good toes curled. Fay breathed deeply. Renee took her hand. 'Just take a minute, please, Fay. There's no rush.'

Charlie's frantic checking of his watch belied her words. Fay breathed again.

'Okay? Come on, then, tell Auntie Renee.' Gently, she coaxed it out of her.

'It's just – well, he's become incredibly – over-protective. He hardly wants to let me out of his sight, he's so worried something else might happen.'

I shifted slightly in my seat. Renee's radar picked up the minuscule movement. She dashed to the middle of the floor; was on me again before I knew it.

'Maggie, have you got something to say? What about your partner? How has *he* dealt with your accident?' Renee looked directly at me. She knew damn well about my partner; she must do. It would have been all around the office immediately. I met her eye.

'I'm single at the moment, Renee.' I forced a smile. 'Like you.'

She smiled right back, her face a mask. Venom seeped out of the tiny lines round her eyes, out of her glossed mouth, down through the hair extensions bought for hundreds from her celebrity stylist, which had been traded for pennies by skinny East Europeans, and originated from starving Asian street-kids. But she kept right on smiling.

'Do you have some advice for Fay, Maggie?' Renee clamped her hand down on my shoulder.

'Not really,' I muttered.

Charlie coughed again, loudly this time. Renee's acrylic nails indented my flesh. I sighed.

'Right. Well, Fay, how do –' I swivelled round in my seat to look directly at the girl, who smiled back in encouragement. '– how do you feel about Troy's protectiveness?'

She considered the question gravely for a moment. 'I don't know really, Maggie.'

This was starting to feel like a bad edition of *Oprah*. I prayed fervently that no one I knew was watching.

'But we are considering getting some counselling to get us through the bad patch.'

I was sure Troy would be overjoyed to hear her admitting this on national television.

'I mean, I've read some stuff, you know, like from Relate or marriage guidance people, you know, and they say the best thing is not necessarily to stay together. I mean, if you have counselling, they won't always advise that. If, you know, things aren't right.'

'No, well, I don't mean to be rude, but I'd say that was pretty obvious. Any counsellor worth their salt would tell you that.'

She looked at me. 'Would they?' There was something incredibly intense about her expression. 'Do you really think they would?'

'I mean, like I said, I don't want to offend you. But if you find him – stifling – why would you want to stay?'

'I guess you're right,' she said, very slowly. 'I just hadn't thought about it like that. I thought he was just being, you know – nice.'

'Well, I'm sure he is nice. But that doesn't mean he's doing the right thing, being over-protective. Some men are just like that, aren't they? They like control.' For the first time today I felt almost impassioned. Almost. 'They want to know where *their* women are at every moment, whether –'

Renee was bearing down on me. She had absolutely no time for what she'd term 'feminist claptrap' on her show: too worthy, not enough blood and guts.

'So, Maggie –'

I recognised that tone.

'You've had to have some help yourself, eh, sweetheart?'

I couldn't field it in time. The air crackled around me and my face froze. She knew. I stared at the floor in front of me as she paced before my chair. But what exactly did she know? Her leather boots were very high, as pointed as a cartoon witch's.

'You shouldn't be ashamed, babes.'

Charlie had betrayed me: he must have done.

'Are you all right?' she asked, so terribly caring, they thought. 'You look a little tearful.'

'Oh no,' I blurted. 'Sorry. It's just the flowers.' I waved vaguely behind me. 'Lilies. I – I don't like – I get a weird reaction, you know.' I would never tell the truth here. 'Hayfever.'

'Share your feelings with us, Maggie. Come on, don't be shy.' Her voice dropped to a singsong lilt; its cruelty wrapped up carefully in coruscating kindness. 'Perhaps we can help you, eh, Maggie?' She raised her eyes to the audience. Her audience.

The air felt electric now; it sizzled round my head. Everybody waited. I could sense Charlie on his haunches, as expectant as a gundog waiting to collect its kill. Panic began to build in me.

Fernandez was sick of being overlooked. He pulled his lip over yellow teeth and unwittingly dispelled the tension.

'So this is exactly what I mean in my latest book, *Shadows in a Modern World*. Often we ignore situations that we are –'

Renee held up an imperious hand. He'd blown it. 'Thank you, Mr Fernandez –'

'Doctor Fernandez.'

'Sorry, *Doctor* Fernandez,' she spat each syllable out like a small piece of dirt, 'but I think we really need to know a little more about how tragedy affects the everyday life of our guests. How exactly do you drag yourself out of bed in the morning if you've lost the love of your life? Please give a huge round of applause to someone who can tell us – let's welcome Lesley Quentin, widow of Stan, the brave driver who gave his life so heroically that night.'

I didn't think poor old Stan had had much of a chance to prove his heroism that night actually. Fay was staring at me with a beatific expression on her gorgeous little face. And it was starting to seriously unnerve me.

In the final break they walked the face-transplant lady on, and the freak-show finally finished me off. Heart pounding, I gestured frantically at Charlie. He was busy eyeing up Transplant Lady's glamorous sister on the sidelines.

'I'm really not feeling that great,' I muttered. 'It's all been a bit of a shock.' I tried to sound reproachful, but he was impervious. 'Do you still need me?'

'For God's sake, Maggie. There's only another fifteen minutes to go. You need to pull the bloody stops out, okay? The reunion was fantastic, don't let it go flat.'

'Please, Charlie. I – I really do feel a little bit – queasy.'

He frowned, stepped back quickly in his Gucci loafers, just in case... Then Fay beamed at him and I saw him drowning blissfully in her violet eyes. She wasn't even his type.

'Okay, Maggie. Go and take five in the green room.' Baring his perfect teeth at Fay, he straightened his tie. 'We'll talk later.'

I grabbed my crutches and hauled myself out of there before

29

he could change his mind. Funnily enough, Renee didn't bother with a goodbye.

In the deserted green room I sloshed some more wine into a glass and downed it with a not-quite-steady hand. Then I poured myself a strong coffee and sat down to wait for Charlie. I wished I was anywhere but here. I thought desperately of Pendarlin, of the soft yellow light and the space and the clear, clean Cornish air. It calmed me a little.

After interminable adverts about loo freshener and nappies, a multi-coloured Renee tripped girlishly through her titles and the show was back on air. She was at her best now with poor faceless Leonora. When Fay reached over and held the poor woman's hand, the audience actually moaned with joy.

'Abso-bloody-lutely sickening.' I snapped the television off with the remote.

'I have to say I agree, mate.'

My coffee went hurtling across the horrible beige appliqué sofa.

'Sorry.' An East-End accent: the policeman. He was disentangling himself from the mike, fishing the lead out of his scruffy white shirt. 'What a complete waste of time that was.'

I delved around for a napkin. 'Didn't you get your chance to shine?'

He grinned. 'Got turfed off before I could make my mark. They ran out of time for me apparently. I'm relieved, to be honest.'

'Oh?' I made a pathetic attempt to wipe up the coffee with a soggy serviette.

'Drummed in to do a bit of police PR, you know. Not really my cup of char. Give me a con over a celebrity any day. What shall I do with this, d'you think?'

'Just shove it on the side.' I gestured vaguely at the table of stale croissants.

'You done this before then?'

His direct gaze never left me.

'I – I work for them, normally. When I'm not, you know –' I tapped my leg again. 'Not injured.'

Did his grin fade just a little? 'Oh right. I see.'

I wasn't sure I did. Since I'd been off sick I felt more out of place here than I ever had before.

The policeman was switching his phone on, checking the time. 'I'd better do one. Nice to meet you.'

I smiled a half-hearted smile. 'Likewise.'

'Hope your foot's better soon.'

'Thanks. And you go get 'em, tiger,' I said, a little groggily.

This time he definitely did grin. Painkillers and booze were perhaps not the most sensible of partners, I reminded myself, as he dropped the mike onto a plate of egg and cress. And it was only as the door clattered behind him that I noticed the blond boy skulking in the shadows.

'God! You frightened me,' I said shakily as he stepped towards me, extending a long white hand from the sleeve of a tweed jacket. How long had he been there? My mind scrabbled like rodent claws on wood as I tried to remember what I'd just said. What I shouldn't have said.

'Sorry. I thought you'd seen me.'

Tentatively I took the proffered hand. It was curiously limp, the rather dirty nails over-long.

'Maggie Warren? Don't you remember me? We met in the summer.'

31

# Chapter Three

There were still quite a few things I didn't remember about the summer, and more that I didn't want to. It was a necessary blank that I'd apparently blocked as best I could.

Last summer I had teetered on a precipice, following my wrung-out heart, and I almost didn't make it back. It scared me now to be confronted with someone I had no memory of.

I looked closer at him. He had a smooth, rather feminine face, a choirboy's pallor, blond hair that fell over his eyes like a child's, although he was dressed like he was fifty. He was swaying slightly. In fact, the whole room appeared to be swaying slightly. I really needed to go home now. I certainly didn't need to be any more unsteady on my feet than I already was: I'd be rendered '*Drunk in charge of a crutch*'. I stifled a rather hysterical giggle. It was definitely time to leave.

The boy looked a little nonplussed. 'Don't you remember me? Joseph Blake. I did some research for you in May. There was a couple of us. University placement.'

'Oh God, yes, of course.' I clapped a dramatic hand to my clammy brow. 'How stupid of me.' I had absolutely no memory of him whatsoever – and it frightened me. 'Joseph – Joe, is it?'

'No. Just Joseph.' He was scowling now. 'You *don't* remember, do you?'

'I do, Joseph, honestly. I've just had a bit of a morning of it. An early start, you know, and this –' I wobbled my crutch around, 'this doesn't help my brainpower. How . . .' I tried to focus on him properly, 'how are you?'

He relented, his smile lighting up his smooth round face. I relaxed a little.

'I'm well, thanks. Oh, and thank you for the reference.'

What was he on about now? 'You're welcome,' I murmured.

'So, I'm back for a bit. Charlie gave me a job. Well, I'm on a trial anyway. A three-month trial.'

'Great,' I smiled back, trying to mask my insincerity. *Please God, get me out of here.*

The door swung open and Charlie swaggered in, his arm round a crowing Renee. I was stuck between a rock and a hard bitch. Oh dear.

'Fantastic, darling. Fantastic bloody show. Leonora was absolutely worth her weight in the proverbial, and Fay's tears. God!' Charlie caught sight of me attempting to dissolve into the sofa. 'All right, Maggie, darling. Feeling better? I told you this show would help heal the wounds for good.'

By the time I remembered him again, the boy had gone.

An apologetic Sally wanted me to go for a quick drink with her, but by now I'd realised that if I didn't sober up I'd be throwing up. I needed to eat and lie down; more importantly, I wanted to get away from Charlie – fast. I'd see them all soon, I promised Sally. I'd be back at work in a week or two (or more like four, if I could help it).

Out on the busy street, I breathed a sigh of relief and lit a cigarette. The lunchtime rush had begun on Grays Inn Road, and I perched on top of the imposing studio stairs to wait for my cab. November's chill was truly in the air, and I huddled down into my coat, shivering despite its warmth. The skeletal leaves from the ornamental trees in the studio's planters skittered round my feet. Chip wrappers cartwheeled in the gutter. A Number 45 crawled past, spewing noxious fumes out below an advert for Renee's memoirs, her smug face resplendent on its bright red rear, as big as a potting shed. I shuddered. I watched a very old man pull his tartan shopping-trolley up the road, his head wrinkled and jutting like an ancient tortoise's. With a great lurch, I thought of Gar. I'd neglected her since the accident.

My cab pulled up and beeped. Hauling myself to my feet at the top of the stairs, an arm snaked through mine suddenly, sending me off balance. Panic coursed through my veins as the concrete rushed up towards me. Just in time I righted myself.

'I'm so glad I caught you.'

I looked round at the voice, struggling to regain my equilibrium. Fay Carter was gazing up at me. 'Does your foot really hurt? I've had loads of problems with my arm. They have to keep re-setting it.'

'Oh dear.' I tried to disengage myself without causing offence. 'No, I'm fine, really.' But I moved too fast; my crutch went crashing down the bloody stairs. I bit my lip, swallowing my pain and irritation.

'I'll get it.' She pattered after the crutch. 'It's nice to help each other, don't you think?'

'Yes, of course,' I replied uneasily.

'After all,' Fay returned the crutch to my freezing hand, 'I'm only returning the favour.' Her huge eyes were so serious, too serious, as she looked up at me. 'I'm sorry I didn't get the chance to thank you before today for saving me.'

'Look, I'm sorry, but I really don't think I did.' I heard the screaming metal on the motorway again and blanched. 'You must have me confused with –'

'No, Maggie.' She just kept staring. 'It was you, it was definitely you. They told me after, the rescue-workers. They pointed you out. And now you've just helped me again, in there.' She indicated the television studio. 'So I *really* owe you now.'

'You don't, honestly.' I hopped down the steps as fast as my

34

leg would carry me. 'I'd better – you know. The cab's waiting. I'll see you –'

A metallic car with darkened windows pulled up opposite the studios, sounding its imperious horn.

'That's me,' Fay smiled dreamily. 'I was going to say', she tapped lightly down the stairs beside me, 'we should get together some-time, don't you think? Give me your number, yeah?'

My heart sank, but she rattled on, not seeming to notice my reticence. 'A few of us were thinking of starting a survivors' group. I'd love you to be part of it, Maggie. You'd be great. Really helpful.'

Fay was too near me now, right in my space, peering up into my face. Was the girl always this upbeat? I felt truly exhausted. How could I explain that the idea of being in any sort of group right now filled me full of dread, least of all one that would reminisce endlessly about that hideous night? The silver car hooted again. Fay waved a little pearl-tipped hand.

'Coming!' She turned back to me. 'Look, here's my number, yeah?' Fishing around in the sequinned handbag that dangled from her own plaster-cast, she handed me a small shiny pink card.

*Fay Carter, Entertainer Extraordinaire*, it announced in black flowing script. A tiny big-bosomed figure high-kicked beneath the words.

'I had them made up when I knew I was coming on the show. Good, aren't they? Give me a call. Don't be shy. You know,' she clasped my freezing hand in her little one, the diamond on her ring finger biting into my flesh, 'I've got the feeling this is the start of something. Something huge.' Leaning up, she kissed me on both cheeks. 'Do you know what I mean? And by the way, I'm so sorry about your boyfriend. Charlie told me.'

I just stood there and stared, speechless, as the small figure drifted across Grays Inn Road, weaving through taxis, beneath the admiring builders ant-like on Café Buena's new scaffolding, earning a beep from an appreciative white-van man.

Across the road, Fay paused at the car door, turning to wave. I saw a spiky peroxide head lean across to help her with the door. 'See you soon,' she mouthed, before a removal van blocked my view. When I looked again, she was gone.

As my driver settled me into the back of his car, chattering about the traffic and the ever-expanding congestion zone, I tried to concentrate politely, but all the time he prattled I felt a gnawing sense of unease, a sense that grew and grew. Deep down I knew I hadn't seen the last of my new friend.

# Chapter Four

I was in bed when the flowers came. Two days after the show and I was still smarting from the shame, still hiding from the world. Sally had tried to reassure me that it had been fine, that I'd been fine, honestly – but then she would. That was her job.

I knew it really wasn't fine when Alex rang. I hadn't heard from him for months. He didn't speak but I recognised his silence. His silence that made me almost breathless.

'Alex,' I said urgently to the air, to the static on the phone, 'I know it's you.' But he didn't speak. He didn't ever speak, but I felt his presence down the phone, solid, tangible. After a while, after I'd just sat there clutching the phone and hoping, he'd hung up.

I hadn't been out of the house since the cab had dropped me back from the studio. My father had left for a three-day teaching conference on the morning of the show, so I'd hardly even bothered to get dressed since I'd slammed the front door safely shut behind me. I knew I should see Gar, I must see her, but I couldn't quite bear to go. Not yet. I felt too vulnerable myself.

'You're not dealing with this, Mag,' chided Bel when she called, but then fortunately Hannah had decorated the kitchen wall with Bel's new bright pink lipstick and Bel needed to go and shout at her, so I escaped yet more psychoanalysis by a whisker. For the time being, at least.

37

I did realise that I must get up sometime. Digby kept nipping at the duvet, desperate to escape our four walls. I ignored him as he ran in rings round the bed, gazing at the dinosaur-shaped stain on the ceiling, the stain that had existed for as long as I could remember. But even I was getting bored now. *Woman's Hour* was wittering on about inequality in the workplace and then Jenni Murray announced that next up was the inimitable Renee Owen to talk about growing up in the valleys with nothing but an alcoholic father and seventeen siblings, her amazing success against all the odds – and I groaned with disgust and threw a pillow at the radio. It missed, sending my latest mug of cold tea splashing all over the pale carpet. And then the doorbell rang.

I thumped down the stairs in my mum's old frilly dressing-gown that I'd never had the heart to throw out, and the spotty youth at the front door blushed as bright as one of my father's prize tomatoes. I wondered if I still had it, if I'd ever had it, and then I saw the flowers and nearly gagged. Lilies again.

'For me? Are you sure?'

'Maggie Warren, it says here. That you?' He couldn't quite drag his eyes from the gaping dressing-gown.

'Yes, that's me. Do you know who they're from?'

He drew his hood closer round his chilly crew-cut and gave his clipboard a cursory glance. He shrugged. 'No name, man. I just deliver 'em. Look at the card, why don't you?'

Frowning, I leaned my crutch against the door and fumbled with the flimsy little envelope. It was speared amid the blooms that strained out to the light, that made me think only of death. A gust of wind sent a flurry of raindrops from the withered creeper above me pattering down on my head. I couldn't extract the card until the envelope ripped clean in two, exposing the bald text.

'*To Maggie, with dying gratitude.*' My skin prickled. I turned the card over, but there was no name anywhere. I shivered as the hoody shoved the flowers at me, kept my arms clamped by my side, the card still between my cold fingers. 'Are you sure you don't know who they're from?'

'I tol' you already.' He was surly with offence. 'I'm not lying. Do you wan' 'em or not?'

'I suppose.' Reluctantly, I took the waxy flowers. Pollen from the swollen stamen speckled my naked arm. 'Thanks.' I licked my finger but I couldn't get the pollen stain off.

Hoody leered. 'I 'spect they're from a secret admirer.'

I'd just spent ten minutes easing my tracksuit bottoms over my bad foot only to realise I'd put them on the wrong way round when the doorbell pealed again. I scraped my frankly filthy hair back off my face as someone insistently held the bell down.

'Have patience for the cripple,' I muttered, reaching for the banister, Digby nearly unbalancing me as he went scurrying between my feet. I plucked the door back before the bell could sound again.

'Did you find out who the flowers were from?'

My heart jolted painfully in my chest. 'Oh!'

It was Fay, swaddled in glossy fake fur.

'Surprise!' she breezed. 'I just came to see how you are,' and then she was in, dipping under my arm, into my father's house. Uninvited. Digby skittered behind my legs. 'Coward,' I muttered at him.

'Amazing flowers,' she called, already in the kitchen where I'd earlier shoved the bouquet into the sink. 'New boyfriend?'

'No.' I hobbled after her, trying to keep up. 'No. I haven't got a – look, actually, Fay –'

'Are you *still* single?' she breathed, swinging round, her big eyes all compassion. 'Oh well. We'll have to do something about that, won't we?'

'Will we?' I asked foolishly.

She smiled patiently.

'Fay,' I was as polite as I could be, 'it's just – I'm just wondering, how did you know where I lived?'

'Oh, you know.'

'Well, no, I don't really.'

She affected thought, one small finger resting childlike on her pointy chin. 'Do you know, I can't remember now. From the hospital I think.'

I frowned. 'What, they just gave out my address? Just like that?'

'Oh no, maybe not.' A shrug of her delicate little shoulders. Her coat fell open to reveal a rather inappropriate dress. Lacy. A lot of flesh. I looked away. 'Maybe from *Renee Reveals*.'

'I mean – I don't even live here normally. I live –' It suddenly seemed unimportant. 'I did live near Borough Market,' I trailed off miserably. 'This is my dad's house.'

'Oh, Borough Market's fabulous, isn't it? So olde-worlde.' She pronounced the 'e's like 'y's. 'Lucky you. They've asked me back, you know.'

I gazed at her.

'The show.' Her eyes were gleaming.

My heart sank further. 'Oh, have they?' I leaned heavily against the table. My foot was really hurting now. 'Great. Good for you.'

Fay was pacing round the kitchen, picking everything up and giving it a quick but thorough examination. 'I know – brilliant, isn't it? Told you it was the start of something huge.' She had my mother's picture in her hand now, the photo of her pregnant with me, ripe as a peach, her titian hair tumbling over her smocked paisley shoulders, serene and smiling fit to burst.

'Sorry, Fay, would you mind –'

'Who's this? Your mum? Lovely, isn't she? You're very similar.' She picked up another photo of me and my grandmother. 'And this? Must be your grandma, is it? Got the same blue eyes as you.'

'Yes, Gar. She's called Gar.'

'Still alive? Lucky you. All mine are either dead or on the other side of the world.'

40

'She's – she's in a home near here.' I felt utterly steam-rollered, aware I didn't want to share anything with this stranger but helpless to resist.

'Lovely.' She rammed the picture back onto the dresser so hard that the mugs beneath swayed in the ensuing breeze. 'You know, a few people commented on how alike we looked on the TV.'

'Really?'

'Yes, really. Despite the obvious differences!' She held up one of her dark ringlets, giggling. 'And you're so tall, of course – lucky thing! I think it might be our eyes. Although yours are more – more of a cornflower-blue than mine.'

I looked away, deeply perturbed now. 'Maybe.'

'Anyway, look, I expect you're wondering why I came?'

I felt a great rush of relief. At least she realised this wasn't *entirely* orthodox. 'Well, yes, I was actually.' For the first time I managed a genuine smile.

'I mean,' she giggled again, 'it's not just a social call.'

'Oh, right.'

'Sorry! No, look, I brought you this.' She delved into her shoulder-bag and produced a brown A4 envelope, which she held out to me with reverence. I had a flash of my grandmother's favourite priest, of the wine and wafer being offered at the altar. 'I think it will really help, actually.'

I had a bad feeling about the envelope, an extreme feeling that pervaded my bones. I turned it over in my hands. I really didn't want to open it. But it seemed I had no choice.

'God, Fay.' The photo I'd just extracted slipped from my clammy hand, spiralled down onto the tiled floor. Nausea mounted in me until I had to physically force it down. 'What the hell is that?'

'Oh Maggie,' she peered at me, 'you're upset?'

'Of course I'm bloody upset.' I moved away from her. 'Sorry, but I mean, what did you expect?'

41

I thought she was going to cry; I couldn't look at her. 'Honestly, Fay. I just – I don't get it. Why would you give me that?'

She picked up the photo and proffered it again, with less certainty this time. I flinched.

'Fay, for God's sake!'

But it was too late. I'd seen what it was: a photo of the crash's aftermath. A tangle of mutilated metal, suitcases and bags littering the dark and shiny road. Someone's shoes, a high-heeled pair of shoes right in the forefront, as if the owner had just slipped them off to dance barefoot in the rain. The edge of an ambulance, its fluorescent lights flashing. Two firemen walking out of shot, one behind the other, both with heads bowed. And there in the corner of the photo, unmistakable, jutting out as if in a horror film, a pair of stockinged feet, belonging to a body. A body under a blanket, but a body nonetheless.

'I think you should go now.' I slumped down at the table. 'I really don't want to look at that. I don't understand why you brought it round. Where did you get it?' I glanced up at her. 'Is it some kind of joke? Some kind of sick joke?'

'No, really, Maggie, it's not.' She held her coat tight around her now. 'I'm sorry, you know? I just thought – my group that I've been meeting with, they said it would bring closure. It's, like, dealing with the reality. Like that man said on the show.'

'That man?'

'That doctor. He gave me his book.'

'Fernandez? That quack, you mean?'

'Look, I'm sorry. I really am. I didn't think you'd get upset.'

I bit my tongue. She looked so genuinely downcast, so terribly young and naïve, that my heart softened a fraction. 'Fay, it's fine. It's just – it's not for me, okay? If it helps you, well, that's – that's great, I guess.'

'It's just – well, you helped me. So I wanted to help *you*.' She gazed at me with those eyes.

I tried not to squirm. 'Well, thanks for the thought.'

'That's a nice little cottage.' She pointed to the photo on the wall behind me. 'Very pretty.'

'Look, Fay –'

'Where is it? Somewhere by the sea, I'll bet.'

'North Cornwall. It was my grandmother's.'

'The one in the home?'

'Yes. She – I sort of own it now.'

'Wow. Lucky you.'

'Yes, I know.'

'I think I'd better go now anyway. Troy's waiting for me.'

'That's nice.'

She put the picture carefully back in the envelope, smoothing the flap down. 'Though we are – well, there are still problems, you know. With me and Troy. I'm not sure we can – what's the word? – *surmount* them.'

Dr Fernandez's voice echoed through the room again. I smiled despite myself. 'I'm sorry, Fay. I'm sure you'll do the right thing.'

'Are you?' She was suddenly enthused, stepping nearer to me now. 'What do you think that is, Maggie? The right thing?'

I thought of Alex.

'Oh, Fay. I wish I knew, honestly.'

'Please, just tell me what you think.'

'I just think – you have to trust your instincts.'

'Your instincts,' she repeated slowly. 'Yes, my instinct.' She shoved the envelope back into her bag and headed towards the door. 'You know what, Maggie, you're quite right. I'll let myself out, okay? See you soon,' she called from the hall.

'I really hope not,' I muttered as the front door slammed. As I hunted for the *Yellow Pages* to track down the florist who'd sent the stinking lilies, I heard a car start up outside, and Digby barking in agreement. He never liked strangers on his patch.

43

# Chapter Five

While I was still recuperating from the crash, Bel finally plucked up the courage to tell me Johnno wanted her and Hannah to move back to Australia with him after their wedding. I cried, though I tried not to let her know. She said it was temporary, just to try out 'Down Under' – but it was yet another final straw; the same one that broke the camel's back, you know. Bel and I had been inseparable since her mad family had moved in next door to my quiet one when she was eight. We'd soon found a loose board in the back fence to clamber through and we lived in and out of each other's houses. She became the sister I'd never had, her brothers like mine too. The idea of her not being around was truly painful.

Eventually I pulled myself together and offered to help her sort things out, to look after her house when it was let, to mind Hannah while they packed up, that kind of thing. But Bel said that all she wanted, all her and Johnno wanted (such a very close couple now, inextricable), was for me to help sort the wedding and the goodbye party. For me to be there too. She knew I'd say I wouldn't come to the party. I couldn't. Of course Bel took no notice, deep down I guess she knew I'd be there – but the very thought made me feel a bit ill.

I didn't do parties any more. Not since Alex; not since the summer. But your best friend doesn't get married and go across the world to live every day. And I'd hidden away as long as I dared, concealed behind my injuries, wallowing in my pain and misery, trying not to remember things best forgotten. Now Charlie had started to lose patience; he was on the phone almost daily. If I didn't go back to work soon, I'd have no job to go to – whatever deal we'd made.

The truth was, I had to start facing up to a whole load of things. How long could I stay in Greenwich, staring up at the ceiling of my father's house, cocooned by his presence? What I really wanted to do was run away to Cornwall, take Digby and disappear to my haven at Pendarlin, but this was real life. I had to get on with living.

I was staring glumly at the peaked and shiny mountains of perfection in Bel's wedding-cake book and realising I'd probably bitten off more than all the dried fruit I could ever chew with my rash offer, when the phone rang. I thought it might provide escape, but it was Charlie.

'I need to see you,' he purred.

'I'm about to attempt Bel's wedding cake,' I demurred, but the slice of steel through his tone told me I had little choice.

'Order yourself a car and meet me at the club at five,' he said, and hung up before I could protest again. I had a quick slug of the cooking brandy and relinquished my still-pristine apron, admittedly with a flicker of relief.

It was already dark by the time my cab pulled up in Greek Street. As I hauled myself onto the pavement outside Soho House, a Lycra-clad courier whizzed by, frantically ringing his bell at a young girl stumbling, half-dressed, across the road. A man very much like a woman, resplendent in white fur, was redoing his cherry lipstick in the shop window next to me. Signing the driver's docket, my crutch slipped from my grasp; the she-man bowed down to retrieve it for me. As I reached to take it, to thank him for his kindness, a huge silver four-by-four slowed behind him. For one tiny moment the tinted passenger window became transparent beneath the bright lights of the shops. A pale face, turning slowly, all ghostly behind the glass.

Alex. I thought that it was Alex.

I staggered. The she-man thrust the crutch into my outstretched hand – but she wasn't quick enough. I'd lost my balance now, whacking my foot so hard against the kerb as I flailed that tears of pain sprang to my eyes. The she-man caught me before I fell. He smelled of something I recognised; something like my mother. Chanel. For one brief moment I relaxed against this stranger's soft chest. It was the first time a man's arms, any arms, in fact, had encircled me since my father's anxious hug at the hospital, since my days of recovery, and I savoured the warmth. Then I remembered myself.

'Thank you.' I pulled away, embarrassed. He winked one beady spider-lashed eye at me. 'Don't mention it, ducks. I love a cuddle in the afternoon.'

By the time I found Charlie in the room they called The Library (no books that I could see, but a few very drunk actors attempting to read the over-priced wine list), I was thoroughly unnerved. With every hobble, Alex's shadow stepped beside me, until I was almost pleased to see the very real Charlie. He was looking king-like though hardly regal in a great leather armchair, his hooded eyes half-shut against the smoke from his inevitable cigar as he browsed through the latest issue of *Broadcast*. Only his man-tan gave him away. Just the wrong side of classy.

'Fantastic pic, don't you think, darling?' He flicked open the industry paper to show off a photo of himself and Renee smiling sickeningly at one another.

'*DOUBLE-DECKER PAIR CELEBRATE RECOMMISSION OF RATINGS WINNER*', the headline declared.

'It'd be funny if they found out her name was really Enid, wouldn't it?' I mused, reaching for the glass of Krug Charlie had just poured.

46

He frowned. 'Would it?'

I met his eye. '*I* think so.' Images of Alex still floated through my mind. I tried to concentrate. 'So, what are we celebrating?'

'I'd say that was obvious, darling, wouldn't you?' Charlie really was looking spectacularly orange today. He must have bumped up his shares in St Tropez. 'So, when can we expect you in the office?'

'Soon.' I took such an enormous sip the bubbles shot straight up my nose.

'Fantastic.' He ran a hand through his hair, his signet ring glinting under the light. 'How soon? It has been almost five months now, my darling.'

The champagne hit the spot. I forgot Alex for a moment; I smiled. 'Oh, you know. Very soon.'

'Soon enough for this?' He flung a folder into my lap. *Doing Me Wrong: You're Dumped*, heralded the title page.

'What's this?'

'Fantastic idea, darling. You'll love it. It can be your victorious return to form.' He relit his cigar. 'The idea is the opposite of the "Proposal on-air" show. This is the "You're Dumped on-air" show.'

I stared at him. 'You're joking, right?'

He toasted me, then knocked the drink back in one and poured again. 'Darling, I don't joke, you know that. It's a fantastic idea. If it takes off, it'll be the talk of the town.'

'Charlie, this is not what we agreed.' An icy sweat broke out across my forehead; the champagne and cigar smoke combining to make me feel suddenly quite sick. 'You said that if I –'

'I know what I said, darling. But look, I'm sure it was one of your ideas anyway. From the summer. You knew the deal then.'

Confused, I stood up – rather too suddenly. Charlie caught my crutch neatly in his orange hand.

'For God's sake, Charlie.' I grabbed it from him. 'You're completely reneging on –'

47

'Such passion, darling.' Charlie smirked. 'That's what I love about you. That's why you've got to do this programme. Sit down, there's a good girl.'

'Charlie, I can't do it. It's utter crap. You know that.'

'Just this once.' His eyes were wolf-like now, slits behind the cloud of sweet and sickening smoke. 'You still owe me.'

'But it won't be just this once. And I did the trauma show because I owed you.'

'You did the trauma show because it gave you closure, darling. Remember?'

'Did I?' I gazed at him.

'Absolutely. It was your idea to do it, my darling.'

'Was it?' Why did my brain ache so much every time I grappled with memories of recent events?

'And you have my promise.'

'I already had your promise, I'm sure.' I glared at him.

'Please do it, Maggie.' He stopped smiling and checked his vulgar watch. 'Or maybe we should talk about the show you *really* don't want to do.'

I went limp with misery. 'You can't do this, Charlie.'

'Can't do what, darling? I'm just giving your career a little helping-hand. God knows you need it after your most recent fuck-up. Work with me, Maggie.'

'You're playing games,' I whispered miserably.

His face was closing down. I tried a different tack, fighting to keep my voice level. 'Look, I know I did something stupid' (I just wished I could remember exactly what it was) 'but it was only the one mistake, wasn't it? You know you can rely on me.'

'Perhaps I could – once.' Charlie studied the end of his cigar intently. 'But you let me down *so* badly.'

We gazed at one another, the memories I'd blotted out shifting slightly in the sands of time, reshaping, struggling to the surface. I could feel the anger driving through my bones. 'But I've been waiting all this time for the *True Lives* docs –'

But Charlie had already switched off.

'You know, you're quite beautiful when you're cross,' he mused. 'Though that mop needs a thoroughly good cut. Why don't you get it seen to?' His mobile rang. 'John Frieda's not bad.' He stubbed out the cigar and picked something out of a back tooth, snapping open the phone.

Before I could respond, an obsequious waiter had ushered him to the landing where it wasn't quite so hallowed: media-whores milling, fat-cats in suits who spoke too loudly and under-dressed girls who simpered, fingers in ears against all the other loud and self-important chat.

Numbly I stared at *Broadcast*. I was sure Renee's eye-bags had been doctored. Then Charlie was back, swinging his cashmere camel coat from the back of the chair, draping it over his shoulders like he was in *The* bloody *Godfather*. Well. He was a bloody hood, for all his supposed charm.

'As soon as that cast is off, back in the office, okay, darling?' It wasn't an invitation. Charlie raised one perfectly manicured finger and slowly, slowly stroked my cheek. 'You know I need you, Maggie. I miss you. You're the best, despite your little balls-up. But it could be your final chance, darling. Crosswell would see to that in one fell swoop. You do remember Sam, don't you? I'll see you at work.'

When I dragged myself outside again, I searched for Alex everywhere – but there were just early revellers, beautiful toned gay men, excited theatre-goers. My ghost was gone.

# Chapter Six

The day after my plaster-cast finally came off, Bel and Johnno got married. I'd never seen Bel looking quite so alive, as she stood smiling on the Registry steps on the Kings Road waiting to go in, clutching onto Johnno under a great scarlet umbrella like they'd never ever part, white velvet collar turned up high, setting off her blonde urchin cut and her beaming pixie face, a proper winter bride. And Johnno, oh God, he looked so proud, small and stocky but still towering over Bel's birdlike form. Hannah stood tiny in sparkly white beside them, her patent shoes all shiny, holding her mother's hand, beaming, the spit (thank the Lord) of Bel. I was overjoyed that Bel had finally recovered from the utter disaster of Hannah's father: the hippy painter who had promised Bel the world and then vanished to Morocco with his other pregnant lover the week before Hannah was born. The father who'd never bothered to meet his adorable daughter.

I stood on the pavement, filming them with my little video camera – Bel's parents and her brothers all cheering with joy. The way Bel looked at Johnno now was enough to give you hope.

The Christmas decorations were already up, although it was only November. The lampposts fizzed with electric blue stars and Hannah pointed a tiny hand and sang 'Twinkle, twinkle, little Mummy', and everybody laughed until Hannah went beet-red with excitement and overbalanced doing the deep curtsies she'd learned in ballet. And for a moment, for one long moment, I felt happy, happier than I'd been in such a long time.

I was just calling to Bel to describe how she felt on this auspicious day, in her last few moments before she become a Mrs for all time, when her face dropped visibly. Frowning, I lowered the camera. She was looking at something over my shoulder, and then she wrinkled her brow and Johnno looked in the same direction, then stooped and whispered in her ear. And then I felt them both gazing at me, and an icy claw crept down my back and I turned round quickly –

And there he was. Just standing there, just like that, as if everything was fine. He had both hands shoved deep in the pockets of an extremely smart dark suit, a suit he'd never have worn when he was with me, and for a moment he looked guarded – but then he caught my startled eye and slowly smiled. I felt a pain, like someone had just got hold of my heart and was slowly pulling the bleeding flesh out through my chest, as I stared at him. And then, as if in slow motion, I saw him put one long hand out behind him, and I saw a leather-gloved hand slip into his, and he pulled the owner, the girl who wore it, forwards.

A great gust of wind blew down the road. The trees leaned right over under the weight and the blue stars wobbled and Bel's mother's fussy pillbox hat went flying off; there was a big kerfuffle while Nigel ran to fetch it. My hair blew across my face and stuck to my lipsticked mouth, stuck fast, but I didn't bother to remove it. I didn't even care. How could he come here, here of all places, and, worst of all, bring this girl too?

He was still smiling, his short brown hair sticking up on end and his yellow eyes glinting with something I couldn't quite read. Malice?

'Hello Alex,' I said quietly.

'Maggie.' He was ever so polite, of course he was. Charm the birds out of the trees, my Alex could, when he wanted to. 'I'd like you to meet Serena.'

51

Serena was very thin and falsely blonde (how utterly predictable), and her expensive heels very high, though Alex still dwarfed both of us. She looked at me, looked me up and down, and then she smiled too, a slow smile, a smug smile, which spread across her chiselled face. I pulled my old red coat round me but still shivered in the wind. Graciously, the girl offered me her hand. Her gloves were so soft they felt like butter.

I stared blankly at this new pair. If Alex didn't stop grinning like that I'd punch him right on the already skewed bridge of his once-broken nose. I clenched my fists. And then they moved off, towards the happy couple, the four of them all kissing and shaking hands, and I was left just standing there, a satellite on the windy pavement of Kings Road. Alone, despite a thousand strangers rushing by.

And all through Bel's wedding in that little room, the room in muted tones that smelled of Bel's red roses, I couldn't concentrate, and when it was my time to read my bit out from *The Prophet*, the bit about '*Love one another but make not a bond of love – Let it rather be a moving sea between the shores of your souls*', Bel's mum had to nudge me to get up. And I tried not to let the strain show in my voice, or let my hands shake, and I stood very straight and tall – although my foot really hurt now and my heart truly ached – not looking at the row where Alex and Serena sat; and I tried to read the lines about love with sincerity, as if I hadn't very nearly drowned in the bloody sea *The Prophet* was on about. As if I thought love could be a good thing, and was not likely to finish you off for all time.

Alex did at least have the good grace not to crash the wedding breakfast. He knew he'd done enough. He and Serena disappeared into the swirl of Christmas shoppers, big hand in buttery one, waving. I could sense he was elated in his shambolic one-off elegance, while I felt utterly bereft. Somehow I got through lunch – ate a bit of the duck pate starter, picked at the salmon main, managed, somehow, to down lots of the very good wine. I thought of Bel and how sad she'd been, on her own with Hannah, and how she'd turned her life around. A little drunk after all the speeches, I hugged her tighter than I'd ever done before.

'I'm so happy for you, darling,' I said, and her pointy little face was so soft with joy that I almost wept.

'I'm so happy too,' she whispered. 'I can't believe it really. I keep pinching myself.'

'It does happen, you know, Bel. Good people do get what they deserve, sometimes.'

She squeezed my arm. 'Yeah, well, your turn will come, I'm sure. I'm sure of it, my Maggie.' She looked up at me, serious now. 'I'm so sorry about Alex. He wasn't invited, you know. I wouldn't let Johnno, though he did want to.'

'It's okay, Bel. It's hardly your fault that he turned up.'

'Yeah, well, I wish he'd bloody stayed away. He knew it'd hurt you. God, after everything he –'

'Don't mention it, please,' I said quickly. 'It's fine. I've got to get on with it sometime, haven't I?'

She squeezed my arm again. 'Oh God, Mag, I'm going to miss you.'

'Oh Bel, don't start that now. Let's think of nice things.' My sniff was barely audible. 'You're not going quite yet.'

'And it's not forever.'

'It'd better bloody not be.'

'And you'd better be at the party, okay?'

Hannah skipped up, her fairy wings iridescent in the candlelight. 'Why are you crying, sillies?' She observed me steadily. 'You look like a panda, Auntie Maggie. Like what I saw in the zoo when Johnno took me. The fat one that was scratching her bottom.' She slipped her hand in mine. 'Don't cry.'

'I'm not. I'm laughing. I never cry.'

'Why's water coming out of your eyes then?'

'Oh, Hannah.' I picked her up and gave her a squeeze. She smelled of biscuits and fresh laundry. 'You don't half ask a lot of questions for someone so small.'

Then I went home to my father's house, alone. The phone was ringing as I unlocked the door, but by the time I reached it they'd rung off. And as my dad had gone to collect his girlfriend Jenny from the airport, I opened a bottle from his trusty Wine Club collection and drank myself to sleep.

# Chapter Seven

**BEFORE: JUNE**

I had dreamed that I was dying, such a very vivid dream. When I woke, I wasn't absolutely sure I hadn't. A huge weight squatted on my stomach, face pulled back in a rictus grin, gurning down at me until, panicking, I pushed up through its mass. Rearing from the bed, my arms flailed like a sprinter's tangled in the finish line; a great sob of terror scraping through my chest.

I wasn't dead, apparently. Not unless heaven was an ice-cream-coloured curtain drawn round a narrow bed, or a glimpse of rain through a small window in a quietly rumbling room. A room that was grey and regular. A dormitory. A ward. Not unless the woman in blue with smiley eyes who stepped neatly to my side was some bizarre kind of angel in a nurse's uniform.

'You haven't got a halo.' I blinked at the nurse. 'Have you?'

The woman leaned forward to hear me properly, but my voice was apparently stuck in my sore and tired throat. I tried to smile instead, but smiling seemed to hurt me even more. Tentatively I brought my hand up to touch my own face, my hand that felt freezing.

'Your lip's been stitched.'

She caught my hand and moved it gently down. The nurse's skin was beautiful, dark and creamy like a pint of newly pulled

Guinness. I had the impulse to stroke her arm, but before I could she tucked my hand beneath the sheet. And I winced at the touch. My body ached; I was realising slowly that every part of me was tender, every part felt bruised and sore.

'Only a few stitches, though.'

I thought the nurse might have said something next about being right as rain in no time, right as the rain I could see falling in vertical lines through that little window. Rain was never really right, though, was it, not unless you gardened like my father and – I had a revelation.

'Have I gone mad?' I enquired politely. 'Is this the loony bin?' This time the nurse caught my words.

'Not mad, no, Maggie. You've had an accident. You're in hospital.'

'Accident?'

'Just slip your sleeve up so I can take your blood pressure. Can you tell me how you feel now?' she asked me kindly, but actually I couldn't, because I didn't know. I gazed at her blankly. Well, I did know I felt calm. Calm, but sort of bewildered.

'You're in shock, dear. And the doctor's given you something to monitor the pain.' The nurse tightened the band round my arm until it pinched. 'Morphine.'

'Ouch. I can't seem to –' I gazed at the nurse again. 'I can't think what happened. It's funny, though. Was there –' I stopped again.

'What?' the nurse prompted. 'What do you think, Maggie?'

'I keep thinking about a horse. Did I – did I fall off a horse?' But I didn't remember being on a horse yesterday. I could vaguely remember a riding lesson from years ago, somewhere in the countryside; remembered my mother waving gaily from the gate of the school. It must have been a long time ago. I remembered that my hat had been too big, that it used to rattle down over my eyes as I bobbed along until I was pink and out of breath and couldn't see anything – not my mother, not the waving –

only my own small hands beneath me, clutching the pony's mane as valiantly I tried to retain control.

'There was – I think there might have been a horse.' The nurse seemed alarmed suddenly. She paused for a moment, thinking. 'You were on –'

The consultant arrived at the foot of the bed with a flick of his pristine white coat. He was very tall and he had a face rather like an eagle, I thought. Yes, an eagle. His nose was a downward curve, like a cruel beak. He glanced at the chart at the foot of my bed, then at me.

'Ms Warren.'

'Yes.'

'Feeling better?'

Better than what?

'I'm not – I don't know really.'

'Vitals all fine, sir.' The nurse peeled the band off my arm and popped something bleeping in my ear.

'Good, good.' He inspected my lip. 'Nice job with the sutures. Bruising?'

'All external, apparently.' The nurse took the bleeping thing out.

'It's just –' I cut in.

'What?' The doctor seemed impatient, ready to move on to the next bed. The one with the curtains right round it. Tight around it.

'I can't remember what happened. Why I'm here.'

The consultant shot the nurse a look. The nurse looked down at her sensible shoes.

'Does anyone know that I'm here?' I thought of Alex. I sat up in bed again. 'I must let my boyfriend know.'

'I'll get the list.' The nurse seemed grateful for an excuse to move down the ward. There was a sudden commotion from the bed next door, the bed that I couldn't see. Someone was crying, racked with terrible sobs. The noise made my blood freeze.

'I think I might like to get up,' I began, but the consultant was already swishing through those curtains. I knew I couldn't stay here, not next to that wall of sound, that ascending wail. I tried to collect my thoughts. I'd go and find a phone, ring Alex to come and fetch me. Gingerly I swung my legs down to the cold floor. A pain like a cold sharp blade shot up through my left foot but I tried to ignore it. I must escape those sobs.

I managed to limp as far as the first double-doors before I thought the pain might actually make me sick. The nice nurse caught up with me as I leaned on the wall in agony, sat me on a furry old chair by the door and held my hand, just for a minute. A middle-aged couple rushed through the doors, the frizzy-haired woman pressing a tissue to her mouth to stop the tears, followed by a younger man, beanie hat pulled down against the weather, all glittery with silver raindrops. He dropped his phone as he passed; it clattered to the ground near my feet.

'Sorry,' he muttered, sweeping it up again. He saw the nurse. 'We're looking for my girlfriend? She was on the coach.'

'Go to the desk.' The nurse pointed back the way they'd come. 'They've got the list.'

He rushed back through the doors without any more ado, the couple following behind. An old woman in the bed opposite started to groan. Oh God.

'I need to ring my boyfriend,' I whispered when I'd recovered enough to talk. 'He'll be so worried. I never stay out all night.' Did I?

'Go back to bed. I'll bring you the phone.' But then the nurse looked up the ward, at the other nurses flying back and forth between those pastel curtains and then at the crash-cart that came slamming through the doors, and she changed her mind. She wheeled the phone to me where I sat. And I tried very hard not to look at that bed, and concentrated on making the phone call.

It took me three attempts to remember my home number.

First I got the voicemail for some curry-house in Dalston; then some very disgruntled old man whom I'd obviously just woken up.

'Sorry.' I thumped the receiver down again in frustration; glanced up at the clock on the wall. It was ridiculously early.

'Eight-nine-eight,' I muttered to myself. 'Nine-eight-nine.' For God's sake! How could I not remember? I made a third attempt. Somehow, somewhere in the depths of last night's accident, I'd wiped out my home number. I'd wiped out my home.

Of course, he didn't answer. Alex hardly ever answered the phone, even at the best of times. Now it was so early he'd be asleep. Or – I steadied that thought to a shuddering halt. He was asleep. He slept so very deeply once he'd actually dropped off. I'd ring back in half an hour. He'd be getting up then; getting up for work, not knowing anything was wrong. Maybe a little concerned, of course, but –

I replaced the phone carefully on the stand and smoothed my hospital gown down over my knees. I really did feel rather peculiar. And I was freezing now.

When I finally went back to my bed, the next-door one was empty, the wail silenced. The small nurse stripping it wouldn't catch my eye; her jaw was set grimly. I started to shiver, my teeth chattering in my head. The nice nurse came back with her list. She looked at me; she seemed a little worried.

'I'll bring you some sweet tea. The sugar'll do you good. The police are here now. They'll explain things to you.'

As she adjusted my pillow, I caught the typed heading on the paper. 'SURVIVORS', its bold black letters stated unequivocally. My bowels clenched in a strange involuntary movement. How could I be on a list? I made lists, that's what I did, compiled lists of people, and attached those lists to a clipboard, clasped the clipboard protectively to my chest so that no one but me could consult it, and then checked people off that list. I ticked the names off as they arrived, fretted when they didn't, shepherded them around the warren of corridors at the studios, and primed them on what to say down in the dressing-rooms. I couldn't be on a list; I didn't want to be on a list. I wanted to get the hell off the list and out of here. I wanted Alex to come and get me the hell out of here.

On my fourth try, Alex answered.

'Thank God.' I started to cry with relief. Once I started, I found I couldn't stop.

'What?'

'Thank God you're there.'

He was groggy, uncommunicative. He was always terrible in the morning. 'Why are you crying?'

'Sorry.' I breathed deeply to quieten my sobs. 'I'm okay, don't worry.' I stifled another sob. 'Can you come and get me?'

'What time is it?'

He was probably hung over.

'I don't know. It's early. I'm in the hospital.'

Probably hung over? There was no probably about it. There never was these days.

'Come and get me, Alex, please.'

'Are you fucking joking?'

My brain couldn't compute this. 'What? What do you mean?'

'Why should I come and get you?'

'Because I've – there's been an accident.'

'Oh really?'

I stopped crying. The shock stopped me crying. For some reason he thought I was lying.

'Alex,' I whispered.

'Yes?'

'Why are you being like this? I – I need you. I'm in the hospital.'

There was a pause. I could feel him struggling with something. 'Yeah, well.' His voice had thickened. I heard him take a deep breath in. 'Bad luck, Maggie.'

There was a click. My boyfriend had apparently hung up.

In the end, my father came to fetch me. I sat numb in my hospital bed, racking my brain, over and over, and as soon as my father arrived I was out of that bed. God, I would have run down the corridor if I could have. The wheelchair the nice nurse wanted me to use loomed black and heavy by my bed, but I couldn't bear it. Instead I clutched my father's arm like I'd never let it go.

'Please, Daddy, get me out of here,' I whispered. I hadn't called him Daddy since I was thirteen. And he understood my desperation, my fear of such institutions; he probably shared it with me, in fact, but he hid it well. He pulled me nearer to his red anorak that rustled so, that smelled of fresh air and bonfires. He stroked my hair, just once.

'Chin up, hey, Mag,' he said and his eyes were both sorry and kind. And then he put me in his car and took me back to his house – because though I just couldn't remember, I apparently no longer had a home.

# *Chapter Eight*

On the Monday after Bel's wedding I woke early and almost sick with nerves. For a moment I couldn't think why – then I realised that today I was returning to work, to the nightmare of *Renee Reveals*. Pulling the duvet over my head didn't make the fear dissipate. Eventually I clambered out of bed.

For once, the journey into town flashed by, when usually it seemed interminable. Surrounded by a floating sea of free newspapers, we rattled over the arches of Rotherhithe and Bermondsey, the sky a cobweb of intricate cloud above neat tower-blocks that flapped bright washing on plastic lines, and I realised with stomach-clenching clarity that I was actually frightened.

Although I'd seen a few of the team while I recuperated at my dad's, I had no idea how they were going to react to me in the office. I had no idea how much they knew, and that was what scared me most. I could still barely piece it all together myself. And, deeper down, I was frightened I'd lost my touch. Sitting at home alone for months hadn't been exactly morale-boosting.

Of course, this morning the journey was so smooth that I ended up being early. I felt very tiny as I dawdled across Charing Cross footbridge in the freezing autumn air, the skyline hectic, huge cranes soaring above the spires of centuries past. I stopped at the corner café for coffee so strong it made my heart bump and they recognised me behind the counter, but I couldn't manage conversation this morning. Finally I couldn't drag it out any longer. I was so nervous that I almost couldn't sign my own name at security.

But when I actually walked into the office, the initial reception I received was so nice, the girls so pleased to see me, the gossip to catch up with so comfortingly familiar, that I felt an enormous wash of relief; compounded by the fact that Charlie was apparently out all day. It's not so bad, I told myself. Perhaps I can manage, after all.

I was just starting to relax a little, sorting things out in my tiny office, trying not to be overwhelmed by the thousands of emails and piles of paperwork that had accumulated since I'd last been here, when there was a tentative knock at my door.

'Maggie?'

I looked up from the letter I'd been reading. It was the blond boy from the trauma show. Now that I looked at him again, it was funny – he reminded me of someone. Probably himself.

'Oh, hi.' I'd forgotten his bloody name again.

'I thought you might like a coffee.'

He looked so eager I didn't dare tell him I was already buzzing with caffeine. Very carefully, like it was a Faberge egg and not a chipped old mug declaring *You're the best* in hot-pink on one side, he placed it down beside the computer. Then he stood and looked at me.

'So, how's it going?' I asked when I realised he wasn't going to speak. 'Are you settling in? Sometimes it can –'

'Oh I love it,' he interrupted airily. 'The girls have made me really welcome.' That'd be a first. They hated anyone who wasn't their own. 'They remember me from the summer, of course.'

I wished to God I did. 'So, what are you working on?'

But he never got to answer because Charlie suddenly stuck his head round the door.

'Miss Warren. Not before time, some less patient than myself might say.'

'Hi, Charlie.'

'Everything all right? Excited to be back?' He sauntered in holding a folder I didn't much like the look of.

'Oh yes, very excited.' My smile was as genuine as Charlie's signet ring as the blond boy slunk out of the room, obviously irritated that Charlie had ignored him.

'Strange boy, that one.' My boss plonked himself on the edge of my desk, crumpling my '*Welcome Back*' card in the process.

'He does seem a bit odd, yes.' I moved the card.

'Anyway, darling, we need to discuss the show –'

The phone rang and I snatched it up, glad of the distraction. 'Maggie Warren.' No one spoke. 'Hello? Hello?' Eventually I hung up.

'So, look, I've been talking to the team about the *You're Dumped* show.' Charlie admired his reflection in the glass partition and adjusted his collar minutely. 'Everyone's very excited.'

I seriously doubted that.

'But we do need to book a celeb couple pronto, for the kudos. Get Donna on it.'

'Oh Charlie, come on.' I actually laughed. 'No one in the public eye is gonna dump their partner live on air, are they. Not even the Z-list.'

'Really? What about Jade Goody? Or that blond kid from *East-Enders*, the one that's always fighting in the clubs –'

I fought the urge to sink my head onto the desk. 'If you say so,' I murmured.

'Pull all the stops out, Maggie, yeah? You know you can do it.'

'I'm not sure I'm quite there yet, Charlie.' I held his gaze.

'Well, you'd better be, my darling. Because Sally and Donna are chomping at the bit for your job.' Charlie flung the folder onto my desk. A photo fell out of the side. 'I can't stave them off for much longer.'

The photo looked horribly like –

'Is that . . .?' I pulled the picture towards me.

'What? Oh yes, your little friend. She's dying to appear on *any* show, apparently. I do love the fame-hungry, don't you?'

I turned the black and white headshot round to face me. Fay.

Somehow I got through that first day, though I practically willed the clock to strike six. I was hugely relieved to realise I hadn't forgotten everything I knew, although my memory and my concentration were still tested.

Around five I'd taken a deep breath and made a phone call. She was horribly pleased to hear from me.

'Don't worry, Maggie. Charlie's explained it all. It makes perfect sense – you know you love someone, but you also know you're doing the right thing by finishing with them.'

How very ingenious of Charlie.

'I need to talk to Troy first, obviously, sound him out. But Charlie said, well, he said he'd make it worth my while, you know.'

'I bet he did,' I muttered. 'You know, Fay, you should really, really think about this before you do it.'

'I have.'

'I mean, how will Troy take it if you do something like that live on air, in front of an audience? There'll be no going back once it's done.'

I almost couldn't believe my own ears. Me, who was usually trying desperately to persuade, to coax people into doing things on live telly that I'd never ever countenance myself.

Fay was absolutely blithe. 'He knows it's on the cards anyway. I'm sure he'd like to be on TV too, you know.'

'Yeah, but Fay, this is real life. It's not play-acting.'

'Oh, yes, I know.' I could picture her dreamy smile. I had the unsettling feeling that she was actually quite mad. 'He'll be happy for me. He knows I want to be famous.'

'Famous?'

'I've already got recognised in the street since the show. It's so exciting.'

I cringed inside. 'Look, Fay, I can arrange for you to be on another show. You don't have to dump your boyfriend live on air to be famous, really.' I was so tense my head was starting to ache.

'It's not dumping,' she gabbled on. 'It's just telling the truth. And Charlie said he'd take care of me anyway.'

It was too late to save her. She'd been truly brainwashed.

In the end Fay and Troy split up long before the show. Instead she came on an episode that Sally produced called '*I'd Do Anything To Be Famous*', where Fay showed the crash photo reverently and cried a bit, and then performed a rather innocuous pole-dance live, which resulted in one of the glamour agencies signing her up. I watched the show in the office with half an eye, busy signing contracts to secure a drug-addled celebrity set to reveal her addictions on a show next week for an awful lot of money. Suddenly I thought I heard my name. I took a swig of coffee and turned the volume up.

'Yes. As I say, I wouldn't be here now if it wasn't for my new friend. Good comes out of bad, you know, I think that's always true. I'm so glad that I got the chance to meet her.' Fay looked right into the camera, practically caressing the lens with those melting eyes. 'Maggie, I'd like to thank you – not only for saving me on that coach, but for showing me the way. Here's to you.' She raised an imaginary glass to the screen.

The phone on my desk rang as I almost choked on my coffee, but by the time I'd mopped up and answered it, the caller had rung off. On the show, Renee moved swiftly away from Fay's pseudo-psychology; if she had any idea it was me that Fay was celebrating, the bitter old bag sure as hell wouldn't dwell on it. And neither would I.

I had an odd feeling somewhere deep inside. I felt guilty about Fay, about the fact that she made my skin crawl. I hoped this would be the last I saw of her. But I soon forgot her. There were more serious things on my mind by then.

# *Chapter Nine*

Since I'd split up with Alex, Sundays haunted me. They were long and lonely; they reminded me of far happier times. However much I tried to celebrate my freedom, I just felt sad and empty as I dragged myself around the hills of Greenwich Park with Digby, or played gooseberry at Bel's.

This Sunday, as my father dropped me at the nursing home on his way to Jenny's, I was suffused not just with self-pity but with guilt too. I hadn't visited much since the accident, since I'd utterly lost myself in the summer. I'd kept away while I tried to recover. Now, though, I wanted to be with my grandmother, searching for some calm and serenity. I needed to step out of time for a moment.

The staff were as welcoming as ever when I arrived; relieved to see young blood in these corridors of doom, I always guessed.

'How's the wicked Renee?' joked Susan, her broad face still jolly despite the smell of decay and urine that pervaded the air; the perpetual smell that Susan lived and worked in. They thought I was so glamorous because I worked in the TV industry, and I played along with the lie because it *was* a nice job when you compared it to what they did: shovelling food and drink into slack old mouths, listening to the same feeble moans, to the hysteria of the senile and the ramblings of the lonely, the interminable wiping and dressing and wiping again. How could I possibly complain? They didn't know that I hated myself a little more each day.

Angelic in her green dressing-gown, Gar looked as fragile as a powder-puff about to float away. Her soft hair was tied in a bun, silky under the dim light of her room. Someone had tuned her stereo into Radio 3 and she was nodding off to the strains of Strauss, her last cup of tea cold and cloudy before her on the table. I didn't want to wake her – there was little point. Gar was going gaga, that was the awful truth. She was clamped in Alzheimer's relentless jaws, and there was no snatching her back.

I held her hand as she slept, her wrinkly old hand that was so light these days, and gazed almost unseeing at the familiar photos on the wall: me as a toothy baby; me as a fat and naked toddler in a pink sunhat on the beach in Cornwall; me aged about five in my mother's strong, freckled arms – skinny now, just a little curving belly of baby-fat left, our hair as brilliantly red as one another's, my mother beaming with love and my dad just off to the side looking on proudly, very tall and thin, before his stoop began. Before the sadness started.

Susan popped her head round the door.

'Fancy a cuppa, lovie?'

'I'd rather have a whisky,' I joked.

'Vera's got some sherry in her cupboard, I think.' Susan did a double-take. 'Ooh, you've had all your hair cut off. I didn't notice with that beret on before. Very nice. You look a bit like Twiggy used to. All eyes.' She wiped her red nose on a cotton handkerchief. 'Only she was blonde, of course.'

'Thank you.' I rubbed my bare neck self-consciously. 'I'm still not used to it. I just thought it was time for a change.'

'A change is as good as a rest, that's what they say.' Susan nodded her approval. 'I'll get you that tea.'

While I waited, I had a hunt for the sherry.

Gar woke just before I left. 'Did you have some porridge?' she asked politely, and I knew she wasn't sure who I was today, her blue eyes watery and confused – but she let me keep holding her hand, which was something. I stroked it gently and waffled on about this and that.

'I'll fetch that porridge, but don't let it burn,' my grandmother mumbled, and then nodded off again. I gave her a long hug, feeling her frame so frail beneath my arms, and headed back to Dad's.

There was a half-hour wait at the cab office so I attempted a bus, but they were rare at the best of times and it was late on Sunday, so in the end I decided to walk across Blackheath. The physio had said I needed to keep moving as much as possible – but God, I was deathly slow at the moment.

In the middle of the deserted heath it suddenly seemed horribly dark. A breeze sniggered through the trees; there was no sight of the moon, no stars, just clouds scudding across a dark sky. Although I fought it, a knot of apprehension tightened as I walked.

However hard I tried not to, I found myself constantly glancing behind me, disturbed by the notion that someone might be following me. But I was alone each time I turned; of course I was alone. I hummed something jolly, something made up, and wished fervently that Digby was here to bark at my imaginings. I tried to walk a little quicker, but my foot was really hampering me now.

A fox barked in the thicket by the pond, a terrible sound like a baby crying, and I jumped. The leaves rustled and shivered in the wind. Then a car drove by very fast, blinding me with its lights, and I stumbled on the uneven grass. Righting myself, I thought I heard voices but I couldn't work out from where. I picked up my pace as best I could.

Eventually a couple of kids dragging a fat Pekinese came into sight under the lamppost on the corner by the pond. My sigh of relief was audible. I shuffled along, keeping them in my sights until I finally hit the main road.

\*   \*   \*

The next day I raced home from work to collect the car I could finally drive again, and was about to head out when my dad called me into the sitting room. He was immersed in *The Times'* crossword.

'Beautiful flowers, love,' he said, waving his pen vaguely in the direction of the sideboard. 'I stuck them in a vase. You might need to do something with them.'

'Lilies,' I said stupidly, gazing at them. The exact same bunch as last time. 'Bloody lilies again.' I crossed the room to see if there was a card with them, but I couldn't find one. I gazed at the top of my father's bent and balding head. 'Do you know who brought them?'

'Fourteen across. Eight letters. Unwelcome pale beast.'

'Dad!'

'Sorry. No. They were on the doorstep when we got back.'

I pushed the vase back, morbidly transfixed. 'Flowers of death, you know,' I muttered. 'That's what they say.'

For the first time since I'd walked in, my father looked up at me sharply. 'Don't be silly, Maggie.' He frowned. 'Do you mean because –'

Jenny trundled in, wearing a vivid orange kaftan creation. She looked like a small plump carrot. 'Hello, lovie.' She came over to kiss me. She was very tanned.

'You look well,' I said, as brightly as I could. 'Good holiday?'

'Wonderful, thanks, Maggie. Amazing place. I'm going to try to drag your father there.'

I smiled. 'You should.' Somehow I couldn't see him on the beaches of Goa. But that was why they worked well together, my solemn, slightly pained father and the gregarious Jenny. When he'd introduced me to her a few months ago – 'their eyes had met across the crowded staffroom' – I hadn't taken much notice. Well, I hadn't been taking notice of anything, to be honest, and anyway, my father's relationships usually lasted less time than the seasons in his precious garden, as his heart never really engaged. But he and Jenny reflected something in one another, and she was still here. She'd seen him through the recent dark days, and she made him smile. That was the important thing.

'I've made a curry in India's honour. You'll join us, won't you?'

The carriage clock on the mantelpiece chimed the hour. 'I'm sure India will be very honoured, but I'm afraid I'm late already.' Thank God. Jenny's cooking was atrocious at the best of times.

'I'll save you some.' She noticed the flowers. 'New beau, darling? I do love lilies.'

'Just what you need,' my father mumbled. We both looked at him. 'A new beau.'

I blushed. 'I don't know *who* they're from, that's the problem.'

'Perhaps you've got a fan since your debut on TV.' Despite my best efforts, I'd been rumbled when my dad's head of maths, off sick, had caught the show. 'How exciting.' Jenny beamed. 'You could have a fan club and everything.'

'I'm going to chuck them out,' I replied. 'I don't want them anyway.'

'But they're gorgeous,' Jenny protested.

'Take them home, then,' I said. 'Honestly. You have them.'

'Of course!' My father hit the paper triumphantly. 'Elephant.'

I patted his head affectionately. 'I'll see you later.'

On the way out of the room I managed not to look at the lilies again, and I had such a nice time at Bel's – making spaghetti bolognese with Hannah while Bel rang round making last-minute arrangements for Friday night, drinking red wine and listening to Johnno playing the guitar badly, serenading us with silly Rolf Harris songs in his broadest Australian accent – that I forgot all about the bloody flowers.

But on the way home to my father's, the feeling of disquiet began to balloon again. It wasn't just the fact that some freak had taken to sending me horrible bouquets; it was my sense of utter displacement – knowing it was time to leave my father's house, time to leave Greenwich. He and Jenny were beginning to get close, and they deserved a proper chance after everything he'd been through. And I needed my own space again. I needed to finally extricate my life from Alex's. We were going to have to sell the flat in Borough Market, and that would inevitably mean seeing him.

My mobile rang. 'Hello?' I swerved dangerously near the parked car on my left. 'Hello?' I repeated irritably. 'Who's there?'

No one spoke, but this time I swore I could hear someone breathing. With a howl of frustration, I threw the phone onto the floor, where its fluorescent face winked up at me mercilessly all the way home.

# Chapter Ten

The morning of Bel's great party, I found Joseph Blake sulking on the office fire-escape. It was a cold sunny day, the sky as clear and bright as a Hockney print, the air fifteen storeys above the Waterloo streets far fresher than the fumes below. I'd sneaked out to have a cigarette, savouring every guilty drag as I contemplated how desperately I didn't want to go tonight, when I heard a stifled noise.

'Hello?' I called quietly up the stairs. No response. 'Who's that? Are you okay?'

A minute later, Joseph's blotchy red face peered down. 'Oh,' he said ungraciously. 'It's you.'

'It certainly was the last time I looked,' I agreed mildly. 'Cigarette?' I offered.

He stood and slunk down the stairs towards me, shaking his head at the packet, his blond hair flopping across his eyes. 'No. I don't.'

'No, well, I shouldn't. But we've all got to have a vice or two. Otherwise life'd be awfully dull, don't you think?'

He shrugged uncommunicatively, bashing a suede brothel-creeper against the metal step.

'So, d'you want to talk about it?'

He shrugged and bashed again. I felt my skin prickle with irritation. I took another drag of my cigarette. 'If you don't tell me what's wrong, Joseph, I can't help.'

74

He hesitated for a moment, looking out across the rooftops. Two young men smoked out of a window in the building opposite; one waving cheekily when he saw me glancing over. I waved back. Finally, Joseph muttered, 'It's them.'

He flopped his hair toward the office behind us, towards the girls scattered round the open-plan room. I glanced back at them. From outside they looked like an advert for a young fashion house, miniskirted, skinny-jeaned, Ugg boots and stilettos thrust up on desks, expensive messy hair skewered with biros, scribbling furiously and tapping fruity-coloured nails impatiently as they waited for answers from the prey pinioned on the other end of the phone lines. Sometimes the noise inside was so intense, so deafening as they pleaded and persuaded and hammered their keyboards frantically, that you'd have to step out for a moment to literally hear yourself think.

'They don't like me.'

'I'm sure that's not true.' But inwardly I sighed. Actually I was sure it was.

'They never ask me to have lunch.'

'They just need to get used to you. You should invite yourself along.'

'They don't talk to me if I do.'

'Well, talk to them.'

His bottom lip trembled, just like Hannah's did when she was going to cry. Poor kid.

'Look, I know it's really hard, being the new boy. And it's a very female office, I know that. Let me have a word with them.'

He shrugged again. How much of this was his fault? I wondered. He wasn't the most prepossessing figure; there was something inherently arrogant about his stance, despite the tears. The trouble was, he lacked the charm you needed to make it in TV-land.

'Won't that just make it worse? It did when my parents complained to the school.'

75

*Aha.* 'Did it? Were you bullied, then?'

'Yep.'

'Why?'

'They said I was posh.'

He was posh. 'I'll be subtle, I promise. I'm sure it's in your head, anyway.'

But it wasn't in his head, unfortunately. The truth was they despised him.

'He's such a bloody drip,' Donna moaned when I summoned the suspected ring-leaders into my office later that afternoon, having sent Joseph off to get some tapes dubbed. 'Always complaining we give him the dull jobs.'

'Well, do you?'

'Of course we do.' She was defiant, her dark face sulky. I wouldn't have wanted to get on the wrong side of someone like Donna when I started out. Driven and determined, she could persuade Blair he hated Bush if she put her mind to it.

'You know how it works, Maggie. You gotta do your time. You gotta start at the bottom. We all did. Anyway,' she sniffed, examining her pink palm-tree nails rather than looking at me, 'he's weird.'

'What do you mean, weird?'

'It's just, he's always poking around.' She flicked her long braids behind her shoulder, her full mouth set firm.

'He's just a bit full of himself, I think that's the problem.' Sally's broad pleasant face was thoughtful. 'He gets people's backs up because he acts like he's too good for the jobs we give him.'

'And have you talked to him about it?'

'It was like this in the summer.'

The hairs on my arms stood on end. I shook my head as if it would bring memories back.

'I've tried to explain, but he just bangs on about how he's going to be a great auteur, and how this is just a stop-gap.'

I sighed again. Yet another aspiring Nick-blinking-Broom-

76

field, about to save the world with his art. 'All right, look, let's just give him another chance, okay? I'll have a word.' I glared at Donna. 'And be nice, yeah? I know how intimidating you lot can be if you put your minds to it.'

She grinned sheepishly, raising the palm trees in supplication before her tightly T-shirted bosom that read *Respect Me*. 'Okay, okay.'

Sally lingered in my office. 'The truth is, Maggie, I don't think he'll ever really fit in. He's just one of those slightly oddball kids, you know? Like the ones at school who had an imaginary friend they played with at breaktime.'

'Yep, I do know. But that lot can be remorseless, we both know that.'

'I suppose.' She brightened. 'You going to Bel's tonight then?'

'Oh my God.' I clapped a hand to my forehead in distress. 'I forgot to pick up my dress. She'll kill me.' I cast a quick look across to Charlie's empty office. 'If I don't go now, I've blown it.'

'Go,' Sally urged. 'I'll cover for you.'

I dragged my coat on and grabbed my bag. 'With any luck,' I switched my computer to sleep mode, 'Charlie'll be too pissed to notice anyway.'

In a dim little street on the Covent Garden borders I found the shop with the fancy name that Bel had insisted I visit. The window heralded some of London's most expensive clothes – a veritable myriad of gorgeous stuff. Minty greens and frilly pinks, gold silks and silver froth, below which crouched lethal-looking shoes with four-inch heels, poised to spring cruelly onto unsuspecting feet. It was so utterly not me – but my fate was sealed. As I hovered by the door, a size-zero girl with scary eyebrows slithered towards me, and, with disdain ill-hidden, relieved me of my polystyrene coffee-cup. 'Can I help, madam?' she asked, barely keeping the sneer off her face.

'I've come to collect a dress Bel Whitemore has reserved for me.' I looked around nervously, taking in the flounces, the backless and frontless, the micro-mini and the slit-to-the-thigh. 'Lord. I do hope it's something subtle.'

The girl swished through the chiffon, the beribboned and the barely-there to find what Bel had chosen.

'So brave to try that colour. Red hair must be *so* difficult.'

Manfully I ignored the girl as I stepped into the beautiful forest-green floor-length dress, plunging at the front and cut deeply at the back. To complete the outfit she gave me stilettos by someone called Manolo Blahnik, the perfect eyebrows nearly shooting off her face in horror when I said I'd never heard of him.

'Everyone's wearing Blahnik,' she chastised, forcing my feet into what seemed little more than a few skinny straps and another killer heel.

'Sounds more like a space shuttle to me,' I joked, but she didn't laugh – and she only blanched a bit at the scar on my left foot.

I wobbled out anxiously through the curtains to look in the full-length mirror, staring at myself for a silent moment. When I read the price-tag, though, I nearly fainted.

'Thanks very much for your help, but I'm afraid –'

The girl was deep in conversation with another skinny someone – a someone I recognised with a painful thud. Serena. I prepared myself to say hello, but she just gazed at me vacantly, immaculate in a long leather coat, then tightened the belt around her tiny waist and carried on her conversation. I thought I heard her mention a wedding as I slunk back into the changing-room, sinking down on the stool in the corner.

When I eventually came out again, Serena was admiring her many reflections, all clad in a pair of vertiginous snakeskin boots. How appropriate and how very unethical, I thought sourly.

I bought the dress just to prove I had as much panache as

them, and then I let the door bang behind me as I strode purpose-fully out of the shop. Outside, the street was busy, the clamour of Covent Garden loud and vibrant – but I felt like I'd lost my mooring, like I was floating off to sea.

Somehow it took some time to get back to work.

In a show of power no doubt born from my afternoon flit, Charlie had ensured I had a stack of new stuff on my desk to sort out for Monday's programme. I was just putting the phone down from briefing Renee when he wandered in, breathing brandy fumes at me.

'Marvellous lunch with Alan Yentob,' Charlie crowed, pulling a book on the Lost Gardens of Heligan from my shelf. 'He's wetting himself with excitement over my idea for a layman's *Panorama*. Current affairs for the thicko.'

'Really?' I said politely. It was extremely hard to imagine Yentob in Charlie's thrall.

'Yes, darling.' He perched on the edge of my desk. '*The Easy View*, I think we'll call it. You know, I never see you as the country type.' He flicked through the garden book indolently. 'Cornwall's deeply unfashionable these days, darling. So bloody far away, and always raining. Give me Dubai any time.' Charlie shoved the book back, knocking three box-files off the other end that he didn't bother to retrieve. 'Going to Bel's tonight?'

'Um, I'm thinking about it.' I doodled on my pad, holding my breath. 'Are you?'

'Wouldn't miss it for the world, darling.'

I breathed out.

'So sad to be losing one of our very best girls.' Bel had long since progressed onto make-up for drama and film, but Charlie liked to think of himself as a great benefactor, responsible for everyone's career, and Bel was always remembered fondly. 'Don't be late now, eh?' He strolled off around the office to peer down some cleavages.

I was so long at my desk that all the other girls left; they'd wait for me in the bar downstairs, they said, wired with Friday night anticipation. Eventually I headed to the loo with my dress. Mid tights-change, my mobile rang. '*Private number*' flashed up on the display.

'Hello?'

Nothing.

'Hello? Hello?' I repeated irritably. 'Is anyone there?'

Just one long, slow breath – and then the line went dead.

'For God's sake.' I considered the phone in my hand for a second, then I rang Alex's number. It went straight to voicemail. I slammed the mobile down on the side of the sink, and stood for a minute. Then I fished out my eyeliner. 'Bloody bollocks to you, too.'

The frosted window rattled suddenly; one of the cubicle doors banged. I jumped, drawing a great kohl tick across my cheek. Immediately tense, I peered round. I was sure I'd been the last one in the office.

'Hello?' I hated the fact my voice wavered as I spoke.

I thought I heard the shuffle of feet. A clammy sweat broke out on my top lip. I took a deep breath and crept down the row of cubicles to the one nearest the exit. It was shut.

'Is anyone there?'

I stared at it and then quickly pushed the door: it swung open and smacked hard against the wall. The cubicle was empty. Nervously I laughed at my overactive imagination, but I struggled into the dress as fast as I could, not caring that I couldn't reach the zip myself. I wanted to get out of there. As I walked into the corridor, one of the fire-exit doors swung shut.

I took a deep breath. I had to retrieve my stuff from my office, which was in darkness now as I hurried across, just the ghostly flicker of light from the computer's screensaver. As I grabbed my bag, I heard another noise.

'Who's there?' I swung round, my voice sharp with fear.

Silence fell again across the darkened room. Perhaps it was one of the cleaners. Perhaps I'd imagined it.

I hurried towards the lift now – and then I heard a cough. A definite cough. I froze for a second behind the central pillar, my heart pounding. Silence fell again.

I shook my head. I was being silly. Except, if I *was* being silly, why had no one answered when I'd called?

And then a low voice, sullen, wheedling, slunk out across the darkness. Peering round the pillar, I noticed the crack of light under Charlie's door. I took a deep breath and crept nearer. I could hear the mutter more clearly: a lone voice. It wasn't Charlie – that much I knew for sure. Flattened against the wall outside the door, which was slightly ajar, I realised someone was using his phone.

'But what's in it for me? I need some sort of assurance,' I heard. A pause. Then –

'So if I do it, you'll sort the . . .? Okay. And can you put that in writing?' the voice said. Another pause. 'No, I realise that.'

I peered through the crack in the door now. There was Joseph Blake, his legs up on the desk, the phone cord wound around his stubby finger, smug even in the gloom. His shiny face was half-lit; his eyes narrowed as he listened. Fragments of lost memory suddenly floated through my throbbing head – a sudden image of Joseph in evening dress and . . .

I shuddered violently. That night at the –

His voice cut through my memories and they dissolved again.

'Yeah, of course I'll get you good ones. The most important. For the right –'

Craning forward into the gloom I caught my dress on the edge of a desk and jarred my bad ankle. My sob of pain was audible. Joseph leapt up, crashing the receiver down immediately.

'Who's there?' His voice was sharp as he stood behind the desk.

'Oh God, Joseph. You really scared me.' My heart was pounding through the thin material of my dress as I pushed the door fully open. 'I nearly had a heart attack. What are you doing here? Does Charlie know you're using his phone?'

'I don't know.' His overly-red lips turned down in an unpleasant pout. 'I just had a call to make.'

'What kind of call?'

He looked supremely guilty as we regarded one another silently for a second, his pale face striped with luminous colour from the beam of Charlie's desk light.

'It was work,' he muttered eventually. 'Just work. You know I don't have my own desk any more. I just needed a phone.'

'Well, as admirable as working late on a Friday might be, you shouldn't be using private offices.' I pushed down my irritation as he glared at me as if *I* was in the wrong. 'There are plenty of phones out there. Come on,' I gestured to him. 'Zip me up and let's get out of here.'

As Joseph stood, he shoved something into his bag in a fluid movement.

'What was that?' I screwed up my eyes in the gloom.

'What?' Joseph followed my gaze to his bag. 'Oh, nothing. Just my diary.'

I headed towards the door, desperate to get out of there. Frankly I'd been dreading Bel's party, but now I suddenly saw safety in numbers. As far away from creepy Joseph as possible.

# Chapter Eleven

Old friends bobbed about the party like baubles on a Christmas tree, the women spilling out of silk and satin, the men preening peacock-like in their best clobber. The air was thick with smoke and music and expensive scent, and the Dutch courage I'd downed earlier meant I was almost starting to enjoy myself, once I realised Alex wasn't there. I was shouting over the din to my chain-smoking friend Naz, admiring her slinky cream salwar kameez and hearing about the job the BBC had just offered her, when I felt a gentle tap on my back. Gentle, but insistent.

'Nice dress.' Fay looked up at me intently as I turned round. 'Champagne?' In a funky little black and white waitress number that somehow clung in all the right places, her violet eyes ringed with iridescent silver, her ringlets perfectly sausage-like, she looked stunning. I, on the other hand, was simply stunned.

If Fay noticed that my face had fallen, it didn't put her off. 'That colour green really suits you. I'd love a dress like that.'

'Thanks.' I tried to collect my thoughts. 'What are – I mean, I wasn't expecting –'

'I'm a Beautiful Bartender.' She smiled proudly.

'A what?' I managed to suppress a deep sigh.

'It's great, isn't it? It's my other job when I'm not on TV. How funny they wanted me to work tonight, don't you think?

Oh look, there's Charlie.' Fay waved merrily at where he lounged against the bar. 'I'll be straight back,' she promised me.

'There's no rush,' I muttered as she floated off, 'really.'

'Old friend?' asked Naz cheerfully, offering me a cigarette. 'You don't look too pleased to see her, I must say.'

'Don't I?' I took a drag so deep the acrid smoke made me cough.

'Nope.'

'I just don't quite understand why she keeps turning up everywhere.'

In the middle of the dance floor, Bel and Johnno were kissing, oblivious to their pogo-ing neighbours, oblivious to everyone around them. I wasn't envious. I really wasn't. Taking a slug of my cocktail, I was surprised to find my glass was empty. 'Oh, I don't know. I'm not sure if I'm just being paranoid.'

'Why? Who is she?'

'She was on the coach when it crashed, and now – well, she just keeps turning up all over the place.'

'Like a bad penny.'

'Something like that, yes.'

'I know what'll cheer you up.' Naz grabbed my hand and pulled me towards the Ladies. 'Come on.'

'I'm fine, Naz, honestly.'

She was determined. 'Oh, come *on*. Don't be a spoilsport.'

'I'm not. I'd rather have a drink, that's all. You go. I'll be at the bar.'

Fay sidled up to me as I waited to get served. My foot was throbbing painfully from bashing it outside Charlie's office door.

'I'm off now, Maggie. I was only booked for the first two hours. Got a party of my own to go to now.'

I felt inordinately relieved.

'My new agency – their party.' Fay said the first words with great pride.

'Oh right. Well, have a good time.' I resisted the temptation to slide my finger through the middle of her perfect ringlet.

'I always do.' Fay took both my hands in hers and squeezed them rather like a vicar might. 'I'll see you soon.'

'Champagne, darling?' Charlie's hot breath caressed my naked back and I shuddered, watching Fay skip towards the stairs.

There followed an hour of polite-if-rather-dazed listening to Naz's friends from one of the big channels. They were all wired, admiring themselves in the mirrored walls with the complete assurance that they had never looked better, slimmer or taller than right now. Frantically they jostled for air-time, each absolutely convinced that what they had to say was far more fascinating than the next person's offering. I stifled a yawn. The only thing more boring than taking coke was listening to people bang on about it.

'Let me talk,' one heavy girl with a thick black fringe kept insisting, scowling if anyone interrupted her. I felt like the needle in the middle of a badly tuned radio, voices vying for attention. 'No, no, listen,' the girl was saying now. I realised hazily that she was talking to me. 'Naz told me you're doing the Renee Owens show. I don't know how you can work on that rubbish, I really don't. It's so bloody rigged.'

'Rigged?' I really couldn't be bothered to defend myself. 'And what do you do?'

'I'm series producing this year's *X Factor*,' she announced proudly. 'It's a corker – beating *Strictly* hands down.'

'What, and *X Factor*'s all about the talent?' Naz scoffed. 'Come on, Nat! Pull the other one.'

'It *is* based on talent!' Natalie was outraged. 'Absolutely. And, God, Simon's *such* a scream to work with.'

'Whose talent?' I raised an eyebrow. 'Sharon Osbourne's? You're shoving the walking wounded straight into the cannon's mouth.'

'We only –'

85

I zoned out. The couple next to me couldn't keep their hands off one another; the bloke kept thrusting his hand down the back of her jeans. Mournfully I thought of Alex and looked away.

'You do look fab, Maggie – just like a Christmas present,' Naz said kindly. 'Someone's bound to tear you open soon!' Only her streaming nose rather ruined the sentiment. As her boyfriend snaked a lascivious arm around her, I fled to join Bel on the dance floor.

She was extremely drunk. After some rather terrifying disco-squats she ricocheted round the dancers surrounding her, finally cannoning into me so that I fell against a group standing on the edge of the dance floor. An arm shot out to steady me.

'Sorry.' I staggered in the heels I wasn't used to, my bad foot sore again where I'd awkwardly righted myself. 'Ouch.'

'Do you want to sit down for a second?' The dark-haired man who'd just caught me led me to a seat tucked in the corner, where I plonked myself down inelegantly and slid my shoe off. 'Oh God, that hurts.' I rubbed my toes. 'Thanks for saving me.'

'No problem.' He offered me a hand. 'Sebastian Rae. Seb.'

'Maggie. Maggie Warren.' And then I looked up at him directly as I took the proffered hand, and for the first time since Alex, the first time in such a very long time, I felt a surge of something, something like life, and it almost winded me. I looked up at this man again, and afterwards I had the horrible feeling I might have been mouthing stupidly, sort of fish-like, saying nothing.

He was studying me intently, his dark eyes inscrutable. So intently. I looked away again very quickly and prayed I hadn't just blushed like a schoolgirl.

'You all right now, then, Maggie Warren?'

'Oh yes, I'm fine.' He was going to walk away. Please don't walk away. But he moved off – and then he turned and looked at me again.

'Can I get you a drink?'

Oh God, absolutely. 'Oh, thanks – if you're sure,' I mumbled.

I liked his suit. It would have looked rather odd and out of place on anyone else amid this mayhem, but something about his leanness, about his stance, meant he pulled it off. I'd quite like to pull it off, I decided. I looked at my feet, and back up again. He was still waiting.

'What'll it be then?'

'Oh, sorry! I'll have a – a glass of red wine please.'

By the time Seb had battled to the bar and back I'd had time to come to my senses. I definitely wasn't ready for this again. And he – well, he wasn't Alex. He sat beside me, his dark hair tousled, his shirt very white, and I stared at the razor-sharp creases in his grey trousers and tried desperately to think of something interesting to say.

'What do you do?' I'd failed. The flashing lights and the banging music were beginning to confuse me; I breathed deep and tried not to succumb to his crooked smile. Trust in myself and any ability I had to choose a man well – a good man – was long gone. My heart was still lumpen in my chest, still jagged and torn. I couldn't imagine a time when it would be whole again.

'I'm an actor, actually.' He raised his glass to me. I had the uncomfortable feeling he was sizing me up.

'How exciting.' Did I sound star-struck? I'd met so many celebrities in my job, but he seemed a little different; somehow aloof from it all. 'I thought you looked a bit familiar.'

He had a very small scar running vertically above his upper lip, the skin there paler than the rest. I sat firmly on my hands, resisting the temptation to reach out and touch it. 'Have you been in anything I'd have seen?'

'Oh, you know. *EastEnders*, *The Bill*. The usual crap.' He smiled, and I smiled back. I liked the way the corner of his mouth twisted as he grinned. I liked the fact he had a sense of humour about himself, which most actors I'd met lacked, and most of all I liked his dark eyes, eyes that were almost black in this dim light. Like melting tar on summer roads. I looked away.

'I'm about to do some Shakespeare actually.'

'Oh really? Personally I never really got to grips with the great Bard. Too much flouncy language, not enough sex.' *Where had that come from?* I winced at myself. *Quit while you're ahead, Maggie,* a little voice muttered.

'No, well, he's not everybody's cup of tea. But, actually, there's quite a lot of sex, I'd say. A lot of people ruined by broken hearts and jealous lovers.'

*Me too,* I nearly said. I am utterly ruined by my last love. My lost love. I caught myself: drunk and maudlin, a fatal combination. I tried to focus; to place his accent. Very faint. A burr, maybe Midlands, West Country perhaps. I felt a pang for Pendarlin again.

'Which play are you doing?'

'*Twelfth Night.*'

I vaguely remembered it from A-level English. I could just see him as the handsome angry prince who bangs on about music being the food of love, fighting desperately for the girl he wants. How romantic. I found I'd drained my wine.

Seb grinned. 'Actually, if you want a bit of sex, there's even some cross-dressing going on in *Twelfth Night.*'

'It's not sexy, cross-dressing, though, is it?' I frowned, concentrating hard. 'I thought it was about disguise and hiding. You're not playing the one who burps, are you?'

'Sir Toby Belch? No, not this time, sadly. He's very funny, though.'

'Or the one that wears yellow socks?' I hiccuped gently and contemplated him. 'I see you more as Hamlet, you know.'

Seb smiled inscrutably. 'I guess most of us "thesps" like to think we've got him in us.'

I was steeling myself to ask whether Seb would like another drink when he stood up. 'I've got an early start.' He smiled at me as I bit down the disappointment, squinting up at him. 'So, Maggie Warren.' He was very gorgeous, and I was a bit drunk. I might be ruined by Alex, but I was still capable of rebounding heavily. It was definitely better that Seb left immediately. There was no telling what I might do when I was in my cups. My C cups. I started to smile.

Taking my hand, he held it for a minute. Or perhaps it was my imagination; perhaps it was a mere second. His skin was very cool against mine, which was burning hot. 'It was nice to meet you.'

I stood up too. 'Oh, yes. Likewise.'

He stared at me for a second, and then he grinned. 'And watch out for that dance floor. It's got a mind of its own.'

This time I did blush. 'Oh yes, I will. I mean, it was Bel. You know Bel when she gets going. She knocked me over.'

But he'd already been swallowed up by the heaving throng, which was getting wilder by the minute. I gazed after him – and then suddenly Bel and Johnno were standing before me – or, rather, Johnno was standing, holding a slumped Bel upright. 'Bit tired and emotional, you know. I think I'd better take her home.'

'Who was that?' she slurred.

'Seb. Sebastian Rae. The actor.' His name sounded unwieldy on my lips.

'Oh yes,' she nodded, then turned a gentle green. 'You know, I actually really don't feel too good. At all, actually.'

After Johnno had removed Bel in some haste, I realised I had little inclination to join the hysterical shrieking fracas that was the last hour or two of a good party. There was really no one left who I even wanted to talk to. For one insane moment I contemplated calling Alex. Because of that, I knew I must go home to bed. Grappling with my coat and bag at the cloakroom, Charlie wafted up beside me and scooped up the confetti packets I'd just knocked off the side. 'Oh.' I gazed at one sadly before plopping them back in the bowl. 'We forgot to throw the confetti.'

'What a shame,' Charlie said insincerely. 'Need a lift, darling?'

'It's the wrong way, isn't it?' I concentrated on not slurring. 'A cab'll be fine, thanks, Charlie. There'll be loads around I expect.'

'Suit yourself.'

It was freezing outside, the frenetic hubbub of nearby Piccadilly not lessened by the late hour. On the edge of the kerb I shrugged my coat round my shoulders and looked hopefully for a taxi, for the usual hustlers hoping for a fare. Of course, tonight there were none to be found. The cold air made me realise just how tired and hazy I really was, and I was suddenly desperate to be home now; for the quietness and serenity of my own room and the sanctuary of my father's house.

A car snapped on its headlights, catching me in the blazing beam. I put a hand up to flag it, and in response he snapped his lights again to full-beam. The glare was so strong it blinded me. I threw my arm up to shield my eyes against the light, relieved to have found a cab, stepping towards the edge of the kerb to wait for him to pull up alongside me.

There was a huge roar as the car over-revved. 'Easy, tiger,' I was about to mutter, but through the glare I could make out that the vehicle was moving – fast now, too fast – driving directly towards me.

Confused, I took a step back. Disoriented by the headlights, I staggered in my spindly heels. I could smell the diesel now as I smacked into the lamppost behind me, and somehow I lost my balance and suddenly found myself falling, falling forward toward the acrid stench of fumes. I shouted something in desperation, I don't know what – but I knew I was about to go under the wheels, wheels that moved relentlessly toward me –

'I've got you.'

An arm grabbed mine and pulled me back. Charlie – Charlie was holding me up now, and I clutched him as the car roared past. With a screech of tyres it took off round the corner. I stared after it, Charlie's signet ring biting into my naked arm. When he took his hand away, his fingerprints had stained my pale skin.

'Bloody boy-racers,' he swore. For once, his slicked-back grey hair was dishevelled, falling across his face. He pushed it back irritably as, dazed, I let him lead me to his silver Alfa. 'Come on, I'll take you home.'

'I think – that car, it was driving straight at me.'

'Don't be so silly.' He manoeuvred me down into the low seat. 'You're pissed. It was just some kid showing off.'

The lights of London slid by outside. Buckingham Palace was an oversized dolls' house, the road around it a great red skating-rink, Big Ben as magical as ever beneath a silver moon. For a moment I imagined I was Peter Pan silhouetted against the clock-face, flying off into Neverland.

I heard my mobile ring in the depths of the bag at my feet, but by the time I'd hauled it out it had stopped and the screen just read 'one missed call'.

And gradually, as my pounding heart slowed, I began to feel safe; like I was in a David Gray video, muffled from the cold, driving in a car so smooth it felt like floating in an armchair, anaesthetised from my own pain by alcohol – until suddenly I realised I was far from home. In Vauxhall, in fact – outside Charlie's penthouse on the river.

'I've had rather a lot to drink, darling, thinking about it.' He smiled at me wolfishly and bleeped the security barrier with the control in one apparently steady hand. 'I forgot you were staying out in the sticks. Come up for a snifter, and I'll call you that cab.'

In the lift up to his penthouse, he moved a fraction nearer – or perhaps it was just the gentle bouncing of the shiny lift. I backed into the corner anyway, feigning interest in my appearance. My reflections in the many mirrors showed me rumpled and slitty-eyed from booze, and as the lift door pinged open I rubbed a fuchsia kiss-mark from my cheek. Charlie stayed close by me as we walked into his flat, as if he was worried I'd make a sudden break for it.

I gazed around, intrigued. All this time I'd known him, and yet I'd never seen his lair. It was so very masculine, such an archetypal bachelor pad, that I nearly laughed out loud. He put some music on, *easy listening* I think they call it, and dimmed the lights. Above the living fire, two naked women rolled on the stone-coloured wall, wrapped tightly round each other. I tilted my head, trying to focus on the print. Perhaps they weren't rolling: perhaps they were fighting instead.

'Like it, darling?' Charlie followed my gaze as he propelled me towards a squashy leather sofa where my bottom was distinctly lower than my knees. He poured me a large Cognac. 'Your sort of thing, eh, Maggie?'

'God, no.' I took a slug of brandy and nearly choked. They definitely weren't fighting, I realised from this angle. 'I'm pretty straightforward really.'

'Really?' His hooded eyes were gleaming like a snake about to strike. 'You can never tell, darling. I thought I had you sussed until the summer. I thought perhaps you were game-on after –'

I changed the subject quickly. 'No tiger-skin rug then, eh, Charlie?'

'What?' He frowned.

'Oh, nothing.' The brandy burnt my throat. 'Can you ring that cab please? I'm knackered.'

'I already did, darling.' Charlie sat right next to me, inching his arm behind my head so I had to lean forward not to touch him. I could smell his hair-oil as I edged away until I was rammed up against the sofa-arm.

'Does Jeffrey Archer still live next door?' I asked rather desperately.

He raised an eyebrow. 'Fan of his?'

'Hardly,' I said indignantly. 'Look, I think – if you just give me the number, I'll call again. I really should be getting home now.'

But Charlie wasn't listening; Charlie was preparing to pounce. Charlie, my supposed bloody mentor – who I'd worked with for years, who I'd never had to fend off before, despite his boringly lecherous ways. I'd never been his type – I wasn't blonde or busty enough. Before I could move, he lunged; stuck his tongue into my mouth until I couldn't breathe. It seemed to have a life of its own. I felt quite sick.

'Charlie, for Christ's sake! Get off!' I managed to push him away, wiping my mouth frantically.

'I thought you liked a bit of danger, darling.' Entirely unperturbed, he pushed his hair back with the signet-ringed hand and topped up his brandy from the decanter on the coffee table. He didn't spill a drop; nor did he replenish mine. 'Don't pretend you didn't enjoy that, Maggie.'

I stared at him. Then I began to laugh. I laughed and laughed until I cried. And then when I cried, I found I couldn't stop. My make-up dripped in black rivulets onto the cream leather, my nose began to run. Charlie shifted slightly in his seat. Then he stared out of the window at the lights of London, at the glitter of the night Thames and the majestic Tate Britain opposite, twiddling his ring.

'I'm sorry,' he said eventually, as I began to calm myself, fishing out a monogrammed hanky and offering it to me. 'Perhaps that was rather crass. I must say, though,' he patted my leg through the thin silk of my crumpled green dress, 'I've never found you so attractive. You've got a kind of vulnerability these days that I've never noticed before'.

I blew my nose loudly. 'That you thought you could exploit, you mean.'

'Hardly, darling. I'm not a predator.' He stood now and reached for the phone. 'Where's that bloody cab?'

Charlie didn't say goodbye as I fled into the lift, and he banged the door shut so hard behind me that it rattled in its frame.

The next morning, feeling hungover and rather queasy, I took Digby to Greenwich Park in an attempt to clear away the cobwebs of the previous night. I tramped up the hill to the Observatory and then across the wild and matted grass to look down on the city, seriously worried about the implications of rebuffing Charlie, especially in the circumstances. I was distracted by the delighted squeaks of a tiny blond boy in an enormous green coat, kicking through the autumn leaves beneath the chestnut trees. The top layers of the pile were a gorgeous mixture of golds and reds, russet and shades of orange. But underneath, as Digby joined the toddler to scavenge there for treasure, there was just nasty rotting mulch. I called the dog away as the boy's father scooped him up, and wandered home again.

Opening my father's gate, I stopped in my tracks, confused. Had I got the wrong house? I stopped to listen, a sickening pain searing through my stomach.

For the first time in years, the piano was being played. My mother's image twirled through my foggy head, and for a peculiar moment suspended in the midst of memory, I thought she might actually be in there.

I dropped the newspapers I'd just bought and flew up the path. Someone was playing the piano and my flesh was crawling with loneliness and need and the knowledge that no one was here to catch me any more, to salve the wounds.

I ran towards the music, gasping and breathless as I took the stairs two at a time to reach the fluid climbing notes, but when I flung the study door wide open, the room that no one ever visited, empty except for my mother's piano looming large and obsolete, it was only Jenny sitting there, playing a jolly waltz. Jenny beamed up from the piano-stool, her fringe very shiny, her rosy cheeks as round as apples – but when she saw my face, she trailed off.

'I'm sorry, love,' she said a little nervously, 'you don't mind, do you? You did say it was all right.'

But it wasn't all right. Had I really said that?

'It just – it seems like such a waste.'

It hadn't been played for years; even I couldn't bear to any more, although I had tried.

'I couldn't resist any more.'

I knew it would be wrong to yell *don't touch*. I bit my lip hard. 'You carry on.' Managing a feeble smile, I shut the door carefully behind me. Alone on the landing I put my hand to my mouth and brought away blood. Bemused, I wiped it on my coat. Then I went to the kitchen to make some lunch. There was half a bottle of Shiraz open on the side. I shoved a pan of parsnip soup onto the hob and stood there clutching a glass of the dark red wine and I felt stupid and bereft again, like I had when I was thirteen. How stupid I was: I'd forgotten Jenny taught music, of course she did – that's how she'd met my father, teaching at his school. Of course she'd bloody play. Although I put the radio on loudly to drown the music out, I could hear how out of tune my mother's piano really was. As I slathered bread with thick yellow butter, I realised it was finally time to leave.

I took a deep breath and rang my ex-boyfriend.

# Chapter Twelve

My dad and Jenny came for Sunday lunch on the weekend I moved back into the flat in Borough Market. My dad said it was a sort of housewarming, but I knew really it was to check up on me, to make sure I was coping.

It felt extremely odd and rather uncomfortable to be there again, but I had little choice it seemed. Alex had just accepted a huge job in Glasgow, so our old flat above the cake shop in the market was sitting empty for the time being. I couldn't afford to rent a new place as well as pay my half of the existing mortgage. In a series of terse and cursory emails and messages to one another, Alex and I eventually established I'd move back in alone while I worked out what to do next.

In an attempt to dispel the ghosts that had lingered since I'd arrived the previous night in a flurry of debris from the market's busiest day, I put on a Beethoven violin concerto very loudly, made coffee strong enough to stand a spoon in and spent the morning cleaning the kitchen and conjuring up a lemon roast chicken with garlic potatoes, and a rhubarb crumble with homemade custard that even Nigel Slater would die for, whisking the eggs to within a second of perfection. Then I opened the wine ready for my dad's arrival. I'd pulled out all the stops; I wanted to show Jenny there was no ill-feeling about the piano. I liked her a lot and, crucially, this time I didn't want to be responsible for spoiling what might be my dad's last chance of real happiness.

At the front door, Jenny presented me with a large cactus.

'Oh, lovely.' I hugged her, hoping fervently it wasn't a symbol of something unspoken. 'Thank you so much.'

'You're welcome.' She smelled nice and homely; of shampoo and L'Air du Temps. Of motherly things. 'It doesn't need much looking after, that's why I chose it.' She was a little shy. 'I thought it'd be perfect for you busy media types.'

'So how do you feel about being back here?' my dad asked later, polishing off the crumble as Jenny washed up.

'It's fine, Dad, really.' I jumped up to collect the remaining plates. I couldn't admit that the memories gouged agonisingly at my brain – that every time I moved across the room I saw Alex sprawled on the sofa sketching, his headphones on, winking at me as I happily threw together a bolognese or a chilli, humming to Mozart; that I felt his constant presence; that I waited for him to bound up the stairs with Digby snuffling at his heels and kiss me like he'd just remembered what living was all about. I couldn't admit that some of the happiest days of my life had been spent here. I was desperately fighting the memories myself.

I fought a sudden rush of tears, keeping my head down as my father passed me his bowl. 'I just need to get on with things now, don't I? No looking back, that's what you always say, isn't it?' My words were brittle and empty and I felt truly haunted actually – but my father's look of apprehension faded.

'That's my girl.' He patted my arm fondly just as I tripped over his chair-leg and dropped the crumble dish.

As I cleared up the shards of china, Jenny offered to take Digby out; she'd often walked him for me while I was recuperating. I hated this biting cold and I had work to do for next week's shows so I accepted gladly. I suddenly felt exhausted and my leg hurt. I sank onto the sofa, closing my eyes, just for a moment . . .

I dreamed I was playing croquet with my mother on

Pendarlin's lawn, and someone was hammering the hoops into the ground and urgently calling my name. I woke up with a start, my sweaty face stuck to the leather cushion I lay on. It took me a second to realise someone really *was* knocking and calling my name.

Hauling myself off the sofa, the phone began to ring. I picked it up, my eyes still half-shut. A click; a dialling tone. Gormless with sleep, I dropped the receiver back into the cradle and staggered towards the persistent hammering.

'All right, I'm coming.' I flung the door back in bad temper.

'About time.' Alex pushed past me into the flat.

'Come in, why don't you,' I said to the empty street, to the glowering grey sky, to the single tree stripped naked by November's chilly wind and the train clanking overhead. 'I thought you were in Glasgow?'

'Going back on Wednesday. Can I get a cup of coffee?' He was already bounding up the stairs into the kitchen. 'It's bloody freezing out.' He blew on his hands.

I followed him more slowly, still hampered by my foot. 'Hung over?' I was waspish because I didn't know how else to be; fighting myself already.

'Hung over?' Alex actually grinned, his long eyes creasing up. I used to love the way they did that. Oh God. I was fighting the part of me that wanted to run across the kitchen and launch myself into his arms, to breathe in his familiar smell, the smell I couldn't get enough of in the old days. And I despised myself; I held myself in check, telling myself firmly it was my mind just playing tricks.

'No, I'm not hung over. I'm on the wagon.'

I stared at him without comprehension.

'Yeah, it's been about five months now.' So very proud of himself. He ran a hand through his short scruffy hair.

'Five months?' I intoned dully. Five months ago I had nearly died. Five months ago we separated forever. Abstinence that he'd refused for me, he'd managed in his new-won freedom. For a moment I didn't trust myself to speak.

'Yep.' He leaned against the kitchen counter, crossing his trainered feet smugly. His sweatshirt was paint-spattered as ever and there was a big rip in the knee of his jeans. Alex's clothes were always dilapidated. 'Thought it was about time I got into this clean-living lark. Everyone else is.' He eyed the empty wine bottles left over from lunch. 'Well – nearly everyone. You're not embracing it yourself, then, Mag?'

Since when had Alex become all smug? I caught sight of my sleep-creased face in the mirror behind him; it just made me more cross. Half-cut and crumpled, I felt at a disadvantage.

'No, that's right, Alex. Can't live without a drop, me.' I tried to keep my hand steady as I tipped instant coffee into a cup, absolutely awake and completely sober now.

'Don't you run to the real stuff? I'm sure I left some in the cupboard.'

'How kind.' Very deliberately I added water to the Nescafé and slopped it towards him along the counter, past the half-full coffee-pot. 'What do you want, Alex? My dad'll be back soon.'

'Great. It'd be nice to see Bill.'

'I'm not sure Bill would agree.' With a shudder I recalled the soggy heap I'd been upon leaving the hospital after my final operation, crying intermittently for a solid week, refusing to leave my old room, forcing the occasional slice of toast down to appease my anxious father. He'd held my hand, folding his awkward height to perch on the edge of the bed like he had when I was thirteen. He'd listened while I'd rambled on; when I'd sworn I'd never love another man again he'd promised that I would. He'd driven me back and forth to the flat to collect my things when I knew Alex wouldn't be there. Patiently he'd accompanied me to the physio, taking time off to drop me there every other day for a month. My father had let me rant and rail when I thought I'd never walk properly again, never walk without a limp.

'No, well, perhaps not. Look, Maggie –' Alex stopped. He was struggling with something now, the smug façade slipping until it eventually crumpled. He jangled his car keys from one finger, his nails chewed down to the quick as usual. 'Maggie.' His voice was very quiet now as he stared at his dirty old trainers.

My heart was thumping painfully in my chest.

'This is really difficult.'

'What is?' I was impatient now. *Just get it over with.* 'Don't tell me. You're marrying that girl.'

'What girl?' Alex frowned.

'The anorexic blonde from Bel's wedding.'

'Serena?' He grinned. 'Are you mad? Why, would you come?'

His lack of sensitivity was no surprise. I ignored him.

'No, Maggie, it's just – I thought we should –'

He was interrupted by Digby, who flung himself at Alex like an animal possessed.

'All right, Diggers!'

The show of mutual appreciation was so lavish I had to turn away. 'Traitor,' I muttered at the slavering dog, and began to scrub an already clean roasting-tin as if it were Alex's head.

My father appeared in the doorway, lead in hand.

'Ah,' he said, rather pointlessly. 'Alexander.'

'Good to see you, sir.' Alex sprang forward, hand extended.

*Sir?* The creep.

'I think – shall we leave you to it, Mag? Jenny was going to come up to say bye but I'll intercept her – unless –' My father looked at me closely. 'Is that all right?'

I tried to smile. 'It's fine, Dad, really. Thanks so much for coming.'

My father kissed me, hugged me tight for a moment. If there was anything good to have come out of the past few months, it was this new intimacy with him. It was an intimacy born late, but one that I'd waited a lifetime for, which I appreciated deeply now.

'Ring me later?'

'I will.'

'Bye, Bill. Good to see you.' Alex looked up from tickling Digby's tummy.

'Yes, well –' My dad was so very British sometimes. 'Likewise.'

As the front door closed, I turned back to Alex. 'Leave that bloody dog alone, will you? You haven't been the slightest bit interested in seeing him in the past five months so don't bother now. Poor little thing. He's forgotten what you look like.'

'Obviously,' said Alex dryly as Digby slobbered all over his face with great enthusiasm.

'Yes, well. He's not very bright.' I slammed the tin into the drying-rack where it wobbled for a minute before falling onto my bare foot. 'Ow!' I bit back tears of pain and anger. 'For God's sake! Look, Alex, what exactly do you want?' I kept my back to the room, desperately trying to collect myself.

Alex picked up the tin. 'It's just – well, we haven't really spoken properly since your –' His voice faltered.

'Accident, Alex, is the word you're looking for, I think.'

'Yes, sorry. I know I've been a bit crap.'

'A bit?'

'Okay.' He held his arms up in submission. 'Very crap. But when you said you didn't want to see me, I –'

'You know why I said that.' I frowned. 'But you still could have come.'

'I didn't think –' he faltered, 'not after – I mean, when Bill –'

'Whatever.' I hated Alex's half-truths with a vengeance. 'It's a bit late now.'

'I'm so sorry. I just couldn't face seeing you in the hospital.' He took a look at my face. 'Right. Well, also, I wanted you to know I've been trying to – you know – clean my act up.'

101

'Great,' I muttered ungraciously.

He gave up. 'Okay. Right, well, let's just sort the practical stuff out, shall we? Splitting bills and things.'

I stared out of the window into the dark, at the glimmer of the train-tracks disappearing into the gloom above us like snail trails.

'And also, Maggie, I just wanted to know how much you –' He ground to a halt again. It was most unlike him to be lost for words.

I looked around for my cigarettes. 'What?'

'How much you remember.'

'How much I remember about *what*?' I looked at Alex now, and he held my gaze for a moment before dropping his. His yellow eyes were tired and ringed with black; he'd always struggled with insomnia.

'Of the accident, you mean?' It made my heart beat faster just to think of it. 'It's all a bit fuzzy.'

I finally unearthed my fags from a pile of paperwork. My hand was trembling as I tried to light one.

'Right. I'm sorry. I really meant, though, of what happened – before.'

I chewed my lip. One of these days I'd chew right through. It was all a blur, that day, the few weeks before, a muddy midnight-blue tangle of tears and recriminations and shouting at each other in desperation and fury and absolute sorrow. We'd been in Cornwall together, I knew that, trying to sort things out, trying to find a solution once and for all, and then – then I couldn't remember much at all about before or after. Then I was on the coach to London. Alone. So much of that period was still shadowed that the doctors talked grandly of 'traumatic amnesia' – but I was sure, oh I knew I must have blocked it.

'What happened with us, you mean?' Perhaps the memories were necessarily vague – but I knew it was only a matter of time before they surfaced. 'I'm still struggling to remember.'

'I just wondered, you know, that night when – my mum's birthday –' He looked a bit sick.

'Oh God, I still can't see it clearly.' I finally lit the cigarette. 'I try and piece it together, but it's all so bloody vague.'

Immediately before the accident was clear: a lot of swearing in a service-station car park just outside Bristol. Alex, covered in engine oil, kicking the driver's door in fury. Yet another heated argument. Silent tears sliding unchecked in the darkness. A cab. Sitting alone in a fluorescent-lit coach station with orange plastic chairs. 'I know we had a row and that's why I got on the coach.' I considered him for a moment, took a lungful of smoke. 'I just can't remember why we were there in the first place.' I exhaled slowly.

Alex looked almost relieved for a second as he turned to put his coffee cup down. 'Why are you smoking again, Maggie? I thought you'd given up.'

I shook my head impatiently. 'Why do you want to know all this now, Alex? About the accident. Did you do something terrible before it?'

'Don't be stupid. I just wondered.' He busied himself with Digby, clapping for the little dog to jump to his clicking fingers. He didn't look at me. 'I need to get on, actually. Can we talk about the flat now?'

'What about it?' I ground the fag out hard.

'Well, Serena and I –'

'Oh.' The penny dropped with a great big clank, rolled around the floor between us. 'Oh, of course.' I clapped a hand to my head. 'You want to move her in.'

'Look, just forget about bloody Serena, will you? Living with her isn't really working out.'

Did he read the relief in my eyes? I cast them down as he went on. 'So I need to – I'm just thinking about the future. After Glasgow.'

The future. I'd never known Alex plan for anything other than

103

where he was drinking that evening. I thought of Serena; of Alex in his beautiful suit at Bel's wedding – her glossy perfection set off by his rangy height. 'You looked pretty loved-up to me the other week.'

'Hardly. I mean, she's beautiful, but – well, you know.'

'What?'

'Maggie –' His voice was so quiet as he stared at me, and he almost said it and I could practically hear the ice cracking in my chest; feel my heart starting to thaw as Alex took a step towards me, his scarred hand extended. I froze for a second and then I forced myself to take a step back. I picked up a dishcloth and began to wipe the counter energetically. My mind was racing, rushing down alleyways that turned out to be dead-ends. He always did this to me. Could charm the birds out of the trees, Alex, on a good day.

'I mean, Serena's all right when I've had a drink or –'

It was a bad day, though. I stopped wiping. 'I thought you *weren't* drinking?'

'I'm not.' Too late. He wouldn't look at me, searched desperately for any fragment of nail left to bite. 'Well, hardly at all.'

'Oh God, Alex. Why do you always have to lie?'

'What – and you never do?'

My foot was hurting from standing too long; I sat heavily on one of the chrome kitchen chairs that he'd insisted we buy one drunken Sunday afternoon on Upper Street; chairs I'd always hated in the cold light of day. He always knew best, though. The silence spread between us like ripples in a pond. I felt so tired, so sad, so tired of being sad.

'I'd rather – I think it's better if we don't see each other right now, Alex,' I whispered eventually, staring at a hole in his trainers. 'I don't want to know about your new girlfriends, really.' I felt a great depression soaking me, a depression so greedy and black it engulfed me entirely. *Nothing*, it whispered, its tentacles crawling, *there is nothing for you here*. Nothing loomed in my future apart from loneliness and my best mate leaving the country and working for bloody Charlie against my better judgement. I was trapped. 'Could you really not just have been on your own for a bit?'

'You're hardly the Virgin Mary yourself, now, are you, sweetheart?' Alex snapped, pushing a hand through his hair.

I narrowed my eyes at him. 'What the hell does that mean?'

'Nothing.' He turned away to pick up his keys. 'Look, this is all bollocks. I only came to say let's put the flat on the market.'

'Oh, right.' I stared at him. 'Bloody great. So you want me homeless as well.'

'We're gonna have to do it sometime, so why not now?'

'And that's what you came all the way round here to say?'

'Yep.' Digby was worrying at the scarf that Alex had stuffed in his back pocket. 'Leave it, Dig.'

'Why didn't you just phone?'

'I did.'

'Did you?' I was sure he hadn't. Had he?

'I came –' The dog still wouldn't let go. 'I came because', Alex swiped at him half-heartedly, 'I thought it was the decent thing to do.'

'You never do the decent thing.'

'I do.' He looked like a belligerent teenager. 'Sometimes.'

I looked back in disbelief, and felt the sudden urge to laugh. It was the moment the tension that twanged so tight between us could have been dispersed. He sensed it too, grinning sheepishly at me, and my heart did a tiny forward-roll.

But I didn't laugh, because Digby finally freed the stripy scarf from his master's holey jeans, trailing it victoriously round the kitchen in his mouth like a trophy. Something followed the scarf, tumbling out of Alex's back pocket, floating to the ground between us. We both watched it as it hit the floor: a packet of gold and silver confetti stamped with the immortal words '*Bel and Johnno Forever – You Betcha!*' Confetti they'd been giving away at their party the other night. I picked the tiny packet up and turned it over, frowning again.

'Where did you get this?'

'I don't know,' Alex shrugged, biting the skin round his thumb now. 'It must be yours. Look, I've got to go.'

'It's not mine. You weren't at Bel's, were you?'

He kept on at that thumb.

'Alex! Were you at the party?'

'No.' He rubbed a hand through his short hair so it stuck up on end. I shook my head in confusion. '*Hardly the Virgin Mary,*' he'd said. I didn't understand. I remembered Sebastian – definitely the first man I'd so much as flirted with since I'd split with Alex.

He jangled his keys. 'I need to get going. Serena's expecting me.'

'Alex, tell me the truth.' I stepped towards him. 'Were you there?'

'Well, I was going to drop in, but then –'

'What?'

'I couldn't face it, so I – I just sat outside in the car for a bit.'

With a shiver, I remembered the car that had nearly run me down.

'Did you see me come out? Did you – you didn't try to run me over, did you?'

Alex looked at me like I was mad. 'Christ, Maggie! Are you insane?' He retrieved the scarf from Digby's slobbery mouth. 'I'll have that, buddy, okay?' His voice softened talking to the dog, and I winced as I thought of all the times he'd talked that way to me. With a great ache in my chest, I considered the violence of change. I remembered the row that had propelled me onto the coach – and then, suddenly, something else. Slivers of that humid night in town, piercing the fog in my brain, slivers of a broken mirror unable to reflect an image accurately any more. I clutched my head – but they'd gone again.

'I'll be in touch about the flat.' He broke through my thoughts. 'Is it okay for the agent to come round to value it tomorrow?'

'I suppose so.' My turn to shrug. 'But I might want to stay.'

'Fine – if you want to take over the whole mortgage.'

'Fine. I might do that. I'll put the rest of your stuff in boxes, shall I, and you can collect it sometime.'

'Fine.'

'Fine. Sometime when I'm not here, obviously.'

'Obviously. No problem. See you around.' And he was gone, loping down the stairs with not so much as a backwards glance. Digby watched his departure mournfully.

'I know, silly thing.' I scooped up the trembling dog. 'Too much excitement for one day, eh?'

On the kitchen counter, the little packet of confetti glistened in the artificial light. The phone began to ring again. When I picked it up, no one spoke.

The first time I met Alex he was in the middle of a huge row with his father. Back in the day when I still had zest and ambition, I'd finally convinced Charlie to give me my first show to produce alone. I was still a novice really, and impressing my boss mattered massively to me.

Those were the halcyon days of believing I could make some kind of difference in my work; striving to bring great entertainment and vital information to the masses. My future soared out before me, rainbow-like: my future, chasing fool's gold. It wasn't so long ago but it felt like an eternity. With the bit truly clamped between my teeth, I'd spent days agonising over a subject I thought was imperative and timely for debate, and then I went with all guns blazing to persuade Malcolm Bailey to appear.

Malcolm Bailey was a thug-made-good – though it took me a while to fully realise it. Infamous for championing unfashionable causes, he'd originally made his money with a raft of

107

innovative computer equipment in the eighties; then he'd used his business clout to buy airtime for his controversial opinions. He was truly Left, left of left, old Left: his political heart belonged in Russia circa the Revolution, though he certainly wasn't averse to a bit of what money could buy, principles or none. And he was full of the things – principles, that is. Chock-full.

I needed Malcolm desperately for the show I was producing on domestic violence: I had to prove to Charlie that I could come up with the goods, and Malcolm would be a truly contentious booking. Unfortunately he'd already sensed my desperation and, calling the shots, arranged an early breakfast meeting on a Monday morning at his new offices in Clerkenwell. I'd spent a hideous weekend working all hours, and then had finally slid into bed on the Sunday night only to be woken by the phone. In the first stages of Alzheimer's, Gar was not well at all, and in the end I'd slept in the chair by her bed in the nursing-home, waking stiff, sore and late, not to mention terrified by my grandmother's fragile state.

By the time I'd screeched into the foyer of Bailey's building a minute before eight, I was beside myself with exhaustion and ill humour. The offices were part of a new block that was causing a huge row – ecological triumph or eyesore, the jury was still out. Frankly, this morning I was past caring. I was more interested in the offer of coffee that Bailey's ferocious PA Charlene made as she escorted me humourlessly to the tenth floor.

'Strong as you can make it, please.' Light-headed with lack of sleep, I collapsed onto a boomerang-shaped leather chair outside Bailey's office and, spotting a big glass ashtray, delved for my cigarettes.

'It's strictly no smoking.' Charlene pursed her thin lips and thrust a paper cup of very weak coffee at me. She had a hairy mole just below her left nostril. 'Mr Bailey's first meeting is over-running.'

I smiled wanly. It was only eight a.m. The man was obviously possessed.

I was nursing the unpalatable coffee when a door was flung open somewhere out of sight, smacking against a wall; angry voices crashing into the lobby. Charlene busied herself, loudly ordering a car for Bailey in ten minutes (my heart sank further at the little time this left me) – but, despite her best efforts, I caught every word.

'You're fucking mad, Pa. You'll make yourself a laughing stock. You only do it to be provocative, that's what pisses me off so much.'

An imperious Cockney drawl replied, rough as a rake on gravel, the words drowned by the phone now ringing on Charlene's desk. She snapped into it officiously.

'Of course it's my right.' The first voice again. 'I'm embarrassed you're even considering it. It makes us all guilty by association. Mum'll go mental.'

'You get on with what you're good at, all right, Alexander, whatever that might be, and let me get on with what I'm good at.' A chair scraped across tiles. 'And when I want your opinion, or your mother's, I'll ask for it.'

'You couldn't give a toss about either of our opinions, that's exactly my point. I give up.'

A tall man strode out into the lobby and then stopped at the sight of me. Furious yellow eyes blazed down at me, a newspaper rolled tightly like an offensive weapon in a rather scarred hand, knuckles grazed on two fingers. He looked like he was contemplating hitting me over the head with the paper. I attempted a charming smile.

The other voice was on the phone now. 'And get that fucking *Big Issue* git out of my doorway, all right? It don't look good for business.'

There was the clatter of the receiver being dropped into its cradle, then a barrel-chested man strolled indolently out of the office, hands in pockets.

109

'Aha.' Malcolm Bailey leaned in the doorway, studying me. 'Maggie Warren, I presume.' A statement: a man who always knew he was right; a strong, cruel face, a prize-fighter's stance.

I stood quickly, aware that my flaming skin was now clashing with my hair most unattractively. 'Yes. Yes, hello.' I stepped forward to shake Malcolm's hand, my cigarettes falling to the floor as I did so. The younger man and I both bent to retrieve them, clashing heads in the process.

'God, sorry.' I rubbed my forehead with an embarrassed smile. He didn't speak; just handed me the packet inscrutably. I noticed how chewed his fingernails were.

'So you've met my son, Alexander,' Malcolm smirked. He was much shorter than the younger man, but he seemed giant-like now in his superiority. 'This is his place, you know.' Was that pride or contempt in his tone? I couldn't quite fathom it.

'Alex Bailey.' Alex shoved the rolled copy of the *Daily Express* into the back pocket of well-worn jeans, and rubbed his face tiredly. I had the uncomfortable notion that the paper he'd just pocketed was the copy that had originally attracted me to Malcolm Bailey. A strongly worded article on the reasons behind male-on-female domestic violence, and the rights that Bailey felt the perpetrators deserved, despite their criminal actions.

'Pleased to meet you,' I lied, offering Alex my hand now. He didn't want to take it, I could tell, but eventually good manners overcame his anger. 'Are you the owner of the building? It's amazing.' Desperate now, I tried flattery.

'Hardly. I'm just the architect.' He didn't look like an architect. He looked like a workman. 'One of them, I should say.'

'Pa' ignored us both, looking at the fag-packet I clutched. 'You don't smoke, do you, Maggie? Tut tut. Not a nice habit for a young lady. We don't like smokers, do we, Alex?'

'Oh, only occasionally, you know.' I shoved my cigarettes away. Tiredness was slowing my brain, my grandmother's delicate coughing frame my main concern. I didn't have the energy for a bully like Bailey right now, and this situation with his furious son was making me nervous. They'd obviously been arguing about my show. I'd built my career on coolness; on the ability to keep calm in a stressful situation. Axe-murderers, paedophiles, soapstars – I'd met the lot without so much as stuttering. So it was bizarre that I was struggling right now. As I tried to collect my thoughts, Malcolm's gaze penetrated me like Clark Kent's X-ray vision.

'What can I do you for then, Ms Warren?'

I cleared my throat, wishing his son's eyes weren't boring into me like two yellow flints. 'Well, Mr Bailey,' I began my pitch, 'it's more what you might like to share with us.'

'You're desperate to hear my thoughts, you mean.'

Another statement. Unconsciously I took a step nearer his son, who considered me for a moment before heading towards the door. Then he stopped, running a hand through his short dishevelled hair so it became a mountain range of tufts and spikes.

'Actually, you know what,' he turned back. 'I'll join you, shall I? I'd love to hear what exactly my dad's got to say.'

*Oh, marvellous.* I forced a smile as Alex grinned at me, his strong face illuminated suddenly, his eyes shining. 'And I'm dying to know how you're going to persuade him.'

'Right. Well, yes, of course, please do join us.' I managed to hold the false smile as I followed the two men into Bailey's office. The fact that at least one of them possessed some kind of morals was small help. I felt exactly like I was off to face a firing squad.

During that first meeting Alex eyed me like I was an irritating child. He slumped on the sofa in his father's office, dirty old boots on the coffee table, half-asleep, apparently oblivious to me giving it my very best shot. When I saw his eyes were actually shut, I felt incredible relief. I was suddenly struck by the uneasy

111

feeling I was prostituting myself for my goal – but I shook it off as I got into my stride, increasingly passionate and enthused by my subject. Still, Malcolm refused to agree to anything; the most he'd promise was to consider appearing.

As I shook Malcolm's hand, Alex opened his eyes and stretched broadly, shaking himself rather like a long shaggy dog would. He muttered something to his father as I headed out, and then he followed me, lounging opposite me in the lift. We didn't speak as we travelled smoothly down, but when the lift spat us out, Alex ran his hand through those tufts again.

'Good luck,' he murmured as the doors to the street slid open, stepping back to let me go first.

Outside it was sharp and crisp, a blast of much-needed fresh air to my addled brain. 'Thanks.' I dug out my travelcard, just relieved the whole ordeal was over. I was buying a paper at the news-stand when I saw Alex lope across the road, a small scruffy dog at his heels now, and whistle loudly.

'Oi, Ron!'

A bent old geezer in a filthy duffel coat and half a balaclava shuffled out of an alleyway beside Pret a Manger, clutching his stash of *Big Issues* and a quarter of a croissant.

'You can go back now.' Alex handed him a tenner. 'Tell them Malcolm's son said it was fine, okay?' He clocked me as I collected my change. 'Still here?'

I flushed angrily. 'Not for much longer.' I turned on my heel.

'Hey,' he called. I glanced over my shoulder. He was standing like an island in the midst of a stream of harried commuters. 'I don't suppose you fancy a quick drink?'

'A drink?' I repeated stupidly. I looked at my watch: it was only just nine. 'It's much too early for a drink.'

'Oh, live a little,' he grinned. 'I've been working all night. I need to unwind.'

'I don't think so, thanks,' I said rather primly. I'd never skipped school, much less work. 'I've got to get to the office.'

'But this can be your office, can't it?' He walked towards me and I realised just how tall he was. His dog sniffed my shoes with enthusiasm. 'Perhaps you can persuade me to be on your show.'

'I don't want you to be on my show.'

'Charming.'

We stood on the pavement amid the flow from Farringdon Station, commuters with heads down, hurrying, scurrying to their burrows for the day, no time to glance up, no inclination. We contemplated one another for a moment – and for some reason my tummy rolled with apprehension.

'And you don't want to be on it either,' I said eventually.

'How do you know?' Alex shrugged. 'I might have very strong views on domestic violence.'

'Have you?'

'Maybe. They won't be the same as my dad's, though.'

'No, well, I have to say that would be a relief.'

'Yes, I expect it would.' He zipped up his jacket and looked down at me. 'Well, don't say I didn't offer.'

I tried to read the expression in those sloping eyes that crinkled at the corners.

'Last chance, Blue Eyes.'

My computer, my office, Charlie beckoned. 'Nowhere will be serving at this time anyway.' What was I on about? It was nine a.m. on a Monday morning and I had a show to produce with not a single guest booked yet. 'I can't. Really.'

'You can if you want to.' Alex smiled at me again. I was sure I was just a challenge he was setting himself. I bit my lip.

'Come on, Maggie, don't be a spoilsport. First round's on Digby.' He picked the dog up.

I took a final drag of my cigarette and chucked it away. Slowly, against my better judgement, I followed them.

# Chapter Thirteen

In the early hours I woke shivering with cold, back on the sofa, my coat draped over me and a wineglass empty on the floor. Digby had been huddled at my feet, but he was gone now. He was gone – but there was someone else in the room, I sensed it.

I lay stock-still in darkness so inky I couldn't make much out, my heart pounding so hard I thought it must be visible to the intruder. I tried desperately to gauge the distance to the stairs and the front door. How long would it take me to get down them, champion sprinter (now crippled) that I once was?

A soft footstep. Fear gripped me round the throat. Should I play dead or should I run? And where the hell was Digby? Oh God, where was he? A sob of terror escaped me as the footstep trod nearer.

'What do you want?' My voice sounded tiny in the darkness of the night. 'My purse is in –'

There was a crash, followed by a laugh. 'Don't be stupid,' a voice said. More than a little drunk.

A fury more pure than any I remembered seized me now. The voice banged into something else in the darkness – something that fell with a clatter – and swore softly. I threw my coat off and stood to snap on the lamp. Alex swayed gently in the shaft of light that fell towards him now, the dog clutched like a baby in his arms, the key bowl upended, keys all over the floor.

'You're drunk, Alex.'

'I'm not.' He swayed again. 'Not very.'

'What the hell are you doing here? You absolutely terrified me.'

'I came to get my stuff, like you said.'

'What are you talking about?' My brain was scrambling. 'What time is it?'

He dropped Digby onto the sofa, and I felt him summoning something. 'Actually, I was wondering – would you mind –' He blinked sleepy and unfocused eyes at me. 'Can I stay here tonight?' he muttered eventually.

'What?' I snapped, rubbing sleep from mine.

'Please, Mag. I'll go in the morning, I promise; I won't make a fuss.'

Speechless, half-dressed for the freezing autumn night, I stood and stared at him.

'*Please* let me stay. I don't want to be on my own,' he pleaded pitifully. But he *would* make a fuss; and I was exhausted by it, by my love for him. It had lacerated me for too long.

'Alex, please.' I turned away. I hardened the heart which he'd shattered so long ago. 'You're doing my head in. You've had loads of time to see me. Why now, in the middle of the night?' There was too much alcohol under the bridge anyway, a veritable flood of the stuff. 'I'll ring you a cab.'

'Maggie –'

'Alex –' I summoned every ounce of willpower I possessed, clenching my fists unconsciously. 'Alex, please, just go.'

He looked at me then, and I looked straight back. I realised what had been scrawled across his face when I'd switched the light on. It had been hope – and it had gone now. Now his eyes just looked dead.

I had a sudden glimmer of what I'd tried so hard to forget, that terrible night in June. I grew more resolute.

We stared at each other for a minute and then, on a sudden

whim, I reached up and for one short indulgent moment I pressed my palm against Alex's face. He smelled of beer and the chill November air.

'Your hands are cold,' he murmured, 'they're always cold,' and for a moment he closed his eyes. But I pulled back, setting the chair that he'd knocked over on its legs, and walked upstairs without looking back.

'Let yourself out, Alex,' I said over my shoulder, and called Digby to heel. I felt like I was acting in someone else's play, watching myself go through the motions of telling the man I'd loved more than anyone else in the world to leave me be.

Upstairs, I lay down on the bed that we used to share, pretended I was very calm, and held my breath as I waited for him to go.

A few minutes later the front door slammed, and I began to breathe again. I didn't cry; I was still too angry for tears. I lit a cigarette instead. After a minute I got up, zombie-like, and went to the window very slowly, like I was sleepwalking. I watched Alex as he opened the door of a silver car I didn't recognise, probably one of Malcolm's. I knew it was pointless trying to stop him driving in his state; I'd learned the hard way that it was impossible to ever stop Alex doing exactly what he wanted. In a pool of light under the lamppost, he stopped at the car door – then he ran back across the street. My heart missed a beat. It wasn't over; of course it wasn't. It couldn't really be over, I'd known that all along . . . He disappeared from sight, and I held my breath again . . .

Then I heard something thud through the letterbox. And I knew without even going to check what Alex had just posted: his keys to the flat. He got in the car and slammed the door shut, then he drove off. He hadn't looked up once.

I lay down again. I couldn't deny that I'd been hoping that when he turned around he was about to come running up those silly steel stairs and be the funny, decisive Alex I'd first met two years ago. Before he'd got too drunk to even make it to the bedroom.

But really I knew that if that had happened, it would only have prolonged the madness.

# Chapter Fourteen

The purr of my mobile woke me but by the time I'd scrabbled to find it, the ringing had stopped. My head was pounding as hard as my heart had last night; my hair was stuck all sweaty to my cheek; my mouth felt like I'd just licked an ashtray clean. Digby was running in ever-decreasing circles at the foot of the bed, whining frantically, desperate to be let out. Through one bleary eye I checked the time on the phone's display. I'd over-slept again.

After Alex had gone I'd found I couldn't sleep so eventually I'd opened a bottle of wine to calm me down. I'd forgotten to set the alarm, and I'd left the heating on, desperate to get warm again after the chill that Alex had left, a chill that pervaded through my bones to my heart. Now I felt like I'd just slept in a sauna; I was sweaty and horribly headachey.

Another Monday morning yawned in front of me, another week, another month of nothing to look forward to except a lonely Christmas. I stumbled into the shower and set the temperature as cold as I could bear it, but it just made me feel grumpy. Goose-pimpled and shivering, I was towelling my hair dry when I thought I heard a door creak downstairs.

'Digby?' I croaked. But I could hear him barking at the pigeons on the roof-terrace. Dragging on my jeans I tiptoed to the top of the stairs. A shadow fell across the oak floorboards below me.

'Alex?' I whispered. But it wasn't him; I could see that straight away as the top of a man's head came into view. A shorter, fat man, with a balding crown, holding a bunch of lilies. An icy sweat broke across my top lip. Desperately I sought a weapon – the nearest thing to hand was an Art Deco ashtray on the landing that had belonged to Gar. I picked it up and crept down a few stairs. The lilies were so pungent I could smell them from here. Suddenly the top of the ashtray detached itself and clattered down the stairs. The man looked up, startled.

'Ooh, you scared me! I thought everyone was out.' He held his heart with a rather camp hand. 'Sorry – you must be Ms Warren?' Collecting himself, he extended that pudgy hand towards me, the lilies clamped beneath the other shiny-suited arm.

'And you are?' Half-dressed, still clutching the ashtray stand, I felt a little ridiculous now.

'Stefano Costana of Costana and Mortimer. I've got a card somewhere.'

I frowned. 'Costana and Mortimer?'

'Estate agents, Borough High Street. Mr Bailey asked me to pop round for a valuation. He gave me a set of keys.' He patted his pocket cheerily. 'Said you'd be at work, said he'd told you.'

'Oh.' I tried to recall yesterday's conversation. 'Well, he didn't.'

'Oh dear. I didn't mean to scare you. I tell you, if you'd seen some of the things I've stumbled across –' He trailed off, catching the look on my face. 'Right, then. I'll – I can come back another time.'

I shook my head miserably. 'No, it's fine. I'll just finish getting dressed.' Digby was hurling himself against the terrace doors. 'Sorry – you couldn't just let the dog in, could you?'

Stefano Costana looked nervous. 'Is he – you know? Dangerous?'

'Hardly.' I laughed. 'Just a bit overenthusiastic.'

'Found these on your doorstep, by the way.' The estate agent looked around for somewhere to put the bouquet. 'Beautiful, aren't they? I do love a lily. So regal.'

'Oh, right.' My heart sank. 'So they're not yours?'

'No, no.' He plopped them cheerfully onto the kitchen table. 'You obviously have an admirer, Ms Warren. Very nice.'

'It's not, though, actually.' I trailed wearily up the stairs to finish dressing. 'It's not very nice at all.'

I didn't bother to check the card. I already knew what the message would say. The same as the last bunch had. *In Loving Memory of Maggie.*

By the time I reached the office, two strong cups of coffee later, I was feeling revived enough to have punched Alex's previously deleted number into my mobile with some considerable aggression. He didn't answer, so I left a short sharp message about keys and estate agents and how being grossly inconsiderate was his absolute forte. I was pretty sure he hadn't told me about the appointment.

I'd shoved the lilies into the wheelie-bin outside the flat as I left and tried to forget about them, determined that today I'd explain to Charlie why I couldn't work for him any more, whatever his threats. It was time to take charge.

But in the foyer I couldn't find my pass anywhere, and the new security guard refused to let me through. I rang up to the office to get someone to fetch me, and then I upended my bag on the floor. I was fumbling through the debris of a few months when I heard my name.

'Maggie, isn't it?'

I peered up at the owner of the shoes hovering beside the pile of bus tickets, old ChapSticks, newspaper cuttings and bar bills that detailed my recent life.

'Sebastian Rae.' He was smiling down at me, that small scar very white above his lip, his dark hair tousled over his dark eyes. 'We met at Bel's party. Need a hand?'

'Of course. I mean – no, sorry, I'm fine. Thanks.' I pushed my own hair off my face, wishing desperately that I'd bothered to put make-up on this morning or had actually dried the stylish new cut which was no doubt sticking out at odd angles by now. 'How come – what are you doing here?'

'I just had a casting upstairs, with Granada. New detective series. Sure I can't help?'

'No, really, thanks.' Shoving everything back into the bag, a solitary tampon rolled along the marble floor towards Sebastian's foot. I scrambled to retrieve it, blushing as red as the Royal Mail van pulling up outside. 'Just lost my pass, you know. I seem to lose everything these days!' I stood up. 'How did it go?'

He looked puzzled.

'The audition.'

'Oh, fine, I think. It's always hard to tell. The ones you think went brilliantly are never the ones you get.'

'It must be so hard. I can't think of anything worse.'

'You get used to it. And you . . .?'

'What?'

'What are you doing here?'

'I work here.'

'Oh, I see.'

'Yeah, I'm – I work on *Renee Reveals*.' I found I was actually ashamed to admit it, but he looked vaguely impressed.

'Aha! The deadly Renee!'

'Deadly? You got that right. Have you seen it?' I was surprised.

'I watched the show every day for a week once a long time ago when I was going up for a part as a talk-show compere. A Spike Jonze film – a kind of post-modern take on the evils of television. It's kind of addictive, isn't it? Your show, I mean.'

'Is it?' I said miserably.

'Don't look so sad.' He smiled at me again. I flushed once more as he checked his watch. 'God, is that the time? I'd better get going. It was nice seeing you.' He held out his hand, then changed his mind, kissing me on the cheek at the exact moment Joseph Blake stepped out of the lift.

'Maggie!' Joseph's voice was high-pitched and querulous. I turned, a little irritated.

'Yeah, all right, Joseph, thanks. I'm just coming.'

'So, take care, won't you?' Seb headed toward the doors and I swung my bag onto my shoulder. Joseph was beside me now, holding something in his hand.

'Maggie –' he started to say as Seb turned back.

'Look, Maggie, I don't suppose you –' His shirt was very white against his tanned skin, unbuttoned to exactly the right point, his dark eyes bright. He really was stunning. 'Do you fancy dinner one night?'

I smiled shyly, surprised. 'Oh!' Oh God – a date. I took a deep breath before I could think any more. 'Yes, thank you. That'd be nice.'

Seb gave me a card. 'Here's my number. Give me a call when you're free.'

I was always free these days. 'I will. Thanks, Seb.'

And then he was gone, outside, whistling for a taxi. I turned to Joseph, who looked even more sullen than usual.

'Let's go, shall we?' I said, glancing down. Joseph was clutching a shiny white oblong: my missing pass. The pass I was sure I'd pocketed last thing on Friday.

Joseph swore blind that he'd just found my security pass on my desk *after* I'd rung from downstairs – but I had an uneasy feeling. In fact, I felt constantly uneasy about Joseph these days. The truth was that things just weren't working out – there was only so long I could keep him on, doing a not very good job. The girls were still frosty with him; he'd made little effort to fit in despite our best efforts. Worst of all, his research was slapdash and poor, his work not up to standard in an industry where people were queuing round the block for jobs.

'They still don't trust Joseph,' Sally said that afternoon, handing me the guest-list for tomorrow's show like the efficient head-girl that she was, 'though I'm not exactly sure why. Goodness, what's this?'

She picked up a cutting on the children of war-torn Congo: a picture of a little boy covered in weeping sores, a grave-faced girl a little older standing behind him holding a machete, stared out at us.

'Poor little mite.' Sally looked appalled, her jolly face falling.

'It's leprosy. It's just – it's something I discussed with Charlie once. You haven't seen my Filofax, have you, Sal? I can't think where I've put it. God, everything keeps disappearing at the moment.'

'No, sorry. Speak of the devil – *mein Führer* is back.'

Charlie strolled across the office with Double-decker's MD, Philip Lyons, and that dreadful snooty researcher Daisy whom I'd met when I was on the trauma show.

'Poor little sods.' Sally sifted through my pile of cuttings. 'Can't see Renee agreeing to any of this, though.' She unearthed one that screamed '*BABY MARKET*', an investigation into foreign adoption in Britain. 'Far too worthy.'

'It's nothing to do with bloody Renee. God, Sal, we all know if she had her way she'd spend the entire season doing DNA tests and breaking some poor bugger's heart every day. Let's just get on with your list, shall we?'

But I was distracted by Charlie's arrival. I'd spent the morning planning how best to deliver my ultimatum to him, so I was relieved to see that both men looked – unsurprisingly – well-oiled. The time was probably as ripe as any. My stomach rolled nervously as the smug pair stopped outside Charlie's office, Lyons's bald head gleaming under the lights, his frill of hair setting off the shine beautifully. They shared a joke with Donna, who was by now flashing her most wicked smile, thrusting her pert chest out just a little further than necessary, giving Daisy a run for her money.

'What's that girl doing here?'

'Daisy? Lyons is placing her in the LA office. Can't think why, can you?' Sally raised a sceptical eyebrow. 'She's almost as bad as Joseph.'

I flicked through her list. 'Blimey, not this bloody footballer *again*. Honestly, Sal, does he really not have anything better to do than appear on our crappy show?'

'Apparently not. It is about ageing lotharios, though. So what shall we do about him?'

'The footballer?'

She laughed. 'No, silly. Joseph.'

I stared disconsolately out of the window. 'I don't understand why Charlie keeps Joseph on. It's just prolonging everybody's agony.' I sighed hard. 'I suppose I'd better talk to Charlie again about him.' I passed back the guest-list. 'And listen, don't book this guy again for at least a month or two, okay? It's lazy. He's just too – obvious. I don't want anyone else from Man U either. Try to get Calum Best instead.'

Sally looked excited, her splendid bosom almost heaving with anticipation. 'You don't think – Joseph and Charlie –'

'Don't be so ridiculous. Charlie might be a letch,' I watched Donna throw her head back and laugh throatily as my phone began to ring, 'but he's definitely not into boys. Not unless I'm losing my instinct as well as my marbles.' I eyed the phone warily. 'Can you get that please, Sal?'

'Sure.' Sally's dimples deepened. 'Trying to impress someone?'

'Hardly,' I muttered, keeping one eye on Charlie.

'Oh, right,' she said knowingly. '*Avoiding* someone?' Her hand hovered over the receiver with great nonchalance. 'Alex, perhaps?'

'It won't be Alex.'

Perhaps I *was* losing my marbles, though, I thought. I certainly felt pretty odd at the moment, cornered by life and circumstance. My phone was still ringing at all hours in the last few weeks – at home, at work, the mobile going day and night. Too often there was silence on the other end: too often to be a coincidence. It was starting to seriously scare me.

'I'll just see if she's here.' Sally clapped her hand over the mouthpiece dramatically. 'Someone called Seb,' she stage-whispered. 'Nice voice.'

I felt my skin go hot as I flapped my hands at her, shaking my head fervently.

'I'm so sorry, Seb, she's in a meeting. Can I take a message? Okay, sure. I expect she'd love to. Eight o'clock. Bye.' She hung up with a triumphant look. 'Now let me see. He said it was nice to see you this morning. And, more importantly, he said he's got two tickets for a screening of *Love All* at the BAFTA cinema tonight, the one on Piccadilly. He'd love you to come, he said. How exciting – a film star!'

I frowned. 'I can't go tonight. I'm cooking dinner for Bel.'

'Bel'll understand, won't she?'

'She might, but she's leaving next week.'

'So?'

'So I want to spend as much time as possible with her. God knows when I'll see her again.'

'How very honourable, Maggie – and how very dull.'

'It's not dull to put your mates before men.' I was indignant. 'Is it?'

'No comment. And what exactly were you up to this morning with the lovely Seb anyway, you saucy minx?' Sally's round face was beaming with complicity.

'Sally, for God's sake! I just bumped into him downstairs. It's hardly Cathy and Heathcliff. I don't even know him.'

'Oh yeah?'

'Yeah.'

'You know what, Maggie, it may be none of my business, but you can't keep hankering after Alex forever you know.'

'Hankering?' I felt my brows knit. 'That's hardly fair.'

The MD was taking his leave with Daisy now, clapping Charlie

125

on the back with great effusion, the two men looking not so much like the cats that had got the cream as the cats who'd gorged themselves until they were fit to burst. I sprang up from my desk just as my phone rang again. Sally swept up the receiver.

'Maggie Warren's office,' she winked at me. But her face quickly fell again, the torrent of abuse audible even from my position by the door. 'It's Alex, I think.' She thrust the phone at me like it was too hot to hold.

I considered the lesser of two evils and made a run for it. 'I'll call him back, thanks.' I pulled my door open. 'Charlie? I need a word.'

Charlie rolled his unlit cigar between two fingers and considered me carefully. Then he checked his Rolex. 'You've got five minutes before my conference call with HBO.'

'That's ample.' I followed him into his den. He'd stopped short of writhing women on the walls here but still it was all leather, dark wood and a furry rug that screamed *'lie naked on me'*.

'There are a couple of things actually.' I cleared my throat bravely.

Charlie poured two glasses of whisky from the crystal decanter on the desk. 'I know what you're going to say, Maggie. You can't do this any more, ya da ya da ya.' He yawned widely – so widely I saw all the gold in his mouth. 'Well, I'm here to tell you, you can. One more month, darling, just while we get the ratings back up there – and then I'll keep my end of the bargain.' He picked up the bronze desk-lighter, so heavy it looked like it was an effort to lift, and lit his horrible cigar.

'But, Charlie –'

'One more month, just to the end of the season – and one more show from you.'

'I don't understand –'

'The crash show was a huge success – you know that. You and Fay being reunited – it melted hearts nationwide! Lyons is over the moon. It's even been nominated for a Viewers' Weepie Award.

126

If we can net one more hit like that, then he secures the American series, and all our dreams come true. You produce the *You're Dumped* show, plus a *Survivors' Reunion* with your pretty little friend Fay et al, and then you're free to do your doco. That's a promise, my darling.'

'I can't, Charlie. I'm never appearing on TV again. It was hideous.'

'Don't be so wet.' He puffed smoke at me like an old dragon. 'I mean, granted, you were hardly an on-screen natural, but I don't know – there was something about you. The viewers love all that doe-eyed vulnerability.'

'I'm not being wet. It just confirmed to me all the reasons I hate the programme so much now. And that *Dumped* show is completely immoral, you must know that.'

'Since when did you grow a conscience, darling? You never complained before.'

I flushed angrily. 'Yeah, well, people change. I've had my eyes opened.'

He laughed without humour. 'What – by that loser boyfriend of yours?'

'Who?' I shook my head in confusion. 'Alex? He's not my boyfriend any more, and it's nothing to do with him. Can we not bring him into it, please.' With a sinking feeling, I remembered pushing Charlie away the other night after Bel's party. I realised I was about to pay for denting his pride. I took a deep breath.

'Look, the point is, I can't do it, Charlie. I won't. Let me do something I believe in – or let me go.'

He looked bored. 'Maggie, you fucked up so badly in the summer, darling, you're hardly in a position to negotiate.'

'That's not fair, Charlie.' My skin was scalding. But God, I wished I had better recall of the events. However hard I racked my brain, the episode in question escaped me in its entirety. Each time I imagined my apparent ignominy I winced inside.

Harder still was accepting my memory was so impaired; it made me feel incomplete and broken.

'Isn't it? I'd say it was. I'd say it was *extremely* fair.'

'I still can't remember it properly.' Which wasn't absolutely true any more.

'How convenient. I'm more than happy to remind you if it helps. And remember this, darling. You blew it – and then you left me in the shit. So you owe me.'

'It just – it got a bit out of control, that's all.'

'I thought you couldn't remember?' He smiled malevolently. 'Listen, darling.' He leaned forward and blew smoke directly into my eyes, speaking very quietly and levelly. 'You'd be nothing without me in the first place. Lyons would have had you out on your ear in June if he'd got a whiff of any of it. Your domestics should not affect your work, you know that, Maggie. Now it's payback time.'

'And if I refuse?' I whispered.

'If you don't do my show, I won't hesitate to use everything I know. And you wouldn't want that now, Maggie baby, would you?'

I stared at him, appalled. 'But I didn't do anything really bad. I'm sure I didn't.'

'Didn't you?'

'They didn't charge me in the end, I know that much,' I said stoutly. The cigar smoke in this airless little box was making me feel ill.

'So what? The industry loves a victim of their own kind – you must realise that. They'll bring you down quite happily – *if* they find out.' He studied the end of his cigar with great interest. 'And you'll never work again if they knew what came next.'

I gazed at him in disbelief. 'Christ, Charlie, what's this all about?'

But I knew the answer really. Charlie had created me – so he'd only let me go on his own terms. The closeness that we'd built as colleagues stood for nothing, I realised now, if it wasn't all up to him. And if it wasn't, he'd rather destroy me first: he was that power-hungry.

I thought miserably of Gillian Router, the series producer before me. She'd fallen out with Charlie so badly there'd been talk of legal action at one point when she left *Renee Reveals*. With some considerable guilt I remembered that I'd simply seen the debacle as a weakness in her, and a great opening for me.

'Can't do without you, Maggie darling. Straightforward as that.'

There was a knock on the door.

'Maggie Warren?'

I swung round as a familiar smell pervaded the small room, fighting with the pungent smoke that swirled visibly in the air. The post-room boy stood in the doorway brandishing a huge bouquet of flowers – of gloriously reeking lilies. My heart hit the floor.

'These are for you,' the boy said to me proudly, as if he'd just grown them himself.

Twice in one day was a first. Reluctantly, I opened the card.

'*In Sympathy.*'

My blood turned to ice.

'How charming.' Charlie ground out his cigar and smiled wolfishly. 'You don't look very pleased, I must say. I do wonder who they're from, eh, darling?'

# Chapter Fifteen

Somehow I got through the rest of the afternoon. I signed off Sally's show and viewed a VT of Renee's best bits (the back of her as she walked away, in my opinion) for the National TV Awards. In between tasks, I tracked down the florist who'd delivered the latest flowers. She just confirmed what all the rest had – a man had rung through the order, paying on a card in the name of Steven I. Sweeger. It sounded American to me, and I had racked my befuddled brain quite desperately, but it rang no bells.

'Can you describe his voice?'

'Not really.' The florist sounded bored. 'Hang on – the red ones are three pound a stem, love.' She came back on the line. 'Kind of posh, I s'pose. Look, sorry, but I'm busy –'

'If you remember anything else about him, can you please call me? It's really important.'

'Sure.' I felt her shrug down the line. I knew damn well I'd never hear from her again.

As I stared mournfully at the phone and contemplated calling the police, not for the first time, Charlie stuck his head round the door and flung the *You're Dumped* proposal on my desk with a sly wink. Leafing through it despondently, Joseph Blake ambled across my vision and I realised I still hadn't broached his future with my boss. Right now, though, it could wait.

I watched the clock incessantly all afternoon, pretending to study the Christmas schedules until finally it was late enough to

130

get the hell out of there. Like most TV companies, Double-decker promoted the entirely masochistic idea that the later you stayed, the better you were at your job. Most of the girls looked incredibly diligent right now, beavering away at their computers; in reality they were probably buying dresses on Net-a-porter and updating their Facebook profiles, biding time.

At six I grabbed my coat, muttering something about a meeting, in truth desperate to open a bottle of wine with Bel. But in the deli on the South Bank, as I filled my basket with fresh tagliatelle and rosy tomatoes and fat white mozzarella, Bel rang.

'I'm so sorry, Mag, but Hannah's come out in some really odd rash. I'm taking her to A&E. Really sorry, babe.'

I stared sadly at my basket before dumping the lot. I strode out into the cold night air of the Embankment, the wind whipping around my face, my newly shorn neck feeling cold and exposed. I wrapped my woolly scarf tighter and tried not to feel sorry for myself. Everyone else looked like they were rushing, like they had somewhere interesting to go – everyone except me. The lights of the Jolly Sportsman on the corner twinkled enticingly, and I thrust my hand in my pocket to check what change I had. My fingers closed round something else – Seb's card. I glanced at my watch. It wasn't even seven. I still had plenty of time to get to Piccadilly if I fancied it. Fancied Seb. But first I slipped into the pub.

I was halfway through my first glass of wine when someone snuck up and grabbed my arm, spilling my drink all over my bag.

'Maggie!'

'For God's sake, Fay!' I nearly choked on my Merlot.

'Shall I get one in?' She gazed at me. 'It's never fun to drink on your own.'

'Sometimes – sometimes it's all right,' I said stiffly.

'Oh, Maggie, don't be silly!'

'Please, Fay. I've had a bit of a bad day. I just – I could really do with some time alone.'

'I don't believe you!' She grinned at me. 'Anyway, I brought this.' She handed me an envelope.

I gritted my teeth. 'If this is another photo of the bloody crash –' I said, placing it unopened on the bar.

'It's not, I promise. Something *much* nicer,' she giggled. She caught the barman's eye instantly. 'A spritzer please. And one for yourself.' He was practically salivating as she slid the envelope towards me through all the sopping beer rings. 'Go on.'

I peered inside nervously. A couple of baby photos gazed up at me, a solemn blue-eyed child with a mass of black ringlets, and a younger one, six months or thereabouts, with one tiny tooth. Then a child of about six in a Holly Hobbie-type hat, gazing adoringly at the camera, great violet eyes shining. A shiver went down my spine.

'Do you know who they are?'

'I could hazard a guess,' I muttered, closing the envelope. 'So –'

'So, I just wanted you to see how alike we were as babies.' She smiled happily.

I frowned. 'How do you know?'

'Because you had some photos at your dad's. I saw them, remember?'

'Fay,' I stared down at the envelope, 'I'm sorry, but this is really a bit weird –'

'Why?' She stared at me like it was me that was insane.

'Because,' I took a deep breath, 'because we're not even friends.'

'There's no need to be rude, Maggie.' I'd never seen her pretty little face sullen before. 'I just want us to *become* friends, that's the point.'

'Well, I don't, to be really honest.' It had to be said. 'I've got plenty of friends already, thanks. And I'm sure you have too.' Beating about the bush had got me precisely nowhere so far.

'Fine.' Her bottom lip quivered like a small child's.

132

'Fine.' I steeled my stony heart and pushed the envelope back into her hand. 'See you around.' Then I relented a little. 'Take care.'

Fay turned and flounced out of the pub.

In the end I didn't ring Seb. Fortified by half a bottle of wine, and pushing thoughts of Fay out of my mind, I felt suddenly excited by the unknown. I could be single and spontaneous, I told myself, hurrying through fur-coated Christmas shoppers on Piccadilly, past the moss-green grandeur of Fortnum and Mason's, fat chocolates stacked in mouth-watering mounds that glistened behind star-dusted windows. Being spontaneous was something positive, something to celebrate about losing Alex, I told myself, as the great flags of the Royal Academy shivered in the wind. If Seb looked pleased when he saw me, I'd stay. If not, I'd pretend I was just passing. I was just drunk enough to believe that I could be convincing.

But outside the BAFTA cinema I lost my nerve. As I watched the elite arrive, I realised with a sinking heart that I was horribly under-dressed, and suddenly my courage faded. I lingered under a shop canopy in the chilly wind and lit a cigarette, debating what to do, so cold my teeth were almost chattering, the wine that had warmed my core ebbing away.

A beautiful dark girl in a shimmery dress and pearls flung her arms around a very gay man in sealskin and air-kissed him passionately.

'Alberto, baby!'

'Darling! I am so excited. I hear you are fantastic.'

'Silly!' She simpered. 'I'm so not.'

'I'm sure you are, *mon ange*. You will light up the screen. I hear it is like Woody Allen at his best.'

'God, well let's hope it's not at his worst!'

'And your co-star, he is quite gorgeous, *non*?' Seal-skin nudged the girl conspiratorially. 'All that brooding darkness, that fabulous body.'

The girl went pink. The door swung shut behind them and their giggles faded. I took another desperate drag and wished I'd gone home to get changed. Into what, though? Yet another battered pair of jeans? Exhaling, I knew I couldn't stay. I didn't belong here.

Perfectly on cue, Seb stepped out of a black Mercedes that had just pulled up on the opposite side of the road. He hadn't seen me yet. I held my breath, hovering – unable to decide –

'Maggie!'

My blood ran as cold as the night around me. Fay was tripping lightly toward me, her long coat falling open to reveal the same green dress I'd worn to Bel and Johnno's do. I was truly astounded.

'Fancy seeing you here,' she said, and she smiled – but she was cooler than she'd ever been before. 'Have you come for the film?'

'Umm, sort of.' With considerable effort, I composed myself. 'Have you?'

Over her shoulder, I watched Seb cross half of the busy lanes of Piccadilly, patting his jacket pockets, then turn back to the car, frowning. He disappeared behind a bus; I wished fervently that Fay would disappear too.

'I was going to suggest we got seats together, but in the circumstances –' She turned those huge eyes on me reproachfully.

I smiled feebly, but she was already through the door and pattering up the stairs as Seb strolled across the road again, clutching a phone and a fat book.

It was now or never. I took a deep breath and, chucking my cigarette away, stepped out of the shadows. 'Sebastian.'

He turned on the second stair and a flicker of recognition crossed his face, followed by a huge grin. 'Maggie Warren. What a lovely surprise!'

'Oh, is it?' This time my smile was truly sincere. 'That's nice.'

'Yes, it is. I didn't think you were coming, I must say. Why didn't you ring me?'

'I was – you know.' I felt ridiculously nervous. 'I was just passing.'

'Really?' He was courteous enough not to look disbelieving. His smart suit hung immaculately on his lean form, his sky-blue shirt complementing his olive skin perfectly.

A couple of braying Sloanes pushed between us with great self-importance, followed by a Kate Moss look-alike in sunglasses and a skirt that barely covered her pants, her bare legs so cold they were a mottled red, hissing something about standing-room only into a mobile phone. I caught Seb's eye and we both burst out laughing.

'You know what,' he murmured thoughtfully, his hand finding mine.

I shivered, with cold or excitement I wasn't sure. 'What?'

'I hate these occasions.' Now his fingers gently circled my wrist.

'Do you?' I asked shyly. His touch was lovely and warm on my cold skin.

'Shall we go and get some dinner instead?'

'But – don't you want to see yourself up there on the silver screen? I don't want to ruin your big moment.'

He let go of me, pushing his hair out of his eyes, staring into the distance for a moment. 'I hate it really. It makes me very uncomfortable actually, watching myself.' He looked at me. 'I'd much rather talk to you instead.'

'Oh!' I felt a small bubble of pleasure form deep inside. 'Okay. Well, it's entirely up to you.'

'Hopefully the car's still there.' He grabbed my hand impulsively and swung me down the stairs. 'The driver was meant to wait. Do you fancy some Thai?'

Food was absolutely my thing. I loved eating; liked cooking even more. I could drum up a meal fit for a king from just a few ingredients and no recipe, a gift I was proud to have inherited from my mother. I collected cookery books; read them in bed for fun, treasured scrapbooks full of Gar's old recipes for lamb casserole and Cornish fish-pie. My father had always said I should have cooked professionally; he thought I should have avoided the media entirely and concentrated on feeding bellies rather than brains. Feeding brains or rotting them was my current internal debate.

But tonight my usually reliable appetite had completely deserted me. I sat opposite Seb in the latest fashionably over-booked restaurant – where it was so dark I could hardly read the menu, and the maitre d' was positively obsequious, calling Seb by his first name; where the waiters rushed forwards to pull out your chair before you even knew you wanted to stand; where most of the other diners were famous or certainly looked as if they'd like to be – and I found I could only drink champagne and grin foolishly. I watched Seb polish off his tom yam soup and green-curry-by-a-frilly-name with great relish while I just picked a bit at some very fat prawns and dropped my fork once or twice, oddly beset by nerves. There was a shiny baby grand piano wedged in behind the door, and every now and then a rather elegant blonde in a trouser suit came and played Gershwin songs. It was all very kitsch, and I loved it. And in between eating Seb asked me all about myself, which I hated, and I managed to steer the conversation towards him, although he was quite meas-ured and discreet about his achievements.

'What are you reading?' I asked, nodding at the book he'd put on the seat beside him.

'What?' He licked his sticky fingers. 'Oh, that. It's just a film book. I'm a bit of an anorak about old movies. If you want a bit of trivia, I'm your man.'

'Okay. Who played –' My mind went blank. For some reason I could only think of Alex's favourite film. 'Who betrayed Harold Shand in *The Long Good Friday*?'

'That's easy. Derek Thompson, playing Jeff. He's in *Casualty* now, actually. Good film, *The Long Good Friday*.'

The blonde came back, dark lipstick reapplied, and started up again. I recognised the tune immediately.

'Maggie?' Seb waved a hand in front of my face. 'Hello? You're a million miles away.'

'Sorry,' I was startled for a moment, 'my mother used to play this song. I remember it from my childhood, I'm sure.'

'Your mum?' He looked at me intently.

I rolled my napkin up, then unrolled it again. 'Yes.' I didn't want to appear rude. 'Tell me about your family, why don't you?'

'There's not much to tell really. My mother died recently.'

'Oh God, I'm sorry.'

'We were – it was just us two.' I could tell he wasn't keen to discuss it either. I changed the subject quickly.

Seb was making me laugh with stories about filming a trainer ad where the French director had kept screaming, 'Dance, damn you, dance' at the cast, and topping up my glass with the last of the Cristal, when my phone bleeped.

'I'm sure I've seen that ad, you know,' I said, ignoring it. Then it began to ring, stopped, and then almost immediately started again. I fished it out.

'Sorry. I should have switched it off.' Glancing down at the screen, I realised it was Alex. With a heavy feeling in my belly I remembered I hadn't returned his earlier call to the office.

'Answer it, why don't you?' Seb drained his own glass. 'I don't mind, really.'

'It's no one important.' I rejected the call and ignored the text message as well.

'So do you fancy coffee – or shall I get the bill?'

A cloud passed over the evening's sun. I realised I didn't want this to end – and I didn't want to think about Alex either. 'I'm not very good at coffee so late. It always keeps me awake.'

'Is that such a bad thing?' He had very straight teeth, I noticed, as he smiled at me, and my stomach lurched horribly; lurched with what I hated to admit was desire.

The blonde was playing 'Let's Call the Whole Thing Off' as Seb wandered off to get the bill. I checked my reflection quickly in the back of a dessert-spoon. Slightly flushed with drink, my hair was ruffled and my eyes were bright and wide with excitement and – there was no other word for it – lust. I hadn't had such a nice night in –

Seb sat back down and smiled at me and I felt like he'd just read my thoughts. My mobile bleeped with Alex's voicemail message. 'Sorry,' I murmured again, and this time I opened the text.

One word:

**WHORE.**

Just that, brutal and harsh.

Shakily I checked the number, but it wasn't Alex's. I didn't recognise it. I hesitated as the waiter brought Seb the card-machine, and then, taking a deep breath, I called the number. It went straight to an automated voicemail. Seb was finishing up now and handing the man some notes extravagantly, and I was feeling horribly flustered. I put the phone away, my hands suddenly clammy with fear.

'Okay, we're all paid up. Shall we go?'

'Sure.' I stood quickly, my heart pounding, my face suddenly tight. 'Thank you so much for a lovely meal.'

'Thank *you* for such lovely company.' Seb came round to help me with my coat. Then he looked closely at me. 'Are you all right, Maggie?'

'I'm fine,' I said in a small voice.

'You don't look fine.'

'I am, really.'

'Are you sure?'

I felt poised on a precipice. The text *must* be from Alex – and I was damned if I was going to let him ruin my night. He'd ruined far too many before. But I couldn't tell Seb the truth, drawing him into a situation I didn't yet understand myself. It

138

was too early to involve him in such ugliness. With a tangible effort, I pulled myself together.

'I'm fine, really, Seb. I think I just need some fresh air, that's all.'

He took my hand and led me through the restaurant and his touch reassured me, calming my nerves. I felt glad that I was with him, happy and proud, happy in a way I hadn't been in such a long time. And then outside Seb looked down at me – he wasn't so much taller and his eyes were burning into mine, and he took the two ends of my scarf and pulled me gently forward till we could be no nearer. I realised I was pretty drunk now and I was glad to lean into him. He cupped my face in his hands, and then he said my name.

'Maggie.' He whispered it like it was a strange, foreign word, staring at me like he wanted to drink me in, and then finally he leaned down and kissed me – and for a moment I felt bewildered. I hadn't kissed another man since Alex, since I'd fallen so violently in love with Alex – and Seb was so very different: smooth where Alex was scraped and scarred, his smell of aftershave and soap not builder's dust, his lips not chapped like Alex's always were. And then I stared at that small scar, and as Seb kissed me again I shook off all thoughts of Alex; I forgot about my ex and melted into this other man.

The freezing air wrapped round us, the streetlight shone on us like we were centre-stage and I forgot the stinking alley we clung together in and the drunken revellers catcalling from the other side of the road. I felt quite giddy with booze and lust and I realised just how badly I wanted this man, how badly I wanted him to take me home and make me forget, to undress me slowly. And I was just wondering whether it was very bad form to demand that he did so immediately when he stopped kissing me for a minute and stepped back.

'Jesus, Maggie.' He looked, for the first time since I'd met him, less self-possessed than normal, his breathing slightly ragged, his dark eyes almost fierce. He pushed his hair back out of his eyes. 'I don't know what it is exactly about you, but you do something very odd to me.'

'Odd?' I tried to control my own breathing a bit. 'That sounds a bit scary.'

'To my head, I mean.'

'Just to your head?' I looked up at him from under my lashes and he smiled.

'No, not just my head. Most definitely not just my head, Maggie. Shall we get out of here?'

And he pulled me against him now and kissed me harder than before, more urgently, and I felt myself spin into the vortex of desire and drink that meant I didn't care whether nice girls did or didn't on the first date, I was most definitely about to.

We went back to my flat – it was nearer and it felt like there was no time to waste. Seb had let his driver go earlier so we got a black cab across the river, across London Bridge, kissing all the way back until I felt like a teenager, like I was going to explode into Tom and Jerry stars, and then the cab dropped us among the debris of the wooden crates and cabbage leaves and old coffee cups which was Borough Market on a Monday night, and by now I was desperate to have him near me, in me, his bare flesh against mine. Most of all I was desperate to stop thinking. We slammed up against the door as I fumbled with the keys and we were in the stairwell, tearing at each other's clothes. Seb pushed me against the wall, unbuttoning my jeans, pushing up my top, and I was shaking with desire now and pulling at his shirt and he was groaning my name and we didn't make it to the bedroom but did it right there on the velvet sofa, which had been very expensive once but had definitely seen better days.

Afterwards I wrapped myself in the silk throw from the armchair and lit a cigarette, smiling shyly at my new lover. 'I'm not normally so forward, you know.'

'It is the twenty-first century, babe. Come here, why don't you.' He patted the sofa where he still sprawled, his shirt unbuttoned. He hadn't even got his trousers off, we'd been so frantic. His body was good, toned and lean, his olive skin so smooth I was tempted to lick it like an ice-cream. But I lay on the other end of the sofa and he lifted my feet and put them in his lap. Suddenly self-conscious, I froze as he traced the livid scar on my left foot with one finger.

'What's this from?' He frowned. 'It looks new.'

I hid behind the smoke from my cigarette. 'It is quite. I had a – I was in an accident.'

'What kind of accident?'

'A crash. It was a – a coach crash.'

'Recently?'

'Yes. Pretty recent.'

He looked at me. 'Not the M4 one? When the horses got out?'

I nodded bleakly. I still couldn't bear to talk about it really, not even to someone I'd just had sex with.

Seb leaned down and kissed my foot softly. 'Poor baby.'

I shivered.

'Is it still sore?' He looked worried.

I shrugged. 'Not the scar, not really. It's more inside, like deep inside my foot.' I killed my cigarette in the ashtray. 'And it's weird, you know, but I'm sure it hurts more when it rains.'

Seb pulled me towards me until I straddled him, and slid his hands under the silk, cupping my breast, breathing gently on my neck until I squirmed with pleasure.

'Let me see if I can take your mind off it, shall I?' He lowered his head and my last sane thought was poor Digby. I must let him in very soon.

In the morning I woke up on the sofa to the smell of fresh coffee and the jolly twittering of breakfast radio. Blinking against the light, I couldn't think where I was – until Seb appeared in the kitchen doorway, shirt still unbuttoned, coffee-cup in hand. I stared at him for a second, feeling confounded; as if he wasn't the person I'd expected to see. As if Alex might step up behind him and come and get his coffee.

'Morning, beautiful.'

I blushed. 'Hello.' I yawned widely, hiding behind my hand. 'God, what time is it?'

'About eight. I didn't want to wake you before – you looked so peaceful.'

Oh Lord. And ridiculous, no doubt – sleep-soaked and tufty-haired and panda-eyed, still wrapped in an old throw.

'Coffee?'

'Oh, yes please.' Considering the level of intimacy we'd achieved last night, I felt absurdly shy. Digby pattered out behind Seb, wagging his tail happily; a welcome distraction. 'Aha. I see you've met.'

'Yeah, I let him in from the roof terrace. Poor thing, he was very glad to see me.'

'Oh God, Digby. Sorry, darling.' The dog jumped up on the sofa and slobbered all over me as Seb handed me a cup of steaming black coffee. I was too shy to ask for milk.

'Thank you.'

'I'm really sorry, but I've got to get going.' He was buttoning up his shirt now. 'I've got a meeting about publicity for *Twelfth Night* on the other side of town at ten, and I really should get changed first.' Slipping his jacket on, he bent to lace his shoes. 'Turning up in Armani might get everyone's backs up, don't you think?' Seb grinned that crooked smile at me. 'Thanks for a great evening.' He planted a kiss on my neck that made me squirm rather like I had last night. 'I'll call you, okay?'

'Okay.' This was all going too fast for me and my poor befuddled brain. I was barely awake yet, and feeling quite peculiar – which may or may not have been the hangover. Seb winked at me from the top of the metal stairs I'd always hated, stairs Alex had designed in a fit of modernism and insisted on; and then he was gone.

With a nasty twinge, I realised I would mind if I never heard from Seb again. I scooped Digby up in my arms, waiting for the door to slam downstairs. I'd mind – but, conversely, I also felt a bit dirty: like I'd just let myself down. I wasn't ready for this yet; these feelings, this man. I stuck my face in the dog's soft back. 'Oh God, Dig. What have I gone and done now?'

A buzz at the intercom was followed by another two short sharp bursts; a voice calling my name urgently. 'Maggie.'

Perhaps Seb couldn't bear to leave after all. I pushed up from the sofa and limped over to the intercom, smiling to myself despite my sore foot, always most stiff in the mornings. 'What have you forgotten, silly?'

'You'd better come down here. Quickly.' His tone was insistent enough to make me drag on my jeans and rush down the stairs, Digby barking behind me. I tore open the door to reveal a troubled-looking Seb standing on the pavement. He held a hand out to me. 'Maggie.'

A man unpacking crates of flaming clementines from a van opposite glanced across and then stopped in his tracks. I turned. Violent red letters defaced the pale green door, the paint running like dried blood towards the floor. I had to step away to read what they spelled; to read the letters that spelled out the words: **MEDDLING WHORE**.

Unconsciously I stepped back in horror, knocking into something by my feet. I glanced down. There, propped against the wall by the front door, made out of hideous white chrysanthemums tightly knit together, was a large wreath. A funeral wreath that said: '*DAUGHTER*'.

# Chapter Sixteen

'You can drop me here, thanks.' I took a deep breath and swung down from the cab, squeezing through the gap between a silver Merc and the monstrous maroon Bentley parked outside the imperious Belgravia house. I stopped for a moment, gazing up at the glossy white pillars, the huge black number shiny in the glass above the solid oak door, the sash windows like unblinking eyes amid the russet creeper hanging shaggy as a beard. It was a house that screamed 'old money' but was lying; a house every bit as arrogant as its owner. I'd hoped I'd never set foot here again.

Turning the collar of my coat up in search of protection, I shot up the stairs before I lost my nerve. The wrought-iron gargoyle set into the enormous door-knocker sneered down at me.

'And you can sod off,' I muttered, before pounding him hard.

An hour ago I'd stood outside my flat staring at those bald words scrawled across my own front door, at that horrible wreath, utterly incongruous before the cosy cake-shop where iced confections in the luminous window proclaimed '*Happy Birthday*' and '*Congratulations*'; the shop Alex had once commissioned to make me a '*Can't Get Enough of You*' cake on a weekend where we didn't get out of bed. I had stared and stared at the wreath until Seb had taken my hand very gently, and slipped his arm around me.

'All right?' He kissed the top of my head.

'Been better actually, you know.' I was shivering with cold and distress, aware that we were attracting attention in the street now. The van driver's eyes were practically popping out of his head as he dropped a crate; the clementines rolled like small missiles into the road, nearly bringing down an old lady who was trundling past.

'Shame.' She shook her head sadly at the wreath, and trundled on.

'Let's go inside, shall we?' Gently Seb propelled me towards the doorway. 'It's freezing out here. You can call the police upstairs.'

I shook my head vehemently. 'No police. Not yet.'

Seb frowned. 'Why not?'

'Just because. It's nothing, I'm sure.' I started up the stairs, my mind ticking over furiously. 'What are they going to do about it anyway?'

'Er – find out who did it?'

'It's just some random nutter, Seb.'

'Oh really? Doesn't look particularly random to me. And what do you mean "not yet"?' He looked at me closely. 'You know who did this, don't you?'

'No.' I flopped onto a kitchen chair, my voice tight and strained. Digby placed his front paws on my knee and stared up at me beseechingly. 'I really hope not anyway.'

Seb switched the kettle on. 'So who *might* it be?'

Shakily I stroked Digby's head. 'Fine guard-dog you are, mate.'

'Maggie,' Seb's voice was urgent, 'whoever it is, and you don't have to tell me if you don't want to – well, it isn't good, is it?'

'No, obviously. But I don't know who did it.' Like a monstrous worm a horrible thought was inching into my consciousness. 'I wish I did.'

'So call the police then. Otherwise I will.'

The police. Other than a brief statement after the crash, I hadn't encountered the police since – since the summer. My lost summer. My stomach heaved; I stood up quickly. 'Sorry. Excuse me –'

In the bathroom I stood queasily over the basin until I felt a little better. My reflection showed a ghostly white face, my freckles livid against my pallor, my eyes round and glassy blue with fear.

'Maggie?' Seb was outside the door.

'I'm fine, really.' But my voice came out a whisper. I felt hunted.

'Maggie, please, let me in. I'm worried about you.'

I smoothed my maddened hair down as if it would soothe my nerves, and sprayed some perfume on. My hands were still shaking; it was a bit like having the DTs. The summer flashed through my head again. Oh God. I plucked open the bathroom door and tried to smile at Seb.

'Great first date, eh? At least someone's warned you what I'm *really* like.'

'Don't be silly.' Seb pulled me towards him and hugged me. 'It's obviously bollocks. I don't believe a word of it.'

I tried to concentrate. 'You don't believe either of them, you mean,' I joked, but my mind was racing now; things slotting together neatly like cards in a dealer's pack.

'What?'

I couldn't say them. 'Either of *those* two words.'

Seb played along gallantly. 'No, I don't believe *either* of them. And you know, perhaps –' he held me away from him for a second and searched my face with something like hope, 'perhaps they've got the wrong house?'

I thought of the lilies, the car outside Bel's party, the text last night. *Hardly the Virgin Mary*.

'Maybe,' I said brightly. 'Maybe they have.'

\*   \*   \*

At Malcolm's house I had apparently arrived at the most inopportune moment – in the middle of a family brunch. Most peculiar for a Tuesday morning in November, and definitely most unorthodox for this dysfunctional family.

The housekeeper, one of Malcolm's many ostentations, a flat-faced Filipino woman who always looked terrified, led me into what Barbara termed the drawing room. (Malcolm's wife Barbara, Alex's mother, was the only class in this marriage.)

There was no Alex, but the rest of the family were huddled around a groaning drinks-table at the far end of the showy room, all thick pile carpet and polished dark furniture, expensive dull paintings of stags in the glen and stony-faced women in pink crinolines clutching hairy lapdogs. Were we meant to think they were Malcolm's ancestry, I'd always wondered, because they sure as hell weren't. I lingered in the corner, trying to fade into the frightfully tasteful William Morris wallpaper, until Malcolm greeted me as if he'd actually been expecting me. In fact, I could have sworn he looked almost excited as he kissed me heartily on both cheeks.

Behind Malcolm was the silver-framed photo of Alex as a lanky boy, proudly holding a cricket bat, his hair on end as usual, his white jumper much too big, his younger brother Tom grinning behind him, both missing a few teeth – the photo we'd had framed for Barbara's sixtieth. I winced at the memory of the night that was slowly seeping back into my consciousness – the night it all went wrong.

I spotted Serena draped around a rather flushed Tom, and with a sinking heart I recognised the gleam in Malcolm's eye. He was obviously anticipating a scrap.

'Drink, Maggie?' Malcolm held up a jug of Bucks Fizz, beady eyes glinting.

'Don't mind if I do, thanks,' I said pleasantly. My adrenaline levels were already so high I was practically flying. 'So, this is a first, isn't it?' I accepted a glass. 'Brunch. What's the occasion?'

'Oh, you know, old girl.' He clinked my glass with his, his East-End drawl as gravelly as ever. 'My merger with Stebsons, Barbara getting out of hospital, of course.'

'Oh, I'm sorry, I didn't know. Is she all right?' I turned to smile at his wife, a smile she returned warmly. Poor mild-mannered woman, I'd always thought, married to the crude Malcolm. Squashed by him.

'She's fine, love, just fine.' He considered me mildly over his drink as Alex came through the door, looking as shambolic as ever despite a shirt and tie. A badly tied tie. 'Oh, and of course we're toasting Alexander. Off to Glasgow – *and* engaged.' Malcolm clapped his son on the shoulder. 'Just need a baby now, Alexander, eh? Complete the trio.'

I choked on my Bucks Fizz.

'Piss off, Pa,' Alex said tiredly. He didn't look like someone celebrating anything. He looked exhausted and lifeless. 'Do you need a bang on the back, Maggie?'

I shook my head vehemently.

'I'm not being rude – but what are you doing here?' Alex loosened his tie as I recovered myself.

'You weren't answering your phone so I rang your office.' I couldn't look at him. 'They said you were here.'

Serena swiftly uncoiled herself from Tom, who was looking rather dazed, his poor girlfriend Clarissa utterly terrified and as horsey as ever in the corner by the canapés. Serena wafted across the room to drape herself round the other brother now, her dress frighteningly low-cut for this time of day, the powder-pink of her silk bra just peeping through the sheer fabric. She raised one curved eyebrow at me.

'Maxine.'

'Maggie, actually,' I said pleasantly. Her ring finger was still bare. I tore my eyes away. 'Hi there, Selina.'

Alex grinned. Then he saw my face and stopped.

'I need to talk to you, Alex.' I drained my glass.

'We're kind of busy right now, aren't we, Allie darling?' Serena said, inspecting her perfect manicure.

'Yes, well,' I put my glass on the polished sideboard where it left a wet ring, 'sorry about that. I just need a quick word with Allie darling,' I smiled amiably at her, 'about why he keeps ringing me.'

Serena shot me a look that could have felled me on a different day.

'Oh dear. I am sorry,' said Malcolm, looking absolutely anything but. 'You been a naughty boy again, Alexander?'

Alex chewed his thumbnail, showing no vestige of emotion. His father brandished the jug again, his bushy brows practically dancing with delight. 'Top-up anyone?'

Barbara joined us now, clad in beige Jaeger, her limp fair hair only accentuating her washed-out appearance, her opulent tones a direct contrast to her husband's.

'Hello there, Maggie. Lovely to see you. Are you well?' She adjusted her large, owl-like glasses. 'Serena, do come and see the piccies of the house in Provence. They've come out so well. I'm really pleased.' She linked her arm expertly through the girl's silk-clad one and guided her away, Serena's skinny back bristling, unable to resist Barbara's charm.

Alex swigged his drink and raised an eyebrow at me. 'So?'

'Nice glass of vodka?' I asked sweetly. I knew his tricks.

'Water, actually,' he said shortly. 'Let's go next door.'

'I don't believe you, Alex.' I paced the room in front of him, pacing until I thought I'd wear a hole in the marble floor. I couldn't stop, couldn't stand still. Round and round the conservatory I went, like a panther I'd once seen in a zoo: maddened by my enforced entrapment. 'This is a complete waste of time. Just admit it.'

'You said it.' Alex's fists were clenched in two tight balls of restrained emotion. I stopped for a second and stared at him.

'You're lying, I know you are.'

149

'For fuck's sake, Maggie.' He met my eye, standing upright for once, not slouched as he usually was. 'I can't believe you'd think I could stoop so low.'

I laughed – but there was less mirth in this room than in a morgue. 'I've seen you lower, Alex, remember?'

His eyes flared with something unfathomable. 'That's not fair, Maggie,' he said quietly. 'I've been a bit fucked-up maybe – but nothing like this.'

He turned away, leaning his head against the glass, and stared out at the dying garden. The rigid borders of flowers were a little pathetic, just a few Michaelmas daisies and rows of fat-headed chrysanthemums whose number had recently been culled, judging by the bare stalks.

'Yes, well, life's not fair, Alex, is it? You spent a lot of time telling me that, I seem to remember.' I watched a scrawny pigeon attacking the empty husks beneath the bird-feeder in desperation, pecking frantically like they were live things. 'If it's not you, who *is* it?' I felt increasingly desperate, and I tried to push the panic down. 'Someone's got it in for me – and I can't think of anyone apart from you.'

Although that wasn't entirely true any more. Suspicion seemed to suddenly fit everyone I knew like a snug glove. Perhaps *everybody* hated me. Scrabbling in my bag for my fags, I looked out at the garden again – at those chrysanthemums.

By the time I had tracked down Alex at Malcolm's house, my pendulum had swung between fear and fury infinite times, and being here now was only compounding my confusion. It felt utterly odd, to get straight out of bed with Seb to find myself threatened so unpleasantly, immediately into this bizarre confrontation with my ex. I stared at Alex and he stared back, his face a mask of indifference.

'What do you want me to say? I can't admit to something I didn't do.' There was a small arrow-shaped bruise on his forearm. He was always in the wars, Alex; usually alcohol-invoked. 'It's probably some nutter that saw you on TV. You shouldn't smoke, you know, Maggie.' He turned away again, biting his nail fervently.

'Yes, well, needs must.' I lit a cigarette defiantly, the smoke curling between banana plants and sweet-smelling jasmine towards the glass ceiling. It was warm in here, humid even, but the sky above was dead, utterly devoid of any kind of colour.

I stared at the smoke, at Alex's long, broad back, and realised I simply didn't know whether to believe him. He'd always had a strained relationship with the truth, and ultimately I'd stopped trusting him some time ago. He'd told one too many stories, and so now . . .

Piano music drifted suddenly into the room; a familiar haunting melody whose notes wrapped themselves around me and squeezed painfully. Mendelssohn's *Song Without Words*. I felt a huge wave of sadness engulf me, infinite misery that this was our reality; that the sum total of my relationship with Alex was being here, now, snarled up in this mess.

'Turn it off, Alex, please,' I whispered.

'What's wrong with it?' He turned from the window.

'For God's sake.' I sat clumsily on a bamboo chair. 'Do you really not remember?' It felt like someone had just poured concrete into my veins. 'Did nothing we ever did together, Alex, did *nothing* ever really matter to you?'

'Of course it bloody did. But why should I remember it?' He looked unworried still. 'You know I'm crap with music.'

I thought miserably of Santana and the Kaiser Chiefs and Led Zeppelin, of all the lost iPods that I'd given him as presents that he then left in taxis and buses ('I'll get another one, Mag, and I'll get you one too this time,' he'd cajole, and he'd tickle my feet, and I'd sigh and forgive him yet again). I remembered the new stereo we'd bought that he'd kicked to bits one night when he was hideously drunk, during a row about Iraq. Ostensibly about

151

Iraq, anyway. Always believed in things a little too fervently, Alex; always took things too personally when drunk.

I didn't trust myself to speak now, grinding out my cigarette in an ashtray so ornamental it couldn't be meant for use.

'Is it, this music –' he looked contemplative, 'is it the one that – when we went down to Pendarlin that first Christmas and –'

'You're really cruel sometimes, you know.' I stood. At the door I turned to gaze at him for a moment, at his familiar craggy face, trying desperately to tune into the Alex I'd first known, the one who hadn't succumbed to all his demons.

'If it is you, Alex, doing these weird things, *please* stop. You've made your point and you're really scaring me now.'

'Maggie, I swear it isn't.' Alex walked towards me now. 'But it all sounds horrible. A bit mad. I'm worried about you.'

'That makes a first.'

'I mean, if someone *is* after you, like you say –'

I flinched. 'I didn't say *after* me, did I?' I hauled my bag onto my shoulder. 'And that reminds me – *please* don't send people like Costana round when I'm not expecting them, okay? I nearly had a heart-attack yesterday morning.'

'I thought you'd be at work. And you'd better get used to it.' He refused to look contrite. 'Estate agents need access. I did tell you.'

'You didn't. And I just don't want anyone I don't know prowling around the flat, okay? Not at the moment.'

He shrugged. 'I'll make sure they warn you next time.'

Serena stuck her head round the door. 'We're about to eat, Allie darling,' she purred. She was so thin I doubted a morsel ever passed her lips – unless it came back up again.

'I'm just coming, beautiful.'

'The croissants smell divine,' she leered at him, all teeth and eyes. She was quite obviously starving.

'I'll be there in a minute.' For a second they locked eyes. Serena surrendered first.

'Don't be long, darling.' She blew him a kiss, entirely for my benefit, I was sure. As the door shut behind her, I couldn't help myself.

'God!' I expostulated.

'What?'

'How can you, Alex? She's so – so –' Words failed me. 'So very – not you.'

He looked at me steadily. 'Needs must, Maggie, as you say.'

'And what needs are those?' I felt queasy again. Fingers on the door-handle, I said, 'You know, I really thought you hated the idea of marriage.'

'I do.'

'So why, then –'

'He was winding you up. You know what Dad's like.' Alex ran his hand back and forth through his short hair, back and forth it went. 'I've got no intention of getting hitched any time soon.'

I felt a fresh rush of anger. 'God! You bloody Baileys and your mind games.'

Rushing out of the room, I went flying over an overnight bag and a pair of workboots so big and dirty they could only belong to Alex. He followed me into the hall, tried to help me up from where I'd crumpled inelegantly. Malcolm wandered out, hands deep in his pockets.

'Easy there, girl. Good trip?'

I smiled wanly as I clambered up.

'You always was a klutz, I seem to remember. Nice to see you, anyway, Mag. Drop in any time.'

*To stir up some sport?* 'Thanks, Malcolm,' I muttered, my hand on the latch now, desperate to get away.

'We'll send you an invite, won't we, Alexander?'

I frowned. 'To what?'

'To the wedding.'

I looked at Alex, confused.

'Jealous?' Malcolm winked at me. I bit my lip. 'I mean to *Tom's*

153

wedding, of course. To little Clarissa. Her of the child-bearing hips.'

Luckily Clarissa was out of earshot.

'Pa!' Alex snarled. 'For fuck's sake!'

'Language, Alexander.'

'You know what, Malcolm –' I had the door open by now, freedom beckoning me into the freezing November morning. He looked so bloody pleased with himself, swollen and pigeon-chested with pride, the Englishman in his self-made castle. 'It's no wonder your family have such terrible problems. You're such a complete shit.'

It wasn't until I was sitting on the tube to work, sandwiched between a large group of hijabed Ethopian women who squawked across me uproariously, that the worm crawled back into my brain. I stared at the greasy youth opposite, who was listening to such loud thrash-metal I was surprised he didn't have a nose-bleed; I stared at his spray-painted boots.

Despite all his protestations, those other boots – Alex's filthy Timberlands that I'd tripped over in Malcolm's hall – had been splashed with something bright, something that in my haste to leave I hadn't registered properly. Something suspiciously like red paint.

## Chapter Seventeen

'Bacon, egg, chips.' In the café on The Cut, the skin around the waitress's vermilion-painted mouth was crepey, the bright colour seeping vertically into the fan of fine lines above her top lip as she leaned over Sally to bang my plate down. I gazed miserably at the insipid-looking bacon that curled wetly up at me.

'On second thoughts, I'm not that hungry. I might go and have a fag.'

'Don't be silly.' Sally pinched a soggy chip. 'You need to eat. It's good for shock.'

'I thought that was sweet tea? That's what they always have in soap operas.' I poked the rubbery egg with my fork; the yolk surprised me by exploding. 'Oh, bollocks. I was saving that bit.'

'Maggie.'

I actually jumped. Joseph slid into the seat opposite us, slightly out of breath. 'The police are here, Maggie. They're asking for you.'

'Police?' I scrunched my brow at him. 'Here?' I glanced around. The tattooed builder on the next table bit lustily into his egg sandwich and gave me a wink. 'Where?'

'At the office, I mean.' Joseph was flustered.

I stared at him. 'I didn't call the police.'

'No, but you should have done,' Sally said tartly, pinching another chip. 'Not very crispy, these.'

'You didn't, did you, Sal?'

'What?'

'Ring them.'

'No, I didn't. But I think it's a bloody good idea you talk to them. Unless –'

'Unless what?'

'Unless you're – well –'

'What?'

'You're, you know. Imagining it.' Sally couldn't quite meet my eye.

'Er – imagining foot-high letters on my door? Hardly.'

'No, of course not.' She looked relieved.

But I wanted to deal with things my way. I wanted to pretend it wasn't happening today. Or any day, actually.

'Maggie.' Joseph's colour was high. 'I think you should come back.'

'But I'm having lunch,' I said forlornly, and ate a chip to prove it.

'Maggie!' Sally pushed me out of the booth. 'Go on. I'll get a doggie bag for you.'

Muttering, I scrabbled for my cigarettes and, dodging cyclists, followed Joseph across the busy road to work.


The small, wiry policeman waiting in my office stood politely as I came through the door. 'Maggie Warren? DI Fox.'

'Hello.' I took his proffered hand. Then I looked at him again. 'I – have we met before?' I asked anxiously.

'We have met, yes.'

My stomach clenched as I peered at his sandy face. 'Really?'

'Don't you remember?'

Oh God. Not again. I bit my lip.

'At the studio.'

'Oh yes.' It suddenly fell into place. The trauma show. 'Of course.'

'Your foot better now, then?'

'Yes, thanks. Much better.' I was so relieved I felt almost cheerful as I sat down at my desk. 'So, how can I help you?'

'That was my question actually.' He took out a small pad and perused it briefly. I noticed the cuffs of his shirt were rather threadbare. 'We had a call from a – a Sebastian Rae.'

I flushed, wishing my office were a little bigger, that I wasn't so very near DI Fox. 'Oh yes?'

'Mr Rae seems to think you received some sort of threat this morning.'

'Right.' I supposed I was pleased Seb was so worried about me.

'So?'

'What?'

He was infinitely patient. 'Tell me about it, please.'

'Honestly, I'm sure it's nothing. Just kids. You know. Graffiti.' Or my jealous ex-boyfriend. I'd rung Alex as soon as I'd got off the tube, but I was still waiting to hear back about the paint on his boots. He was probably busy, sharing some divine croissants with Serena. I sniffed and adjusted the photo of Digby the girls had framed for me last Christmas.

'And you're sure that's all it is?' The policeman had very orange hair that he'd slicked back; it gleamed in lucozade-coloured pools under the nasty strip lighting. 'No other incidents that have worried you or alerted you?'

'Alerted me?'

'Well, those words: *Meddling whore . . .*' He was watching me very intently. I blanched. 'They're very specific, aren't they?'

'I suppose so.'

'Often in these kinds of cases – you know, vandalism on private property – often they're caused by a dispute with neighbours. Have you had any sort of problems like that? No late-night parties or anything anyone's objected to?'

'Not that I know about.' I shook my head. 'We don't really have many neighbours. I don't really have many, I should say.

157

It's mainly shops where I live, and businesses. I've never fallen out with anyone there.'

I swear his ears literally pricked up.

'Who's "we"?'

'Sorry?' I was losing the thread.

'Who is the "we" you just referred to?'

'I used to share the flat with my ex-boyfriend, Alex Bailey. We – we're not together any more. And, actually, I've only just moved back. I was at my dad's for a couple of months.' I considered my neighbours for a moment. 'There's the Forlanis – they own the flat above the shop next door, but they're in Verona most of the time. And there's Melvin who runs the Fresca Deli, God knows what goes on in his place. He, er – he has a lot of boyfriends who come and go.'

'So there's no one you've had a row with at any time?'

'God no. Everyone's pretty friendly round us. You have to be, to cope with the crowds. The tourists, you know.'

'And your ex, is it amicable?'

I tried to keep my face inscrutable. 'Kind of.' I could feel the heat suffusing my cheeks. 'As amicable as I guess most splits are.'

'Which, quite often, is not very.'

'No. But it's fine, really.'

We looked at one another steadily. Inside I didn't feel very steady, though. DI Fox's eyelashes were tipped with sand, I noticed.

'Right.' DI Fox stood up. 'I should probably tell you, Maggie,' he closed his pad, 'I looked you up after Mr Rae rang. I wanted to see if you'd reported any other incidents. Which you haven't, have you? But it means,' he tucked the pad away neatly in an inner pocket, 'it means I've read your file, love.'

My face turned to stone. 'I see.'

'I know you weren't charged in the end. But you're – everything okay now, is it, after the summer? You're all right?'

It was almost dark outside though it was barely four o'clock.

I turned away from his gentle scrutiny, ostensibly to switch the overhead lights off and the desk-lamp on. 'Absolutely fine, thank you.' My voice was just about even. *Please go now*, I prayed.

'I'm glad to hear it. Well, listen, here are my numbers.' He pressed his card into my hand. 'Please, don't be scared to ring me if you have any need to. If you have any more – problems.'

Turning the card over in my fingers, I wondered which problems Fox meant; apparently I had a lot of them right now. 'Okay. Thank you again.'

'I mean it, Maggie.'

To my horror, tears sprang to my eyes for the second time that day. I forced myself to meet his eye. 'I will, if I'm worried. But I'm fine, honestly.'

'Good. Well, I'll see myself out.'

For about half an hour after the policeman left I sat in the dim light of the desk-lamp and stared at the small painting of the cottage in Cornwall. Something really bad was brewing, I felt it in my belly. '*Something wicked this way comes*' – Macbeth's three witches stamped round the midnight cauldron that held my life, and for some reason they were summoning evil against me. Something wicked that threatened to suffocate me. I had to escape.

Bel was leaving on Friday, so I had to stick around till I'd dropped her at Heathrow. But if I could get to Pendarlin, I was sure I would be safe.

# Chapter Eighteen

It was raining hard. The rain had started the very moment I'd left work, and of course I had no umbrella, and then outside the tube I'd slipped off the pavement into the river running through the gutter so my trainers were completely sodden, and then my phone rang as I opened Bel's front gate and I dropped it as I fumbled to answer it. When I bent to retrieve it, water cascaded down my neck, then down my back, so by the time Bel opened her front door I was thoroughly soaked and equally irritated.

'You left me a message.' The voice on the phone was curt. 'What *now*?'

My eyes stung as my waterproof mascara slid down my face. 'Alex.' I was curter. 'About time.'

Bel pulled a face. 'I'll be in the bedroom,' she whispered.

'Sorry,' he said, sounding less than contrite. 'I'm pretty busy.'

I waited for him to qualify his busyness until I realised he wasn't going to.

'You had red paint all over your boots this morning.' I rubbed at my panda eyes in the mirror. 'Why?'

'What? What boots?'

'In the hall. At your dad's.'

'For Christ's sake, Maggie.'

A girl laughed in the background and it was like a knife in my belly. 'It *was* you, wasn't it?' I said sharply.

'I'm getting really bored of this,' Alex sighed wearily. 'We've been through it a million bloody times. I've told you, it's nothing to do with me.'

I heard a drink being poured and suddenly I felt like screaming. I bit my lip painfully.

'Look, I've got to go.'

'No, Alex, wait.'

'What?'

Hannah appeared in the hall in a pair of patent tap-shoes and a Snow White outfit two sizes too small. 'Watch this, Auntie Maggie.' Some very loud and unrhythmic tapping began.

'So where were you last night, Alex?' I gave Hannah a thumbs-up. 'You never told me that.'

'Last night? Let me think.' That silly silvery laugh chimed in again, as if someone had once told the owner she sounded bell-like and she was pealing for her life. 'Ah yes. Most conveniently, between the hours of twelve and three I was screwing Serena, at her place. Which is in Kensington, Maggie – i.e. on the other side of town from where we – where *you* – live.'

I recognised the serration in his voice, the invincible blade of alcohol that cut his words. He spoke very slowly, provocatively, in a stupid Sean Connery accent. 'Postcoitally, I crashed out in her delectable arms.'

My grip on the phone tightened. *If you laugh again, you cow, I will scream.* Hannah did some inelegant but extremely flamboyant turns up the hall.

'How lovely for you,' I muttered, and I thought of all the times Alex hadn't made it to bed with me. 'I'll be up in a minute, baby,' he'd promise, but when I got up for work the next morning he'd still be slumped on the floor, inert, surrounded by cans and, quite often, later on, porn.

'I'm sure Serena will be more than happy to corroborate my story.' His voice faded as he turned to speak to her. 'Won't you, sweetheart?'

'Oh, I'm quite sure she will,' I said tightly. Hannah began a complex tapping-backwards routine that resulted in her flying over a packing-crate and landing on the cat, who squealed indignantly as loud tears ensued. 'Ow!'

I rushed to the little girl's side.

'Who's that?' Alex stopped showing off.

'It's Hannah.' I put my arms around her as best I could. 'I'd better go.'

'Is she okay?' He sounded worried and my heart softened a little. 'Send her my love, won't you? And tell her to mind out for those boomerangs.'

'I will,' I mumbled ungraciously.

'And Maggie –'

'Yes?' I savoured the child's solid warmth as she sniffled softly against my chest.

'I might be a bastard, but I'm not a stalker.'

There was a long pause. I squeezed Hannah tighter, burying my face in her silky hair until she began to wriggle.

'Be careful out there, Maggie,' he said quietly, and rang off.

'What's going on? Are you off the phone from that idiot? I'm still waiting to hear what you've been up to, Maggie, you minx.' Bel appeared at the top of the stairs, her hair tied up Mrs Mop-style, packing-tape in hand, and clocked her dishevelled daughter. 'Gawd. I'm only upstairs five minutes, Han, and you're in the flipping wars again. Come and show me what you want to take on the plane.' She held out a hand to the little girl.

Reluctantly, I released Hannah, following her upstairs slowly. I was still tempted to believe Alex. But then, believing him had always been my downfall.

I didn't tell Bel everything about Seb. She was my oldest friend; we'd shared every secret since I was eight, and a new man was definitely a subject usually up for debate – but for some reason I kept silent now. Perhaps I was a little ashamed by my rash actions and the fact I hadn't heard from Seb yet. Perhaps I knew I wasn't ready: I wasn't at all sure it was time to get involved with someone new; I didn't want Bel to emphasise my doubts. Or perhaps we were simply distracted by Hannah's whinging.

'You're not going halfway round the world dressed as Snow White, so don't even bother, okay?' Bel snapped when Hannah threw her tracksuit trousers down the stairs in a fit of pique. 'Sorry, Mag. It's so hard to concentrate right now.'

'S'okay,' I said, and topped up my wine. 'I'm knackered anyway. I need to go home and look for the key to Pendarlin. I can't find it anywhere.' I peered out of the window, through the old magnolia tree in the front garden, looking for the cab I'd called. It was still pouring outside and the street was empty apart from a man unloading shopping from his car and making a dash for his front door. 'I keep losing everything at the moment. My memory's still terrible.'

'You're not being very forthcoming about this bloke, Mag,' Bel chided me as I turned back into the room. 'I want all the juicy details.'

I pretended I hadn't heard her, pulling the curtain back again. It was so dark and wet and the branches were flailing around so energetically in the wind that I couldn't make out if my cab was there or not. I kept imaging Alex lying in Serena's arms. I was suddenly exhausted, desperate to be home, alone.

'What are you looking at?' asked Bel. 'Right, bed for you, young lady.' She pushed Hannah gently towards the bedroom door.

'My cab.' I squinted down at the street. 'I wish it'd hurry up.'

'But Mum –'

'But Mum nothing.'

I spotted what must be the cab driving slowly down the road.

'Johnno,' Bel shouted downstairs, 'go and tell Maggie's car she's coming, can you?' She pushed a suitcase shut with her foot. 'Go on, Hannah, before I get *really* annoyed.'

Dropping the curtain, I went down the stairs. Johnno had left

163

the door ajar and the wind rattled the safety-chain. Shivering, I shoved my feet into my sodden trainers again. 'Yuk.'

Bel carried a black bin-liner down and shoved it in the cupboard under the stairs. 'God, it's freezing. Why's he left the bloody door open?'

'Er – so he can get back in? It's like something from *Halloween* out there.'

Bel went to the door now. 'Johnno?' she called. 'Hurry up.'

But the pathway was empty, the gate banging in the wind.

'God, where is he?' she muttered, peering into the rain. I picked up my bag and stood behind her, waiting. A sense of unease pervaded me slowly. Something didn't fit.

A huge gust of wind savaged the old tree so it bent its branches to the ground in supplication, and Bel and I unconsciously huddled together in the doorway. A small hand suddenly snaked in between us and we both jumped.

'Hannah,' Bel snapped, 'get up the stairs NOW.'

And then Johnno burst through the door, soaking, his hair all stuck up in clumps.

'God, it's foul out there.' Grabbing a fleece off the peg, he towelled his head. 'I don't know what that bloke was playing at but as soon as I came out, he screeched off. He's gone, I'm afraid, Maggie.'

When I rang the cab company they said there was still a thirty-minute wait because of the rain. They hadn't sent anyone yet.

# Chapter Nineteen

On Wednesday it rained all day. I'd slept badly, hounded by nightmares involving rain and flowers as big as Triffids, and DI Fox telling me off. During the day my mood only got bleaker as I worked up the ridiculous *You're Dumped* proposal. I stared out of my tiny office window at the sheets of rain, despising myself, longing for the sandy beaches of North Cornwall. For the umpteenth time this week, I considered hurtling into Charlie's office and resigning, never mind the consequences – but he was in Paris for the day, so my plan was foiled.

I went to get coffee around eleven, walking behind Joseph's desk to the machine. He was swinging back and forth on his chair, talking loudly, oblivious to my presence. I heard him say, 'Yes, seriously, I'm the director. We need a pair of Bose earphones, yeah, that's right. Yeah – and the Sony. Fabulous. I can send a bike if it helps.'

I put my hand on his shoulder and he nearly fell backwards off the chair in shock.

'I'd like a word, Joseph, please.'

He couldn't have been more sulky if he'd tried as he stalked into my office. 'What?'

'What do you mean, what?' I raised an eyebrow. 'Who were you talking to?'

He shrugged. 'Just someone. About props.'

'And what props are those then?'

165

Joseph met my eye with watery grey ones.

'You were on the blag, weren't you?'

He scuffed his foot on the nylon carpet.

I sighed wearily. 'Joseph, it's the oldest trick in the book. Everyone does it, and it's fine for a ticket to a concert or a club – but use your head. Don't blag really expensive stuff – and *don't* tell people you're the director of a network show, for God's sake. You'll only get rumbled.'

He glowered at me and I was aware of a new emotion beginning to emanate from him. Adulation was turning to serious dislike.

At lunchtime I ate a cheese sandwich at my desk, and avoided Joseph's daggers, reading an article from yesterday's *Guardian* on child labour in India until I felt quite tearful. Guiltily I glanced down at my high-street top and pushed away the *Dumped* proposal in disgust, the limpid eyes of a little boy in the Calcutta sweatshop gazing blankly at me from my desk. I thought despairingly about booking a psychologist to make sure Darren from Wembley would survive once girlfriend Sandra had dumped him live before the nation because he wouldn't ever clean the loo. Given that he'd also shagged Sandra's sister three times behind her back, Darren was probably tough enough to survive the ordeal, but I found I'd lost my appetite anyway.

I chucked my crusts in the bin and checked, for the first time in five whole minutes, that my phone was actually working, which of course it was. I was pretending really hard that I wasn't waiting for Seb to ring, and that I didn't mind that he absolutely indisputably hadn't. Then, galvanised finally by my indecision over flying Charlie's coop, I phoned Naz to ask about a *Dispatches* programme on childcare that I'd heard was crewing up. She promised to make enquiries.

To compound my misery that afternoon, I was just going into a meeting with Renee and her stylist when Susan rang from Gar's nursing-home.

'Is everything okay?' I asked anxiously.

'It's fine, lovie. Your nan's tickety-boo, honest. It's just –'

Renee tapped her Cartier watch officiously at me through the conference-room window.

'I'm so sorry, Susan, but could we talk later?' I interrupted apologetically. 'I'll call in after work. Will you still be there?'

'Course, lovie. Mustn't keep those celebs waiting, eh?'

I tried to laugh in agreement, but my guilt at not visiting my grandmother again in the past week was already intense. Susan's remark only made my crime seem worse.

To me, Gar had signified a peace, a kind of sanctuary, since I'd lost my mother at the age of thirteen, and now I desperately missed the grandmother who'd half brought me up. Part of me feared the vacant look in her eye as she skimmed over me, the feeble smile she sometimes managed. I had to remind myself that she was still there somewhere deep down; that, like a shiny little onion under the browning outer layers of illness, she was the same Gar at heart. I could still just about find a vestige of that sanctuary as I sat in the quiet of her room, and it was vital for both of us that I kept that going.

After work it was still raining. I dashed through the rush-hour to pick up my car, tensing in anticipation as I neared the flat. I hoped fervently the painter I'd called had made it while I was at work.

Rounding the corner, I saw the foul graffiti had been covered. But, sliding the key into the lock, I was sure I could still see the shadow of those words through the fresh cream paint that smelled so strong, and I fled through the front door as quickly as I could.

Grabbing the car-keys from the bowl, I tried not to mind about the distinct lack of flashing lights on my answer-phone. Despite Seb's call to the police on my behalf, the fact I hadn't heard from him since we'd parted yesterday was compounding the increasingly sick feeling I had with myself. I really wasn't ready to start worrying about a new man ringing me; I wanted to be strong, free and single. I caught my eye in the mirror and nodded at myself coolly, like the strong, free, single woman I was. The phone rang. I leapt on it as if it were a live thing about to escape.

'Hello?'

'Goodness, Maggie, you sound a bit breathless.'

Crashing disappointment, followed by a creeping sense of disquiet.

'How did you get this number?'

Fay laughed breathily. 'You're always so suspicious, Maggie. Honestly! You gave it to me when we met a while ago. Don't you remember?'

I wrinkled my forehead. 'No, I don't.'

'Anyway, it's only a quickie. I'm sorry about our little spat. I never saw you at *Love All*. Are you avoiding me?'

'Oh.' I thought about Seb's lips on mine and I blushed. 'I never made it inside actually. Something, er, something came up.' I smiled to myself. Oh yes, it had most definitely come up.

'It was very good, you know, the film. But look, never mind. I was just ringing to tell you I've forgiven you and we're having our first meeting next Monday.'

I felt a sudden pain.

'Do you want to come? I wish you would.'

I realised I was clutching the car-keys so hard they were digging into the soft flesh of my palm. 'What meeting?'

'You know, the trauma survivors' meeting. I'd love it if you came.'

'Fay, I don't want to be rude again, but I thought I'd made it pretty clear I'm not interested.'

'Oh, I know you said that, but a girl can change her mind, can't she?'

I glanced at the clock and pulled myself together. 'I've got to go, Fay. My grandmother's expecting me.'

'Of course. But look, if you change your mind, yeah, you will come along? It's at the Tabernacle in Notting Hill. There are quite a lot of us. It'll be fun. I'll be really, really cross if you don't come.'

*Just get her off the phone now, Maggie.*

'Right. Thanks for letting me know.'

'You're welcome, Maggie.' She sounded like someone off *Oprah*. The girl was a natural, everything she said was imbued with all the sincerity of a psychopath. 'Take care out there, won't you.'

'I will.' I rang off. As I left the flat, I cast a look up and down the street first. Nothing but a group of twenty-something girls in their finest Burberry, splashing arm in arm through the puddles to the Oyster Bar opposite the flat. I had a nasty gnawing feeling in the pit of my stomach as I got into the car. A feeling I was getting used to – but a whole new suspicion.

Susan's cold was still streaming when I arrived at Elmside House an hour later.

'Ooh dear, sorry.' She sneezed loudly. 'I just can't seem to shake this off.' She blew her nose energetically and then tucked her hanky up her sleeve. 'You go on to Vera while I get us a nice cuppa. She'll be so pleased to see you.'

She wouldn't really, we both knew, it was unlikely she'd recognise me at all, in fact – but I acquiesced politely and started up the hall. On the way I passed Emmeline. She was at least ninety but insisted on wearing smocks in little-girl pink, velvet bows in her hair, and was always accompanied by her imaginary poodle Toy-toy on a lead.

'Hi, Emmeline,' I smiled at her.

'Have we met? My dance-card is full, you know,' she simpered back and wandered off to stretch Toy-toy's legs.

The apricot-coloured corridor didn't smell quite the same as normal. There was the usual stench of disinfectant, but something else was fighting it hard; something sweet and rather sickly.

As I rounded the corner my skin rose into goose-pimples. Through the partially open door I could see Gar slumped awkwardly in her chair, her radio tuned to something sombre, something that I knew and had reason to hate. It took me a moment to recognise it as Mozart's *Requiem*. Gar's hair had come loose from its usual bun, flopping across her veiled face, the strange light dappling her skin. My heart skipped a beat and I started to run.

'Gar,' I shouted, but she didn't move and I was beside her now, my hand on her shoulder, shaking her as vigorously as I dared. She was so thin she felt like a rag-doll, like I might snap her clean in two, and I realised the horrible smell was the smell of lilies. 'Gar, wake up!' I cried, and then she did, she started and looked up at me, bewildered and confused, blinking her faded rheumy eyes. 'Lily?'

I shocked myself by bursting into tears. 'Oh, Gar.' I hugged her frail form, pressing my face against her crumpled cheek, her skin as soft as ash. 'It's Maggie, not Lily. I thought – I thought you were dead.'

'Don't upset yourself, Maggie.' Susan came in bearing a tea-tray. 'She's as right as rain, honestly. Aren't you, Vera, love?'

'I'm sorry.' I was embarrassed by my loss of control. 'She just gave me a bit of a fright, that's all.'

Gar patted my hand kindly as I wiped my eyes, although I knew she still had no idea who I was. 'Pretty girl,' she murmured. Her wedding ring was so big these days that it rattled round her bony finger, clicking on my skin as she patted me. Susan shook her head as she set the tray down on the table.

'I'm glad you're here.' Susan offered me a tissue from the box by Gar's bed. 'I didn't want to panic you on the phone, but I've been a bit worried by these calls she's started getting.'

'What calls?'

Susan pulled Gar's hair gently back into its bun, hairpin between her lips. 'Someone keeps ringing and asking for Vera

Knowles. They wouldn't say who it was until this morning, when they finally announced they're a friend of yours.'

'A friend?' I frowned. 'Is it a man or a woman?'

'A woman. She's perfectly polite but – I don't know. I don't want to be rude, but she gives me the willies, you know.' Susan patted Gar's head fondly and stooped to pour the tea.

'What does she sound like?'

Susan pursed her lips, her big face ruddy with disapproval. 'It's hard to say really. Quite posh, I suppose. And she just won't say what she wants. But she's rung every day for the past three days now, the bugger, and this morning she rang four times before lunch. We've explained you don't live here, and we've offered to take a message, but she just keeps ringing back. She's becoming a bit of a pest, to be honest.'

Exhausted suddenly, I flopped into the small armchair opposite my grandmother and accepted the tea Susan passed me. 'Thank you. How weird.'

Gar suddenly turned and smiled at me, and her eyes held that lucid light that I had come to long for. 'Is Alex with you?'

My stomach lurched again. 'No, Gar.' I tried to smile. 'Not today, I'm afraid.'

'He was here the other day, you know. Such a dear boy.' She leaned back and closed her eyes again. 'He read me something.'

I looked at Susan and smiled sadly. 'She gets more and more confused, doesn't she?'

'She's right actually. He did come.'

'What?' I sat bolt upright. 'Alex was here?'

'He's come a few times, bless his heart. Actually, it was after he left the other night that these turned up.' Susan moved over to the lilies and pulled off a broken stem. 'I mean, they're lovely, aren't they, cheer the room up no end – but it did seem a bit odd.'

'You've lost me, Susan.'

'To leave them here. I suppose he's shy. Now you've split up.

171

You know, to say how he still feels.' She dug down into her pocket and came up with a half-packet of Tunes, a stub of a pencil – and a small envelope, instantly recognisable. My stomach turned over as if someone had flipped it like a pancake. 'It's addressed to you, lovie.'

I glanced at my grandmother, nodding back off to sleep, as oblivious to this threat as a newborn baby, and I wiped my damp eyes resolutely. I'd kill anyone who laid a finger on my grandmother. With unsteady hands, I opened the sealed envelope – but I already knew what it would reveal.

*'In Loving Memory,'* it said, next to a badly printed spray of purple flowers. *'In Loving Memory of Maggie – and Vera.'*

That night I slept in Gar's armchair again, after accidentally polishing off the end of her sherry. I didn't turn the light off till I woke up the next morning.

# Chapter Twenty

I arrived at work with a cricked neck, a sherry hangover and a truly foul mood. Sally was waiting outside my office, flicking through *Hello!*.

'Your friend's in here.' She waved the magazine under my nose.

'What friend?' I scrabbled in my bag for my key.

'That Fay girl, at some perfume launch. She's very photogenic, isn't she?' Sally pointed at a small photo. 'She looks a bit like you in this picture.'

I shuddered. Donna shot past, snarling into her phone. 'You cannot be serious, Max. You promised me Kerry was hot to trot, not about to bloody OD.'

'We need to talk about Joseph Blake, Mag.' Sally dropped her voice theatrically. 'You'll never guess what he's done now –'

The post-boy knocked on my door, bearing a beautifully wrapped basket of fruit and champagne with a glossy white envelope. My heart beat faster, my instinct screeched *don't open it* – but to my huge relief, inside were two tickets to a concert at the Festival Hall that night and a handwritten note from Seb.

*'Guess what? Gershwin's playing tonight, 'specially for you. Come with me, please.'*

I wondered if he knew Gershwin was long dead. At the foot of the note there was a PTO.

*'I want to lick every inch of you,'* he'd written. Lord! I blushed as hot as the boiling radiator and shoved the card into my

bag, knocking the grapes and lychees all over the carpet in my haste.

'Clumsy Maggie!' Sally picked up a peach, already bruised, and handed it to me, her broad face intrigued. 'You've gone all red.'

'I have not.' I blushed hotter.

'Who's that little lot from then? Lover boy?'

Donna flounced into the office without knocking. 'It's him or me, all right?'

'Fine, thanks, Donna,' I said dryly, 'and how are you today?'

'You don't want to know. That flipping PR's giving me brainache.'

'Right.' I switched my computer on. 'So what's the problem?'

'It's not the PR – it's bloody Blake. He's been going through my drawers.'

'How exciting.' I raised an eyebrow. 'Lucky you.'

Sally giggled. 'I'll leave you to it.' She shut the door behind her.

'This is serious, man.' Donna scowled at me. 'He's been nicking all my contacts.'

'What do you mean?'

'First of all my Rolodex went missing, and so did Lisa's. Then we found them in the bogs. God knows why. Some of the pages are missing.'

'How do you know it's him?'

'Because then my address book, the one I keep everything in – email addresses, private mobiles – it went missing last night, out of my desk drawer.' Donna slumped onto the sofa. 'God, there's numbers in there I've had to do you-don't-wanna-know-what to get hold of. There's all sorts in there, and Christ, if any of them lot find out their numbers are floating around London, they're going to go NUTS!' She was practically crying now, her head in her hands. 'I'm talking big celebs, agents, addicts, politicians, convicted paedos. The blinking lot.'

'All right, Don, calm down.' I sat beside her on the sofa. 'So why do you think it's Joseph?'

'Because he was the only one here with me last night. He said he was doing some "extra research". God knows on what, cos he's so bloody whack anyway.' She looked disgusted. 'My drawer's always locked – but I left my keys on my desk when I went downstairs to have a fag. When I came back, he'd gone, and so had the book when I came to look for it.'

'And the keys? Are they missing?' I felt like DI Fox.

She shrugged. 'No. They were still on my desk.'

'And you're sure the book was in your drawer?'

She sucked her teeth. 'Positive. Come on, Maggie, you know what he's like.'

I sighed. 'Okay, granted, he's a bit of an – oddball –'

'That's an understatement. *And* I caught him skulking around your office.'

'Really? When?' I frowned.

'The other day. He said he was finding some file, but he looked proper guilty.'

'Well, maybe, but that doesn't mean he's a thief. Are you absolutely sure your book's not at home?'

'I checked. Believe me, I turned the place upside-down. I didn't get to bed till two.' Judging by the state of her desk, she'd turned that upside-down too.

Joseph Blake walked into the main office at that moment, wearing brothel-creepers and a huge pair of earphones, clutching his brown leather briefcase. He'd quiffed his floppy hair today; he looked like a ten-year-old Teddy boy wearing his father's clothes.

'Bloody bastard.'

I restrained Donna from marching straight out and confronting him. But, gazing at Joseph thoughtfully, I wondered again why Charlie didn't want to let him go. 'It could be him, I guess.'

175

We watched an oblivious Joseph take off his Crombie coat and hang it carefully on the coat-stand in the corner. He smoothed back his hair and sat down at his desk, opening up a copy of the *Daily Telegraph*.

'Jus' take a look, man. He's well pretentious. There's a name for types like him down my way.' Donna glowered at him through the glass. 'I'm going to give him a piece of –'

'Let me deal with this, Donna, okay? It's not good, I know – but it's hardly the crime of the century.'

'Whatever,' she shrugged. 'It's just – he makes me properly uncomfortable, d'you know what I mean? It's not the same vibe out there since he came back.'

'Look, go and get yourself a coffee. I'll have a chat with him.'

'I can't leave now. I'm waiting for Fergie's people to call back.'

So in the end I took Joseph out with me, dodging the black cabs and the couriers, back to Crepey Lips's café on The Cut.

'Are your eggs free-range?' Joseph asked the waitress, whose roots were oily-black against the bright peroxide.

She smirked. 'They're out of a box, pet, that's all I know.'

'Yes, but is it a free-range box?'

'Joseph, it's a caff, not the flipping Ivy.' I suddenly felt like a mother with a truculent teenager in tow. 'Have something else. Have a bacon roll.'

He looked at me like I was mad. 'I don't eat meat. I'll just have tea and toast. Brown toast, green tea, please.'

'You can have white bread and brown tea or none at all, pet.'

I fumbled for my cigarettes to hide my smile. He looked at them pointedly and gave a little cough. Every bit of sympathy I had left for him flew out the door.

'Actually,' he said, 'I was thinking, we could do a show about intensive farming.'

The waitress plonked my coffee down in front of me.

'Have you seen the way animals are treated in this country?

The hormones the cattle and pigs are injected with, the terrible cruel transportation, the –'

Crepey-Lips slammed my bacon roll and Joseph's mug down with such gusto that tea sloshed onto the Formica top. 'One brown tea. With white milk in it.'

I smiled at her politely.

'White sugar, brown *and* red sauce are on the side.'

Joseph rattled on oblivious. 'The immoral pens, the fat on the animals that shouldn't be there. I mean, bacon's a prime example. They're given such high-energy food that they swell to twice their size.'

I looked down at my roll miserably, and had a slug of coffee instead. 'It's an admirable idea, Joseph, but can you actually see Renee going for it? It's not really her style.'

'I don't see why not.'

'Why don't you make a list of your ideas for me?' I put my mug down carefully. 'But look, what we really need to do is talk about your future at Double-decker.' I tapped my fingers against the china. 'I mean, it's not really working out, is it?'

He paled visibly. 'Don't sack me, Maggie, please.'

My heart went out to him. He really was pathetic. 'I don't want to sack you, Joseph, really I don't – but I am worried. There's been a few allegations against you now.'

'What kind of allegations?'

'Have you been – borrowing stuff? Like the girls' address books?'

'No.'

'Are you sure?'

'Yes.' He wouldn't look at me.

'Is that the truth?'

'Yes, seriously.' He looked up at me defiantly. 'Why would I steal phone numbers?'

'I don't know. You tell me.'

'I can't, because I didn't.' But he was screwing a twist of sugar very tight. There was a pause. 'You should be nice to me.' It sounded rather like a threat.

'Should I? Why?'

'You know why.'

'Remind me.'

'Because my uncle will be furious if you don't treat me correctly,' he declared. It *was* a threat.

'Your uncle?'

'That's right, my uncle.'

'And he is . . .?'

'Philip Lyons. But you knew that.'

I thought of Lyons, Double-decker's MD; of his unprepossessing ways, his lack of social skills, his love of a fast dollar, the utter moral vacuum that he was. I remembered Charlie's reticence to let Joseph go. It all fitted suddenly.

'Oh, I *see*.' I caught Joseph's rather protuberant eye. Steadily we regarded one another. 'I suppose there is a family resemblance, now you mention it.'

'Had you forgotten, Maggie? Just like you've forgotten everything else.'

'What everything else?' I frowned.

'If you can't remember it's not my place to remind you.' He stared me out. 'Can I go now?'

'Joseph, just because you've got relatives in high places, it doesn't mean you can just do whatever you fancy. It doesn't work like that.'

He smiled. 'Doesn't it?' It was a greasy, queasy kind of smile.

'No.' I ploughed on. 'You still have to work hard, you still have to earn respect.'

With a great ache, I thought suddenly of Alex. He'd been so desperate for Malcolm to be proud of him for his own achievements – whereas his younger brother Tom had taken the easy route, going straight into Malcolm's business out of school. Malcolm's inexplicable contempt had only served to fuel Alex's demons.

178

'I do work hard.'

I pulled myself back to the present. 'Not hard enough really, Joseph. You have to start at the bottom. We all did.' I tried for schoolmarmish jolliness now. 'So come on,' I patted his hand awkwardly, 'show me you can do it, okay?'

He shrugged morosely. 'S'pose.'

'And if you did take that book, Donna's book, just put it back, all right?'

'I didn't, Maggie, seriously.' He glared at me. 'I said I didn't and you should believe me.'

I considered my bacon roll for a moment, then reached for my cigarettes. 'All right, Joseph. You go on back. I'll be over in a bit.'

He stood up. 'You smoke too much. I told you that in the summer.'

My stomach plunged. 'I don't remember that.'

'Yeah, well, I'm seriously not surprised.'

I looked up at him. His old Crombie coat smelled of moth-balls, pungent and acrid. 'What does that mean?'

'Forget it.' He made a big play of doing his buttons up.

'No, go on, Joseph, please.'

'I just meant – well, I know what happened.'

'What are you talking about?'

'You can't hide much from me. Though obviously you did try. You're just lucky I didn't tell my uncle.'

I couldn't tell if he was bluffing. 'I'll see you back at the office, Joseph.' I was desperate for him to go now. I didn't want to remember any more.

Ordering another coffee, I watched Joseph scoot across the busy road, a solitary figure weaving between the camera-crews smoking outside our building, leaning on their tripods, joking with one another in a way I could never imagine Joseph ever being part of. I felt a sudden wave of nostalgia for the business I'd signed up for all those years ago, for the excitement and novelty and camaraderie.

My telephone bleeped. Idly I opened the text message.

**I WAS RIGHT. YOU SLUT**

Oh God. I dropped the phone like it was hot. Then I cancelled the coffee and went across the road to the pub instead. Standing at the bar, I had a huge slug of nasty thin red wine and then I rang the bloody number back, just like I had each time before. But no one answered and of course there was no voicemail. The phone just rang and rang – until someone cut it off.

# Chapter Twenty-One

'Bring Seb along,' Bel said on the phone, evidently distracted. 'Hang on a sec, Johnno, can you? ...The more, the merrier, I say. It is the bloody Last Supper, after all – might cheer things up . . . That one next, please . . . And I'm dying to meet him properly before I go . . . Oh my God, no, not that one . . . Look, sorry, Mag, but I think the removal men have just packed Hannah in a crate as a truly hilarious joke. I'll see you later, all right?'

I put the phone down slowly. I wasn't sure I was ready to introduce Seb to the curious throng at Bel's farewell dinner. I was so dreading these goodbyes that I would have much preferred the Gershwin gig, but I couldn't abandon my best friend on her last night in the country. Seb said he quite understood of course. I'd known he would, he just seemed that type of man. He said that rehearsals were over-running anyway, they were having problems with the blocking (whatever that was). I very nearly asked him to meet me when he finished but as I teetered Seb said, 'I'll call you soon', and I said 'Great', when what I really meant was, 'Wait' – and by then he'd already gone.

When I left work the rain had stopped at long last, the pavements glistening like molasses under the streetlights. It was freezing again, a proper winter chill cutting through the air, and for once I was glad, my masochistic side craving the cold tonight. My head felt fusty, almost dirty, after the last few days' events – the graffiti and the texts, the calls to Gar, coupled with creepy

Joseph and Donna's missing book. The icy bite outside roused me again. It wasn't far to the gastropub Bel had booked for dinner. I stuck my headphones on and set off for Clerkenwell.

I'd spent the afternoon in the office pretending to ignore that last text, although DI Fox's sandy face kept popping up to chide me, my hand hovering over the phone constantly to call him until I decided not to be so weak. But now, tramping alongside the rush-hour traffic, the chill here thick with fumes, those vicious words resonated round and round my head ... *SLUT, WHORE, SLUT, WHORE.*

Who hated me enough to try to scare me witless? Whoever it might be, they were succeeding.

I crossed the road, squeezing between a minibus and a small lorry, a cyclist skidding past in a luminous vest like a raver from the nineties. With Elgar's *Cello Concerto in E Minor* soaring in my ears, I was starting to feel quite trippy myself, my mind speeding from one suspicion to the next. Joseph? Charlie? Philip Lyons? *Don't be ridiculous, Maggie.* I shook my head again, impatient with myself. None of them, surely. But – Alex?

I kept arriving painfully back at him.

Mesmerised by my own feet, their steadfast tread belied my fears as I reached the junction and hesitated, unsure of the right way through the maze of Dickensian streets. With a nasty lurch I realised I was horribly near Malcolm's office; the office where I'd first met his son. It was painful to find that everything still reminded me of Alex. Shoving my numb hands deep into my pockets, I chose a small alley on the right and marched on. I was going to have to face facts sooner or later; Alex was obviously punishing me. He might be a clown when comedy appealed, but I knew he was deeply hurt. And I'd started to remember more clearly the events of that terrible summer night; often in the early hours now I'd wake sweating and a little more would have clawed its way into my consciousness. And I'd bite my lip against the painful memories, praying they were just bad dreams.

The signs that it was Alex were all there. I sighed hard, my breath condensing before me, and realised I'd have to phone Fox back.

Stumbling slightly on a jagged paving-stone, one of my earphones dropped out. About to slot it back in, I thought I caught distant footsteps somewhere behind me. I turned Elgar down and glanced behind me quickly. Nothing. I tried to laugh my fear off, but that wobbly laugh was interrupted by what were most definitely footsteps: they echoed eerily up the small cobbled street. The dark buildings loomed high above me and I had a sudden vision of Bill Sikes prowling after poor old Nancy with vengeance in his cruel heart. With a jolt, I realised how very quiet the street was, how utterly deserted – just how far the pub was, its lights barely visible at the far end. I realised I was completely alone – alone, apart from those footsteps. All I needed was a pea-souper and I'd be truly done for. I sped up.

So did the footsteps.

This was the point where the audience shouts 'run'. My foot ached as I pushed myself forward; my teenage self blazing past me. Lord, I had been fast back then. Jacqueline du Pré's cello bow flew with such valour, such vigour now, and with it the thought flashed through my head that this was a perfect score to die by.

I peered over my shoulder; a cloudy-edged figure was gaining on me now and I sobbed with something like real fear. And then the pub door came in sight, and I thought I'd be safe – until something shot out of the shadows at my feet and I went flying, landing heavily on my knees, losing my earphones so I could just hear du Pré's crescendo rattling tinnily from the ground. There was a crash of metal beside me and I almost assumed the foetal position as a mangy old fox slid out of the dustbins beside me, his back scabby, his tail a pathetic wisp. Unblinking, he regarded me for a second, his eyes green glass in the streetlight, before he slunk off into the night.

The footsteps were so near now I couldn't bear to look. I just jumped up quickly, my hands grazed and bleeding from where I'd blocked my fall. Abandoning the iPod on the floor, I started to run again.

'Maggie!'

Did I know that voice? I didn't care.

'Maggie, stop! Please stop!'

But I couldn't now. I couldn't stop; I daren't. I sprinted the last fifty yards up the alley and dived through the pub door, nearly taking Bel down with me.

'Blimey!' She took one look at me and started singing *Bat Out of Hell.*

'Yeah, all right.' I tried to catch my breath. 'I was just worried that I was late, that's all.' I attempted to smile; I didn't want to ruin her night with my fears, but I kept one eye firmly on the door as she kissed me hello.

'God, your cheeks are cold.' Bel held out her hand for my coat. 'I'll hang it up.'

'Thanks.' I passed it over.

'Oh, your hand, Maggie.' Bel took mine in hers, frowning. 'It's bleeding. Ouch! They both are. How on earth did you do that?'

'It's fine, honestly.' I cased the room quickly. 'Alex isn't coming, is he?'

'No way,' Bel was starting to say, and I was just relaxing a little – and then Joseph Blake walked through the door, his pale face flushed, his nose bright red from the cold. I felt like screaming, but I didn't. I swiped a glass of champagne off a tray on the bar instead and drank it in one gulp, which made me cough. Bel was still talking about Alex as Joseph walked towards me. I realised he was holding my iPod.

'I warned Johnno, anyway, Mag. Not to invite him this time, I mean. But what *have* you done to your hands?'

'Nothing. I just tripped. You know me and coordination.' I put my glass down and searched for another.

Joseph had almost reached us by now. I felt like my pet rabbit when I was ten, his run on the lawn being circled by the neighbourhood cats, crammed into one corner, praying for survival.

'I was calling you, Maggie.' He reached me. 'Outside. You didn't stop. You dropped this.'

'Thanks.' I held my hand out for the player. 'I – I didn't hear you.'

'You're bleeding,' he said.

'Oh God, not you as well.' I looked around desperately for that drink.

'Blood.'

'Yes, I'm bleeding blood, Joseph. It's quite usual, I think.'

'Maggie!' Bel reprimanded softly.

Joseph's white face was even paler than normal. 'I'm not very good with blood.' He started to sway.

*Brilliant.* 'Well, let's go and sit down, shall we?'

Bel's brother Nigel crept up behind her, sweeping her into an enormous bear-hug. 'Let me go,' she giggled, kicking her legs like a toddler, and I caught the expression on Joseph's face as he watched. Something I recognised as longing.

'Come on, you,' I said, propelling Joseph to a corner, pulling my sleeves over my still-stinging palms in an attempt to stop him from fainting. 'Okay now?'

He nodded. We sat there for a moment in silence, two lost souls in a sea of revelry.

'So?' I prompted eventually. 'I don't mean to be rude – but why exactly are you here?'

'It's just,' Joseph was murmuring, so quiet now I could hardly catch the words over the crowd's babble. He was staring at his feet. 'I couldn't go home without – well, I just wanted to explain something.' He looked like he might cry.

I took a big slug of wine. 'Go on.'

'I wanted to own up.' He met my eye for practically the first time today, and his forehead was all sweaty. 'It was me. I did take Donna's book.'

'I see.' I felt no emotion at all. 'Why?'

'I dunno.' He picked at the bright label on his beer-bottle, droplets of moisture rolling down the brown glass, more droplets rolling off his head. 'I was showing my initiative.'

'And how was that then?' And then the penny dropped. 'Oh God, Joseph. That's what you were doing the other night in Charlie's office.'

'What?' He stared at his drink.

'You were selling Donna's numbers. Oh, you stupid, stupid boy.'

'Don't call me that.'

'Well, weren't you?'

'I get a bit – a bit kind of confused sometimes.'

'Confused?' I stared at him.

'I have a bit of a problem with depression. I have to take a – a medication, you know.'

That word: depression. How it stalked me.

'What's that got to do with stealing numbers? Who were you selling them to?'

'It doesn't matter.' He shrugged. 'I just mean sometimes I don't know what I'm doing.'

'It does matter, I'm afraid, Joseph. I'm sorry for you, really, if you're depressed, but it's hardly an excuse. What you've done is thoroughly dishonest, and highly illegal too, I'm sure.'

Behind him Bel and Johnno were preparing to go through to the dinner table.

'Look, now is not the time. We'll talk about it in the office tomorrow, okay? I just – I need to –' I inclined my head towards my friends.

Joseph stood up, quick to grasp his reprieve. 'Of course.'

'Stay and finish your drink if you like.' I stood too. Despite my pity for him, I couldn't deny the fact he made my skin crawl.

'No, seriously, I should get home anyway. My parents will wonder where I am.' He put out a clammy hand to shake mine. My graze smarted where our flesh met. We both winced.

'I can't believe you followed me all the way here just to confess,' I said, following him towards the door. 'It was brave, though, I'll give you that.'

'I didn't follow you.'

'What?'

'No, seriously, I didn't.'

My blood ran cold. 'That wasn't you running behind me in the street?'

'No, seriously. Don't get cross with me again.'

If he said *seriously* again, I would scream. 'How did you know where I was then?'

He dug deep in his coat pocket and produced it like a trophy, though the colour mottling his pale pudgy face belied his emotions. 'This is yours, isn't it?'

My Filofax. The Filofax that had disappeared last week. I took it wordlessly.

'The pub address is in it,' he explained. 'I'm just a bit of a detective, that's all, Maggie. Seriously.'

'Right. A detective.' My mind was flitting about like a demented dragonfly. 'So you weren't – behind me when I was walking just now? Trying to catch me up?'

He shook his head. 'No. I got a cab almost right to the door.'

The thought my stalker was real and not just a figment of my overactive imagination, coupled with the knowledge that he had been so close to me, was nearly enough to send me into the loos with some of Bel's more excitable friends; those who were rejecting food for other delights. But I restrained myself. I sat at the table and pretended fervently that everything was fine, all the while feeling flushed and panicky. I talked to Bel's devastated mother Lynn about how cheap and easy, honestly, it was to fly halfway round the world. At one point I thoughtlessly mentioned carbon footprints, but luckily Lynn thought they were a type of shoe. I chatted to Nigel about Bristol University and all the nice girls he'd met, and the fact he preferred the nasty ones.

From time to time Alex crossed my mind, but I just had another sip of wine and made my mind go blank; not letting myself dwell on him or Joseph Blake or pounding feet that got ever nearer. Or the fact that Bel was leaving England tomorrow for God knew how long. I sipped the wine and forced myself to think firmly of nice things like being at Pendarlin or seeing Seb, and after another drink I started to relax for the first time that day, until eventually I realised I was having a lovely time.

Then Charlie and Sally walked in, Sally in an ill-fitting wrap dress that strained over her generous bosom. I pulled a face at her.

'He insisted on giving me a lift,' Sally hissed on her way over to Bel. 'Sorry.'

I thought about hiding, but Charlie, all blazer and tan loafers, intercepted me at the bar, where he redeemed himself a little by buying me a drink. I considered him over the rim of my glass for a long moment.

'Why have you got it in for me?' I was impressed by my own serenity, sipping my drink elegantly.

'I haven't got it in for you, darling, I really haven't.' Charlie smoothed back his hair, that bloody stupid signet ring catching the candlelight. 'Don't be so paranoid. I just don't want to lose you, that's all. There are so very bloody few who can actually do their job, Maggie. You're the best I've got.'

'Can you get me another drink then?' I waved my half-empty glass at him. 'It's a nice glass, isn't it?' I gazed at it. 'I think Alex and I had some glasses like this once.' *Before he threw them all at me.*

'I think you might have had enough.'

I gazed at him now. 'Don't be silly, Charlie. Silly-billy Charlie. I've only had about two. Most certainly not enough.'

'Despite what you may think, Maggie darling,' he drawled as I attempted to focus on him, 'I do care about you – really.'

'Rubbish.' Someone bumped my back and I turned, tipping my entire drink down Charlie's front in the process.

'Whoops.' I dabbed his shirt ineffectively with a beer mat. 'Sorry about that. Quite a nice effect though.' I stood back to admire the stain. 'Sort of – marbled.'

'For God's sake, Maggie.' He grabbed my hand. 'This is pure silk.'

I laughed, happy to know it was possible to rattle Charlie. Then I had a thought. 'Why didn't you tell me Joseph was Lyons's nephew?'

'You did know. But it's irrelevant. He deserves a chance.'

'Charlie, you and I both know that if he wasn't Lyons's blood, you wouldn't give him the time of day.' I leaned forward conspiratorially, and tapped him carefully on the shoulder to emphasise my point. 'After all, he's not blonde and big-boobed, is he now?' I paused to reflect. 'Well, he is blond, I suppose.'

Charlie stared at me with dispassion; then he smiled roguishly. 'No, and more's the pity.'

'You know, Charlie, you really are incot— incomp—' I couldn't seem to grasp the word. 'Terrible,' I finished lamely.

He waved a fifty-pound note at the barman. 'Top us up, there's a good chap. Call me an old fool, Maggie –'

'You ol' fool.'

He ignored me, '– but I feel sorry for that boy.'

'Oh come on, Charlie,' I spluttered. 'Bene— bene—' The word just wouldn't come.

'Benny who?' he frowned. 'Spit it out.'

'*Benevolence* is hardly your forte.' I swayed backwards triumphantly – and then, luckily, after a second or two, forwards again.

189

Bored now, Charlie's hooded eyes darted over my shoulder to see what better prospects lay in store. 'I really must go and clean up, darling. Blake's got a bit of a dark past, that's all I'm at liberty to say. His family are rather desperate, and we're giving him a chance. But don't be taken in by him.'

'What do you mean?' I suddenly felt rather more sober.

'Let's just say he can be a bit –'

'What? Disingenuous?'

'You managed *that* big word, didn't you? Clever Maggie.'

I glared at him. At least I hoped it was a glare. I was having some trouble actually seeing.

'Let's not split hairs, shall we?' Charlie ran a predatory finger down my cheek. 'You're very sexy when you're cross, you know.' And he moved off like a sleek cruiser through a throng of pedalos, a nubile blonde in his sights.

The music was getting louder, the pub crowd more rowdy. Bel's guests were leaving the table now, mingling with the few dancers by the speakers. Digging my phone out of my bag, I squinted at it nervously. It was text-free, thank God. Before I could think about it too hard, I rang Seb, but he didn't answer so I left a message.

'If you've blocked, can you come down? I want you to meet my very best friend in the world, she's called Bel. And I'd love to see you, lovely Seb. Whoops.' Someone knocked the phone out of my hand. I retrieved it from the sticky floor without *quite* falling over, fortunately. 'Are you still there? Did I mention that Bel's my very best friend?'

Half an hour later I was contemplating a spin round the dance floor with Bel when I looked up to see Seb grinning at me from the bar. My tummy went all funny as I realised how pleased I was to see him, and how relieved I was to be pleased. He waved and mimed a drink and I waved my glass back.

'There's Seb.' Bel poked me in the ribs. 'He's very hot, isn't he?'

'Do you think so?' I said nonchalantly.

'Why – don't you?' she teased. 'Nothing like Alex.' She caught my eye. 'Sorry, sorry. Forget I said that.'

'I will. I do quite like him.'

'I'm glad.' Bel hugged me impulsively. 'God, I'm so pleased you're finally getting over that idiot. Promise me you won't go there again.'

'I won't.' I smiled foolishly until I registered her words. I yelled over Blondie, 'Sorry, what do you mean "*getting*" over him?' Then I stumbled slightly as someone pirouetted past me. 'Whoops. Sorry.'

'Honestly, Mag,' Bel looked all serious suddenly, 'I think you ought to take it a bit easy now. Especially now I'm not going to be around to keep an eye on you.'

My head was starting to spin now. 'Explain "easy", can you?'

But Johnno's mates from work struck up a chorus of '*For they are jolly good fellows*' and everyone joined in, and cheered a lot, and then Bel got all tearful as Nigel presented her and Johnno with a brand-new digital camera that we'd all chipped in for – 'so you can email us on your great travels' – and then Bel started on about how Sydney really wasn't that far away, and her poor mother burst into the tears that had been brewing all night long. And I felt myself get quite teary too; God knew what I was going to do without the girl I'd shared everything with since we'd learned hospital corners at Brownies. (Bel's were terrible, mine immaculate.)

And then Seb was behind me, his arms around me, and I felt the heavy cosh of alcohol strike me round the head, clutch me in its velvet hold. I leaned into his body with sudden exhaustion. 'You called the police yesterday, didn't you?' I mumbled.

'Yes,' he murmured back. 'Someone's got to keep an eye on you, babe.'

And the thought made me want to cry. 'Take me home, Seb, please,' I whispered in his ear. 'Would you mind?'

191

'I'd be honoured, Maggie. Do you want to say goodbye first?'

'I've got to take them to the airport tomorrow. I can't face another farewell now.'

And so he drove me home in his sleek car, and as we travelled across Blackfriars Bridge, the OXO tower looking like a neon rocket about to blast off into the electric fug that hid London, I had a brilliant thought.

'After I drop Bel off tomorrow evening, I'm going straight on to Cornwall.' I raised my head from the leather headrest to peer at him. 'You could come too, if you like.'

Before he could answer, I nodded off, and when we arrived at mine, Seb half-carried me upstairs and I passed out straight away.

So I missed the message on my answer-phone. The message about the stranger lurking by my door.

# Chapter Twenty-Two

In and out of troubled drunken sleep, I slipped between horrid dreams where Joseph tried to kiss me all covered in blood while Seb watched us intently, except he looked like Charlie, his hooded eyes malevolent. And then I dreamed of Alex, laughing at the kitchen table, hollows for eyes, the night I'd come back early from filming in Cardiff and found him bare-chested and snorting grams of cocaine with his old college mate Riff, not long after our first Christmas together.

Somewhere deep down, perhaps there'd always been a tiny germ of doubt, of fear, about a man like Alex who could happily drink all day – but I'd surrendered without much struggle to something that felt so right. To something I'd never felt before – something I think I'd been waiting for since my mother had gone.

Alex never brought me flowers, or took me to fancy places. He wasn't king of lavish gestures (though he did quite like the cake-shop downstairs), he was just him – shambolic, master of silly voices; every opinion held hard and argued for. But God, I knew he loved me. He'd hold me in his arms and stare at me, those sleepy eyes unblinking, and I'd gaze back. We were like children, discovering something new and mesmerising, some-thing we couldn't get enough of. For a while we almost did become one, clinging to each other like you would a life-raft; like we'd found the way home. Slowly Alex lured me in – he was looking for a companion to join him in his decadence, although I didn't realise it at first.

A month after we'd met, I took Alex to Pendarlin for the best week of my life. Bursting with happiness, with love and joy, I felt invincible, giant-like in my delight. I sat in the window-seat upstairs one day, basking in the warmth of the spring sun soaking through the old glass, and I realised I was almost euphoric. I watched Alex and his faithful friend cross the pea-green lawn with firewood, Alex waving up at me and Digby barking happily amid crowds of creamy yellow daffodils – and I ran down the higgledy-piggledy stairs and flung myself at my boyfriend just like his beloved dog did. I hadn't known it was possible to feel like this.

The only trouble with getting quite so high is that you must inevitably come down again. And the crash is painful and hard. It's a long way down from bliss.

At the start I think Alex saw me as his salvation – as perhaps I saw him as mine – and he hardly drank. Then the novelty wore off. I didn't know he was already battling with an addiction that had its avaricious fingers clasped right inside his core; a greedy bastard of compulsion that wouldn't let him go, that clung on like a succubus.

It took me a while to realise quite how steadfast that hold was – and when I did, it was too late to get out. It had been easy to let Alex become my mainstay. Before him, it had been work, always work, but years of suppressing my childhood pain now imploded, and I was distracted by his debauchery. I was sick of being sensible – perhaps that was the problem.

After only a few months we bought a flat together in Borough Market, much to my father's politely alarmed surprise. Alex was already in the process of buying it when we met and, on a whim, asked me to come in with him. On a similar whim, I said yes. Initially I worried about leaving Bel's, but Alex had just introduced her to Johnno, and so for a while my best friend and I celebrated our luck, our most fortuitous timing.

194

Alex and I spent our first Christmas alone in Cornwall. I cooked goose and red cabbage with apples and the most perfect roast potatoes (even if I did say so myself) on Christmas Day, although we probably drank more than we ate. I gave Alex a stocking full of silly stuff, false teeth you could wind up, bubble bath and tangerines. Alex bought me mittens because my hands were always cold, he said; a dustpan and brush because I was always breaking things – and a battered oak piano.

Maybe that was the beginning of the bad stuff. I didn't want a piano; I didn't want any reminder of my mother; though most of all I didn't want to spoil Christmas Day. I tried hard to pretend I was glad, but I couldn't overcome my dismay. On Boxing Day, after we'd walked Digby on the blustery beach, Alex asked me to play. I'd been dreading this moment.

'I can't,' I said stiffly, slicing the Christmas cake with a shaking hand, 'I don't play any more.'

Alex tried to put his arm around me. 'But I've been dying to hear you. Your dad said you're great. He said he hoped you'd start again.'

It was a conspiracy, I realised, shrugging him off angrily. 'I won't play it, Alex. You might as well get rid of it. You shouldn't have spent all that money on me anyway.' I went to poke the dying fire, refusing to catch his eye. 'And if you've talked to my dad, which you obviously have, then you know why I won't go near it.'

'I don't know, Maggie. I really don't know what you're on about.' He looked so confused that I felt a great stab of guilt. But I couldn't explain. I sat on the footstool in front of the fire and lit the first of many cigarettes, though I was meant to have given up, and Alex went out to the kitchen and came back with an enormous glass of wine which turned into the whole bottle, and we had the most horrible row about me not letting go, of suppressing the past. I said I didn't want to let go if it meant getting as drunk as he did, though I think I was quite pissed myself.

Then Alex suddenly let rip about my job, about the show I'd done with his dad all those months ago, telling me I shouldn't be so moral about his drinking when I had no morals myself. I told him that was rubbish, that I just wanted to help people, but he said I was 'fucking naïve' – and that I shouldn't try to change people, especially not him. And then I went to bed alone for the first but not the last time since we'd been together and cried piteously.

In the morning Alex brought me fresh coffee and burnt toast in bed – another first and certainly a last – and stroked my hair wordlessly, and I didn't say anything about how drunk he'd been the night before, and he didn't mention my job. In front of the fire, I tried to read a book I'd got for Christmas on old royal chefs, but I couldn't concentrate.

It had snowed in the night and everything was white outside, rounded and smooth like the icing on the Christmas cake I'd made weeks before. Where there should have been hard edges there were none, and it looked quite magical, belying the harsh truth beneath: the naked trees and scraggy shrubs of bleak midwinter. Mendelssohn was playing on the stereo and Digby was chasing his tail in the snow as Alex came in. The coldness from the garden emanated from him; he was freezing despite his thick jumper, the snowflakes melting on the wool wet against my skin, and I wiped one from the bridge of his slightly skewed nose, and wrapped my arms around him to try to warm him.

'I like this music,' Alex said quietly. 'I can imagine you playing it.' He looked so sad as he leaned down to kiss me, and that kiss, I can't describe it. It was like he was a drowning man, like he was fighting to survive. I was frightened by his desperation, frightened but entirely acquiescent as he pulled me onto the rug in front of that fire and tugged my nightie off. He made love to me like he wanted to destroy me; he was so fierce that I was literally breathless, crushed beneath his whole weight but not caring, wanting suddenly to disappear beneath him. To disappear with him, or into him, perhaps.

'I never want to let you go, Maggie,' he whispered into my hair afterwards as we lay in the dusk, the room quiet now except for the hiss and snap of the fire, the only light the orange glow that flickered across our bodies. 'I just want to stay here forever. It's weird, but I'm –' He trailed off.

'What?' I twisted my head to look at him. He was staring at the ceiling, where shadows danced. I'd never known him quite so melancholy.

'I don't know how to describe it. Scared?'

'Of what, Alex?' I clutched him tighter.

'Scared I'm going to lose you, I suppose.' And there was something in his voice I'd never heard before, something like desolation, and it scared me too. I hugged him hard and almost cried again and promised he wouldn't lose me. And any fears I had about going down a path I didn't like, well, I pushed them right away. I told myself he'd change, despite his words last night; I'd help him change if need be. I didn't realise it would be me who did the changing.

We lay in silence listening to the fire until I promised I'd try to play the piano, I really would. Digby appeared suddenly at the window, grinning toothily, drooling, snowflakes like tiny crystals on his fur, begging to be let in, and we both jumped, then laughed shakily. But deep down I think we both knew the idyll had been shattered.

Alex got up. 'I'll get us a drink,' he said, and I smiled, though with a sinking heart I knew he didn't mean a cup of tea. He sloped off to open the door for the dog – and that was it. We had entered a new phase, without even realising it. The next phase. It was the beginning of Alex trying to bring me down with him, deliberately or not. And I never did play that wretched piano.

*   *   *

197

Just before dawn I snapped out of my dreams and sat bolt upright in bed, feeling nauseous and, as I gradually regained my memory, mortified. Even Digby looked vaguely embarrassed from his watchful position on the armchair. My skull felt like it was being hoovered from the inside. Digby slipped his nose onto his front paws and regarded me with plaintive eyes. 'And you can shut up,' I muttered at him, clutching my head.

My heart missed a beat as someone rolled over in the bed. Oh God. Seb. I flopped down again beside him – too fast; closed my eyes tight against the spinning world. Against Seb. His breathing was that of the happily unconscious. I listened miserably to the lone bird trying to summon dawn, attempting to get my head comfortable on the pillow – but whichever way I turned, I couldn't place it quite right. I slipped an arm around Seb as he slept, then slipped it off again. It felt overfamiliar. Eventually I drifted into the weird land of still-drunken half-sleep and worry.

It wasn't until Seb offered to drop me at work later that morning that I remembered with a heavy heart my invitation of the night before; and, with heavier heart, the fact he hadn't answered. I sure as hell wasn't going to repeat the request.

'Okay?' he asked, lacing his boots in the kitchen as I slipped my coat on. His dark eyes were twinkling in an I-know-you-feel-rotten kind of way.

'Oh yes.' I nodded my head with vigour and immediately regretted it. 'Fine, thanks.'

We walked from the flat in silence through Green Dragon Court, towards the roar of rush-hour London Bridge, me concentrating hard on not being sick, and on concealing the fact I might be. An angelic-looking Asian child was leaning against a bollard under the railway arch, eating crisps, regarding us with great solemnity as we approached. I smiled down at him. He blinked eyelashes like velvet caterpillars at me and crunched up his final crisp.

'Excuse me, miss.'

I stopped.

'Do you want to see something?' He licked his salty fingers carefully.

'Okay,' I smiled, with beneficence this time. I was pretty good with small children. The boy folded up his crisp packet very tight and tiny and tucked it into one anorak pocket. From the other, he fished out a pretty little pill-box, all greens and blues and sparkles.

'Oh, that's nice,' I was enthusiastic, 'isn't it, Seb? Lovely treasure.'

Seb grinned politely. We started to walk on.

'Do you want to see inside?' The boy's skin was like caramel, his cheeks a dusky pink as I looked down again, and shrugged. 'Okay.'

The boy looked up at me, as solemn as the night is long. Then he wrenched the lid right off and thrust the box beneath my nose.

'Oh,' I exclaimed, and nearly threw up. Inside were three long and dirty yellow fingernails.

'Wow,' said Seb, peering down. 'Impressive stuff.'

I managed to quell the nausea. 'Are they yours?'

Devil-boy nodded. 'They are now. But they were Sanjit's. He didn't want them no more. He gave them to me, and I gave him my Wayne Rooney poster, innit, cos I don't like *him* no more.'

'I see,' I said a little shakily. 'Well, thanks for showing us.'

'Thassallright.' The boy pocketed them again and, pulling his fluffy hood up against the morning chill, wandered off towards the chilly planes of Southwark Cathedral. Seb grinned at me, and for the first time that morning I felt a little more human.

'Christ.'

The smile was instantly wiped from Seb's face as we rounded the corner.

'What?' I followed his gaze to his car. His car that now had two, three – no, four, we saw as we circled it – flat tyres. He swore softly.

'Oh God.' I held onto the wall for a moment, bracing myself. 'All four,' I said numbly. 'That's a bit of a coincidence, isn't it?'

'A coincidence?' he muttered darkly, walking round the car. 'Don't be stupid. Look.' He pointed at the back tyre. A chisel lay in the gutter; a screwdriver with a great shiny red handle protruded from a tyre's rubber skin.

'Oh.'

'The fucking bastards.'

'I'm so sorry,' I said rather helplessly. I kept staring at the chisel; at its worn wooden handle.

'Yeah, so am I.' He sounded all Midlands suddenly, his features set and stern, pushing his dark hair back with a quick angry movement – a Seb I'd not seen before.

'I'll pay for them to be fixed, of course.'

I'd only seen him smiling.

'Maggie, babe, there's no fixing this little lot. They're fucked.'

'Well, I'll – I'll pay for the new tyres.'

He came back round the car and pulled me gently towards him. 'Why should you pay? Is there something I should know?'

I felt my skin burn. 'No,' I muttered.

'I mean, did you creep out and slash them last night? Are you Secret Slasher Maggie?' He grinned at me; finally, he grinned. I felt my legs go weak with shock and relief.

'No, of course not.'

'Well then. What's it to do with you?'

'I dunno. I suppose I just thought –'

'You mean, cos of the graffiti?'

I shrugged. 'Well, someone's got it in for me. Now it looks like they don't like you much either.'

'That's true.' Seb gave my fingers a squeeze. 'But there's safety in numbers, isn't that what they say?' He let my hand go and dug in his pocket for his phone. 'I'd better get this sorted, babe.'

I didn't tell him I recognised that chisel. That I was sure it belonged to Alex; that he kept it in a toolbox in the back of his old Land Rover.

We went back into the warmth to wait for the tow-truck, much to Digby's great excitement. He hated spending his days alone; despite the fact Jenny had started to walk him regularly while I was at work, I felt guilty whenever I left him at home. Seb offered to take him for a trot round the block while I made some coffee and scrambled eggs. If I didn't eat soon, I'd be sick. I chopped mushrooms like my life depended on it, narrowly avoiding slicing my little finger off in rage. Switching the kettle on, I noticed the red light flashing on my answerphone.

There were two messages: one from Stefano Costana asking if he could bring an 'interested party' round to see the flat – the other from an extremely agitated Mrs Forlani, who lived opposite. She was worried, she said, *mia bella* Maggie, she didn't want to appear nosy but there'd been a stranger lurking by my front door for much of the evening. A couple of times he'd even tried the handle, but when Matteo had gone down to see if he could help, he'd disappeared. Then they saw him again before they went to bed, about ten last night, which is when she'd rung me.

Abandoning the mushrooms, I sat down at the table, head in my hands. I lit a cigarette, jumped up, paced up and down the kitchen, thinking. I wasn't very certain of a lot of things right now, but one thing I knew for sure: this just couldn't go on. Something had to give – and soon it would be my brain.

'The tow-truck's here.' Seb bounded into the kitchen, Digby at his heels, bringing the cold in with them. I shivered.

'Good.' I stared out of the window at the tail-lights of a train.

'Look, Seb,' I turned back, 'I'm going to call the police, okay? I think you were right to do it last time. This is all starting to really freak me out.'

'I'm not surprised.' He kissed the top of my head. 'Whatever you think, babe.'

'And then I'm going to get out of London.'

He looked quizzical.

'After work, I'm going down to Cornwall.' I contemplated my feet. 'I think I might have mentioned it last night.' I had nothing to lose – especially if my stalker got me first. 'You could – I was serious about you coming with me, if you like.'

I tore my eyes from the floor to find Seb looking rather awkward.

'Thanks, babe. It's a really tempting offer. I'm just not sure –'

I cut across his words, grinding my cigarette out briskly. 'It's fine, Seb. Really. You don't have to explain.'

'Maggie, honestly, I'd love to come. It's just, with rehearsals and everything at the moment, I'm not sure I can get away. The show goes up next week.'

'Up where?'

'It starts, I mean.' He smiled that charming crooked smile. 'It's a technical term. What's in Cornwall, anyway?'

I gave a diffident sort of shrug. 'I've got a little house,' I said. I'd gone off the subject now. 'Well, not a house. A cottage.'

'Oh, right. How nice. Very *To the Manor Born*.'

I flushed angrily. 'Hardly. I inherited it.' That didn't sound much better. 'I mean – it was my grandmother's. Her home. Her only home.'

'And she doesn't live there any more?'

'No. She's gone a bit – she's got dementia. She's in care. She left it to me. In her living will.'

'Lucky you.'

'I know,' I said stiffly. 'I'm very lucky. I do know that. Though I'd rather have my gran back.' I turned towards the sink and swilled my cup out. 'I'm her – I'm her only surviving relative, you see. Since my mum –'

Like a dragon rushing from its lair, a train to God-knew-where went speeding past. I wished vehemently that I was on it.

'Since your mum what, Maggie?' Seb asked quietly. He was behind me now.

'Forget it.'

'Maggie!' Seb tried to turn me round, but I shrugged him off. The eggs had congealed horribly on the hob.

'Maggie, babe –'

'That reminds me. I still can't find the bloody key for Pendarlin.' I ransacked the pottery bowl for the fiftieth time this week. 'I just can't think –'

'Maggie, look at me. What's wrong? What happened to your mum?'

'Nothing.'

'You're hiding something. You have been since I met you.'

'Hiding? Me? Why would I be hiding anything?' I met his look full-on this time with challenge in my eyes.

'You've got to let me in, Maggie, if you want this to work.'

'For God's sake! You sound like the great Renee Owens, you know.' I laughed with derision, without mirth. It always came down to this and I loathed it; hated being backed into this claustrophobic corner. Seb just looked bemused.

'Why are you being like this? I don't understand –'

'You want to know about my mum? I'll tell you, shall I?' I caught my reflection in the mirror behind him: my hair all up on end, my eyes blazing, two spots of colour scalding my cheeks, the rest of my face as pale as death.

Seb stared at me like I was crazy.

'Don't look at me like that.' I almost stamped my foot in frustration.

'Like what? Maggie, this is ridiculous.'

'Like you know what's inside.'

'Inside what?' He pushed his hair back distractedly, utterly perplexed. 'I'm lost, babe.'

'Inside me. Inside my mother. The thing you want to know is this, you see.' I nearly stopped but I couldn't. It came flying out like that high-speed train. 'My mother – my beautiful, my wonderful mother – she went quite mad.'

# Chapter Twenty-Three

After that, it wasn't really a surprise to be driving out to collect Bel alone that evening. I'd managed about two hours in the office and then I'd pleaded a migraine. I'd gone to see Gar at the nursing-home instead, lying my head down on the quilt while she slept. When I left I had the strangest feeling; a sense of foreboding, as if I might not see her again.

'Look after her, Susan, won't you? Don't let anyone you don't know in to see her.'

Susan patted my shoulder fondly. 'I won't, ducks, don't worry.' She blew her nose. 'We never do anyway.'

And then I drove to the police station and asked to see DI Fox. Only he wasn't there. Day off, of course. Apparently he'd told me.

'Do policemen have days off?' I asked stupidly, and the nice police lady offered me a cup of tea in the interview room and asked me what was wrong, why did I want to see the Detective Inspector anyway, and could she help instead?

I turned down the tea though I was sorely tempted. 'Could you ask him to call Maggie Warren, please?' I called over my shoulder as I rushed out again.

I collected Digby from Jenny's, went home to get some clothes, and then drove to Bel's, ringing my dad to make him promise to visit Gar tomorrow. Charlie kept trying to call me; I didn't listen to the message he left.

'You all right, Mag?' Bel let me in, looking incredibly spaced-out. Before I could answer Hannah flew down the hall in tears. 'Can you look after Cagney and Lacey? Please, Maggie, please.'

Squeaking hysterically, Cagney and Lacey both looked terrified. Bel prised the guinea pigs from her daughter's hands.

'Hannah, Maggie can't have them because of Digby, you know that. Amelia's going to look after them for you.'

'But she won't give them back, I know she won't,' Hannah wept. 'She'll keep them forever.'

'Oh, Han,' I said, bending to hug her, and I felt like my heart was cracking all over again. 'I'll check on them for you, okay? I promise I will.' I tried to muffle the sob in my sentence. 'And we won't let Amelia keep them, I swear.' I felt my phone vibrate and then it rang.

It was Seb. 'Maggie, babe, I'm sorry about this morning.'

'No, *I'm* sorry,' I said a little stiffly, moving off down the hall to stand alone in the shadows.

'Are you okay now?'

'I'm fine, thanks.'

'I was quite worried, I must say.'

'I'm fine, really.'

'Good. Look, I don't have much time cos we're about to run the last act.'

'I understand. You'd better get on.'

'Maggie, listen, I just wanted to say – if that invitation still stands – I'd love to come with you tonight. Unless you've changed your mind?'

'Oh,' I said foolishly. Slowly the world slid out from beneath its enormous storm-cloud. 'No, of course not. But we're about to leave.'

'I was thinking – I could get the Heathrow Express from Paddington, if you like, and meet you at the airport. Would that work?'

'Yes,' I grinned. 'That's a great idea.'

'Blimey,' said Bel, marching down the hall with the trembling Cagney and Lacey in her arms. 'You look like the Cheshire cat.' She peered at me. 'Have you just eaten the White Rabbit?'

The M4 was heavy with Friday-night traffic, and I was heavy with foreboding. I hadn't been on this road since the coach crash and I was struggling with the memories now. We weaved slowly between row after row of fat four-by-fours driven by complacent second-homers with double-chins and stripy shirts, until a lorry lost its load of feathers in front of us and everything ground to a complete halt in a bizarre snowstorm of goose-down. By the time we reached the terminal, Bel was almost out of time to check in.

'For God's sake,' she hissed as fluorescent-jacketed officials waved us on each time we tried to set down, 'do we look like Jihadists?'

When I finally pulled up, Johnno leapt out, piling bags onto a trolley as Bel necked yet another Valium behind his back. 'If I have any more of these, I'll overdose,' she muttered.

Hannah clutched her Barbie rucksack, a mini-Bel under the bright airport lights. 'Aren't you coming, Auntie Maggie?' Her eyes were huge and owlish.

'Not now, darling, no.' I smiled cheerfully, but inside I felt like howling.

'Why not?' Her bottom lip quivered.

'I'll be out to see you really, really soon, I promise. And, look, hang on a sec.' I delved in my bag for the book I'd bought Hannah for the plane. She ripped the wrapping off in a flurry of excitement.

'*Little Red Riding Good*,' she read carefully, '*and other Tales*. Did Riding Good have a tail?'

'Red Riding *Hood*.' I swept her up into a big hug. 'She didn't have a tail, but the wolf did.'

Hannah looked worried. 'There are no wolves in Austria, are there?'

'Australia. No, of course not.' I kissed her soft little cheeks; I didn't want to let her go. 'Just lots of koala bears.'

'It's you who should be watching out for wolves, young lady, now I'm not going to be around,' Bel said rather primly, fluffing up her hair in the car window. 'Don't rush into anything on the rebound, okay? You know, I'm sure there's something I needed to tell you, Mag. I just can't for the life of –'

'Bel,' Johnno's tone was sharp, the trolley stacked high, 'I know this is painful and all that, love, and your hair's very important – but we'd really better get on. Have you got the passports?'

Bel patted her pockets rather vacantly. ''Spect they're here somewhere. God, I haven't even done my make-up.'

I clutched Hannah tighter. 'Can't she just stay with me?' I whispered to Bel over Hannah's shiny little head. 'I'll bring her out in a few months, I promise.'

Bel prised the little girl out of my arms and set her down by Johnno. 'You're as bad as her with those bloody guinea pigs.' But my best friend's eyes were full of tears now as she hugged me.

'Christ, Bel, what am I going to do without you?' I muttered.

'Come with us,' she said, and we were both crying now. 'I'm serious. Why don't you?'

'I can't. What about Gar? And Dad.' Then I thought of Jenny. Of Alex. My life was changing slowly.

'Bel!' Johnno shouted.

'All right, all right.' She wiped her face fiercely and relinquished her hold.

'Look after them, Johnno. They're precious,' I mumbled.

'I will.' He gave me a squeeze. 'And you look after yourself, Maggie.'

Hannah ran at me and clutched my legs, her head buried in my jeans. I stroked her hair wordlessly until Johnno scooped her up.

208

'Seriously, Maggie,' Bel grabbed my hand and forced me to meet her eye, 'take it easy, yeah? Remember the summer and stay strong. Remember you are strong.'

And then Johnno tugged Bel's other hand gently and they began to move away. I stood and hugged myself, suddenly realising how cold I was, and I waved and waved as they retreated, and they turned and waved too, and I could see Bel was crying, and then they were gone, the little family, swallowed up by the crowd so I couldn't see them any more. My family – gone.

Numb, I walked back to my car. I got in and stared blankly at the windscreen. Digby licked my hand several times valiantly – but I felt nothing. I watched the people come and go across the car park; waving goodbye, hugging hello. I saw people unloading, rushing, clinging on or desperate to cross the world to reach their loved ones. Goodbyes were anathema to me. I remembered my revelations to Seb that morning. I remembered my beloved mother. I buried my face in Digby's springy back.

Goodbyes could only ever be poisonous.

# Chapter Twenty-Four

I was in a world of my own when someone smacked the roof of my car. I'd been listening to the news, about the BBC faking a programme, while I waited for Seb in the airport car park.

'Christ!' I jumped, and locked all the doors immediately. Another knock. I craned round to see Seb grinning through the passenger window.

'That's not funny.' I let him in crossly. 'You gave me a real fright.'

'Sorry.' He threw his bag onto the back seat and slid in beside me, looking dishevelled and not very sorry at all. 'I thought I'd surprise you.'

'Terrify me, you mean.' I started the engine. 'You look a bit hot and bothered yourself, I must say.'

He pulled his grey cashmere jumper over his tousled hair. 'Yeah, well, it was a close thing. They suddenly announced the suspension of the whole bloody line at Paddington. I just managed to get on the last train out. It was a bloody bun-fight though.'

'So how was the big farewell?' he asked, yawning widely as we eased onto the motorway. 'God, sorry. I'm knackered.'

'Don't ask,' I said, as we shuddered in the slipstream of a lumbering juggernaut. The motorway was quiet now, the frenzy of London's Friday night exodus apparently over for another week.

'That good? I'm sorry, babe.' He offered me a piece of chewing gum, flexing his shoulders. 'God, I'm sore. I can't wait to get out of bloody London. A whole weekend of sea air and doing nothing.' He shot me a mischievous look. 'Well, nothing *too* strenuous anyway.'

I was searching for an appropriate response when my phone rang. Seb picked it up from the glove compartment. 'Someone called Fox,' he said, peering at the display. 'Shall I answer it?'

'Yes please. Would you say I'll call back.'

At a service station somewhere in deepest Wiltshire, Seb went to buy coffee while I called Val to check she'd left the spare key under the geranium pot, as I'd never found mine. Cheery Val was my nearest neighbour in Cornwall, apart from the pub – though she was still a good mile down the road. She kept an eye on Pendarlin and did the occasional bit of cleaning for me. After I'd spoken to her, I lit a cigarette and, leaning against the car, rang DI Fox back. I told him about the anonymous texts, and he took a note of the phone number they had come from.

'I'll get it checked out, Maggie.' He was calm and matter of fact. 'It might help a lot if it's linked, because so far the evidence is all circumstantial.' I could sense the wariness in his explanation. 'Until we actually catch someone in the act of vandalism, there's very little I can do. Much as I'd love to put a plod outside your door –'

'Don't be silly,' I laughed. Out in the dark I suddenly felt free for the first time in weeks. I breathed in the cold country air, the vast sky above looking like someone had chucked a bucket of stars into the blackness, the night that went on forever now we were out of London's grime. I always felt like this on the long road to Cornwall – like I was being reborn. Through the glass, I watched Seb at the counter of the coffee shop and felt a rush of optimism.

'Honestly, it's probably nothing. It's probably just some

211

random nutter.' I squashed the memories as best I could. 'I'm sure it is.'

'We have had a couple of complaints from property owners around you who've been harassed by a local family called the Frenches. Have you come across them?'

'No. I don't think so.'

'They seem to think the area's being taken over by –' slight embarrassment crept through his tone – 'by what they call very politely "a load of ponces". We're keeping an eye on them, believe me. Just got to catch 'em in the act, you see.'

'Really? You mean, like a grudge?' I grasped this information gladly; I was in desperate need for some respite. 'Well, that might make sense. I'm out of London for a few days anyway, so I should be fine.'

'Right. Well, look, just keep in touch, okay?'

'I will, DI Fox. Thanks very much.'

Seb appeared out of the darkness bearing steaming coffee. He kissed my neck and I squirmed with pleasure, hardly concentrating on Fox's final words. 'I'll speak to you sometime not *too* soon, I hope.'

It wasn't until my mobile rang again halfway down the M5 that I realised I hadn't mentioned my worries about Gar to DI Fox. Seb picked up the phone again.

'Hello?'

There was a pause, then he held the phone out to me, his face darker suddenly. 'Someone called Alex. He doesn't sound too happy.'

I took the phone. 'What do you want?'

'What do you mean, what do I want? You rang me.'

'No I didn't,' I muttered.

'Yeah, you did.'

'When?' I frowned.

'From Bel's party last night, from what I could establish. Who the fuck just answered your phone?' he snarled.

212

'I'm driving, Alex,' I said, 'I can't talk now.' I didn't want to draw Seb into this.

'Well drive this, baby. Get the keys to the flat to Costana because I want to sell it fast before the market crashes. Okay?'

Even I was taken aback by Alex's ferocity. By the hatred in his voice. 'Don't talk to me like that. What's wrong with you, Alex?'

'None of your fucking business.'

Digby barked suddenly as a Porsche whizzed by and was sucked up by the darkness.

'Is that my dog?' I recognised danger in Alex's tone. 'Have you got my dog with you, Maggie?'

'Well, where else would he be? Should I have left him at home for you to feed?' I was too close to the car in front; I braked sharply. 'Just like you did in the summer. Are you drunk, Alex?'

'No, I am not fucking drunk,' he howled. 'I gave up, I told you. Look, just get the estate agent the keys, would you?'

'I can't. I'm on my way to Pendarlin.'

'With who?' His tone was icy now. 'That bloke who just answered the phone? And *my* dog.'

'None of *your* damn business, Alex.' I swerved slightly in the fast lane; Seb was starting to look worried now. 'I've got to go.'

'Just get Costana the keys on Monday, all right? And don't ring me again.' Alex hung up.

'He didn't sound like he was in a very good mood,' Seb joked, but neither of us laughed. After a minute, he reached out and squeezed my thigh gently. 'Okay?'

'I'm fine. Sorry.' I wasn't fine, though, not fine at all. I was so angry I was practically crying with rage. I dashed away an imaginary tear. 'Can I – do you mind if we don't talk about it right now?'

'Of course,' he said softly. 'I understand.' He patted me. 'Exes are a funny thing, eh?'

'What makes you think he was my ex?' I asked carefully. I pressed the cigarette lighter in like it was Alex's face.

'Isn't he?' Seb looked at me and I nodded silently. 'It's easy to tell, you know. They have a strange hold over us, I think, sometimes, our ex-lovers. Even if you don't want to be together any more.'

I didn't trust myself to speak right then. I just didn't know how I could have reached such utter depths with someone I'd loved so much. I thought about the moment I'd finally realised that Alex and I *weren't* together any more; that he *was* now my ex. After that disastrous first call from the hospital I'd tried to ring him several more times in the following days – to no avail. I had no recollection of a problem between us at first and I was stupefied. It took two weeks before the fog lifted even a little and the day of the crash began to take shape. And Alex had refused to see me; it was Bel who'd sat beside me and listened as I finally drew what had happened from the depths; it was Bel who filled in the excruciating blanks as best she could, and assured me it might hurt like hell-pains, but it was definitely for the best.

I threw my fag out of the window and tried to forget Alex. Now Seb was here instead.

It wasn't until hours later, when we were on the moor road running through the wind-farm, the farm Alex and I had always joked looked like something from *Alien*, that I had a sudden thought. The estate agent must have keys already. He'd let himself in the other day.

# Chapter Twenty-Five

I had such a nice weekend with Seb that I managed to banish most thoughts of Alex and his strange behaviour from my mind. We drank pints of Tinners and local cider in the crooked old pub and shared fat chips on Polzeath Beach, jumping between the busy rivulets to watch the reflections of the winter sun on the glossy golden sand, while Digby barked at the surfers paddling madly to catch a wave. In the tiny village of Port Isaac that tumbled toward the sea, we bought the fishermen's fresh catch before walking out between the deep rock-pools onto the harbour wall, the sea a great aquamarine eiderdown beneath a clear blue sky. Later I cooked Seb a Breton bouillabaisse for dinner. We lay by the fire after eating and listened to the old jazz that he liked, and I felt comfortable with him in a new way, a way I hadn't before.

On Sunday morning Seb brought fresh coffee and smoked salmon up to bed, and I tried not to make comparisons between this new man and Alex, who couldn't even boil an egg. He ran me a bath and filled it with bubbles, and then he dragged me out again and made love to me under that wobbly ceiling and I felt like I was starting to heal; like fresh skin was growing over my heart, over the deep chasm where old sticking plaster had once been.

But as the clock ticked on remorselessly we grew ever quieter. I cooked roast lamb for lunch, and then Seb took Digby outside and threw sticks for him while I washed up. On the radio they were discussing the BBC story again. I laughed at something irreverent Russell Brand said.

'What?' Seb leaned against the kitchen table and unlaced his muddy boots. 'What's so funny?'

'Oh, nothing really. Just this story about TV producers trying to make it look like something happened that didn't.'

'Why's that funny?' Seb looked puzzled. 'It's bad, isn't it?'

'Well, yes, I suppose. But it's so typical.'

'Is it?' He frowned. 'It shouldn't be, though, should it?'

'No, of course not.' I turned the casserole dish over to dry. 'But everyone knows TV bods make stuff look like *they* want it to look, surely.'

'You really think poor old Joe Public understands that?' Seb flung his boots over by the door. 'Of course they don't, poor bastards. They're just the unsuspecting victims of your power.'

I gazed at him, perplexed. 'God, Seb. That's a bit strong.'

'I don't mean *your* power, individually.'

'Well, no, I realise that.'

'Sorry.' He recovered himself a little. 'It's just all so bloody manipulative.'

'I had no idea you felt like that.' I dried my hands slowly, considering his words. 'I mean, granted, it's bad. It's not something that sits comfortably with me, all the manipulation.'

'Really?' He looked back at me, his face blank.

'Yes, really.' I was beginning to feel irritated. 'But come on, Seb, actors are hardly paragons of virtue. You're all pretending to be something that you're not.'

'Yes, but that's for entertainment.'

'So – supposedly – is what I do.'

'*Supposedly*, Maggie. You said it. I just think it's – it gets abused sometimes.'

'Can we discuss this another time? I've got to go and make the bed.' I put the tins back in the oven and shut the door, hard.

'We need to leave in about an hour if we're going to miss the traffic.' I strode out of the room before he could answer.

'Maggie,' he called up the stairs a minute later. 'I'm sorry if I offended you. Do you want a cup of tea?'

'No thanks.' I stomped into the bathroom and pulled the airing cupboard open to find clean sheets. Something fell out with a crash. I picked it up slowly. It was a photo of me and Alex kissing under the mistletoe that first Christmas. I looked horribly adoring. Horribly in love. God knew what it was doing in the airing-cupboard; I couldn't have put it there. Could I? Anyway, it was broken now, the glass in smithereens – just like our relationship. 'Bollocks.'

'All right up there, butterfingers?' Seb was trying for jolly now – too late. I tried to think why this photo would have been in there. I thought I'd removed all traces of Alex months ago, but surely I hadn't stuffed them in the airing cupboard?

'Okay?'

I jumped as Seb put his hands on my shoulders. 'Oh God, you scared me.'

'Sorry, babe. Can I help?'

'You could get a dustpan and brush if you fancied.' I tried to hide the photo, but too late, he'd seen it.

'Friend of yours?' he asked calmly, taking the frame from my hand. I still hadn't spoken about Alex and, fair play to him, Seb hadn't asked. 'You're bleeding, you know.' He took my scarlet-stained finger and put it to his mouth; he sucked it slowly.

I breathed deeply. I breathed long and hard, then I looked up at him.

'I was thinking, actually,' he pulled me into him now, dumping the picture on a chair, 'I was thinking, actually, you might be coming down with something, mightn't you? A bug, you know. You feel a little warm.'

Slowly I ran my hands up beneath his sweater, ran them over

217

his bare flesh. 'I think it's called Monday-itis.' His skin was smooth, his shoulder-blades taut under my hands.

'Ah yes,' I said gravely, 'Monday-itis.'

'I've heard it can be serious. Let me take a look.' He led me towards the bedroom, and suddenly he didn't look that calm any more; suddenly he had a blaze in his eyes that I'd begun to recognise. I felt my legs go rather shaky, so it was lucky that he picked me up and practically threw me on the bed. I'm glad I didn't bother making it, was my last coherent thought.

I woke up in Seb's arms about an hour later. My mouth felt tender and slightly bruised, my skin bore traces of his finger-marks. I felt satiated and slightly dazed. This sex had been different from any we'd had before, a tension in Seb that I'd not known before. He muttered in his sleep now, a lock of hair falling across his forehead, his wide mouth almost smiling as he dreamed.

The wind had got up while we had been distracted. Downstairs the kitchen door banged in the draught; the dying wisteria tapped against the window. I'd never felt nervous in Pendarlin, it was my true home – but recently I never seemed able to quite relax anywhere.

I reached for a cigarette but the packet on the bedside table was empty. I suddenly felt starving again. I eased myself out of bed and pulled the duvet up around Seb just as the phone rang.

I clattered downstairs to pick it up, but whoever it was had rung off by the time I reached it. Letting Digby out and putting Handel's *Messiah* on the stereo, I unpacked the remains of the fish stew and whizzed it into a thick soup. I made a spinach and radicchio salad to go with the cold lamb, and then I eyed the pot of double cream left over from lunch and the half-dozen eggs we hadn't eaten. Far too much food, as usual – I always worried my guests would go hungry, a habit I'd learned from Gar.

When Seb wandered down a while later, yawning and stretching like a cat, I was just pulling eight perfect little meringues from the oven.

'My, my, Nigella, you have been busy.' He kissed the tip of my nose. 'Mmm, whipped cream. I'll light the fire, shall I?'

I blushed happily, happier than I had been in a very long time.

After supper I switched the television on.

'Seb,' I called, 'they're about to review *Love All* on *The 8 O'Clock Show*. Quick, you might be on it.'

He strolled into the room, wine bottle in hand, Digby at his heels. 'Top-up, babe?'

'Thanks.' I offered up my glass. Seb sat in the armchair and I watched him for a moment as the television bleated on in the background about Russian art.

'What?' He suddenly turned to me. The scar above his mouth was paler than the rest of his skin as he smiled. 'Does my hair look funny or something?'

I blushed. 'No.' I took a big slug of wine. 'No. It's just, I was thinking how – how sort of, relaxed you look. Here, I mean.'

'Well, I am, babe. This is a very comfortable chair, I must say.'

'No, I mean, comfortable in my home.' I was getting a bit muddled now. 'You just sort of – fit in.' I bit my lip then. 'Sorry. You probably think I sound a bit mad.'

'Not very.' He lowered himself to the floor where I lay propped against the sofa. 'But I do know where I'd like to fit in.' He picked up the remote and snapped the television off. The phone started to ring again.

'Leave it,' I murmured, as Seb idly unzipped my sweatshirt and ran his wineglass down my naked skin. Digby wandered off in disgust. The fire crackled and the wind moaned. Quite soon after that, so did I.

# Chapter Twenty-Six

Seb had to be back by Monday afternoon for the tech run of *Twelfth Night*, so we left at practically dawn, heading up the motorway to London with *Don Giovanni* blaring in a vain attempt to cheer us up. The sky was grim and flat and the clouds menacing. I felt a curious tightening in my chest as we approached the capital. Seb read the paper he'd bought at the garage, and then some book about Shakespearean film adaptations. I was wrapped up in thoughts of how much I was dreading going back to work, and how I was going to have to take my chances with Charlie's threats and get the hell out – although what to, I didn't know.

My mood grew ever bleaker as we left my beloved hills and beaches far behind; as the landscape became greyer and more suburban by the minute, sucking us into the metropolis like a huge magnet. Even Digby looked miserable, twitching in his sleep on the back seat. Somewhere in Somerset we slowed behind a convoy of army trucks, crawling beside a great muddy field of grazing horses in their green blankets, and I gritted my teeth as a huge grey stallion wandered towards the fence. From time to time Charlie called my mobile but I ignored it. I'd sent him a text saying I was ill and sleeping.

*Don Giovanni* ended. A depressing debate on Radio Four about Care in the Community came on, which I promptly switched off, suddenly aware that Seb was scrutinising me.

'What?' I felt a prickle of discomfort.

'Nothing.' He chucked his book into the bag by his feet. 'It's just – you never finished telling me about your mum, you know, after you mentioned her the other day.' That was a polite way of putting it. 'You never really explained what you meant.'

'Nice juxtaposition, Seb.' I overtook a rusty Beetle.

'What do you mean?' He frowned.

I nodded at the radio. 'Care in the Community and my mum.'

'I didn't mean it like that, babe. Sorry. It was a bit crass, I suppose. I just – it just reminded me, that's all.'

There was a pause. 'Do you mind if I smoke?' I muttered eventually.

'No, of course not.' Seb lit a cigarette for me in a smooth gesture that reminded me a bit of Cary Grant. I inhaled deeply and opened the window a bit, the car suddenly full of white noise from the road.

'What do you want to know?' I asked quietly.

He craned to hear me. 'Well, whatever you want to tell me, I suppose.' He raised his voice against the shudder of the wind.

'Which isn't much.'

'But you – you did say – your words were – she was mad.'

'She was severely depressed. Not mad. Nowadays, I think they call it being bipolar. It's quite fashionable, apparently.'

'Like manic depression, you mean?'

'I guess so. But back then, they didn't seem to be able to get a handle on it. She was misdiagnosed.'

'So, what happened?'

'She was institutionalised. Because she was misdiagnosed, they gave her the wrong medication and it didn't agree with her. It – it kind of made it worse. Turned her into a – a sort of zombie.'

I felt him trying to find the right words. I sensed he wanted to comfort me, but didn't know how. I withdrew into myself. 'I'm sorry, Maggie. I really am,' he said eventually.

'Thanks. So am I.' I threw the cigarette-end out of the window.

It was whipped against the glass for a moment, a tiny glowing spearhead. 'She was – in the end, she became –' the word still stuck in my gullet, even now, 'suicidal.'

My phone rang. Saved by the bell: this time I answered it, balancing it precariously between ear and shoulder. It was Sally.

'Where are you? Charlie's going ballistic.'

'I'm ill.' I cast a guilty look at Seb, who raised an amused eyebrow. 'Tell him I'll be in tomorrow, would you?'

'You do know the *Dumped* show is on Wednesday, don't you?'

'Yes, Sal. I scheduled the bloody thing in the first place. Look, I'll see you early tomorrow. I'm not feeling too good right now.'

Seb didn't mention my mother again. But when we passed the crash site, marked with a plaque, bouquets of flowers and photographs still festooning the grass bank, he put one hand gently on my leg as he gazed out of the window.

I had last seen my mother when I was thirteen. Swamped by adolescent hormones and utterly confused by circumstance, I must have seemed hideously ungracious. In truth, I was just lonely and more than a little lost; longing for my mother's love and unable to express it.

My father collected me from school one afternoon near the end of term. It was horribly humid that day, and I was cross even before I got in the car, annoyed to be missing both my running meet and Madonna on *Top of the Pops*. Then Alison Jackson, standing by the railings with her miniskirted cronies and their Slush Puppies, started to chant 'Daddy's girl' with blue-tinged lips as I clambered into the Granada. I felt my cheeks flaming with shame; I flicked her a V when my father wasn't looking, surprised by my own daring. Alison blew a contemptuous pink bubble in response. I stared ahead. I'd pay for it tomorrow.

We drove out to the home in virtual silence, through the bosky July lanes of Kent, through the tunnels of dappled light falling through the trees; honeysuckle and wild roses peppering the lush hedgerows. The beauty of the afternoon didn't ease our trip at all. My father stopped to let a sturdy young woman on horseback cross into a field; she waved her crop cheerily, the chestnut flanks of her small mare gleaming like my dad's cricket bat when it was oiled. I thought of the fat ponies I used to ride as a small child, my mum leaning over the gate, watching oh so proudly; the two of us drinking Tizer afterwards on the bench beside the paddock.

I thought she'd always be there.

Why wouldn't I?

No one had explained to me how very sick my mother was. Perhaps they hadn't realised. Gar was visiting friends in Cornwall, unaware of how irrefutably our lives were about to collapse – and my father, my poor father, he was so lost himself, now my mother was in this strange place.

Walking into her room, I struggled with the fact that she found it hard to even smile, although she sort of tried – and I, well, I couldn't bear to see the shell she had become. She sat in that wicker chair in the corner like she'd given up, her beautiful red hair limp, stripped of its vibrancy, her body shrivelled. Trapped by her own depression, abandoned by her spirit.

As ever, my dad had brought her a pile of books, a new tape of piano music, the latest school photo of me, self-conscious and rather spotty, my hair carefully pushed back to show my newly pierced ears. She took the picture and held it in her hands without looking at it. She clutched it hard. Dad talked about our forthcoming summer holiday to Brittany; tried to joke with my mother, asking her if she was looking forward to snails and frogs' legs, telling her he'd ordered up the sun especially. At one point she held her hand out to him and he took it gladly. But it wasn't long before her fingers slipped from his grasp again. She was so monosyllabic, kind of curled up and sunken, that in the end he gave up entirely.

'I'll go and get some tea, shall I? I'm parched.' He was too bright, practically backing out the room, his angular frame starting to stoop as he always would from this time on.

As the door swung shut, my mother looked at me properly. I picked at the hem of my school skirt.

'Come here, Maggie, would you?' Her voice was little more than a whisper as she patted the bed next to her, placing my photo carefully on the table. I scuffed my way across the room and sat. She took my hand in her skeletal one.

'Did you see my earrings?' I twisted my head this way and that to show off my gold studs proudly.

'Oh, they're lovely.'

Actually my ears were red and angry, a crust forming round the small studs every night.

'I wanted – I wish I could have taken you,' she said, forlorn.

'S'all right.' I was generous. 'Gar came. And Bel. They do crosses on your ears with felt-tips, did you know? It did hurt.' I spun one round. 'I didn't cry, though.'

'Darling Maggie, you know –' she cleared her throat like it actually hurt her to, 'you do know how much I love you, don't you?'

'S'pose,' I mumbled. I rolled one white sock up; I rolled it down again. I looked at a younger me, at the happy family photos of us being normal. I studied the watercolour Gar had painted for her only daughter of her beloved Pendarlin, trying to bring the light back to her life. I looked anywhere but into my mother's great blue eyes because I couldn't stand to see the pain.

Her grip tightened on my hand. It was the most energy I'd known her to exert for months, but I didn't understand. Freeing myself, I crossed the room to fiddle with the net curtain.

'You've got so tall. You're getting like a willow.'

'I know. Dad says I've got to stop growing cos I'm costing him too much. He has to keep buying me new uniforms.'

I thought my mum looked anxious then. 'Don't worry, Mum. I think he's only joking.'

Although the windows were all open, there was a peculiar calmness here; an enforced silence. An enervated hush. The perfectly shorn lawn was green like the glassy emeralds in my mother's engagement ring. A few croquet hoops were placed at strange angles, but no one played. A bee hummed across the quiet, and, unnerved by his lone noise, hummed off again.

'My Maggie.'

Why didn't she tell me she was saying goodbye? Sometimes still I wake in the middle of the night and I want to scream at her. If only I'd known.

I could have stopped her.

Couldn't I?

Instead, I watched an old lady sitting in a stripy deckchair on the lawn. She seemed quite normal; a grandmotherly type, though not like Gar. But gradually I saw that she muttered to herself, constantly adjusting her straw hat like it hurt her.

'Tell me something, Maggie.' There was desperation in my mother's tone; it made me feel panicked.

'What?'

'Just something. Anything you like.'

My mind darted around like a minnow looking for a way between fat tunas. I wanted to land the right thing at my mum's feet – but I didn't know what that was.

'I've been doing the cooking. I'm learning shepherd's pie. Gar helps sometimes, but mainly I do it all now.' Which wasn't really true; Gar did nearly everything, though I helped a lot. 'Mainly I cook for us now. I'm good at scrambled eggs. I'll cook you some when you come home.'

I didn't say I'd nearly burnt the house down with my first solo effort. I was just trying to make my mother proud; reassuring her that we were coping without her guiding hand. Only, as I've got older, I'm haunted by my own words; fearful she thought I was saying I didn't need her any more.

Because, actually, I was utterly lost without her, floundering

225

around, frantic that she should come home. I loved my dad but he didn't dance around the kitchen with me to silly pop, or play Chopsticks on the piano, or teach me duets; he couldn't plait my hair just right, or cure my tummy-aches with magic hands.

I needed my mother desperately; I just didn't know how to say it.

'I'm so glad you love to cook, my Mag. Just like me.'

One tear crept down my mother's freckled face – and even that tear was dull. My smile froze. Right then, I didn't want to be like her. Her tears embarrassed me; I was thirteen and bewildered.

And God, that haunts me too.

My dad arrived then with a floral tea-tray that looked faintly ridiculous in his large bony hands. 'And how are my two favourite girls in all the world?'

His jovial tone smashed empty on the ridged brown carpet as we stared at him.

'Dad!' I scowled. 'What about Gar? She's your favourite too.'

My mother looked away.

Perhaps she was deciding then.

In the car on the way home, I asked my father, 'Can I go to Bel's when we get home?'

'No,' he snapped, so unlike him, 'you can't. It's too late. It's a school night. You've got homework.'

I sulked ferociously until I realised he hadn't even noticed. Then I put my trainers up on the dashboard and read *Just Seventeen*. He didn't tell me to stop reading that rubbish, like he usually would. He didn't even tell me to put my feet down again.

The next week my father had to cancel the holiday to France.

Somewhere between Reading and London, fog began to drift across the road, hanging in the air like wet icing-sugar. By the time we arrived at the city's outskirts the fog was so thick we'd reached a virtual crawl. Near the Chiswick roundabout, Seb started to put his coat on. My heart sank.

'Can you drop me at Hammersmith tube?' he asked.

So this was it. Another man down the tube – literally, driven off by my family history.

'Sure,' I said brightly, as we slid to a halt at a red light. 'Thanks for a nice weekend.'

He laughed. 'Is that it then?'

I looked at him. 'I don't know. Is it?'

'I wouldn't have thought so, would you?'

I smiled. 'Okay then.'

He regarded me for a moment. 'I don't know what it is about you, Maggie, but you're not at all what I expected.'

'Oh.' The lights turned green. 'I'm not sure that's a compliment.'

'It is, babe, it is.' He swung his bag from the back seat. 'See you, Digby. Look after Maggie for me.'

He kissed me once, hard – and then he was gone, into the traffic, weaving elegantly through the blur of shiny-backed monsters, before disappearing into the tube. I switched the stereo back on and headed home, though I felt like I'd just left my heart in Cornwall yet again.


Monday morning in Borough Market was always quiet after the frenetic weekend, and the street was deserted as I pulled up outside the flat to unload. The cake-shop, its lights normally a welcoming beacon, was still shuttered; the fog meant I couldn't see much further than the next lamppost. Digby had shot off the minute I'd opened the car door and I whistled for him now, a shiver coursing down my spine. I wanted to get inside quickly.

I dug around in my bag for the keys, fumbling as I hurried, annoying myself with my clumsiness. I put my overnight bag and the carrier of groceries from Pendarlin by the front door, which still smelled of fresh paint. And it wasn't double-locked. I frowned. I was quite sure I'd left it locked – but maybe in my hurry to collect Bel on Friday...

The rank and fetid air hit me hard as soon as I pushed the door open. I whistled for the bloody dog again, but still he didn't come. I took a deep breath and steeled myself against the foul smell, propped the street door open with my bags and slowly crept up the stairs.

At the top of the stairs I froze, my hand already sweating where I clutched the metal banister. I stared and stared, but I couldn't quite absorb any of it.

'Oh my God.' My voice was a cracked and empty husk.

What lay before me was utter carnage – a car crash, a train-wreck of a living room. The flat destroyed, my world turned upside-down: ransacked by someone who could only mean me harm. Rubbish from the bin lay strewn across the kitchen floor, rotting vegetables, old teabags, meat-bones – worse. Alex's painting of dawn over Waterloo Bridge was slashed to pieces above the fireplace; my framed photos smashed. Every book and CD had been pulled from the shelves and flung across the room; clothes were scattered all down the flight of stairs from the bedroom. I looked closer. No, not my clothes – my under-wear.

And across the back wall, once a stark and brilliant white, were huge words: scrawled in that red paint again, looking like the letters had just bled:

I'M GETTING CLOSER

What was that smell? I could taste it in my mouth now, hot and meaty. I gagged as it pervaded every pore.

And then I heard a noise. My top lip went all clammy. 'Digby?' I whispered, but I couldn't see him. There was a creak on the stair, followed by a footstep. My heart began to gallop faster.

What the hell did I do now? I looked around desperately; the bread knife was on the floor about five feet away. I made a lunge for it just as I heard another footstep.

Alex appeared on the stairs below me.

'What the fuck's happened here?' He looked horrified. 'And what the hell is this?'

In his hand he held an envelope, from which tumbled a stream of long black curls.

I burst into tears.

# Chapter Twenty-Seven

Once DI Fox had established that neither the roof-terrace nor the front door had been forced in any way, he wanted to know who had keys to the flat.

'Only me and my dad. Oh, and Alex's estate agent.' I dried my tears fiercely and tried to drink the coffee Alex had brought me from the café across the road. I wanted to get the hell out of the flat as soon as possible, but I had to wait for Fox to finish his questions.

'Estate agent?' Fox crooked a sandy eyebrow.

'It's on the market with Costana and Mortimer.' Alex looked shifty, towering over the smaller man. 'But actually – the estate agent's lost his keys, apparently. That's why I called Maggie the other day.'

'Lost them?' The policeman frowned. 'That's not very professional, is it?'

'Nothing to do with me, mate,' Alex snapped.

'I didn't say it was, sir,' Fox replied mildly.

'He said they were in the office somewhere; they'd probably got mixed up with another set.'

'So you don't have keys any more yourself?'

'No. I gave my last set back to Maggie, the others to Costana.'

'Right. And what about you, Maggie?'

'I've got a set, so has my dad. And there's the set Alex gave me back. They're in the bowl on the side.'

But they weren't. The bowl my mother had made so many years ago was in tiny pieces, the phone ripped out of its socket, wires protruding like plastic guts. I felt like I'd been violated. I sipped my coffee miserably; it tasted as bitter and foul as I felt. 'Can I go now? I'd really like to get out of here.'

DI Fox smiled patiently. 'Yes, of course.'

'I'll help you clean up.' Sifting through the debris, Alex picked up a pair of frilly pink knickers he'd once much admired. The crotch had been completely ripped out. 'Nice.'

'Oh God.' I stared at the flimsy bit of silk. 'This is doing my head in.'

'Can you leave everything alone, sir, please,' Fox's blonde Detective Sergeant interjected, 'until the SOCOs have done their stuff.'

'The SOCOs.' Alex dropped the knickers back on the ground. 'Right. Sorry.'

'Have you seen the dog?' I asked Alex.

'No. Not since I got here.'

'Can you go and call him?' I said urgently, peering out of the window onto the street below.

Alex shrugged. 'Sure.'

'Just one minute, sir,' Fox apprehended him. 'I just wondered – you and Ms Warren are no longer an item, are you?'

'No, we are no longer "an item".' Rudely, Alex mimicked Fox's cockney accent. Fox drew himself up to his full height, which was still way below Alex.

'So what were you doing here this morning?' the policeman asked him in a neutral tone.

'I'd come to get the keys. For the estate agent. And to pick up the rest of my stuff.'

'And what stuff might that be?' Fox glanced round.

And it was only then that I noticed the two boxes of Alex's junk which I'd packed up in misery the other night were still by the door.

'There,' I mumbled, pointing at the still sealed and apparently untouched cardboard cartons, Alex's name scrawled on both.

Our eyes were all drawn to the spot.

'That's funny.' Fox knelt down by the boxes and ran a finger over the masking tape that held them shut. 'No one's had a go at these, sir. Though everything else has been turned right over. How very fortunate for you.'

'What exactly are you insinuating?' Alex's voice dropped dangerously low.

'Nothing at all, sir.' Fox stood again, reaching for his mobile phone from the pocket of a mac that had seen better days. 'Not yet, anyway.' He turned away as his call connected.

My heart began to hammer again. 'Alex, where the hell is Digby?'

'He's probably scavenging outside. You know Digby.' I imagined that Alex's face softened as he looked at me. 'Come on, Mag. We'll go and find him – and then I'll give you a lift to work, if you like.'

I ran down the stairs. 'I'm not going to bloody work. I just need to find the dog.'

Outside, the fog was still wafting down the street like a grand dame on her way to a ball. There was no sign of the dog anywhere, although my bags were still leaning against the wall.

'Digby,' I called, 'Digby. Here, boy.' My voice was sharp and cracked. 'Oh God, Digby, where the hell are you?'

Mrs Forlani appeared through the fog like a ghastly apparition, in a pink dressing-gown and fluffy slippers, her dark hair wild. She never got dressed before three.

'*Bellissima*, are you all right?' She eyed the police car with its top light still flashing through the strings of fog as if it might leap forward and bite her. 'I 'ave been so worried about you.'

'That's nice. I'm fine.' I was gabbling. 'Or, no, I'm not fine actually. Have you seen my dog?' I couldn't stop. 'I can't find him. Someone's broken into the flat. They cut up my underwear. It's all a terrible mess.'

'Oh my God.' Mrs Forlani clapped her hands to her face in horror. 'I say to Matteo, I told you how I was so worried on the telephone the other night. *La giovinastra* – how do they call them now in the news here – that hoodie waiting around your door. It give me the creep.'

'Creeps,' I corrected absently, vaguely recalling her message. 'Have you seen the dog, though?'

'She was very strange.'

'Who was?'

'Her. *La ragazza* I talk about. This stranger.'

'He,' I corrected again, walking towards the corner to call Digby. 'You said it was a "he".'

There was a massive crash and a yelp. I nearly jumped out of my skin as Digby shot out of a pile of butcher's crates. 'Oh, thank God.' Falling to my knees, I grabbed him before he could run off again, burying my face in his back. 'You silly boy. You really scared me.'

Mrs Forlani was shaking her head fervently at me, her bulgy eyes all wild and starey. 'No, no, Maggie. It was not an 'e outside your flat. *Mio Dio, ma perche' questi inglesi non mi capiscono mai?*'

Or perhaps it was me that was mad. That was more likely, in fact.

'*Ho detto una donna, intendevo una donna! Buon Dio!*' The fluid Italian washed over me as I looked up vacantly from the pavement. 'Most definitely not a man,' Mrs Forlani finished crossly, wrapping her dressing-gown tighter around her drooping bosom.

'Get the hell up, Maggie.' Alex appeared above me. 'It's wet down there, for God's sake.' He tried to help me up but I felt all crumpled, like a rag-doll, quite happy to be on the floor, next to the dog's sinewy warmth. I would just lie on the pavement for a while and let all this hideous strangeness go on above me. Without me. But Alex leaned down and grabbed my hand, pulled me to my feet.

'Ouch,' I complained. He forced me to stand; otherwise I think I might have lain down again. Mrs Forlani had recommenced her babbling. 'Sorry, but you've lost me.' I looked at her.

'It was most definitely *una ragazza* that I saw. A girl who was trying to enter your flat.'

And as I stood there gaping at her, trying to comprehend it all, Stefano Costana rounded the corner in a cheap shiny blue suit, his belly straining against his pink shirt.

'Morning all! Sorry if we're late,' he said cheerfully. A curl of dark hair poked through the gaping buttons above his waistband. I looked at Alex; Alex looked rather ashen. My mouth dropped open further. Pitter-pattering behind Costana, her face framed perfectly by her black fur hood, was my worst nightmare.

And as she smiled winningly at us, her hood fell back, and I heard my own sharp intake of breath echo in my ears. It was Fay standing before me, but with newly short hair, cut just like mine and dyed the same shade of red.

# Chapter Twenty-Eight

'What the hell is she doing here?' I asked no one in particular. And as no one answered, I asked Fay herself. 'What the hell are you doing here?'

She smiled beatifically. 'I've come to see your flat.'

'My flat,' I repeated numbly. 'Why?'

'I've heard it's lovely.'

'It's not lovely any more. It's a tip. Literally.'

'I don't understand.' She frowned very slightly. 'It looks very nice on the details. It is for sale, isn't it?'

'You're not –' I stared at her, 'you're not thinking of buying it, are you? Not seriously?'

Stefano Costana looked a little uncomfortable. 'Sorry – do you two know each other?'

'Oh yes, we're old friends, aren't we, Maggie?' said Fay, at exactly the same moment as I replied, 'No, not really.'

She gazed up at me. 'Do you like my hair, Maggie? I really hope so. I've brought you the rest of my curls.' She tried to hand me an envelope. 'I posted some the other night when I called round, but now I think it's best if you have them all.'

'Why would I want them?' I refused to take the package.

'It's like a kind of bond. You know, like blood sisters at school. I think the Red Indians used to do it as a sign of friendship.'

'Well, the Red Indians can have them then.'

'It is a bit chilly, though, I must say, round the old ears.' To my huge relief, she pulled her hood back up.

'Aren't you going to introduce me to your twin?' Alex muttered, thrusting his hands deep in his pockets. I felt like someone was kneeling on my chest.

'I don't think we've met. Fay Carter. Maggie is my saviour.' Fay offered her hand to Alex now. She didn't quite flutter her eyelashes, but . . . He was so tall and she was so tiny, so doll-like, they looked incongruous next to one another. I had a sudden vision of Alex scooping her up and sticking her in his pocket.

'Did you know about this?' I muttered, stupefied.

'What, about freako here? Stefano told me he had someone seriously interested in the flat, that's all.'

'It's such a fabulous area, isn't it? Borough Market. Ever since Maggie told me all about it, I've wanted to explore,' Fay breezed.

All about it? I felt my brow knit anxiously. I hardly remembered mentioning the flat to her. I gazed at Fay. Droplets of fog lingered pearly on her fur-hood, her eyes so enormous with innocent enthusiasm that I could practically see the male hearts around me melting.

'Stefano says it's very up-and-coming. And when I heard it was your flat, Maggie, I was just so excited. It's like it was meant to be.'

'But *how* did you hear it was my flat?' I shook my head slowly. 'I don't understand. How could you possibly know?'

'Stefano must have told me, mustn't he?' Fay patted the estate agent's portly arm with a dainty little hand. 'After all, it's not every day you get a famous TV producer's flat to sell, is it, Stef?'

'That's right.' He smiled fondly down at her, his goatee practically quivering with testosterone.

'Oh, for God's sake,' I muttered. I glanced at Alex to see if she was having a similar effect on him, but he was savaging his nails, almost scowling, staring over at the florist as she put another bucket of greenery out on the pavement.

DI Fox suddenly materialised at the front door, his pretty DS close behind him. 'Morning,' he said coolly. 'DI Fox. And you are?'

'I'm Stefano from Costana and Mortimer, and this, this is Fay. She's a prospective buyer.'

Fay stuck out that willing hand again. 'Hi.' Then she screwed up her little nose in thought. 'You look kind of familiar, DI Fox.'

'Oh yeah?' He considered her briefly.

'I know.' She clapped a hand to her heart. 'From the TV show: *I Overcame a Trauma*.'

I groaned quietly.

'I 'spect that's it. Weren't my finest hour, it must be said.' Did DI Fox wink at me then? The DS's radio crackled loudly and she stepped away.

'Anyway, in the circumstances, I'm afraid you can't go in,' Fox said. 'This is currently a crime scene, while we wait for finger-prints to be taken. I'll have to ask you to come back.'

'A crime scene?' Costana shifted from brogue to shiny brogue, scowling slightly.

'There's been a break-in,' Fox explained. The DS was now signalling to an unmarked car pulling up through the dispersing fog.

'A break-in? I see.' Impatiently Costana tapped a glossy set of details for the flat against his thigh. 'It's not exactly a great selling point, is it?' He glared at me and then smiled apologetically at Fay.

'So sorry about that,' I muttered.

'Are you Maggie's boyfriend? You're lovely and tall, aren't you?' Fay was smiling up at Alex. 'I thought you were single, Maggie, you naughty girl.'

I bit down so hard on my lip that I tasted blood.

'Ex,' Alex said wearily. 'Ex-boyfriend.'

Fay twinkled knowingly. 'Aha.'

'Excuse me,' I said faintly, 'but I'm not feeling all that

237

wonderful.' If I didn't leave immediately, it might just become a murder scene. I gathered up my various bags. Perhaps it was the fog; perhaps it was just sheer desperation to get away from Fay, but somehow I went flying as I stepped off the pavement in search of peace.

I whacked my head on the kerb as I fell, and my mobile went straight down the gutter. There was a big hullabaloo, I remembered afterwards, with potatoes and Cornish Yarg and little tomatoes rolling all over the road, and then someone phoned my father and asked him to collect me as I sat with my head between my knees for a while. The DS gave me the once-over but nothing was really damaged apart from my pride.

'Get some ice on that when you get home,' she advised, and gave me a brief rundown of the symptoms of concussion while I looked mournfully up at the flat and wished that I actually had a home these days.

Fay picked up the tomatoes. She returned my collection of bags to me, and then eventually she and Costana dissolved into the chilly day, although Fay wanted to stay, I could tell even in my dazed state.

'Please go now, Fay,' I said, and she tried and failed not to look put out. I heard Alex assuring her he'd take good care of me. Fox patted my hand and said he'd talk to me later.

Then Alex practically carried me to the pub on the corner and bought me a double whisky and, after I pleaded, cigarettes from the machine. He ordered fruit juice for himself. The landlord greeted Alex like a long-lost friend, which he was, I supposed sadly. Sitting in the corner booth, I hugged Digby to me. My teeth kept chattering though it was warm and fuggy in the pub.

'What's going on, Mag?' Alex asked, eyeing my drink.

'You tell me.' I lit a cigarette. 'Can you get me another whisky please?'

'You haven't finished that one yet.' He frowned. 'So why weren't you at work?'

'Why weren't you?'

'I'm meant to be getting on a plane back to Glasgow in about', he checked his watch, 'an hour.'

'You'd better go then.'

'Yes, I better had.' But he showed no sign of moving. 'And you?'

'I'm having a crisis,' I said, and drained my glass. 'Another one. *Please* get me that drink now.'

So he did. And another orange for himself – apparently. I was so suspicious I even tasted it.

'What kind of crisis?' he asked, ignoring the insult, pushing my whisky towards me.

'An everything crisis,' I said mournfully.

'Right. One of those.'

I stared at the wall opposite, at the little etching of a knife-grinder on London Bridge serving a bonneted lady. 'My life's falling apart, Alex.'

He sighed deeply. 'It's not, Maggie, honestly. It just – it probably just seems a bit like that.'

'Someone's out to get me and I'm really scared. Sometimes I think I might be –'

'What?'

I couldn't bear to say it. *Turning out like my mother.* I shook my head. 'And I don't trust any of you –'

'Thanks very much.'

'It's a strange way to live, isn't it?' The world seemed to be retreating. Or perhaps it was due to the whisky. 'And I wish that bloody girl would get off my case.'

'Which girl? The redhead?'

'She's not a bloody redhead. She's a nutter.'

'I thought she was a friend.'

'Hardly.'

He chewed his thumbnail. 'She's very –'

'Don't say it, please.' I held up a hand. 'She's very pretty. The kind of girl you just want to take care of.'

'Yeah, she's pretty,' he grinned. 'She looks a bit like you actually.'

I groaned.

'But I was going to say – odd. Kind of – spaced out. She looks like she's – I don't know. Almost nervous of you.'

'Nervous? Of me?' I was incredulous.

'Like – in awe. Like you might turn round and bite her.'

'You're making it up.'

'If you say so,' he shrugged. 'So why else are you having this crisis?'

'I want to leave Double-decker, that's the main thing. I've remembered that I hate it.'

'Well, do it then. You know what I think.'

'Yes, I do know, thanks.' I took a big slug of my drink. The whisky fumes burnt the lining of my nose. 'But it's not that easy.'

'Why not?'

'Well, what else would I do?' I looked at him. I took a deep breath. 'And also – it's Charlie.'

'What about him?'

'He won't *let* me go.'

Alex's face closed down. 'Fuck Charlie.'

'I'd really rather not.' I swirled my whisky round the glass. It was very golden under the ceiling light. I wasn't sure I even liked whisky, but I seemed to be quite enjoying it now. 'Although he did try it on with me the other night, I think.'

'For Christ's sake.' Alex banged his own glass back on the table. 'Just tell him where to go, Maggie, why don't you?'

'I can't,' I mumbled. 'He's kind of threatening me.'

'With what?'

I looked at him very directly. 'I imagine you know perfectly well what with, Alex.' I couldn't pretend I didn't remember any more. The early-morning nightmares had become reality as my brain finally filled in the gaps. Relieved as I was to have not lost my memory for all time, the images of the night that precipitated my downfall were so unpleasant I'd rather not have recalled them at all.

Alex shifted slightly in his seat, gnawing his thumbnail in that oh-so-familiar gesture. 'Because of –'

'Because of the summer, yes.'

Alex looked away like the memory actually hurt him. In the corner by the fruit machine, two stallholders were arguing about the most lucrative kind of tourist. The taller one had wiry hair that looked like it had been neatly folded on top of his head.

'And what's Charlie going to do about it?' Alex asked grimly. His eyes were slanted half-shut against the overhead light.

'He's angry. He says I let him down, and he says he'll make sure I don't work again. He'll ruin my reputation.' I picked at a cardboard beermat. 'Whatever reputation that might be. I don't think it's a very good one any more, do you?'

'For fuck's sake, Maggie.' Alex stood up too quickly and whacked his forehead on the lampshade. 'The bloke's a fucking bully.'

'Sit down, Alex. He might well call you the same, you know.'

'He might, I suppose,' Alex muttered, rubbing his sore head almost violently. 'Why the hell didn't you tell me about this? I could talk to him –'

'It's nothing to do with you any more, Al. I'm not your problem now, you know that.'

He looked down at me and suddenly I felt like I was on a keeling ship, as if I was pitching up and down; as if I needed to grab for Alex. If I grabbed on, perhaps I could haul myself back up to safety.

Alex sat down beside me now. Digby grinned up at him happily.

'You'll always be my problem, Mag,' he said quietly, fondling the dog's silky ears with his long, nicked fingers.

'Why's that then?' I peeled the whole colourful top layer off the beermat.

'Because,' he rubbed his craggy face tiredly. 'Because you're my best friend.'

'Really?' I stared at my drink. My heart felt like it was somersaulting across that deck. 'Well, you're not a very good best friend, Alex.' I looked at him again. 'In fact, you're an extremely bad friend. You've practically cost me my career.'

And he looked at me and I looked back, and suddenly it was like we were connected again, just like we used to be. It was a strange sensation, and I tried to remind myself of all the black days, the violent rampages, the terrible despair, but –

Alex took my hand in his; the hard skin on his fingertips just as I remembered, the blister from where he held his pencil too tight when he drew, the scars and scratches from where he simply didn't care enough. 'Cold as ever,' he muttered, turning my palm up. I felt most peculiar, like I was about to lose myself.

And then my dad walked in.

'Maggie, love!' His eyes found me, his long face all consternation, his anorak crackling damp from the fog and drizzle that had started outside. He suddenly looked old, and I felt a huge rush of guilt over all the stress and worry I kept putting my poor father through.

Alex stood up. 'Hi, Bill.' He shook my dad's hand.

'Alex. Thanks for looking after her.'

I snorted. 'I'm not a child, you know.' But the way they both looked at me then made me doubt my own words.

'Can I get you a drink?' Alex asked my father, almost hopefully.

'No, better not, thanks all the same. I'd like to get you home, Maggie. I'm double-parked outside.' He patted Alex's shoulder absently. 'Another time, old chap. I'll be in the car, Mag.'

My father returned to his car while Alex went to the loo and I finished up my drink. The stallholder with the folded hair was ranting now. 'You can't trust those middle-class prats,' he informed his milder companion ferociously, wiping a beer-foam moustache away, 'they always buy one poxy mackerel after you've just priced up lobster.'

Some middle-class prats soaking up the local atmosphere over half-pints of cider looked around rather nervously. The other man conceded.

'I suppose so, though they spend more than the bloody Japs, thank God, and they don't bleeding photograph you all the time. Got fifty pence for the machine, Fred?' He slotted the money in, followed swiftly by the clank of winning coins.

I finished my own drink and picked up my bag. The handle was tangled round Alex's portfolio; I shook the bag to release it until the case fell open on the faded velvet seat. Some glossy photos of an apartment complex in Chicago slid out, a batch of mathematical-type drawings that looked like lots of black lines to me with Alex's little squiggles everywhere. A sketch, upside-down, that I peered at; that I thought for a funny moment might actually be me. And then, as I heard a rattle, another clank, Alex was behind me, pulling the portfolio roughly out of my hand, snatching up that sketch.

'Ow! That hurt.'

It was too late, though, the set of keys tumbled out onto the table.

Keys that Alex had just told DI Fox he didn't have in his possession any more; keys to my violated flat. Alex swiped them up as I stared at him, and then I grabbed Digby's lead and ran.

'You shouldn't interfere with what's not yours,' Alex snarled behind me, and Digby barked in confusion, but I tugged him on.

My father's car was waiting outside the shut-up fishmonger's. I jumped in the passenger seat, and Digby, highly excited by all the running, flung himself onto my knee. 'Can you just drive, Dad?'

He frowned, adjusting his mirror; he could see Alex standing in the doorway.

'Dad, go – please!' I implored. 'I'll explain later.'

'Maggie, really, the poor boy is –'

'Dad!' I shouted, and my bewildered father, shaking his head, pulled off.

'I can't keep up with you, Maggie. You're starting to seriously worry me, you know.' He indicated to turn left onto the main road. 'We don't want to head down this path again, do we?'

I watched, utterly miserable, as Alex's tall frame dwindled, as we picked up pace; and then we turned the corner towards London Bridge – and he was gone.

'I'm sorry, Dad,' I muttered. 'I don't mean to worry you, honestly. I'm fine.'

And it was only later I realised I'd left the shopping and my overnight bag under the pub table.

# Chapter Twenty-Nine

'Bel's been trying to ring you from Thailand,' Sally said, plonking a steaming cappuccino in front of me early the next morning. 'She says your mobile number's dead. It's thirty-eight degrees in Bangkok apparently, the jammy cow!'

'My phone went down the drain,' I said flatly, glancing at the guest-list for the *Dumped* show tomorrow that lay on my office desk, my stomach churning unpleasantly at the very thought of the travesty that would ensue. 'Literally.'

'Ah, poor phone,' Sally said. Then she looked at me properly. 'Goodness, Maggie, are you all right? You look bloody awful. What's happened to your head?'

Whichever way I'd tried to rearrange my short mop, it just wouldn't cover the by-now aubergine-coloured bruise resplendent on my forehead.

'That looks really painful.' Sally peered at it. 'Perhaps you should go home.'

'I can't,' I muttered, 'home's out of bounds for now.'

'What? Why?' she frowned.

'I've had a break-in. I'm back in Greenwich, at my dad's.'

'Oh God, Maggie, I'm sorry. What did they take? You didn't disturb them, did you?'

Charlie sauntered in, his grey hair looking particularly bouffant today. 'Nice to see you found the time to drop in, Ms Warren.'

I smiled feebly. 'Sorry.'

He was about to lay into me when he looked at me properly. 'What the hell's happened to your head?'

'I fell. Can you get someone to sort me out a work mobile, please, Sal?' I chucked the *Dumped* list back at her. 'This all looks fine.'

'Really?' She wrinkled her snub nose at me. 'I thought you might be worried that Kevin bloke is a bit old hat.'

I'm absolutely beyond caring, I nearly said. I managed to restrain myself in time. 'Why?'

'He's done *Trisha* and *Jeremy Kyle*. Oh, and the orange man.'

'Lucky old Kevin,' Charlie said dryly. 'Let me see.' He held out a manicured hand for the guest-list.

Sally and I exchanged glances. Charlie never looked at lists – it ballsed things up every time he got involved.

'On second thoughts, Sal, I'll recheck it now.'

'You get on now, Sally dear. Go and whip up some enthusiasm from young Blake,' Charlie said silkily as she passed me back the list. He pulled up a trouser leg creased sharp enough to cut yourself on and settled on the edge of my desk. Sally backed out nervously, her chest flushed with anxiety.

'Sorry,' she mouthed at me.

As the door shut, I pretended very hard that I was reading the list, although the words kept swimming around like little black fish.

'I get the feeling, Maggie darling, you've been avoiding me.'

'Don't be silly.' I gave him a wan smile.

Charlie examined those perfect nails. 'Not thinking of flying the coop, are we? A little bird told me you've been asking around.'

My mouth went dry. 'Asking for what?'

'*Dispatches*, no less. Very grown-up. Not really your thing, I would have said.'

How could he possibly know?

'Could you really hack it, though, with your history? That's what you need to ask yourself. Especially when you know I'd

246

miss you, don't you?' Charlie placed his forefinger under my chin and forced me to meet his eye. 'Let me take you out to lunch and explain exactly how much.'

'I've got so much to catch up with,' I mumbled, my smile frozen now. 'Another time would be great.'

'Leave it, darling. It can wait. I'll get Monica to book a table at Le Caprice.' Charlie brushed one finger along my forehead, grazing my bruise so I gasped in pain. Then he tucked my hair behind my ear as if the tender gesture had been his sole intention.

'I can't, Charlie. The girls need me here today.'

Our eyes locked for a moment until Charlie stood. He made a big show of brushing his trousers down, retying his Ralph Lauren jumper round his shoulders as he battled to control his temper. He so hated being told no. Strolling to the door, Charlie turned with his fingers on the handle.

'Remind me – what exactly's been wrong with you *this* time?'

I refused to let him rile me. 'I just had a bit of a bug,' I said mildly.

'Oh, a bug! A bug like in the summer?'

I gazed at him calmly. 'No, not like in the summer, Charlie. Thanks for asking, though.'

'Right.' Charlie plucked the door open. 'Well, have your bloody bugs on your own time, please.' He slammed the door behind him.

After I'd rung Seb and left him a message with my new mobile number, I sat and stared at the painting of Pendarlin on the wall for what seemed like hours. I'd spent the whole sleepless night at my father's debating whether to shop Alex to the police. Every day, memories of the last fight, of his actions before the crash, became clearer . . . I didn't know how long I could fight them any more.

At lunchtime I declined an offer to go to the pub with the

girls, but after half an hour of reworking Renee's sickly script listing all the ridiculous reasons for dumping your unsuspecting partner on live television, I began to eye the new bottle of Smirnoff on the filing cabinet. It was strictly for emergencies – but if this wasn't one, I didn't know what was.

As I unscrewed the top, a panicked-sounding Sally rang. 'I think you'd better get over here now,' she stammered. 'We're in the Windmill.'

The lifts were full of the lunchtime news team knocking off, so I sprinted down the fire-exit stairs, past the smokers, across the tiny park to the busy Cut, where I found Donna and Joseph Blake standing on the pavement outside the pub. He was practically crying as she berated him, waggling a finger at him, her other hand on her hip. Sally was trying valiantly to stop the row like the jolly prefect she was, and failing miserably.

'But Maggie knew,' I could hear Joseph imploring. 'Maggie said it was okay.'

'Yeah, well, I ain't no soft-touch-Maggie,' Donna spat at him as I panted up beside them, my foot aching now. 'She's out of control herself these days. And it weren't Maggie's bleeding book in the first place, was it?' Then she realised it was me standing beside her.

'Oh,' she finished feebly.

'What's going on?' I eyed the two of them like naughty children.

'She found out.' A red-faced Joseph was wavering between anger and tears. 'You said it would be okay.'

'I did not say that, Joseph, and you know it.'

'You knew it was him, man, and you never told me,' Donna accused me.

'I haven't really seen you since I found out,' I told her quietly, holding out a placating hand to calm her. I'd forgotten all about her book. 'That's enough, everyone.' The rest of the girls were gathering in a small intrigued circle around us. 'Get back to the

248

office please.' I flapped my hands at them like a flock of geese. Reluctantly they began to move off.

'But they should know too,' Donna said sullenly. 'It's their right.'

'Donna!' Sally's tone was sharp. 'Come on, you lot. Feeding time's over.' She herded them across the road like a sheepdog would.

I turned back to the stand-off. 'I wanted to talk to you in private about this, Donna.'

I understood why she was upset – fiercely ambitious and competitive, she'd worked bloody hard to get this far. She'd had a tough life and she needed to succeed, just like I had once, when I'd sought something to fill the gaps. But shouting in the street was one step too far.

'Why? Why can't we get it all out in public?' she jeered. 'Or should we just go and have a *drink*, Maggie, and chat about it nicely?'

'Donna –'

'Just sack me, Maggie, seriously,' Joseph Blake interrupted. 'I don't care. I want to leave anyway. I hate the bloody lot of you.' He *was* crying now, tears streaming down his plump soft cheeks, his blond quiff descending as he sobbed.

Donna gazed at him, transfixed with horror as the workmen on the scaffolding above started to hoot and jeer.

'Shut up,' I snarled at them, but they just jeered some more.

'You've never made me welcome,' Joseph sobbed, 'none of you – except Maggie, and you're a fucking loser, Maggie, anyway.'

'Charming.' I felt like he'd just slapped me in the face. 'Why's that then?'

'Why do you pretend all the time? I know you must think about Sam. About how you messed up.' He looked demented now.

My face went rigid; I took a deep breath. 'I don't want to talk about Sam. Not to you. Not to anyone here.'

'You're seriously lucky my uncle didn't find out.'

'Come on, man.' Donna held out her hand now, the crystals on her nails glinting. She took a step towards Joseph. 'Calm down, yeah? Let's go inside. We can work it out, I'm sure.'

'Fuck off,' he whispered vehemently, his voice barely audible above the traffic. 'Seriously – fuck off. I don't need any of you. You're all fucking evil. Television's fucking evil. I should have listened to my parents in the first place.'

'Why, what did your parents say?' Donna asked, fascinated.

'They said that the reason my uncle's such a foul man is cos television's corrupted his soul.'

'I suppose Philip Lyons is a bit of a devil,' Donna grinned. 'But a corrupted soul's a bit harsh. Have your parents got God or something?'

'Don't mock my parents,' Joseph hissed. 'Seriously, don't.' For a second I thought he might actually hit Donna, but he didn't. He just balled his fists, and then turned on his heel.

'Steady on, mate.' A burly Australian tourist moved quickly out of Blake's path as the boy started to run with an odd lumbering gait. 'Where's the fire?'

My eyes met Donna's; she looked deeply embarrassed. 'I'm sorry,' she said, a tinge of defiance still in her tone. 'I wouldn't have said anything now if I'd thought – I mean, I didn't realise he'd take it quite so badly.'

'No,' I stared after him, 'I didn't either.'

# Chapter Thirty

Seb had been appalled when I'd told him what had happened at the flat. When I got back to my desk, wondering whether I should have gone after Joseph, there was a message on my answerphone from him, leaving me an address in Notting Hill. 'I'll see you there at nine, babe,' Seb said. 'Don't be late. I'm going to cheer you up.'

There was also a message from Charlie. 'You missed a treat at Le Caprice. Steak tartare to die for. Now, you realise this show tomorrow's a big one.' His voice dripped with insincerity. He'd obviously regained his equilibrium along with lots of calories and units. 'Don't mess it up, Maggie, will you? Not this time. Just think of that lovely doco.'

I put the phone down hard.

I was about to go into a meeting to prep Renee for tomorrow's programme when the locksmith finally returned my call. He could meet me at the flat in half an hour, he said, but that was his only slot.

I postponed an irritated Renee and jumped in a black cab, trying to ignore the way my palms were sweating at the thought of going home. Outside the flat, I leaned against the wall drinking coffee and eating a brownie, watching the silent skinny locksmith slide the bolts in and out of the door-frame. The reflections in the cake-shop's window played tricks on me as I gazed vacantly into the glass, until I almost thought I saw Alex inside, buying me a hundred chocolate Florentines for our first anniversary, which Digby had unfortunately reached before me, and I actually smiled. Then I shook my head. I made myself think of meeting Seb tonight, and then I realised I had no clean clothes or even underwear to take with me.

'Are you going to be here for a while?' I asked the locksmith, licking my chocolatey fingers. 'I'm just going to pop upstairs.'

He nodded silently. Taking a deep breath, I sidled past him and climbed the stairs. Someone had at least removed the rubbish from the overturned bin and the air had lost that foul and fetid smell from yesterday, but the flat still looked annihilated. Tears sprang to my eyes as I crunched over the pottery shards of my mother's bowl and my fists clenched unconsciously. I needed to be quick.

I glanced down at the locksmith's bald spot, and then, heart hammering, I began to climb up to the top storey. Halfway up, I thought I heard a noise.

'Are you still there?' I called down.

'Yes, mate,' the man answered. 'I'm still here.'

I went into the bathroom and grabbed my sponge-bag and filled it up with what came first to hand. Then I went to the spare room, untouched by the intruder, and pulled down one of the overnight bags Gar had bought me for my twenty-first. I grabbed a couple of jumpers from the chest of drawers, and then I headed to my bedroom and pushed back the door –

I don't think I'd ever screamed properly before. It was an unconscious instinctive reaction and afterwards my throat actually hurt, but right then all I could hear was the blood rushing through my head –

The locksmith ran up the stairs. 'You all right there, love?'

'Yes, yes, I'm fine,' I stuttered eventually. 'Can you just stay there a second please?'

Joseph Blake lay on the bed. Joseph Blake lay on *my* bed,

half-naked, my long green dress from Bel's party wrapped around him, a bottle of vodka empty on the duvet beside him.

He'd opened his eyes when I screamed, and now he giggled as he sat up slowly. From his rubbery movements it was clear he was horribly drunk, his head waggling on his thin neck as he looked at me, his usually protuberant grey eyes rather squinty. He giggled again.

'Hello, Maggie. You know,' he spoke very precisely, his face draining of colour as he did, 'you know, you really shouldn't have ignored me the way you did. It's a sin.'

Then he turned, almost in slow motion, and threw up on my pillow.

I didn't know what to do, so I called the police and an ambulance, who came and removed him. Joseph was so drunk I couldn't talk to him or ask him how he'd got there or why, and for the first time in weeks I found I actually craved the distraction of work. I wanted to get back to the office, to people. I saw an incoherent Joseph escorted into the back of the ambulance with a uniformed WPC for company, and then the locksmith finished up and gave me my new keys and I left, feeling utterly bewildered.

DI Fox called a few hours later.

'We've arrested Blake,' he said bluntly, and my stomach lurched.

'Why?' I asked numbly.

'Maggie,' the policeman sounded tired, 'I thought you'd be pleased we've caught your stalker.'

'My stalker?' The words sounded so strange. Other people got stalked: famous, important people. Not me. 'My stalker,' I repeated.

'Are you all right, mate?' Fox asked.

'I suppose so.' I didn't really know any more. 'How did he get into the flat?'

'He had a set of keys.'

'Keys?' All these bloody keys; I was haunted by them. I saw

them dancing down the hall in ever-multiplying sets – a tech-nicolor *Nightmare of the Keys.*

'He said you gave them to him.'

'Well I didn't.'

'Right.'

'I didn't,' I said indignantly. If one more person said I'd done something I knew I hadn't –

'No, well, I assumed as much, though he's quite a convincing kid. Has he had access to your keys recently? Could he have had his own set cut?'

I thought about the missing Filofax, safely returned; about Donna's book. 'I suppose he must have done.'

'Did you know he has a record for harassment?'

'No.' I was shocked. 'Are you sure?'

'Sure I'm sure. Some kid he went to university with. He wouldn't leave her alone, apparently. She pressed charges but he was lucky; got off with a caution in the end. It's hard to make these bloody cases stick sometimes.'

'Right.' I cleared my throat. 'Did you ask him what – what exactly he was doing in the flat?'

'He says he was waiting to talk to you.'

'Oh God. Poor boy.'

'I must say, Maggie, you're taking this very well.'

'Am I?' I said slowly. 'To be honest, DI Fox –' I paused. I kept seeing my beautiful dress wrapped round Joseph's plump white body, like a butterfly struggling out of its pupae. He really was repellent. 'To be honest, I'm just relieved. Because if you've caught him, if it was him that broke in before and him who's been hounding me, that means – it means it's all over, doesn't it?'

'Yep, I'd say so. At least you might sleep peacefully tonight.'

'I hope so, DI Fox. I really hope so.'

I put the phone down slowly as the truth of the situation began to sink in.

\* \* \*

254

While I'd been having my overdue meeting with Renee, Bel had called again.

'I've got terrible jetlag,' she moaned on my office voicemail. 'I can't sleep at all. I remembered what I wanted to tell you, Mag. Why aren't you answering any of your phones? Ring me on Johnno's mobile in the morning. Your morning. Or is it my morning? Oh God, I don't know. My brain's scrambled – it's so bloody hot. Hannah sends you a hug.'

Everything was squared up for the show tomorrow. I rang Susan to check on my grandmother. My father had been to see her while I was down in Cornwall and had promised me that she was as well as could be expected; Susan assured me now that Gar was doing fine. I'd be out to see her after work tomorrow, I said.

I put the phone down and stared at the picture of Pendarlin again. I thought of Joseph Blake, of how sad and empty his life must have been to do the things he'd done, and I shuddered as I thought of Fox's words about the previous harassment. Poor, friendless boy. How desperate for attention he must have been.

Adrenaline had been pounding my body for so long that I felt truly exhausted, its remains trailing like smoke through my veins: I felt like I'd just run a marathon entirely uphill. I had to give myself some space to breathe now, to make the descent to normality. I'd have to physically force myself to turn a corner and put Alex and poor Joseph behind me.

Printing out the final script, I turned the computer off and got straight into a cab. I gave the street name Seb had left me, not caring if I was unfashionably early, just looking forward to seeing him. Just trying to look forward.

The anonymous address turned out to be a small private hotel called the Portobello Hotel, secreted away in the heart of Notting Hill in a street of grand houses not unlike Malcolm's. The cab driver winked at me as I scrambled out next to two beautifully clipped bushes in giant wooden pots that flanked the entrance.

'Planning a night of passion, then, darling?'

I blushed scarlet. 'Um –'

'You don't wanna be getting up to any of them Johnny Depp tricks here. Cost you a fortune.' He guffawed at his own joke, his belly vibrating as he laughed.

'Pardon?' I was confused.

'This hotel, it's where that Depp bloke bathed in champagne with old whatsername – you know – Cocaine Kate, or so the story goes.'

Lost for words, I over-tipped him and traipsed up the polished stone stairs. Beside the most tasteful Christmas tree I'd ever seen, all silver and turquoise ribbons and tiny flickering candles, a handsome receptionist with puppy-dog eyes welcomed me most graciously.

'Can I take your bags?' he asked smoothly, his eyes sliding over my bruised forehead and away again, and I blushed as I confessed I didn't have a bag. Without batting an eyelid, he led me up to a small room, heated subtropically, the balcony door ajar so that the floor-length white curtains billowed gently in the winter breeze.

'Please ring if you need anything at all.' He indicated the telephone, before shutting the oak door softly behind him.

The room was presided over by the most amazing antique four-poster bed, adorned with fat-cheeked cherubs flying across the painted top, gold trumpets in chubby hands, dimpled naked bottoms twinkling across the azure sky. In awe I slipped my trainers off and climbed two wooden steps to throw myself onto a mattress so enormous I almost bounced. I lay there for a moment feeling like the Princess and the Pea, and contemplated the life of a cherub. Quite nice, apparently, judging by their cheeky grins as they wafted through the fluffy clouds above me.

When I felt myself drifting off I reached for the phone and tried Johnno's mobile, but it was switched off, so I rang room service instead and ordered some sandwiches and a bottle of champagne. Remembering Kate Moss and Johnny Depp I jumped off the bed, padding into a bathroom dwarfed by the most enormous tub. You'd have needed your own vineyard to fill that up with alcohol, so I settled for old-fashioned hot water instead.

The clock said Seb would be at least half an hour. I put some Beethoven on the stereo and sank into the steaming bath, glass of champagne by my side, floating into a doze of exhausted relief.

I came-to thinking I'd heard the bedroom door open. I sat up quickly as the old wooden floorboards creaked beneath the thick plush carpet, the violins soaring through my half-dream. For a moment, I thought someone was creeping slowly across the room, but when I peered nervously through the half-ajar door, I saw only that great bed. Lost in a world of Beethoven and his tortured dark soul, I was obviously imagining things. I'd have to learn not to be so very jumpy. Lowering myself back down into the bubbles, I floated off again.

When the hands went over my eyes, I panicked. Thrashing like a dolphin in a fishing-net, I tried to scream – only this time my voice just wouldn't come.

'Get off!' I panted, trying to get a grip on the hands over my eyes, my hands all slippery with the expensive soap. My flailing arm caught the full glass on the bath's edge, sending it smashing to the marble tiles, champagne fizzing everywhere. 'Please,' I pleaded croakily, 'please, Joseph, please let me go.'

As suddenly as those hands had been placed there, they were gone again. I slipped down, half-submerged, choking, fighting for my breath, and then, gathering my strength, I sprang up in the bath, sending water slopping out of the side, and turned, utterly vulnerable in my nudity, to face –

Seb.

He was grinning at me. He was actually grinning.

'For Christ's sake!' I howled, leaping out of the bath and grabbing a huge white towel to cover myself with. 'What the hell are you doing?'

'I'm really sorry, Maggie.' He held his hands up in supplication. 'I was just being silly.'

'Silly?' I stared at him, nonplussed.

'I didn't mean to scare you, babe.' His smile was fading.

'Well you bloody well did scare me. God, Seb. You terrified me.' My heart was beating so fast I thought it might explode. 'I thought you were trying to drown me.'

'Don't be ridiculous. I was just messing around.'

I pushed past him into the bedroom and sat on the edge of the bed for a minute. My skin was all red from the hot water; I felt dizzy and disoriented from the heat of the room, unsure what had really just happened.

'Maggie,' he followed me, looking contrite, 'I'm sorry, I should have thought. It was just a joke, honestly.'

'Was it? Or were you trying to drown me?' I stared at him. I suddenly felt completely exposed. How well did I really know this man? I looked around for my clothes.

'Drown you?' He began to look annoyed as I slipped my bra on. 'Are you kidding, babe? This isn't bloody Lynda la Plante. Why the hell would I want to do that?'

I stared at him. It did sound ridiculous now he said it. 'Well, all right, not drown me, exactly –'

'Well, what exactly?' His dark eyes were full of something I couldn't read. He looked confused. My anger began to dissipate.

'Maybe – just hurt me then,' I suggested, milder now.

'For Christ's sake! Are you joking?'

'Do you see me laughing?'

'Maggie,' he took a tentative step towards me, 'Maggie, I am sorry, really, but –'

'What?'

'I'm a bit worried about you, actually.'

'Why?'

'You just seem so – jumpy, all the time. And what's happened to your poor head?'

258

'Nothing.' I flinched away from him. 'I'm jumpy for good reason, don't you think?' Locating my trousers, I sat on the edge of the bed to pull them on. But Seb didn't answer, suddenly looking uncertain. It was my turn to laugh, only I didn't find it the least bit funny. 'What, you think I'm imagining all this?'

He still didn't speak.

'Seb!'

He ran his hands through his hair. 'I'm not saying that. But – it's just – a little extreme to think I'm trying to kill you. You must see that, don't you?'

I found my shirt and tried to grin but it was shaky. 'Okay. Maybe you're right. I'm just a bit – wound up at the moment.'

'I can't believe you'd think I want to hurt you,' he said quietly, contemplating me. 'Why would I want to hurt you, babe? God, if anything, I think –' His voice faltered.

'What?' I stopped buttoning my shirt up and looked at him.

'Nothing.' He walked over to the balcony and opened the doors properly. The trees outside were festooned with tiny fairy lights, the sky as black as treacle beyond.

'Tell me what you were going to say,' I prompted quietly.

'If anything, I think you'll be the one to hurt me,' he said, staring out into space, almost talking to himself now.

'Why? I don't understand.' I wrinkled my brow, suddenly chilly in the December breeze.

There was a long pause.

'Because you're on the rebound.'

'I'm not.' I was defensive. 'Of course I'm not.'

'Aren't you? It's just –' at last he turned back to me, 'I think I'm falling in love with you, Maggie.'

'Oh,' I said. I gazed at him, stupefied. 'Are you?'

'Yes. I think I am.'

'Blimey.'

'Yeah,' Seb said, stepping nearer, 'blimey. It wasn't really on the cards, was it?' He reached for my hands and pulled me gently towards him.

'I suppose not,' I mumbled.

'And the trouble is, I think – I think it's beyond my control.'

He put his hands on either side of my face and I didn't flinch this time. He raised my face to meet his and then he bent and kissed me. I felt myself start to relax as his lips met mine. My heart beat faster again, but this time it wasn't with fear. I looked into his eyes and they were so dark, I still wasn't used to such very dark eyes. And as I tried to decipher what lay beneath the surface, Seb ran a hand down my cheek and down my neck and on down, on down . . . He pushed me back onto that enormous bed and ripped the few shirt buttons undone that I'd just done up, and I gasped – but it wasn't a gasp of fright this time. I kept trying to read his face as he stared down at me, as he slid his hands behind my back and undid the bra I'd just done up. He pulled his own T-shirt off impatiently and I dug my hands into his tousled curls and then I put my hands on his bare chest and the pulse there, it felt like it was too fast, as if he was being consumed by something I didn't understand. And I knew that if this was ever going to work, I had to let myself go too.

# Chapter Thirty-One

I slept the sleep of the dead that night. I didn't dream, I didn't stir at all until reception rang around seven, saying they'd been asked to wake me. Seb was already gone, a note on the snowy pillow next to me.

*Morning gorgeous. Didn't want to disturb you – you looked so peaceful sleeping. I've got a big audition first thing. Keep your fingers crossed for me. And sorry about last night: it was really stupid of me. Call you later x*

I lay in bed for a second staring up at Cupid's little face as he grinned down at me knowingly. The thought came to me that last night was the first time I'd had sober sex in a very, very long time; and then, gradually, as sleep finally dissolved, I remembered Seb's murmured confession. The fact he'd said he loved me. Slowly, luxuriously, I stretched, and then, very slowly, I smiled.

When I got to the studios Renee and Charlie were already in the green room gorging themselves on Danish pastries meant for the guests. Renee looked pointedly at her Cartier watch.

'A tardy mind is a lardy mind,' she said tartly, and popped the final corner of a croissant into her ladylike mouth.

'You just made that up, surely, Renee.' I sloshed coffee into a

261

cup. Now they had caught Joseph, I could concentrate on securing my freedom. It had been a long time coming.

'I certainly did not.' She delicately dabbed vividly cerise lips with a starchy napkin. 'Ma used to say it to my da every Friday when he brought home the wage packet.' Her voice dropped into a tragic monotone. 'Before he went and drank it all down at Boyo Dyffd's.'

'Before he came home and beat Ma black and blue, was it?' I added sugar and smiled sweetly at Renee's startled face. 'Before you shouldered every chore, bringing up your thirty-five siblings single-handedly while also going down the mine?'

'My sainted mother was a – a – saint, I'll have you know, Maggie.'

'Renee, with you as a daughter, I don't doubt that for a moment.' I sat so heavily beside her, her own drink slopped out and spotted her pink linen top. 'Whoops! I'm sorry.'

'For Christ's sake!' She glowered at me. 'I'll have to change for the show now.'

'I'm not sure pink's your colour actually, so it's probably a good thing.' I bit into a *pain au chocolat* with gusto. Everything in the room suddenly became absolutely crystalline, as if it had all been washed by super-jets and polished afterwards. I'd had an epiphany; I could almost hear the angels singing.

'Maggie!' Charlie's voice held a warning note. 'Have you been drinking?' he hissed, and I wagged my finger at him.

'Silly boy. At this time of day? Of course not.' I licked the chocolate off my fingers lasciviously. 'Now, shall we get on? Have you been through the guest-list?'

Renee was staring at me like I was something disgusting on her shoe. 'Of course I've been through the bloody list.'

'No need to swear, Renee,' I rebuked her mildly. 'You have got a bit lazy recently.'

Donna rushed into the room. 'We've already got one drop-out and the driver outside Melanie Adams's flat has been ringing for half an hour but there's no answer.'

'Typical,' said Renee, glaring at me as if I'd planned the whole thing. 'This is bloody typical.'

'Renee, we always have no-shows; it's hardly a surprise, is it?' I remembered the days when a missing guest had utterly panicked me; recently I just felt glad that people had the sense not to turn up.

Sally burst through the door, her round face flushed. 'The Scottish lads have gone and done a bloody runner from the hotel.' She stuck her pencil behind her ear. 'I thought they were a bit too good to be true. Willing to dump each other on air but prepared to share a hotel room first.'

'Oh for God's sake, not again. All this bloody free-loading pond-life.' It was Charlie's turn to glare at me now. 'I said we should have done a pre-record.'

'You didn't. You said it wasn't edgy enough, actually.' I cocked my head like an irritating budgerigar. 'You wouldn't want everyone at home to think something was true if it wasn't, eh, Charlie?'

Donna was eyeing me like I was mad. 'So what do you want me to do?' she asked, one hand on hip.

'Wheel in the standby.' I finished my pastry calmly and poured myself another cup of coffee. 'It'll all be fine. Renee's been around so flipping long she could do it standing on her hair extensions. You're an old pro, eh, Renee? In every sense of the word.'

There was a crash of crockery as Renee stood, Sally desperately suppressing a snigger in the corner, Donna's head snapping back and forth as if she were watching a tennis rally at Wimbledon.

'That's *it*, Charlie!' Renee was so scarlet now her face clashed with the stained pink top. 'I'm not doing the show until this – this hussy apologises.'

'If hussy means the marvellous fuck I had last night,' I stirred my coffee, 'you're not *that* far off the mark, Renee. Shame you can't get one.'

'Shut the hell up, Maggie,' Charlie was shouting now, 'for Christ's sake.'

'Yes, shut up!' Renee flounced to the door. 'Shut up – and get one of the girls to sit up front. And get that lovely Joe', Renee always favoured the few male members of staff, 'to my dressing room. Now. He can help me go through the script.'

My high suddenly felt not quite so soaring. 'The lovely Joe's been nicked, actually, Renee.' My veneer cracked just a little.

Renee and Charlie both turned in horror. 'What are you talking about now, you stupid girl?'

'Nicked. As in arrested.'

'What?' Donna asked, aghast. 'Why? What the hell did he do?'

'You know,' I said pensively, standing up, 'there's nothing like the buzz of live TV, is there, folks?'

I strolled out of the green room, letting the door slam behind me. None of them saw my hands tremble as I lit a cigarette on the fire-escape, as I fumbled in my bag for my dad's old hill-walking flask. But, shaking or not, there was plenty more vitriol where that had come from.


Charlie was tapping furiously into his BlackBerry as I re-entered the green room, relieved that Renee had vanished into make-up to be pacified by Kay.

'Are you *trying* to get the sack?' Charlie snapped at me.

'What do you think?' I replied evenly.

Donna burst in. 'I've got her, Charlie. She's in a cab now. I didn't even have to offer her money, she was so keen.'

'Thank God!' Charlie said.

'Who?'

'Your friend Fay Carter,' he muttered.

I groaned. 'Oh for Christ's sake.'

'Well, can you do any better?'

'But who's she going to dump? She's already bloody single.'

He had the good grace to look a little abashed. 'She's going to be our expert.'

'Please tell me you're joking.'

I looked at Donna; at how desperate she was to salvage the programme, the doomed *Dumped* show, and I realised that I really had to do what I should have done months ago. I felt Charlie watching me. 'I'm going to go, Charlie.'

'Donna, go and meet Fay's cab,' he said.

'Okay, boss.' She rushed off.

'Maggie, I need you,' he implored. 'You have to get this off the ground.'

We stared at each other.

'You owe me this much. After everything –'

'I owe you nothing,' I hissed. 'And you damn well know it. There's nothing left to give, anyway.'

Sally appeared with our first guest. We smiled our disingenuous smiles before Charlie grabbed my arm and forced me into the corridor.

'Was that true about Joseph Blake?'

I nodded grimly.

'What exactly has he done?'

'Ow!' I shook him off. 'That hurts. He mounted a one-man campaign of terror against me, that's what.'

'Really?' Charlie frowned at me as I rubbed my arm crossly.

'Yes, really. That break-in, various nasty texts, funeral flowers, missing things, it was all him apparently.'

A spotty young researcher called Cheryl came panting down the hall. 'Maggie, your dad's been on the phone. He says have you got the dog?'

My stomach hit the floor. 'What?'

'He said two things –' She was painstaking in her thoroughness as she tried to remember exactly what she'd been told.

'He said – one,' she ticked it off on her fingers, 'more flowers have arrived for you at his house. And two, he said have you got the dog?'

I stared at her, uncomprehending. Not daring to comprehend.

'Sorry.' Cheryl looked really worried. 'He said you'd understand.'

The show was due on air in twenty-five minutes when I found DI Fox's number and rang him from an empty dressing-room. He sounded uncomfortable.

'Maggie. I was about to ring you actually.'

I felt a sudden tightness in my throat.

'Why?'

'I'm sorry, but we're just about to release Blake.'

I leaned my burning head on the dressing-table.

'Maggie? You still there?'

'Just about,' I muttered.

'I thought you should know. There's just not enough evidence to tie him to the first break-in, I'm afraid. Not a single fingerprint, nothing. Nada.'

'Are you sure? And he has – he's been in jail all night?'

'He's been in custody, yeah. And he swears you gave him the keys to fetch your bag from the flat. We can't charge him.'

'Well, he's lying,' I said, thinking fast. 'Could he have made any phone calls? Like to order more flowers? He couldn't have nicked my – my dog?'

'Your dog?'

'He's –' I felt that constriction in my throat again; I swallowed hard. 'He's vanished. It's probably nothing. He's probably just harassing next door's poodle.' I wished I believed that.

'Right. Well, Blake's been in the cells all night. No access to a phone or a dog.' He was almost brusque. 'Anything else I should know about?'

'I'm not sure.'

'Maggie –'

266

I snapped the phone shut and rushed into the green room to retrieve my coat and bag. Renee stalked past me, head in the air, followed by an extremely obsequious Charlie.

'But you look wonderful in red, my darling,' he was saying. A knowing little smile attempted to cross Renee's Botoxed face. 'You're not going, are you?' he muttered at me.

'Looks that way.'

Fay popped her head round the door. 'Hi all.' She pattered into the room, wrapped in fluffy blue angora like a little Persian kitten. Her new hair made her look even more ravishing than before, like a gorgeous street urchin. I stared at her jumper. I was sure I'd had one like that once.

'Maggie, darling, are you all right? I was so worried yesterday.' She put a hand up to stroke my head and I flinched. 'Oh goodness, I'm sorry. Is it that painful?'

'So what exactly have you come to talk about today on this great show?' I gazed at her, almost fascinated by how much she repelled me now. 'On this fine display of human culture.'

Charlie coughed loudly.

'I'm going to talk about my newfound fame and how splitting up –'

'Dumping,' I corrected.

'*Splitting up*', she smiled at me with pity, 'with my boyfriend was both extremely painful and also fortuitous. I never would have achieved what I have recently if I'd stayed with him. He was too controlling. You want to take a leaf out of my book, Maggie. Don't be answerable to men.'

'Right. Well, good luck.' I backed out of the room.

'Oh, aren't you staying?' Like she cared. Renee was bearing down on her like some hulking great carrion crow as I escaped.

Charlie followed me into the corridor.

'This show can run itself, Charlie. I don't really care any more. I loathe all this so much . . .' I gestured to the falsely smiling celebrities whose pictures lined the walls, at the crocodile of

267

over-excited guests being led into the studio now. 'You promised me a change and I haven't got it, so I'm going.'

'I'll stick to my promise,' Charlie said stiffly. 'Even though what you did in June was unforgivable.' We glared at each other like gun-slingers in the dirt, trying to assess who'd be fast enough to fire that final fatal shot.

'It's funny, Charlie, cos I thought it was exactly the type of thing you'd understand. You're the most immoral man I've ever met. And my only regret is that you think you know the truth about me – and that you abused that so badly.'

Renee swept out into the corridor on her way to the studio. 'Are you going to apologise for being rude?' She glared at me.

'Why would I? You're a rude old bitch yourself.'

Just in time to catch my words, Sally turned the corner with the two key guests. Eyes wide with delighted shock, she didn't know whether to rush the couple through or stay for the fight.

'We work really hard, Renee, and you're nothing but foul most of the time.' I warmed to my subject now. 'As foul as the show. Look at us, paying for some poor sod to have a DNA test. Or encouraging this lot to dump their partners live on air! Fantastic. Let's hope they don't all go and top themselves straight after the show. Don't, will you?' I implored the shocked couple in the corridor.

'Maggie –'

'Get those people into the studio now,' Charlie snarled at Sally.

'I've lost count of how many times my guests have thanked me,' insisted Renee.

'Is that before they have to go home and face real life? It's all a bloody sham, just admit it.'

Charlie laughed.

'Fuck off, Charlie.' I could feel hysteria rising like the tide.

'For God's sake, Charles, the girl's mental,' Renee hissed. 'Get her out of here before she scares the guests.' She gave me a final filthy glare and swept grandly into the studio to tumultuous applause.

There were footsteps behind me now, light little tappings down the corridor – then a gentle hand on my shoulder.

'Maggie, by the way, there's something you should know.'

I turned wearily. 'What's that then, Fay?'

'Do you want to go somewhere private?' she stage-whispered.

I eyed Charlie dispassionately. 'No, not really. I've got no secrets left, it seems.'

'Right.' She looked almost disappointed. 'Well, it's your boyfriend, Alex.'

'My *ex*-boyfriend,' I corrected her. 'What's he done now?'

'Your *ex*-boyfriend.' She wrinkled her creamy little brow slightly as if this was painful for her, her huge eyes never leaving my face. 'It's just – I thought you should know. We spoke on the phone yesterday afternoon.'

I shook my head in bemusement. 'Why?'

She twisted a little pearl ring round her middle finger once. 'Well, he wanted to – we – we met for a drink.'

I started to laugh. 'Perfect,' I said.

# Chapter Thirty-Two

My sole intention was to find Digby and then get the hell out of London. I knew I couldn't take Sebastian with me, the first night of his play was on Friday, and I'd have to miss it now – but I had a desperate urge to speak to him. In the cab on the way to Greenwich I scrabbled around for my phone. Before I found it, it started to ring in the depths of my bag.

'Maggie!' Bel screeched. 'Finally. How are you?'

'Don't ask,' I said. 'Not great.' There was a strange echo on the line that meant my own voice repeated itself three seconds after I spoke. It was eerie. 'Terrible actually (terrible actually).' I shook my head in frustration. 'How's Bangkok?'

'We're not there any more. We're on a little island down on the east coast. It's absolutely beautiful, Maggie. You'd love it. You should see the colour of the sea.'

'I wish I could. How's Han?'

'Bit dazed, I think, but having a good time. Making friends with everyone, getting to grips with a snorkel. The jetlag's a bit full-on though.' There was a pause and I thought I'd lost her. My eyes seemed to be swimming oddly. I blinked hard.

'Bel?'

'Yeah, I'm here. Listen, I remembered what I wanted to tell you when we left. I don't want to upset you, but –' Her voice trailed off.

'Bel?'

'Sorry. It's a really bad connection. The mobiles don't work at all and the island phones are a bit dodgy.'

'So what is it?' To be honest, nothing could get any worse.

'It's just – I thought you should know. Alex has been up to his old tricks.'

'Which ones?'

'I got an email from Anna-Beth. She knows Serena from the fashion circuit. Serena's having serious problems with him now too.'

'I see.' I tried to be droll, though actually I felt almost victorious. 'Poor her.'

'I just wanted you to remember why you left him.' Bel was trying to engage me. 'That it wasn't just you, that Alex has a serious problem. I don't want you to keep blaming yourself, because I know you do. You know what men are like.'

The problem was, I obviously didn't.

Listlessly, I lit a cigarette and stared out at the dreary morning streets of South London. I'd crashed off my adrenaline high; now I just felt tired and sad. I watched a young mother at a bus-stop berating her toddler for taking his coat off, and then cuddling him in remorse when he cried, and I thought about my mother and how desperately I wished she was still here to hug me. I turned my phone over and over in my hand debating whether to ring Seb, but I suddenly felt all shy. I felt like I was losing all the stability in my life, and I despised myself for not being stronger, for not just being on my own when I knew I needed to be, for clutching on to another man when I wasn't really over Alex.

'And next up,' Robert Elms's distinguished voice broke into my thoughts, 'we've got an exclusive interview with Oscar-tipped star and lead of the smash hit that even I enjoyed – *Love All.*'

'Can you turn it up please?' I asked the cabbie urgently.

271

'So stick with me, cos coming up right after a nice bit of funky stuff' – I waited with bated breath – 'we'll be welcoming the exceedingly cool James McAvoy.'

James McAvoy. Not Sebastian Rae. I stared at the driver's bristly neck, at the red rolls of fat as Minnie Riperton began to sing sadly about love. I stared out of the window, but I didn't see anything apart from my own stupidity reflected there. Racking my brain, I tried to think if Sebastian had ever actually said he'd played the lead, but I couldn't recall the details now.

When we pulled up outside my father's, I practically ran up the garden path.

'Is Digby here? Have you found him?'

'Oh dear.' Jenny's anxious shiny face spoke volumes. 'I was really hoping – he's not with you then?' Her perfect hair was ruffled for once. I shook my head miserably.

'Oh dear, oh dear,' she intoned again, talking very fast as I followed her into the kitchen. 'I feel like it's all my fault, though I honestly don't understand how on earth he got out.' A stack of exam booklets looked precarious on the edge of the table; like a paper Tower of Pisa. Jenny pushed them to safety. 'One minute he was here with me while I was marking the mocks, then I answered the door to the flower chap – your bouquet's out there, by the way, it's lovely,' she gestured to the utility room, 'and when I next remembered about poor Digby, he just wasn't here. Your dad's gone out to look for him in the car.'

'Right.' I thought quickly. 'Do you know which way he went?'

'Oh dear, no, I don't. Can I do something? Make you a cup of tea?'

'No, thanks.' I grabbed my car-keys from the sideboard. 'Could you just ring my dad and tell him I'm going back to mine to look for Digby there. Dad should stick to the streets round here. And can you let the local police know, please. In case they've picked him up.'

'The police? Oh dear. Do you really think it's that serious?' Her round face was the epitome of concern.

I nearly screamed in frustration. 'I don't know, Jenny. I wish I did.'

As long as I was looking for Digby I didn't have to think about everything else that was going wrong. But I hit the lunchtime rush and got so snarled up in traffic that my mind began to race through the disasters of the day. I felt increasingly overwhelmed and desperate to get out of London – but I didn't want to leave until I'd found the dog. I was too frightened to think what might have befallen him. I was still too angry to involve Alex; too depressed to call Seb.

'Face it, Margaret Warren.' I looked at my wan reflection in the car mirror, my bruised forehead a splendid mash of colours now. 'Your life's a mess.'

I turned on the radio to hear Danny Baker announce the A2 was blocked entirely by a crash involving a caravan. I'd never get back to mine now. I turned the car around; I'd go back to my dad's and phone Mrs Forlani and ask her to keep a lookout for the dog.

As I drove down my father's road my dad was just hauling his stooped frame out of his car. He looked tired.

'Oh Mag, I'm so sorry,' he said when he saw me, half-opening his arms. I stared at him.

'What?' I croaked. 'Did you – have you found him?'

'No.' He shook his head and my legs went sort of trembly.

'Oh God.' I sat on the garden wall for a second. 'Oh God, I thought you were going to say you'd found him and he was, he was – you know.'

'No, Mag. But –' he dug in his anorak pocket, 'I did find this by the gate.'

Digby's collar, his dog-bone tag that Hannah had given me for a birthday present, with my mobile number on it. I stared at it.

'Oh Dad. I'm not sure . . .' I whispered, 'I'm really not sure I can cope with this.'

My father didn't speak. He put an arm around me and led me home again.

# Chapter Thirty-Three

Desperate for news, I waited for the phone to ring all afternoon. I sat in the warm kitchen drinking endless cups of coffee and watching Jenny cooking a lumpy cauliflower cheese, biting my lip when she didn't sieve the flour or get the butter to the right heat. Eventually I stood silently at the cooker and whisked up a white sauce that I could do in my sleep, and she gave me a quick squeeze. I couldn't even bear to look at the latest bunch of flowers; I asked Jenny to chuck them away and she took one look at my face and didn't argue.

Over dinner we managed to make small talk about the end of term and our plans for Christmas. I didn't tell my father about work and I didn't call Sebastian. After struggling through Jenny's valiant attempt at rice pudding, I shivered outside the back door, staring alternately at my father's perfectly regimented but dying garden and my mobile phone – until I took a deep breath and sent Seb a pretty bald text with lots of question marks at the end. Then I poured myself a big glass of red wine and took it up to wallow in the bath. This time I locked the door.

A while later my father tapped on it gently. 'There's someone called Sebastian on the phone. He's pretty keen to talk to you.'

'Well, I don't want to talk to him, Dad. Thanks.'

I ducked my head under the water. I'd just stay here all night. It was warm and safe and kind of womb-like – and I'd felt so incredibly cold recently, as if my very bones were made of ice.

Sometime later, there was a commotion downstairs. Digby! I jumped out of the bath and rushed dripping wet onto the landing.

'Please, Mr Warren. I only need five minutes.'

He was so beguiling I could sense my father hesitating. I sighed. It just wasn't fair to keep dragging my poor dad into my mess.

'It's okay, Dad.' I stuck my head over the banisters. 'I'll come down.'

I pulled on my pyjamas and drained the rest of my wine before I went to find Seb by the fire in the sitting room, the fake coals glowing red and warm, the carriage clock gently chiming on the mantelpiece. My dad and Jenny had retreated tactfully into the kitchen.

'Maggie,' Seb turned as I came in, his tone urgent. 'I got your message.' He looked a bit like a small boy with his hand stuck in the cookie jar. 'I'm sorry. I'm really sorry – but you got the wrong end of the stick.'

'Did I?' I went to the window in case Digby was outside. 'And which wrong end would that be?'

'I *never* said I played the lead in *Love All*. When did I ever say that? You seem to think I've lied to you, but I honestly didn't. I'm sure I told you.'

It was dark outside except for the flare of the streetlamp – and there was no small dog panting to be let in. I let the curtain swing back as I looked at Seb. I thought of his invitation to the small premiere in Piccadilly. What had his exact words been?

'I'm sure you didn't. And you must have known I thought you were playing the main part.'

'Why?' He pushed his dark hair back distractedly. 'You never asked – I seem to recall you never asked which part I played. And if we'd gone in, if we'd watched the film, you would have seen.'

'But you didn't want to watch it.'

'I hate watching myself, that's why. I never think I'm good enough.'

'So what *was* your part?' I sat on the sofa opposite him. 'Third undertaker from the left?'

He grinned. 'No. A bit bigger than that, thank you very much. I played the hero's brother.'

'I see.' That didn't sound quite so bad.

'It's just,' he sighed, 'he does get killed in Afghanistan about ten minutes in.'

'I see.' I tried not to smile. 'Third corpse from the left then?'

'Something like that.'

We gazed at each other. Then, tentatively, he crossed the room and slowly sat next to me. 'I mean, I had a proper part, Maggie. Lines and everything. I wasn't trying to pull the wool over your eyes, I swear.'

I stood and crossed to my dad's drinks cabinet. 'Drink?'

'I'm okay, Maggie, thanks. Are you all right now, then?' he asked rather anxiously as I poured myself a whisky.

'Kind of,' I shrugged. 'I resigned today, actually.'

He stared at me. 'Really?'

'Yes, really. Well, sort of. I think they got the message anyway. I'm not going back.' I wrinkled my nose at my acrid drink. 'And Digby's –' I swallowed hard, 'he's gone missing.'

Seb looked shocked. 'Oh God, I'm sorry. When?'

I shrugged. 'Sometime this morning. Early.'

'Can I – do you want me to go and look for him?'

'I don't think there's much point. I think someone's taken him. He's pedigree, you know. Maybe it's a trader.'

We both knew I didn't really think that.

'Right.' Seb pushed his hands through his hair, gazing at the fire. 'Maggie, I'm so sorry about this mess. You've got enough on your plate.'

'No, I'm sorry.' I drained my glass. 'I'm just in a bit of a state. I probably overreacted.'

'Well, I should have been more upfront, I suppose – I didn't lie, but perhaps I was trying to impress you.'

'So what about your audition this morning? Was that real?'

'Totally real. For a new doctor in *Holby City*. I've got the script somewhere.'

'And the play you're doing, your big part – is that real? Or are you just a spear-carrier?'

He was starting to look cross now. 'No, I'm not. I'm playing Orsino. Of course it's bloody real.' He dug around for something in his bag. 'God, what do you take me for, Maggie?'

He found what he was looking for – a batch of publicity shots and a well-thumbed script. I peered at the photos: the top one was Seb dressed in a ruffled white shirt and breeches, long riding-boots to the knee, looking very dashing; in the next he was a punk; then a British soldier with a rifle. 'That was my mum's favourite. That's *Love All*.' He pointed to the last one, pushing his hair back again distractedly. 'It was taken just before she died.'

'I'm so sorry,' I said mechanically. 'I'm sure she was very proud. You look very handsome.'

'She thought so, bless her.' He stood. 'You look knackered, babe. Give me a call when you're ready, okay?'

'Okay. Thanks, Seb.'

He moved towards the door, then he turned round slowly. 'We're having a cast party tomorrow to celebrate going up. I did – I really wanted you to come.'

'Wanted?'

'Well, it's just – I mean, after this – perhaps you don't want to.'

I contemplated my glass like the answer to all my problems might lie in the dregs. 'I'm sorry, Seb. I'd love to come normally. It's just – I'm just not in a very good place right now,' I said honestly. 'Everything I thought I knew seems not to be true right now.'

'Really?' He looked perplexed. 'That bad?'

278

'You know I thought they'd caught the bloke who's been doing all this crap to me, Joseph Blake.'

'I know, thank God. They have, haven't they?'

I felt the wall of panic rise in me again. 'But it's not Blake. It can't be. I just got more of those hideous flowers, and it was while he was locked up. Oh God.' I put my head in my hands. 'I was so bloody relieved it was over, and now it looks like it's not. And I'm so worried about Digby. He's never run off before.'

Seb came towards me and took the glass out of my hand, setting it down on the little walnut table beside me. 'Maggie,' he said softly. 'I'm here for you.'

'Thank you.' I couldn't look at him.

'I know you're cross, but I didn't lie. And we're good together, aren't we?'

'I thought so,' I mumbled. I was starting to feel like I wanted to just let go of all this mistrust now. I wanted some kind of oblivion. I wanted someone to hold me; to tell me it would be all right.

He pushed my hair out of my eyes. 'You're beautiful, Maggie, and you're hurt.'

'I'll say,' I joked. 'My head's still throbbing.' I still couldn't look at him.

'I'm serious. You're drowning in misery. I want to help you.' Gently, Sebastian forced me to meet his gaze. 'I came here to save you.'

'Lordy,' I mumbled. 'My hero. Am I really that far gone?'

He bent his head to kiss me. After a minute I came up for air. 'Do you *really* think I need saving?'

He didn't answer.

Seb went home around midnight, once I'd promised to think about coming to the party. But when I woke the next morning, back in the room where I'd spent the demise of my childhood,

I realised I couldn't go. I had to get the hell out of London; I had to before I imploded.

My dad and Jenny had already left for school. I had a cup of coffee, several cigarettes, and then I drove to the office to clear my desk. I wanted to make my leaving absolutely official. There was nothing Charlie or Renee could do to me any more, I reasoned; I had to be adult about the situation.

Sally bounced into my office as soon as she saw my light go on.

'Oh my goodness!' she said, her freckled bosom almost heaving with the drama. 'What *were* you like yesterday?'

'I don't know,' I said dryly. 'What *was* I like?'

'You certainly gave 'em what for – not that they didn't deserve it.'

'I'm glad it was so entertaining. I meant every word. Are there any boxes out there?' I took the picture of Pendarlin off the wall and clutched it to me. 'I need to pack my stuff up.'

'I'll get Cheryl to have a look. So you're really going then?'

But Sally had lost my attention as I switched on the computer. About ten emails down from the top was one from Alex, dated yesterday morning, and headed 'MY BLOODY DOG'.

'Oh my God.' I opened it feverishly.

*Maggie,*

*As we don't seem to be able to have a decent conversation and your mobile appears to be dead anyway, I'm emailing you to let you know I've taken the dog. You're so all over the place I think he'll be better with me – and when I came to collect him from your dad's he was just wandering around the front garden alone anyway.*

*I don't know why you ran out of the pub the other day – you looked like you thought I was some kind of axe murderer. It was a genuine mistake, I'd forgotten the keys were there, but you didn't let me explain. Given the circumstances, I think it's better we don't see each other. I've collected my boxes now, and my mother will look after Digby when I'm in Glasgow should you want visiting rights.*

    *Alex.*

'Bloody bastard. I don't want to see you anyway.' But I was so relieved that Digby was safe I laid my sore head on the desk for a minute.

'Maggie?'

'Sorry. It's nothing. Just that Alex took my dog and I've been worried sick.' From my vantage point I spotted the bottle of vodka on the cabinet. I sat up. 'But he's okay. This calls for a celebration, I think. Pass the bottle, Sal.'

She eyed it nervously. 'Maggie, it's nine thirty in the morning. Do you really think it's a good idea?'

'One of my best.' I held out my hand.

'Maggie.' Sally sat down in front of me, her jolly face serious. 'I'm starting – I'm worried about you, you know. You seem a bit –'

'Mad?' I stood to reach for the vodka.

'No. Manic, I was going to say.' A big crease furrowed her forehead.

I unscrewed the lid. 'I'm fine, honest. I'm in control.'

'Are you?' she asked quietly. 'It's okay to say you need help, you know, Maggie.'

'Are you saying I'm acting mad, Sal?' No one here except Charlie knew about my past, but I was beyond caring now. I looked around for a glass. 'I'm fine. I promise.'

'Please don't drink that, Maggie.' Sally stood too, holding her hand out for the bottle. 'I just don't think it's a great idea.'

I looked at her and then at the vodka. The clear liquid rolled behind the clear glass and I thought longingly of the burn in the back of my throat as the alcohol hit it. Then I thought about the truth of Sally's words and the fact that I hadn't eaten anything this morning and how I needed a clear head, and reluctantly I relinquished the bottle into her hand.

'All right, Sal. I expect you're right.'

My new phone beeped. I picked it up.

'**LAST WARNING**' it said. '**YOU'RE CORNERED.**'

'Oh God.' I looked at the bottle, now in Sally's possession. 'On second thoughts, Sal, I think I might need that after all.'

# Chapter Thirty-Four

Perhaps I was imagining it, but DI Fox seemed to have lost interest in my case.

'Maggie,' he half-sighed. 'How are you doing?'

'Okay,' I said. 'But I just got another text. I think it might be Joseph Blake again.'

'I don't think so. His parents have shipped him off to some nutty monastic retreat in the Pyrenees. Actually, I was going to call you. We're pretty sure now that the perpetrators of your flat break-in are the French family.'

'They sound like something out of the Krays.'

'Yeah, well, they'd probably like to think they are. They're a nasty little lot, running a protection racket in London Bridge; they don't like all the yuppies taking over. They've got various illegal gaming-rooms going on and they resent the buildings being snapped up by all and sundry.'

'Yuppies?' I was offended. 'I'm not a yuppy.'

'Okay, you're not a yuppy. But they are two-bit thugs and the turnover of your place smacks of their style – or lack of it. The trouble is, there ain't a fingerprint in your flat which we don't recognise as one of yours, or your,' he cleared his throat, 'your various blokes.'

'Various blokes?' I spluttered.

'You know what I mean. Your mates. The real point is, Maggie, I'm up to my eyes in all this terror stuff in town – and with the Christmas bomb threat, and bleeding hoaxes coming out of our ears, I just ain't got the manpower to post someone to watch over you. We've upped the plod presence on your patch anyway – but I think you'll be all right now the Frenches know we're on to them. Just stay in touch, okay?' He was ready to hang up.

'Well, actually –' I stopped. For some reason I felt a bit daft. 'It's just – I think, I'm sure I did mention these texts before, quite nasty ones, and now, if you say Joseph is out of the picture –'

'Yeah, we were looking into the texts, weren't we?' It was definitely a sigh this time. 'You got another one?'

'Yes. I mean, it is just a kind of vague threat.' It sounded a little pathetic out loud. '"*You're cornered*", this one says.'

'And you're quite sure it's nothing to do with that charmer I met the other day?'

There was a long pause.

'Maggie?'

'You mean Alex?' I thought about Bel's words on the phone from Thailand. 'I dunno. I really hope it isn't, anyway.'

'You do know he's got a record, don't you, mate?'

'Yes, DI Fox, I do know.'

'Yeah, of course you do. Well, give me the number they're coming from and I'll see if we can trace it.'

Before I left the office I emailed Alex back.

*Alex*
*How dare you take the dog. I've been worried sick and you're in no moral position to judge my care of him anyway. You relinquished all rights when you abandoned him in the summer. I looked at you like that because you had a set of my keys in your portfolio. I'm considering shopping you to DI Fox. He doesn't like you anyway.*

284

*And just for the record, that girl Fay's a loon. So you should suit each other perfectly.*
*Maggie*

Then I picked up my stuff and carried it past the desks to say goodbye to the girls. 'Good luck, everyone,' I said as cheerfully as I could manage, resting the box on a chair. 'Thanks for being so brilliant.'

'Are you really going?' Donna asked, coming round her desk. 'Really truly? What will we do without you?' She hugged me tight, the sweet smell of cocoa-butter enveloping me. 'Aren't we even gonna have a goodbye drink?' A guilty look crossed her face. 'I'm sorry about what I said the other day,' she muttered, staring at her boots. 'It was well rude. I've learned so much from you.'

Sally looked glum. 'Oh God. It's just us against them now.'

I picked up my box. 'You'll all be great. Just don't let the bastards grind you down. And remember – there are other programmes outside the inestimable *Renee Reveals*.'

'What a shame you won't be working on any of them.'

Charlie.

I'd wanted to get out before he arrived. He smiled at me like Judas must have smiled at his good friend Jesus.

'See you,' I smiled rather feverishly at the others, walking quickly to the lift. 'Keep in touch.'

Charlie followed me. 'Don't do this, Maggie.'

'It's too late, Charlie. I'm doing it.'

'Maggie –' He grabbed my arm. I shook him off impatiently and jabbed the lift button.

'Maggie, I –'

'Leave me alone, Charlie. Do your worst, tell everyone about the summer if you want. I'm not ashamed any more.'

The lift doors slid open and Renee stepped out like a ghastly apparition. I stepped in.

285

'Goodbye, Charlie. Renee.' I smiled pleasantly although my heart was thumping. 'I wish I could say it's been fun.' I pressed *Ground*. 'But I'd be lying.'

I drove straight to Barbara Bailey's and thanked God she was out when I arrived.

'I've come to collect the dog,' I said politely to the housekeeper.

She looked worried. 'Mrs Bailey, she not here. I think I check her first; you not mind?'

'Mrs Bailey is expecting me. I'm in a bit of a rush, actually.'

'I try call her.'

As soon as she'd scurried into the back of the house, I opened the sitting-room door. My heart soared as I saw my scruffy little dog rushing around the huge back lawn, barking at the trees that bowed like courtly dancers in the wind, at the wood-pigeons pecking at the half-empty stone fountain.

'Digby!' I rushed towards the French windows.

'Wasn't expecting to see you again so soon, Maggie.' That voice, like nails on sandpaper. I jumped guiltily. 'Can I help?'

'I've,' I cleared my throat as I turned slowly, 'I've just come to get the dog. My dog.'

'And you've cleared it with my boy, have you?' Malcolm sauntered towards me, hands in pockets, his barrel chest as puffed out as the pigeons Digby was hounding.

I stared at him. 'No, actually.'

'Well, I think you better had, don't you?'

I had the strange sensation that my life was flashing before my eyes suddenly, rather like a drowning woman's would.

'Why? Alex wasn't interested in Digby when he left me.'

'He left you, did he? That's not what I heard.'

'What?' I was confused.

'I thought you abandoned him. I think you'd better leave the dog.'

286

'Look, Malcolm, why do you care? You're so foul to Alex anyway –'

'Foul?' His strong, cruel face darkened.

'Yeah, foul.' I moved towards the door, towards my dog. Then I turned back. 'I mean, why exactly *do* you despise your eldest son so much? I don't get it. Especially when he obviously reveres you.'

'I don't despise him,' he scowled.

'You do. You certainly act like you do, anyway.'

Malcolm stared at me as if he'd never even countenanced this before. 'I just get frustrated,' he said slowly. 'He's had every chance I never had, because he had the best education money could buy –' He did so love the sound of his own opinions.

'But I'd say it has served him pretty well, that education.'

'Maybe.' He shrugged noncommittally. 'Maybe I'm tough because I had it so rough myself as a kid – and it shaped me really. If you'd seen the beatings my dad dealt my poor mother –'

Oh, the old boo-hoo. Only Renee could match Malcolm for the working-class hero bullshit, and I was sick of it, quite honestly.

'So you're punishing Alex for your childhood, are you?'

Digby had spotted us now, bounding to the door in great excitement, barking madly. I opened the door and knelt to let the dog slather my face with big pink licks.

'You know, Malcolm, nothing's as valuable as a parent's love. I learned that the hard way too, actually. And Alex needs you.'

'Needs me?' he snorted. 'He's thirty-two years old.'

'Yeah – needs you.' I stood up. 'You're his dad.'

I'd never seen Malcolm stuck for words before.

'It's watching the boy trying to destroy himself that makes me mad.' His voice was gruff but quiet now, almost gentle. For a split second I glimpsed the man behind the posturing.

'Don't you think that you might be just a tiny bit responsible?' I picked up the dog. 'He's trying to fill the socking great hole your contempt has drilled in him. It's just, he's not filling it with the right things.'

The housekeeper appeared, scurrying like a frightened mouse. 'Mrs Bailey, she not answer phone. Please can you –'

Malcolm held up a sturdy hand, his fingers straggly with coarse hair. 'It's all right, Gemi. Maggie can take the dog. I'll square it with the missus.'

'Oh.' Gemi looked hugely relieved. 'Thank you, Mr Bailey.'

I looked at Alex's father and I wondered if my words had made an impact. 'Yes, thank you, Malcolm. Come on, Dig. We'll see you around.'

# Chapter Thirty-Five

When I left Malcolm's I went to see Gar. I felt like I was saying goodbye to everybody; I felt like I was on the run . . . like the predator was closing in.

It was Susan's day off and an insipid-looking redhead called Annette was on duty, reading the *Sun* next to a fake white Christmas tree festooned with gaudy tinsel. She barely raised her eyes as I walked past.

Gar looked more dishevelled than usual somehow, although she managed to pat my hand after I'd hugged her tightly. I felt horribly anxious about the fact I was planning to leave town again.

'Hello Maggie,' she said, and I looked at her in surprise.

'She's been all right, has she?' I asked Annette when she came to give Gar her pills.

'As all right as she ever is, you know.' Insipid shrugged slouchy shoulders. 'Aren't you, dear?' she yelled at Gar.

'She's not deaf, you know,' I said stiffly. 'Just a bit –'

'Senile?' Insipid sniffed.

'She's not senile,' I snapped. 'She's got Alzheimer's. There's a difference, you know.'

'If you say so. She had another visitor yesterday, that perked her up – didn't it, dear?' she shouted again.

I bit my tongue. 'My dad, you mean?' I moved the poinsettia I'd brought with me onto Gar's bedside table, noticing with irritation that beneath the top layer of scarlet leaves, the next layer was already shrivelled and dead.

'No, not your dad. I know Bill, lovely man, he is.' She looked almost girlish for a minute. 'No, this was a lady I think. I'm not sure, I weren't here yesterday. Leanne said.'

My blood ran colder than it had all day. 'Who was she?'

'Said she was a relative. She's been before. I think she left something for Vera.' Insipid had lost interest now. She snapped the lid back on the pill bottle.

'What?'

'Should be over on that shelf. That's it – that big scrapbook.' I picked up a red cardboard book like I'd had in my childhood to record my holidays, and flicked open the first page. I gasped in shock.

There were family photos here, family photos of me and Gar and my mother. Only wherever I should have been, my face had been cut out.


'Dad,' I said urgently, 'can you come and collect Gar?'

'What?' He sounded confused. 'Why?'

'I can't explain now. It's just – I've got to go to Pendarlin.'

'Why?'

'Please, Dad. I just do. I'm worried someone strange has been visiting Gar – and Susan's on holiday. Can you just have her for the weekend?'

'Really, Mag, you're making me nervous. I –'

'I know what you're thinking but I'm fine, honestly. I'd take her down to Cornwall, but I don't think she's fit enough to travel that far.'

'Maggie –'

'*Please*, Dad. Just for the weekend. I'll be back on Monday, I swear. It's not like the summer, honestly.'

'But why do you need to go so badly? Why now? What about work?'

'I've – I've resigned,' I confessed in a small voice.

'I see.' There was a short silence, then a deep sigh. 'Well, I can't say I'm altogether surprised.'

'And I just – I need to get out of London. I just – I really need some space to clear my head. Please.' I heard my voice crack slightly.

Another sigh. 'Well, if it's really that important to you, Mag, then –'

I nearly cried with relief. 'You're a star, Dad, an absolute star.'

'But when you come back, Maggie, we need to sit down and talk properly, okay? I'm worried about you.'

'Okay.' I was sheepish. 'We will. I promise.'

After I'd gone back to Greenwich to collect Digby from my father's – where Jenny had him practically chained to the kitchen table – and listened patiently to her lecture about looking after myself, and eating properly and driving carefully, and that my dad would really like me back on Monday, and after I'd hugged her tight for a moment, clinging on a bit like I was five, I sat in the car in the dark outside the house. The dog panted damp hot breaths down my neck, impatient to be off.

'Looks like it's just you and me, buster.' I started the car, thinking wistfully of Seb and last weekend and a chance for happiness already lost. Then I stamped the memory down and set off across London for the motorway. The sky was the twilight-stained blue-orange of a winter city filled with too much light, busy for a Thursday night, the streets crammed with horns and sirens and atrocious driving.

Eventually shaking off the suburban traffic, we shot along the Embankment, the river a dark and oily flank beside us, the Houses of Parliament on the opposite bank like something from a Gothic fairytale, down plain old Nine Elms Lane, heading for Chelsea Bridge. Passing the Dogs' Home, Digby let out a pitiful whimper, pushing his cold nose into my placating hand.

291

At the roundabout, I realised suddenly how very near I was to where Seb was having his drink. Perhaps it wouldn't hurt to have just one, just to say goodbye. I hesitated until the van behind me started to beep impatiently, and then I found the big pub quite easily – The Latchmere, pinioned by the busy intersection; the billboards advertising the upstairs theatre – a new production of *Twelfth Night*. I stared at the swirly writing for a moment, at the photograph of a grim-faced Sebastian and a jester-type guy and a grand woman with swept-up hair wearing a black veil, and I laughed out loud. It wasn't quite the West End show I'd been expecting, but at least it existed!

A police car screamed past, narrowly missing a young girl in nothing but jogging bottoms and a crop-top despite the December cold. She ran across the road clutching a huge bottle of cider against her jutting ribs, her great gold hoops swinging as she went, and I shivered. The brightly lit pub looked like a cosy oasis in a chilly urban night; through the windows I watched people laughing, joking, toasting one another, rapt in deep and serious conversation. People living. Two men kissed passionately and then I spotted Seb and a tall skinny woman with dishevelled hair leaning across to hand him a pint – then he was gone from sight.

I felt like such an outsider – never more isolated, in fact. I should just leave. But I didn't. I sat there in the car, watching still, like a stalker myself. I'll just pop in for a second, I decided eventually, when Digby started to whine and snuffle. I'll just have one for the road.

I looked for a parking space. Spotting a small side-street under the railway bridge, I turned right across the traffic as a small neat figure, hood up, stepped out without warning in front of me. I slammed on the brakes, the car stalling as the figure slipped safely into the shadows under the bridge without a backwards glance.

My heart had stopped. It couldn't be.

I leapt out of the car and screamed her name – but she'd disappeared already.

I was transfixed, staring after her, blocking both lanes, a transit van beeping furiously somewhere behind me – but I couldn't move. Then Digby barked frantically, and I snapped out of my trance as the Number 44 bore down on me from one direction, an ambulance with all lights flashing from the other.

I was sure I'd just seen Fay.

# Chapter Thirty-Six

My mouth was completely dry, like I'd sucked up a desert. I parked the car badly behind a metallic BMW that I thought might have been Seb's, narrowly avoiding crashing into the back, and fumbled for a cigarette, my fingers trembling with adrenaline. The girl was truly the stuff of nightmares.

I didn't know what to do – but I was going to have to do something. My mobile made me jump as it rang in my pocket.

'Maggie.' It was DI Fox.

'What a coincidence.' My voice was as tinny and bright as a new copper penny. 'I was about to ring you.'

'Really? Why?'

'About that girl, Fay Carter.'

'What about her?'

'I've just got this feeling –' I paused, and then it plopped out, like a big dollop of cream that had been stuck for ages on a spoon. 'I think she might be the one stalking me. She keeps turning up everywhere and she's been slashing photos of me –'

'I don't think it's her, Maggie,' the policeman interrupted, annoyingly calm.

'With all respect, DI Fox, I do,' I said urgently. 'I mean, at first I thought she was just mad, but now I'm seriously starting to think she's bad too.'

'She might well be both – but I don't think she's your stalker. 'Fraid I've got some bad news.'

'You do surprise me, DI Fox.' I took a drag so deep my cigarette practically withered.

'We finally traced that mobile number you gave me. I'm sorry it took so long; I'd given it to my DS and she was off sick, so it got buried. Shoddy, that. I apologise.'

'Go on, please.' An Alsatian lolloped down the narrow pavement beside the car and Digby growled. I checked the doors were locked and pulled my coat closer, craving warmth.

'It's a contract phone; belongs to someone called –' there was a slight pause, 'Steven I. Sweeger, fictitious address. Ring any bells?'

'Um, sort of. I mean, I don't know him but I think he sent me some flowers.'

'Charming.'

'Not really. They were funereal.'

'Right. Well, the name's an anagram. I rang the number about half an hour ago. Did you – had you thought of doing that?'

'Well, obviously.' I was insulted. 'It was the first thing I did. But no one ever answered. What does the anagram spell?'

'It's not very complicated. It spells, I'm afraid, *Revenge is Sweet.*'

I felt foolish for not working it out. 'And did someone answer the phone?' I whispered.

'Yes. Someone did answer. You're not going to like this, Maggie.'

Why did I get the feeling he was almost enjoying this?

'Someone you know rather well. Your mate Alex Bailey.'

My gut rolled over. 'I don't believe it,' I mumbled eventually. 'I'm sure it's that girl. She's definitely after me.'

'Believe it.' Fox didn't quite say *told you so*, but . . . 'It was him, sweetheart, I'm afraid. No doubt about it.'

'Are you really sure?' I said.

'Sure I'm sure, Maggie. He didn't make no bones about it. I mean, he said it wasn't his phone – but then he would, wouldn't he? We're bringing him in.'

I didn't answer.

'Maggie? You still there?'

The Alsatian padded back the other way, towards a big man silhouetted beneath the far end of the bridge.

'I'm not sure, DI Fox, actually,' I said quietly. 'I'm really not sure where I am any more.'

By the time I got into the pub I was shaking with cold and unhappiness and suddenly paranoid about the reception I'd receive from Seb. But I couldn't see him, and my heart sank further. Perhaps he'd already left. Then I spotted him deep in conversation with the dishevelled dark woman.

'Maggie!' He waved from the other side of the bar. 'Over here.'

I raised a nervous hand. Thank God, though, he looked genuinely happy to see me.

'Do you want a drink?' I called, but he shook his head, indicating his own pint.

I ordered myself a large glass of red and managed half of it in one go. Then I had a thought. I took the drink over to a quiet corner and rang my father's house, Digby lying faithfully on my feet. Jenny answered, slightly out of breath.

'Those lilies,' I launched straight in, 'the ones I asked you to chuck away yesterday. Did you see who sent them by any chance?'

'Ooh no.' Her reply came too fast. 'And, actually, they weren't lilies, Maggie.'

'Are you sure?' I was confused.

'Quite sure, yes.' There was a small, embarrassed pause. 'I gave them to Ethel at school actually – the nice lady who does the reading with the kids. I hope you don't mind, but it seemed like such a waste, and she was ever so pleased, you know. No, they definitely weren't lilies. They were a lovely sort of mixed autumnal bouquet.'

She sounded like a florist.

'Right. And you're sure you don't know who sent them?' I slugged back my drink. 'It'd really help.'

'Well,' Jenny was flustered now, 'I might have had just a little tiny peep at the card.'

'And?' I said impatiently. 'I don't mind, honestly.'

'I think it was your boyfriend,' she said apologetically, sure I was furious with her.

'Alex?' I scrunched my brow, watching Seb across the room as he laughed at something his companion said.

'No, the other one. The lovely dark one. Hang on a sec. I'll see if the card's still here. I thought you might change your mind.' I heard a scuffle and a curse. 'Oh damn. That's half the Persil gone! Ah, yes, here it is. "*To Maggie, from your sorry lover.*" I think it's quite sweet, don't you? I always did think he was a –'

'Is it a normal card?'

'What do you mean by normal?'

'Is it,' I took a deep breath, 'it's not a – an "*In Sympathy*" card, is it?'

'Oh no.' Jenny was horrified. 'No, of course not. Just a little pink one with flowers on the bottom. I'll keep it for you, shall I?'

'Yes, please. Thanks, Jenny.' I snapped off the phone.

Seb put an arm around me and kissed my cheek. 'All right, babe. Are you okay? Hey.' He patted Digby's head fondly. 'You're back, good boy. What are you two doing hiding over here on your own? I wanted to introduce you.'

'Sorry. I had to make a call. I just had a bit of a – a fright.'

'Really? What now?' He frowned.

'Aha, yes. That is the question,' I said. 'What now, dear Seb? Or is it Yorrick?' I tried to remember when I'd last eaten. Perhaps I should have some crisps. 'I am truly surrounded, that's what.'

'Surrounded?' Seb looked baffled now. 'Is it too busy in here for you?'

'No, I didn't mean that. I'm just being silly. Or stalked. Depending on how you look at it.' I drained my second drink and shoved the glass back on the bar. 'Look, Seb, thank you so much for inviting me, but I think I'd better go.'

'Really?' He frowned. 'Already? You've only just got here.'

'The thing is,' I said very slowly, 'the thing is, I've just found out my ex is probably an axe-murderer, apparently, or something, you know, something rather charming like that, and so – so –' The enormity of what I was saying hit me suddenly and I reeled slightly.

'Maggie?'

'It's just – I'm not very good company right now. I think I really need to get away,' I mumbled, and picked up my bag, swaying a little as I straightened up. 'I'll call you.'

Seb grabbed my arm. 'I don't think you should go anywhere in this state, Maggie.' He scrutinised my face. 'You're drunk.'

'I am most certainly not drunk. I've only had one drink.' I reconsidered. 'Okay, two drinks. But I'm not drunk. Perish the thought!' Most certainly I was a little confused, though. 'I'm just in shock, that's all. And that bloody girl keeps following me around and it's all just starting to freak me out. I nearly crashed the car outside. I could have been mincemeat.'

'You've lost me. What bloody girl?'

'Bloody Fay Carter, that's who. She turns up like a bad penny just when I don't expect her.'

And then, through the increasingly rumbustious crowd, I saw a figure come through the far door, and the crowd parted between me and her just like the sea did for Moses, and I watched dumbfounded as that little hooded figure tripped over to the bar. I stared at her.

'Maggie?' Seb was shaking me gently. 'Maggie, are you okay?'

'That's her,' I whispered, and he had to bend to hear me. 'Over by the bar.'

'Who?' He shook his head.

'That's Fay.'

He looked over just as the girl turned, just as her hood fell

298

back, and she raised a glass in toast to the group on her left. 'Sorry I'm late,' I heard her call, 'I couldn't find a bloody cash-point anywhere.'

It wasn't Fay. It looked a little like her, a very little bit – but it definitely wasn't her.

'So apparently I really am losing it now,' I tried to joke, but for some reason I was on the verge of tears, dangerously close to falling somewhere very dark, very deep. I sat very still on the bar-stool – thinking. Seb was obviously worried, I could sense his concern, but I couldn't allay his fears, I couldn't think of him right now. I simply didn't know what to do, that was the truth. Vaguely, somewhere in the background I heard Seb order me some soup and a cup of coffee and then he led me to a table by the window and put his arm around me to try to make me warm. I was grateful for the touch but I felt a million miles away as I looked out of the window, and the grim night-lit world seemed to have speeded up outside. Three kids in hoods bowled past, their jeans slung low around snake-hips, their trainers very white against the dark pavement. Brake-lights streamed behind cars like ribbons of coloured water, and I felt like I was losing my mind. Again. What I'd always feared was finally happening.

'Did you ever see that Madonna video where it's all going very fast around her?' I said distractedly. 'I feel like that now.' I leaned my cheek against the cold glass. 'Like I'm here but nothing else is real. Like it's all a – a big crazy blur.'

'Maggie,' Seb took both my hands in his, forcing me to look at him, 'I'm really worried about you, you know.'

'I've got to get out of here, Seb. I think that's the answer.' I glanced around me. 'I don't feel very safe any more.'

'I think it's in your head, Maggie babe,' he said gently. 'You're perfectly safe here. You're just really on the edge.'

And then I remembered DI Fox and what he'd just said about

299

Alex and one tear fell, plump and unstoppered, rolling down my cheek onto my knee, and then another followed. And I thought about that night in the summer and perhaps I should have known then, but I'd believed in him, in my beautiful, terrible Alex, even when it all went wrong. I'd taken my share of the blame because I had believed in his good, deep down. But obviously I'd been so wrong, so very, very wrong. I took a deep breath and staunched the tears.

When the soup came I made a show of eating it but there was still half a bowl left at the end. I drank the coffee and a glass of water to keep Seb happy, listening to him talk about the first night tomorrow and which critics they were hoping would come and how a big West End producer had already shown interest in the production and how Seb had a recall for the junior doctor in *Holby City*. And I was pleased for him, I really was, and I managed to smile a bit at him, but I couldn't concentrate, I just kept seeing Alex's face the first time he'd said he loved me and my mind went round and round like a Ferris wheel thinking, *How could we have come to this, how could he hate me enough to persecute me so?*

In the end I stood up and pushed the bowl of soup away so it slopped onto the table in an ugly mess of little tomato bits.

'Seb, thanks so much – but, look, I'll leave you to it. This is your celebration. I don't want to spoil it for you.'

'You're not spoiling it,' he insisted, but I'd seen his glance gently slide to the group of actors in the snug, and I hugged him quickly.

'I really, really want to be here tomorrow, but I think – I might not make it. Can I come next week instead? Is that okay?' I spoke into his shoulder, his lean warmth reassuring for a moment. 'You will be brilliant,' I rattled on before he could answer. 'Absolutely brilliant, I know. Break a leg and all that kind of stuff, yeah?' Digby snuffled around my feet, scavenging for spilt crisps. 'I'll call you when I get to Cornwall.'

'Maggie, please.' Seb's face was tense. 'I really don't think you should go now.'

'I have to, Seb.' I picked up my bag. 'I need some time to clear my head.'

He didn't know what to do. 'I'll walk you to your car,' he said eventually.

'No, please don't. Stay here. Your friends need you.' I kissed him on the lips quickly. I had to go; I couldn't be sucked in. 'I'll be fine, honestly.'

'Well –' He held the ends of my scarf in both hands, loath to abandon responsibility. 'You know, when you come back, I think maybe you should see someone. You know, to talk. I'll get you some numbers, okay?'

'Seb!' I felt quite desperate to get out of the pub; away from the noise, the heat, the bustle and the smell of beer. The cheerful air that I could not absorb. I felt like a cardboard cut-out among these fleshy rounded mortals. Oh God. Gently I freed myself from his hold. 'Are you saying you think I'm mad too?' I tried to laugh, but his bony face was solemn.

'No, of course not. But – I just wondered – you know, because of your mum –'

'Seb! I've had one breakdown. I'm not going to have another.'

'One breakdown?' He stared at me. Like a stone flying from a kid's catapult, my words hit their target. 'When?'

'Yes, one breakdown. In the summer, after the crash. Look, sorry, Seb, but I can't do this now.'

'Okay.' He was flummoxed. 'Just promise me you'll drive carefully, babe.'

'Of course I will.' I tossed my scarf over one shoulder as if I were Amelia Earhart. Truly carefree.

'And call me as soon as you get there, please.' He rubbed his face wearily. 'I feel really odd about this, babe. I wish I could come too.'

'So do I.' I smiled bleakly. 'But you're better off without me.'

'Don't say that. Look, Maggie, are you really sure you –'

'I'll ring you, okay?' Before he dissuaded me I shot to the door, Digby trotting in my wake. I didn't look round.

When I reached the car, I locked the doors and put the stereo on loudly. The gorgeous strings of Vaughan Williams's *The Lark Ascending*, normally so uplifting, only accentuated the fact that I hadn't felt so desolate for such a very long time. Not since that day in June when Alex and I had ended it; the day I'd climbed onto the coach. I listened to the music for a moment, staring blankly at the damp brick wall beside me, watching water suddenly spurt from a broken pipe below the arched roof. Then I laid my forehead on the steering-wheel and wept. I cried until no more tears would come – until finally I dried my eyes and, grim-faced, picked up my phone to make a call.

# Chapter Thirty-Seven

In the summer, Alex's drinking had hit an unknown precedent. Bowed down with stress at work, setting up the new office in Glasgow, arguing with his partner Patrick about funding, when Alex began to drink, he often appeared unable to stop – or, at least, unwilling. When Patrick decided to pull out of the Glasgow deal, Alex asked Malcolm for a loan in a last-ditch attempt to both salvage the new office and include his father in his life. To Alex's huge surprise and joy, Malcolm actually seemed to be considering it.

With Alex splitting his time between work, familial hang-ups and alcohol, there was little of him left for me. I'd invested everything into my relationship – but it was an investment that was no longer paying many dividends. Without even realising, I'd let my own career flounder while I'd got sidetracked; initially by trying to stop Alex's excessive drinking, and, when that failed, by being slowly, inexorably drawn in. The old adage '*if you can't beat 'em, join 'em*' was like a gong sounding in my empty head.

Why do women so often feel they have to fix their men? I should have asked myself firmly. Unfortunately, though, I'd lost my self-awareness. I was heart-sick: heartily sick of trying to get Alex's attention and failing to reach him, sick of all the nights I went to bed alone. But somehow I just got ever more entrenched in misery; until I was on a constant knife-edge. It was only a matter of time before I fell.

One morning, as I struggled to recover from a night that had culminated in Alex smashing half the crockery when I'd dared to suggest he sober up, Charlie sent a cab for me. Over lunch at The Ivy his approach was almost gentle.

'I'm worried about you, darling.'

'Oh yes?' Charlie's empathy unsettled me far more than his wrath would have done. I stared at the over-pink langoustine lying plumply on my plate, a peppercorn eye staring up at me reproachfully.

'I don't know why I didn't see it before.' Charlie eyed me over his glass a little like the crustacean was. 'It was most remiss of me.'

'Didn't see what? You're making me nervous.'

'I can't protect you for much longer, you know, Maggie.'

'Protect me?' I stared at him. 'Are you joking? From what?'

'Don't be obtuse. The whole office knows something's up, darling.' Charlie helped himself to bread, his hand hovering over the curl of creamy butter. 'But the minute Lyons notices you're below your game, you're finished. You know that.'

'I'm not below my game.'

'Yes you are. Utterly below it.'

'I've just been – I've had a lot on,' I muttered, fiddling with the langoustine's spindly feeler.

'A lot as in bottles of vodka and parties that last all night?' Charlie finally resisted the bread and butter and lit his cigar instead. 'A lot as in forgetting to ever eat, or being hung-over every morning?'

'I never party all night.' I summoned mild indignation with an effort.

'That boyfriend of yours certainly does. Come on, Maggie. We all know everyone canes it in this game –' I winced at the youthful expression, 'and that's fine, as long as you can still deliver the next day. But you're in serious danger of getting demoted. Or worse, darling.' Charlie regarded me coolly. 'Losing your job entirely.'

I pulled the head off that bloody langoustine so savagely that strange liquid squirted into my eye.

Charlie puffed his cigar at me. 'And that would be a shame, wouldn't it? Now drink up, there's a good girl.'

Despite his apparent concerns for my welfare, Charlie kept the champagne flowing throughout lunch – until the truth eventually did out.

'It's not just you that's in trouble, darling – we're in trouble as a show.' I sensed how hard this was for the sanguine Charlie to admit. 'Ever since the appalling Jeremy Kyle came on the scene our bloody ratings have been dropping. We need to totally rethink the brand without alienating our audience, and we need to do it fast.' He ran a weary hand through his luxuriant hair. 'I want to steer away from the mud-slinging Kyle does so well.'

'But we've been doing it so well ourselves for years.' I raised an incredulous eyebrow at him. 'In fact, I thought we started it.'

'Maybe we did,' Charlie shrugged elegantly, 'but it's time to play it differently, darling. The media's picking up on the depravity of the chat-show in general. We need to use it to our advantage. Take the upper-hand morally, you know.' He slid his slightly clammy hand over mine. 'And it'll give you the chance to prove yourself again. I don't want people saying I backed the wrong horse.'

'God, for a minute there, Charlie, I thought you actually cared.' I slipped my hand away.

'I care enough to try to save you from Lyons's ire.'

Oh, the dichotomy of Charlie. Smooth as butter, he was the ever-articulate hood who might appear entirely sure of himself – but he wasn't quite as cool as he made out. I had seen it when he'd been abandoned at the altar the year I'd started at Double-decker. Charlie had laughed it off as a narrow escape, proceeding to bed at least half the office when he returned from his solitary honeymoon in Antigua. But that brief glimpse of humility had forged the bond that had let us work together effectively these past years. For all his debonair suavity, beneath the man-tan, the expensive hair and the royal-blue Ralph Lauren beat the still malleable heart of the son of a bank manager from Sutton – not the impenetrable gold-plated shell of Lord Hee-Haw's son from the Home Counties, as Charlie would have us all believe.

And now, as the champagne drained slowly from the bottle, it transpired that not only did Charlie want me to find a new direction for *Renee Reveals*, he also wanted me to train up Lyons's nephew Joseph and Sam Crosswell, son of billionaire entrepreneur and TV mogul Dickie Crosswell. Sally would be promoted to deputise for me, and I would hand over the day-to-day running of the show to her until I'd proved to Charlie I'd got my act together. By the time dessert arrived, I felt mortified – but I had little choice, it seemed.

'Nepotism's hardly my thing, Charlie.' I traced patterns in the cream on my plate. 'It makes me extremely uncomfortable.'

'You're hardly in the highest of moral positions right now, my dear Maggie. You're wasting yourself.' His smile was positively vulpine. 'You should be much further on by now. What happened?'

I shrugged wearily. 'Love?' I suggested.

'Love-schmove. You look utterly miserable. Grow some balls, darling. You're an extremely capable young woman.' Charlie leaned back to relight the cigar. 'Sort yourself out and I'll give you the *True Lives* documentary strand to produce.'

'Really?' I eyed him warily.

'Really. It's all yours. We're launching the season with a doc about binge-drinking. Right up your street. You have my word as a gentleman, my darling.'

I wasn't at all sure Charlie was a gentleman.

'I will sort myself out. I have to say, though,' I poked at the crust on my lemon tart, 'I don't know what it is exactly that excites you so about these two boys. TV should be a merit-ocracy.'

'Don't be so boring, Maggie.' Charlie exhaled his smoke like the old lounge lizard he truly was, and toasted me lazily with his Cognac. 'See it as a chance to mould this fresh blood. Train these kids up well, blow that smug creep Kyle out of the bloody water – and you'll reap the rewards.'

And, for all his cynicism, Charlie trod so softly-softly that eventually I began to spy an escape from the recent depression I'd apparently slipped into. I'd enthuse Joseph Blake and Cross-well's son Sam with some of the passion I'd started out with; we'd reinvent bloody Renee; I'd show Charlie I was back on track and move on to something I believed in.

By the end of the meal I was so drunk I actually felt happy.


I tried to tell Alex about Charlie's plan and my new charges; I tried to explain that I feared I was on trial, that it felt like starting out again. Alex made a vague pretence of listening but his thoughts were on himself as Malcolm strung him along over the loan – and he was back and forth to Scotland so often that we seemed further apart than ever. Eventually I gave up trying to talk about myself.

My brilliant plan to play the great mentor collapsed at the first hurdle. Joseph Blake arrived alone on a Monday morning, a few days before Sam, who was still doing good in some Malaysian orphanage. I loathed the idea of Sam already, the spoilt rich kid with a pseudo social conscience – but the arrogant Joseph was something else. He came with a briefcase, a copy of the *Tele-graph* and a bad attitude. I kept waiting for him to produce a monocle.

Joseph thought he had nothing to learn; in fact, he was ready to take charge from the moment he walked in. He argued with almost everything I told him; he was sulky when I asked him to chill out. He banged on about 'Oxbridge education setting us up for life' and wanted to make 'radical TV', but had no new ideas. He was a snob and an unutterable old fogey, and, worse, he was supremely unlikeable.

The following week Sam Crosswell sailed into the office like a bright ship on a stormy horizon. To my everlasting contrition, he turned out to be a really charming kid. Sunburnt and sun-bleached, slightly gawky and befreckled with the broad smile of someone who is genuinely relaxed with themselves, he soon had an admiring flank of older girls circling his desk like brilliant piranhas, wanting to know about catching waves in Costa Rica and his dad's celebrity mates, more than happy to perch on the edge of his desk showing too much thigh and flirt all day. And I didn't mind because Sam was smart and enthusiastic, not too grand to make the tea or do the photocopying or bash the phone for hours – plus he fielded new ideas all day long: some bad, some actually quite good. It was refreshing to have him in the office, if only to watch the girls pant after him.

The week after Sam started, the invites to the Vision Awards arrived. I had absolutely no interest in going this year; I'd networked and schmoozed with enough bumptious producers and commissioners to last me a lifetime. More to the point, since my drunken lunch with Charlie, much to my surprise, I was finding the path of abstinence more enticing than I'd believed possible. Award ceremonies inevitably meant copious amounts of anything that took your fancy, accompanied by copious opportunities for making a complete arse of yourself.

'No thanks.' I shook my head at Charlie when he dropped the tickets on my desk. 'Not this time. You go.'

Charlie, on the other hand, had other ideas.

'I want you to represent Double-decker, and I want you to take Sam and Joseph. And keep an eye on Renee.'

'Do me a favour,' I groaned. 'God, why?'

'Let's just say we're keeping Daddy Crosswell and Uncle Lyons sweet.'

'Let Sally take them,' I implored. 'Or Donna. All the girls are dying to go. I'm trying really hard to keep on the straight and narrow – just like you said.'

'They're your responsibility, Maggie, those boys. Don't let me down.'

The morning of the ceremony at the Dorchester, Alex rang from Glasgow airport.

'Maggie, baby, I've completely fucked up.'

'Really?' I said wearily, tucking the phone under one ear to put my mascara on. It was a hot day, unseasonably so for early June, and my summer dress already felt like a fur coat.

'Tom's just rung. It's Ma's sixtieth today. It had kind of slipped my mind.'

'Oh, Alex, honestly.' I wished I was surprised. 'Your poor mum.'

'Help me out, Mag, can you, please? Sorry, hang on a sec.' He put more money in the beeping payphone. 'Look, order some flowers from us, would you? My battery's died and I've just missed my flight.'

'I'm pretty busy myself, Alex. We've got an away-day and then the bloody Vision Awards tonight.'

'What awards? And I also forgot –' He paused as the Tannoy announced an imminent departure. 'We're, er – we're meant to be having dinner with them tonight.'

'For God's sake, Alex. You should have told me before.' I shoved the mascara back into my make-up bag. 'You'll have to go without me. Charlie's got me over a barrel.'

'Why?' He sounded like a small abandoned boy.

'I told you, Alex, at least ten times. I've got to chaperone these bloody kids and the diva herself. We're up for Best Daytime Show. Charlie will go mental if I try to wriggle out of it now.' I didn't add that it felt like my last chance. 'I'm really sorry, but you'll have to go without me. I'll call your mum.'

'But I need you, Mag, I really do.'

'Why?'

'I always need you, baby,' he wheedled.

'Alex!' As usual it was me having to prop *him* up.

'And I think Pa's going to come good with the money, so I've got to keep him sweet.' That boyish charm was oozing down the phone now. 'Maggie, oh my beautiful Maggie,' he coaxed, 'you know how much Pa loves you. I can't go without you. Don't make me, baby.'

I could never resist him, that was the whole bloody problem. I pushed down my resentment. 'I'm not sure about *love*, Al. '

'He loves you as much as he loves anyone. He knows when he's met his match.' Alex was fighting to keep the edge out of his voice now, and it was that plaintive tone that finally won me over.

I sighed. 'I'll come for a quick drink, okay?'

'I'll make it up to you, Maggie,' he crowed. 'I promise. I'll pick you up at six.'

'Just don't get too drunk beforehand, okay?' I pleaded, but he'd already gone.

I went to work with a heavy stone in my stomach. I was looking forward to seeing Alex, I always did when he'd been away, hoping for a return to the normality we'd once achieved. But I was painfully aware that once again I'd compromised myself for him. I despised myself for my weakness.

I spent the day shivering in the air-conditioned conference room of a chichi Covent Garden hotel, drinking cafetieres of gloopy coffee and eating fashionably small bits of fruitcake, brain-storming rubbish ideas. I felt like the great pretender as I smiled blankly at Sam and Joseph and the girls, trying to get enthused while listening to yet another take on the 'Drop Renee into a

310

situation alien to her'; 'Swap Renee's celebrity lifestyle with a crack-addicted hoodie's'; 'Swap Renee's body for that of someone halfway attractive.'

Around five, I shot home to change, shrugging myself into the beautifully cut Prada suit Bel had steered me towards the week before in Selfridges; and into a rare pair of heels that only served to make me stagger slightly.

Just after six Alex arrived in a black cab, his eyes glittering in a way that alarmed even me. He'd promised he'd knocked the coke on the head last year, but I didn't like the look of him tonight. He picked up his stack of post from the kitchen table and flicked through it. Then he pulled me into his arms and buried his head in the crook of my neck. His skin was hot against mine in this sultry night, and I felt the butterflies that still fluttered when things were good. The reason I'd failed to walk away yet.

'God, I've missed you, Mag,' he whispered in my ear. 'You look amazing, baby.'

He rarely noticed how I looked these days.

'Really?' I blushed, stepping back, suddenly shy.

'Yeah, really. Come here.'

In the shadows he pushed my hair back with a kind of rough tenderness, staring at me silently for a moment. A terrible longing suffused me; a longing for what we'd once had. He leaned down and kissed me like he hadn't in months. I felt myself start to dissolve.

'Oh God, Mag,' he groaned.

'Isn't the cab waiting? Your mum will be –' I tried to concentrate as he pushed me against the wall and kissed me harder.

'I don't care,' he murmured, running his hands up my body, 'I just want to fuck you senseless.'

'Alex,' I gasped, hearing the cab beeping outside but suddenly desperate for him, for the Alex I had first known, 'Alex, hang on.' But I didn't really mean it. 'I don't –' I bit my lip as he yanked my jacket open, 'I'm – what's going on?'

'Nothing.' But he was edgy, slightly manic, his hands insistent as he slid one into my waistband. Pulling at his belt, his own breath was jagged as he tugged up my skirt, his fingers on the bare flesh above my hold-ups.

'God, stockings and the lot,' Alex muttered, and kissed me even harder, until my lips were almost hurting and I didn't care any more, I was almost maddened with suppressed desire, desire thwarted recently by his unavailability. I felt a need for him more urgent than I'd ever felt, the ache caused by him habitually ignoring me suddenly as tender as a new bruise. My legs were actually trembling in my stilettos as he yanked me up and shoved me against the sink, fumbling at his own buttons. Impatient now, I reached down to help him as a huge black spider sidled from behind a leaf of the peace-lily on the windowsill. I gazed at it, but I didn't really see it.

'Oh God, Alex.' I bit his earlobe gently with my teeth, wrapping my legs around him now. 'Oh God, I love you –'

And then suddenly he stopped.

'What?' I pressed into him quite frantically, past the point of caring. 'Don't stop now, for God's sake.'

Alex stepped back from me so suddenly that I nearly fell onto my knees, his eyes narrowing as he looked at me. 'Stockings?' He stared at me like he didn't even know me. 'For my mum's party?'

'What?' I was confused, my mood already plunging. 'What are you talking about?'

'Why are you all dressed up like that?'

'For you. I was –' I felt cheapened by his suspicion. 'I've been looking forward to seeing you, you know.'

'Right.' Alex chewed the nail of his middle finger. 'And you expect me to actually believe that?'

'It's too hot for tights.' I pulled my skirt down and started to button up my shirt, my fingers clumsy. 'Sorry – what exactly are you trying to say?'

'I'm not sure, really, Maggie.' He stared at me like I was some peculiar stranger. 'I'm really not sure.' He laughed mirthlessly. 'I could do with another drink, I know that much.' Then he turned and, pulling his wallet out, cut himself an enormous line of cocaine on the kitchen table.

'What the hell are you doing?' I hissed.

'What does it look like?'

'I thought you'd stopped all this?' I shook my head, bewildered.

'For Christ's sake, Maggie, don't be such a fucking prude. It's only a bloody line of coke. I bet you're the only one in your office not bang on it.'

'What?'

'You know what. All your bloody media-whore mates.'

'Shut up, Alex.' I could hear the doorbell ringing now, laughter outside in the street.

'I thought you liked a good time, Mag,' he snapped, rolling up a ten-pound note.

'It's not because I'm a prude, you bastard. You know exactly why it is. My mother –'

'Oh, change the record. I know she was doped up to the eyeballs. So what?' Alex stared at me and then he snorted that enormous line. 'Fancy one?' he mocked, and sniffed massively, pushing the rolled note at me. The queen would blanch now if she could see what she was up to, I thought disjointedly.

'No, I bloody well don't,' I said. The bell rang again insistently.

Alex strode past me, pushing his shirt into his trousers, as unkempt as ever, rubbing his nose. 'Time to face the music, baby.' He bared his teeth in a semblance of a grin, but his yellow eyes were full of menace. 'Tidy yourself up, yeah?'

I looked down to see an enormous ladder running up my filmy hold-up. 'Shit. Alex, wait!' I stumbled in my silly heels as I tried to catch his arm, but he was too fast for me. He was already gone.

\* \* \*

313

In the cab the driver was singing along tunelessly to Dolly Parton's *Jolene*. Alex reached forward and rudely slammed the glass divide.

'I quite like that song,' I protested. Alex gave me a look and started opening his post. I couldn't be bothered to argue: I simply wanted to get through Barbara's party sober; to get to the Dorchester unflustered; to get the whole bloody night over with, in fact.

Alex tossed letter after bill onto the seat, until, with a nasty lurch, I recognised Malcolm's scruffy scrawl on the final envelope he held. Without a word, Alex tore it open. Without a word, he read it once. His eyes narrowed. He looked out of the window. We were in the heart of the City now, heading for some swanky restaurant on the river. Still silent, Alex screwed the letter up into a ball and threw it on the floor.

As the cab slowed at a set of lights, I leaned forward and picked it up, smoothing it out. It was short and to the point.

*Alexander,*
*Regrettably I have decided I will have to decline the kind offer to help your business out. It hasn't been an easy decision but I think it is a fair one. Much as I would like to make the loan, I feel I am doing you more of a favour by not giving it to you at this juncture. I think it is time for you to realise what it's like to be on your own – just like I was at your age. Also, I think you need to knock the boozing on the head. It ain't doing much for you at all.*

*Good luck, son. I am happy to give you any (free!) advice that might add to your business acumen.*
*Yours,*
*Pa*

'Can you stop here, please, mate?' Alex muttered at the driver, and jumped out into two lanes of oncoming traffic.

'Alex, wait.' I paid the driver. By the time I got into the bar, Alex was already halfway through a pint, a whisky chaser glinting on the bar beside it. He handed me a glass. Against my better judgement, I took it. 'What are you doing?'

'I'm not going,' he said. 'I'm not in the mood now.'

'Don't be silly,' I soothed, but I was irritated. 'Your mum will be so upset if you don't show up.'

'I just can't bear to sit in the same room as my bloody father. I don't get it, Mag. Why the fuck does he hate me so much?'

'He doesn't hate you, baby. He – he's just Malcolm.'

Alex didn't answer. He just drained his drink and ordered himself another.

'Look, I'm sorry, but I'm going to have to go. I need to –'

'Don't leave me on my own, Mag. I don't mean to be a shit, I don't really,' he muttered, kissing the side of my neck so that I shuddered with an emotion I couldn't immediately place. 'I need you, baby.'

I slid out of his grasp. 'I can't heal you, Alex,' I said slowly. 'It's got to come from you. You're going to destroy us both if you don't stop all this soon.'

'All *what*?'

The air between us curdled as we glowered at each other. A clot of misery swelled in my chest as he grabbed my arm. 'Maggie? I said don't go.'

I felt that eerie sensation when you peer down from a great height and see how easy it would be to simply step right off. The feeling you get when you're almost tempted to do it.

'I'm going to be late.'

'You know, Maggie, you think you can save the world with your stupid TV show. But you can't, baby.'

'No, you're right. But maybe I can save myself, Alex.'

I turned and walked out.

\* \* \*

315

I arrived at the Dorchester only slightly late, only slightly drunk, unbuttoning my jacket in the clammy night, dying for another drink now to anaesthetise the pain. Sam and Joseph were waiting in the foyer, hands in suit pockets, both looking rather over-whelmed as bright young things air-kissed and hugged all around them.

'Come on.' I indicated the ballroom with my head, suddenly feeling like a Roman general at the Coliseum. Like little lambs, I led those boys to the lions.

Renee was already seated at our table in a hideous gold creation circa 1971, her gnarly hand proprietorial on the arm of a young black guy I vaguely recognised from some music show. I was sure she must have bribed him to accompany her.

'Hello, I'm Maggie. Drink?' I grabbed the bottle of Merlot from the middle of the table and waved it so some splashed down my arm. 'Whoops!'

'Johnson.' He reached out a hand to shake mine; he had a nice smile and silver hoops in his ears. 'Don't mind if I do, thanks.'

Renee simpered at Johnson, who was still grinning at me. Renee's simper turned to stone. Gently, Sam took the bottle.

'Allow me.'

Sam looked very handsome in his tuxedo and much less gawky than normal – if terribly young – his nose still peeling a little from his deep tan, his hair on end, friendship bands peeping from his pristine white cuff. I smiled at him benevo-lently. I knew I couldn't teach Joseph anything – he was already arguing with Johnson about the state of the Tory party today, for God's sake (not Fascist enough for him, probably) – but Sam, well, he might just be the hope of British television. I patted his hand.

'I'm just going to the loo.' He flushed beneath his tan and loped off across the chattering room.

'Bit young for you, Maggie, babes,' Renee hissed.

'He's not *for* me, Renee, at all. And anyway, I could say the same, couldn't I, *babes*.' I looked pointedly at Johnson, my smile as glacial as I could manage in the hot night. An executive producer accepted an award for a particularly car-crash edition of *Wife Swap*, his table whooping and looking inappropriately smug. I yawned widely. My mate Naz materialised from behind a pillar as Sam sat down again beside me.

'Mag! I thought you'd be here.' She kissed me.

'How's it going?' I refilled my glass and offered her a slurp. 'Meet Sam, and this is Joseph, and Johnson. And you know Renee, of course.'

'Hiya all! If you fancy a quick livener, I'm on the *Panorama* table, behind the *Big Brother* lot,' she muttered in my ear. 'Those spoddy types are mad for it.'

A big ruddy-faced man appeared behind Sam. 'All right, Sammy? Enjoying yourself?'

Dickie Crosswell. Sam must have taken after his mother, I thought hazily, smiling at the jolly brick-red face and three chins. He looked like a man who enjoyed life, though he had small eyes sunk like raisins in dough. Sam was flushing gently again.

'Dad,' he muttered, head bowed.

Joseph looked sulky as I stood to shake Crosswell's hand. Crosswell leaned forward and kissed me heartily on both cheeks. 'You must be the lovely Maggie. Sam's told me all about you. Keep up the good work.'

It was my turn to blush.

Somewhere between Fern Britton awarding her mate Philip Schofield for Best Entertainment show and Judy Finnegan's dress NOT falling off – to everyone's enduring sadness – as she awarded a gurning Davina for most Compassionate Presenter for the ten-thousandth year in a row, I cadged a fag off Johnson and snuck out to the courtyard off the ballroom. I could have been a million miles from London as I stood in the dying light, the hollyhocks in wooden planters taller than my head, snail tracks slippery and silver over the frayed lower leaves, and lit my first cigarette in months.

'Maggie,' his voice made me jump as I coughed, 'I didn't know you smoked.'

'I don't really any more.' Hydrangea heads as big as cauliflowers wobbled in the gentle breeze as I ground out the hardly smoked cigarette with my toe, the unfamiliar taste pungent in my mouth.

'Will you wait while I smoke mine?' Sam licked his Rizla.

My phone beeped; I ignored it. 'Give us a drag.' I held my hand out for his roll-up.

'Aren't you going to check your message?'

'I suppose.' Listlessly I opened the envelope on the screen.

**I CAN'T BELIEVE YOU DESERTED ME, YOU TRAITOR. WHERE THE FUCK DID YOU GO?**

Alex.

I shook my head and shoved the phone away.

'Okay?'

I tried to nod – and failed, bowing my head now as Sam gazed at me; as I realised suddenly that I was crying. Slowly, soundlessly, tears slipped down my cheeks, and I covered my face quickly, ashamed of the naked emotion.

'Hey, Maggie.' Sam's voice was quiet as he slipped an arm around my shoulders. 'Don't cry. What's wrong?'

'Oh God, sorry,' I gulped. 'How stupid. I don't know really. Everything. Nothing. Just ignore me. I think – I'm just tired.'

I felt a huge yawning emptiness, like a rushing in my ears and I swayed slightly, wiping my tears away as Sam exhaled his smoke. And then he leaned forward and kissed me. I was so surprised I almost fell into the hydrangeas; his lips were soft on mine and I was hesitant. Then he stopped. I opened my eyes slowly and looked into his very green ones.

'Oh,' I said quietly.

'Sorry.' The flush spread beneath his freckles.

'Don't be,' I murmured. 'I was just a bit – taken aback.'

'I shouldn't –'

'Ssshh.' I put my finger against his mouth. 'You should. It's nice. No one's kissed me like that for –'

He kissed me again. He was so nice; such a boy, so very young. He tasted of tobacco and wine and I felt no lust for him, just a kind of drunken sweetness from lost teenage holidays.

'You always look so sad, you know,' he whispered.

'Sad?'

'You're so beautiful – but you always look kind of haunted.'

I was touched that he'd noticed anything about me at all. 'I thought I just looked – I don't know.' I tried to laugh. 'Knackered all the time.'

'No, just sad.' He pushed my hair back off my face. 'And beautiful. Would you –' he cleared his throat nervously, 'would you like to come home with me?'

'What – back to your dad's?' I laughed. 'I don't think so, Sam, sweetheart.'

He looked embarrassed and I immediately felt guilty. 'Sorry. That came out all wrong. It's just, well, I've got a boyfriend, you know.' I thought of Alex; I realised I didn't feel any guilt about him at all. I looked at Sam again, into his black-fringed eyes that gleamed in the dark, and I smiled. 'You're so sweet.'

'Don't say that.' He scuffed the gravel with his baseball boot. 'It sounds a bit – you know. Patronising.'

'Aha!' Naz popped out of the glass doors, her glossy bob swinging in the candlelight. 'Smokers united!' Then she peered at us in the gloom. 'Sorry, am I interrupting something?'

I moved away from Sam and accepted another fag from her. 'Don't be silly.'

Naz gave me a light. 'Listen, Ben and Jeff from Roar have

booked a suite on the twelfth floor. They've got a sound-system going and everything. Come up afterwards.'

The night seemed to speed up then, as we went up and down in the big lifts between the ballroom and the free booze and the caners in Suite 103 until I realised I was having a positive whale of a time. Johnson left Renee downstairs chatting up a courteous Trevor McDonald and skinned up several enormous spliffs of Sam's skunk that I didn't dare try; my head had started to spin already and everyone was drinking champagne and Mojitos and dancing to Kanye West and then I felt so pissed suddenly that I decided to have a line of Naz's coke. It seemed like a blinding idea at the time, and Sam had one too, and then I felt very peculiar and suddenly much more sober, like I'd just seen everything with great clarity, like the whole room had stopped tilting, was brightening and sharpening into cartoon-like colour. The music was so loud it rocked through my body as Sam pulled me into the ornate bathroom and pushed the door shut behind us and we kissed again, and this time it wasn't quite so innocent. I leaned over him as he sat on the edge of the bath and he unbuttoned my shirt and kissed my neck, and I thought *this is nice, really, really nice*, although it was also rather blurry and this time I had to push away thoughts of Alex in the flat earlier – and then suddenly there was a massive pounding on the door and I jumped. I turned towards the door to see Johnson.

'Blood, there's some bloke looking for you – and that kid Joseph downstairs told him you were up here. He don't look too happy, I must say.'

I thought Johnson was talking to Sam until suddenly there was Alex looming behind him, oh Christ, and I didn't even have time to button my shirt as he pushed past the other man to haul me off Sam's lap, and then he literally picked Sam up by the scruff of his neck and punched him so hard that I heard the bone in Sam's nose crack.

'Sam,' I screamed, far too late. Then Alex lifted me right off my own feet, dragging me backwards towards the door.

'Ow.' Tears sprang to my eyes. He had hold of handfuls of my hair, and Johnson was moving to pick Sam up off the floor, and I tried to speak, to explain, but I was shaking with fear and adrenaline.

'I was just –'

'Fuck off,' Alex snarled.

Sam was trying to stand now, holding his nose, blood seeping through his fingers, and I reached out to him. 'Oh God, Sam. I'm so sorry –'

'Shut up, you stupid cow,' Alex howled, flinging me back so I banged my head against the door-frame. 'What the fuck are you up to?'

'Easy now, bruv.' Johnson was coming towards us now, arms extended, pacifying.

'I'm sorry,' I stuttered to my furious boyfriend, but he wasn't listening, he was squaring up to Johnson.

'Alex, for God's sake.' I tried to pull him back before he punched Johnson too, but Alex grabbed my arms now in an unremitting hold, staring down at me like he didn't know me, like he'd never seen me – and when I looked back into his eyes I saw that they were blank. Despite the heat of the night, I shivered. 'You're hurting me,' I whispered. 'Let go, please.'

The music was still banging, but other people were coming towards us now. Naz was there, and Alex was still holding on to me as Sam leaned over the huge bath, groaning, blood splashing onto the white porcelain – and then Alex suddenly looked at him.

'Sorry, mate.'

I grabbed some loo-roll to offer Sam, to staunch the blood – and then Alex picked me up like a small child.

'Get the fuck away from him,' he snarled, dragging me outside into the suite, banging me against the wall, and he had his hands

321

around my throat, and I could see he was gone, he wasn't there any more, he was in a netherworld. He didn't know what he was doing and I was struggling to get free and then Johnson was trying to pull Alex off, and Naz was yelling at him, and then hotel security were there and suddenly one of them headbutted Alex and I was screaming like I couldn't stop – actually, the thing was I *couldn't* stop – and then I was trying to get in-between the security guard and Alex and somehow my suit got torn and my shirt was still undone, and then I got punched too by a random fist before Naz pulled me away. Then Alex got arrested, and I was so utterly hysterical by this point that for some reason they took me in too.

And that was when Charlie had to bail me out.

Dickie Crosswell wanted to press charges against Alex. Sally told me later that he'd been in Charlie's office the next day with Sam, absolutely furious, and Charlie had been utterly sycophantic – but it was Sam who'd apparently dissuaded his father in the end. Somehow the Awards people managed to hush it all up, paranoid that it would get out that so many industry bods were taking drugs at their do, and apparently there had even been a couple of Eastern European hookers in the room who'd wandered up from the bar, and so it was in everybody's general interest to cover it all up. Thank God no names made it into the press – although a fracas was alluded to in various gossip columns. And thank God Renee never found out exactly what happened. That would really have been the end of me.

I felt mortified about Sam. He never came back to Double-decker, at least not while I was there. I called him a few days after the incident, and he was quiet and apologetic, although I felt it was entirely my fault.

'I hope you will be happy again soon, Maggie,' he said at the end of a stilted conversation, 'you deserve to be.'

Dry-eyed, I put the phone down – but his words haunted me

for a long time afterwards. I felt hollow and truly ashamed; like I'd compromised everything I'd ever believed in, like I'd let him down.

The following Monday I dragged myself back in to work to face my furious boss.

'What the fuck were you thinking, Maggie?' Charlie snarled. He was so angry he could hardly speak, pale beneath his tan. 'Fucking with Crosswell? I mean, why not choose the son of the most powerful man in TV to hospitalise. Give him some coke and a fucking Polish tart while you're at it. I trusted you – and you and your loser boyfriend utterly, *utterly* fucked it up.'

I was completely contrite, tried hard to explain – except what could I possibly say to make it any better? 'My boyfriend's an alcoholic and I'm not far off and I kissed the well-connected work-experience because he said I was beautiful; I kissed him because my boyfriend has forgotten me; because I'm so terribly, terribly lonely.'

Charlie was about to sack me, of that I was sure, and then he seemed to realise I was rapidly falling apart – albeit quietly – by this stage coming into work drunk, black-eyed from that flying fist, Alex's fingerprints visible around my neck – and so he gave me a week off to 'recuperate', as he called it.

'Sort it out, Maggie,' he said, and got his assistant to book me an appointment with the employee counsellor – 'before you have a complete breakdown, you stupid girl.' At the time I was just grateful to still have a job; grateful to have an understanding boss; grateful my father hadn't found out about Alex and me being arrested. It wasn't until later that I realised Charlie was only worried about being sued by Crosswell or rumbled by Lyons or the press.

I made Alex come with me to Cornwall; I said it was make or break, and of course he knew the truth. The night before we went, Bel turned up at ours when Alex was out and told me how worried she was and that I needed to sort it out – I was drinking

323

too much and smoking again and why was I this thin, it wasn't natural, and she loved Alex but the two of us were killing one another. And I defended him, saying he'd never laid a finger on me before, but really I knew we were in freefall over a deep chasm. We were never going to get back from there.

Stubbornly I told Bel to get out, she was no friend of mine, although deep down of course I knew she was, my very best friend, the only one brave enough to actually challenge me.

And despite sticking up for Alex, it was all spoiled, and although I knew I was complicit because I'd kissed Sam, I knew too that I would never have done it if things had been right between us. And although Alex tried to explain his loss of control as stress from work and having to stay up all night to get things done, and he swore he'd knock both the booze and the cocaine on the head – really soon – my trust in him was shattered. I felt sorry for him about Malcolm, I did, really – but hey, at least both his parents were alive and literally kicking. And I couldn't forget because when I looked in the mirror I saw those marks around my neck. I suggested we have a week off the booze while we talked things through – but he point-blank refused.

In the cold light of a Cornish summer's day I realised I couldn't forget that violence; I couldn't forgive the drinking any more.

One evening as we got into bed, Alex tried to kiss me but I pushed him away; I felt I didn't know him any more. We lay side by sleepless side. The next night he moved into the spare room.

That last afternoon we drove from Pendarlin to the small hamlet of Port Quin down on the coast, Debussy's *Clair de Lune* playing on the car radio, and I thought it had never sounded so sad. I dropped a pound in the honesty box, and then we walked up onto the headland and sat in the sun among the bracken and the pink-tipped heather, but we didn't speak. Digby sniffed around joyously in search of rabbit-holes, and I stared out at the brilliant sky, at the tiny fishing boats and the buoys bobbing in the turquoise sea, and I knew that although I loved this man,

Bel was right, he was so damaged I couldn't save him on my own; I couldn't bring him back.

And then Digby caught some kind of field-mouse. He was so proud, but it made me want to cry as its tiny feet flapped from the dog's salivating mouth. I let Alex deal with the corpse.

In silence we packed up the cottage and the car and then we headed back to London. Somewhere along the way the car began to smoke and stutter and then the rain began and we argued until we both began to scream, and I told him he'd broken my heart, cliché or none, he'd stamped all over it with his big shambolic feet and it could have been so different but it wasn't. And I told him I couldn't see him any more, it was over – until he sorted himself out, at least – and he was so angry his bashed-up face was white with rage and he said *fine*, and I nearly said I didn't mean it because I'd never loved a man the way I loved him – but then the AA man turned up and dropped me at the coach station because the car was fucked. The car had died just like our stupid love, and Alex wouldn't look at me as the tow-truck pulled out again, he just glowered into space, although Digby panted happily through the windscreen at me as if he were just popping round the corner; and I climbed onto that packed coach in Bristol with a dead feeling in my heart and head. And then the coach took me to my terrible fate.

# Chapter Thirty-Eight

My chin hit my chest and I jerked awake again. Two teacher's ticks before my tired eyes; two hypnotic slashes that went back and forth, forth and back – although the rain had long since stopped. Turning the wipers off, I opened the window wide for a blast of night air, realising how fast I was approaching the spot. I pulled onto the hard shoulder.

The bitter wind whipped my short hair into peaks as I got out of the car. A supermarket juggernaut thundered by, sounding his horn, and I staggered in the wind-tunnel before wrapping my coat tight around me and stumbling up the bank in the dark.

*Lest we forget: to the brave souls lost on that tragic night.*

I stared and stared at the brassy memorial, at the shrivelled bouquets, at the single rose in a plastic case preserved chemically – but they meant nothing to me. I wasn't the same person who'd been on that coach that night in such a very bad state. I wasn't the person who'd spiralled into the breakdown last summer that Charlie had predicted, despite my very best efforts not to, while I was convalescing at my father's. I wasn't the same person who'd sobbed and sobbed about my mother and my boyfriend and the abyss of loneliness I floundered in, sobbing on the figurative shoulder of the therapist, a kindly older man with sad eyes and a cropped beard and a nose with a knobble on the end that quivered sometimes when he spoke. A man who my frantic father was paying to listen, to assure me that, no, I wasn't mad; I was more than my mother's daughter. That I would be all right, honestly, it might just take some time to recover from this trauma.

The truth was that I was still screaming in silent anguish, screaming into the yearning void my mother had left, and Alex's last actions had finally released the pressure building since my teens.

The last time I'd seen him, the man with the knobbly nose had studied me hard. 'And this boyfriend, this man with all the addictions. Why him, Maggie? Why did you pick him?'

I stared miserably out of the window, where a cloud shaped rather like my mother's floppy wedding hat was scudding by. 'He made me laugh,' I ventured after some time.

'And?'

'And what?' I sought for more. 'Alex is very bright. And I loved his passion for life. He was passionate about everything.' I corrected myself. 'Is passionate, I mean.' He wasn't dead, after all.

'And they are the only reasons?'

'No,' I said slowly, 'I suppose not.'

'So?'

'So.' I took a deep breath. 'He needed me.'

There was a long pause. 'And you wanted to be needed?'

Yes. I wanted to be needed.

And the man didn't say it, but we both knew what he meant. *Like your mother hadn't needed you.*

'Like my mother hadn't,' I whispered.

One day after that, my father collected the dog from Alex's and took us both to Greenwich Park. 'You know, Maggie,' he said quietly, throwing a stick for the scruffy little terrier, 'your mother loved you more than anything in the world.'

We stood next to one another on the hill that overlooked the far-off Thames, sparkling in the early-morning sun, the Queen's House below us a pristine white against the green sweep of grass. The spire of Our Lady Star of the Sea spiked the Indian-summer sky. It reminded me of the first joke I ever told.

'Why did the sky laugh, Mummy?'

'Why, Mag?'

'Because the trees tickled its tummy.'

And then I would slip my small hand proudly into my mother's as she would laugh, laugh just like I thought the sky had. The way I thought she'd laugh with me forever.

'I know she killed herself . . .' My father's voice quietened as it always did when he spoke those harsh words, and he paused. He threw the stick for Digby again. 'But she was in a place she couldn't get out of at that time. Couldn't see out of. You were her life – absolutely. You do know that, don't you?'

This time it was his hand I slipped mine into wordlessly.

Quite soon after that, I decided to call the therapy a day.


I shivered on the bank. Nor was I the person now whom Bel had visited almost every evening in the summer, the person lucky enough to have a friend as patient as her, a very, very good friend who listened as I said I was worried I had lost it. Lost my mind; lost everything.

'Not me,' she said brightly, 'you can't get rid of me that easily,' and she painted my toenails scarlet and blue and brought me pictures Hannah had painted of us on vivid yellow beaches with be-hatted suns smiling happily down.

No. I wasn't that person: I was stronger than that shattered soul. Standing on the side of the bleak dark M4, I pulled my coat tighter round me now. It was time to step forward into something new; time to make peace with my old life and move on with dignity. I could not stay in this ugly place, in this grave-yard of a life. I had to accept that Alex and I had long since been over; that though my foot would always be scarred from the crash, it would keep healing until the scar was very faint. That Seb was a nice, attractive man who I still couldn't quite fathom, and that maybe he would be in my future, but that it wasn't yet. That right now, I had to think alone and for myself. That, most importantly I still had my dad and Jenny and Gar and Digby, and Bel, despite her being so far away.

I *was* the person who had parked my car just off Sloane Square a couple of hours ago after leaving Seb in Battersea, and walked into the café with a name like a bird. The person who had ordered coffee and fizzy water and had sat waiting on the terrace.

And as she tripped gaily to the table, thinking this was a social meet, I was the person who looked at her intently and said, 'So, Fay, what's this all about?'

'What do you mean, Maggie?' she asked lightly, unwrapping her pink pashmina and ordering a white-wine spritzer from a drooling waiter. Such a girlish drink; so apt.

I lit a cigarette and inhaled hard. 'Let's cut the crap, shall we, Fay? Ever since I met you, you've been following me around. Were you in Battersea an hour or two ago?'

She winced as if I'd just poked her in the eye. 'Battersea? No, why? What do you mean, following you?'

'Oh, don't be so obtuse.'

She stared at me, all hurt.

'It means awkward,' I said.

'I know what it means, thank you, Maggie.' Her little chin jutted into the air.

'Look, Fay,' I took it down a notch or two, 'it's just, ever since we met on the show –'

'On the coach, really, Maggie.'

'We didn't, though, did we? I didn't know you existed till I saw you sitting in that studio. And just because we were both on that sodding coach, and the stupid thing crashed, it doesn't mean we are soul sisters now. Perhaps I did turn you over when you choked on your own blood, but I still can't remember it.

Even if your hair is like mine now, it doesn't mean I'm looking for a new best friend.' I ladled sugar into my coffee. Then some more. 'Especially not one who's decided to start seeing my ex.'

'I'm not seeing him. I wouldn't do that to you, Maggie.'

'Why not?' I snapped, grinding out my cigarette. 'You don't owe me anything, Fay. I don't want to be horrible, but all I want is . . . all I ask is that you leave me alone. You're freaking me out. All this turning up everywhere I go.'

'Where? What do you mean?'

'What do *you* mean where?' I wailed. 'For fuck's sake, Fay. At parties, at my work, at my bloody flat the day it's broken into. It's a bit coincidental, isn't it? And more than a bit bloody weird. Have you been stalking me? Do you hate me for some reason? Did you cut my picture out of all my family photos and leave them with my grandmother?'

'No, of course not.' She stared at me, wounded to the core. 'Why would I? I love you.'

'Oh my God,' I moaned, slumping forward, my head in my hands now. 'Please, Fay.'

'Not love you like that.' She patted my hand with her little paw. 'Just in a caring way, silly. That's what I've been learning with my Survivors' group. Don't blame, just forgive.'

'Forgive?'

'Not you. Just generally.'

'Great. Well, you'll forgive me then for asking you to stay the hell away from me.' I took a massive swig of coffee and burnt my mouth. I was rarely this brutal with anyone but I'd reached my snapping point. I couldn't look at her as I said, 'And if you want to date Alex, that's fine – but I don't want to know about it, okay?'

'I don't want to date him. He's very damaged, Maggie.'

'You're telling me.'

'He's still in love with you, I think.'

We gazed at one another.

'Really?' I said quietly, after some time.

'Yes, really. You know, I don't understand why you're quite so angry.'

'Don't you?' But I felt the fury ebb away now, wash up on the beach of my exhaustion like dirty old spume. I watched a middle-aged couple go through the doors, the drizzle that had just begun outside glittering on the woman's cashmere scarf. Her companion was very attentive, taking her coat and carefully pressing it on the waiter before pulling out her chair and seating her like she was made of china.

'I just feel so – well, kind of cornered right now,' I said. 'And very alone. And I probably *need* to be alone, to sort things out.'

'You probably need some friends, you mean,' Fay corrected me pertly.

'I don't. Not any new ones. Not right now. I'd only make bad friends, the state of mind I'm in.'

Fay stirred her drink with an efficient cocktail stick. 'Fine.' She licked the stick thoughtfully. 'But if you change your mind, I'm here for you. You know that, don't you? You changed my life.'

I looked out at the neon words above the Royal Court Theatre, at the hustle of people plunging into Sloane Square tube beneath the fizz of the Christmas lights, at the throng at the bar chattering like birds. Everyone was meeting someone; everyone was heading somewhere. Christmas parties were on the horizon, the buzz that December brings was vibrant in the air. There was no more lonely a time than this, I thought sadly. No time when it was more poignant to be lonely. Were they all wanted, all these strangers? Were they all welcomed?

I shook my head against my maudlin thoughts and dug some money from my bag. 'Listen, can you settle up? I've got a long drive ahead of me, I should get going.'

'Sure.' Fay tried to give me back the ten-pound note, but I wouldn't take it. 'Off anywhere nice?'

I smiled at her wanly and stood. 'I think so. I'll see you around, okay?'

For a moment when I walked away, I thought she called something, but her voice was dragged into the busy night. I didn't look back.

# Chapter Thirty-Nine

Did ghosts patrol this part of the road, the road I stood beside at midnight? Did they congregate here on the M4's hard shoulder, swapping stories of their deaths in this freezing darkness?

Was that Fay lying there in a small heap; was that me being cut free from a jagged mass of deadly metal and pulled through a shattered window? Was that me lying beside Fay, who began to choke; did I turn her so she could breathe before I fell unconscious myself from the pain? Did the motorists directed on to the hard shoulder thank God it wasn't them as they slowed to have a horrified peek at the limp huddles that were being hastily covered over? Was that the body of the Hobbit woman I had just stepped around, *Northanger Abbey* gripped in one pale and lifeless hand, her ever-moving lips stilled for good?

Was that the couple who had whispered in front of me entwined forever in a ghastly screaming death? The tall boy who had gone up to talk to his friends lying on his back near the central reservation, next to a stunned man who'd escaped without a scratch.

The boy who had opened his eyes and stood, slowly, slowly, and hobbled to the side of the road, blood in his eyes, blinking in the police's floodlights. Who, after a while, let a paramedic wrap a blanket around his shoulders and then slumped on the grassy bank, staring at the mangled body of a piebald horse. Dead; dead just like the old lady whose white hair poked in tufts from beneath another blanket. Was that the old Maggie there? Had I left a piece of me forever in the terrible wreck?

I stared at the dark damp road and felt a hot tear trickle down my icy cheek, and I shivered properly now, trying to banish these dark thoughts from my exhausted head. After them chased confused images of Alex and Fay together. I shut my mind down as best I could, and realised suddenly that I was freezing.

Climbing back in the car, I cuddled the dog until I started to get warm. Then I turned the radio on, the heating up, and drove on to the next service station, where I bought tea and chocolate and a copy of *Vogue* in Bel's honour, and threw my fags away before travelling on to Cornwall. And it was only when I got to Pendarlin hours later in the pitch black that I actually exhaled.

In the morning the wind had settled and I awoke late to find a thin sprinkling of frost on the ground and the sun shining, albeit weakly. I made strong coffee, tuned the radio to Radio 3 and ate some cornflakes before letting Digby out.

I watched him chasing imaginary shadows and his tail, cutting zig-zags on the lawn, and I was really glad to see him free again. London life didn't suit the poor old thing. Turning to go back in, I noticed with irritation the fresh tyre-tracks across the frosted grass. I wished the bloody postman wouldn't always cut across the lawn. At the door I looked for letters, but when I bent to check there was just an old postcard from the gas company about reading the meter last week. I felt a fresh rush of unease, but I shook it off and went to get dressed.

Under a soft chalky sky so rich you could scoop it in your hands, I drove down tiny lanes to Pentire Point. The landscape rolled out before me with the barren majesty of December, sheep like so many balls of dirty cotton-wool dotting the fields. The headland was wreathed in sea-mist that smudged the hills and made them vague, but by the time I parked at the muddy farm it was finally clearing. Frost had hardened some of the ground I tramped across, but in parts the puddles were so deep I had to jump them, splashing through the water, skidding in the mud

334

as brambles pulled at my legs. I trekked up and up the hill until I realised how hungry I was. A sudden surge of birds flapped like hope up into the air and I actually smiled.

'Lunchtime, eh, Dig?' I whistled to the dog. Turning back, I could see a figure in a blue anorak heading our way, distant, on the other side of the cliff. Otherwise it was deserted, Digby barking occasionally as the birds swooped and veered above us before sweeping off. The silence was immense, and for the first time in days I felt at peace.

The figure in the blue anorak had disappeared. Digby and I were alone in the world apart from minuscule brown cows clinging to the chequered hillside in the distance. I reached the point where the track narrowed, fringed by a vertiginous drop to the frothing sea – and suddenly the man was there, on the narrow path in front of me, and I nearly screamed in shock because he'd come from nowhere.

'God, sorry,' I said, laughing shakily, my hand on my beating heart. 'That was a bit overdramatic. I just didn't realise you were so close.'

'I didn't mean to scare you.' His blue hood was tightly drawn around his grey curls like an old pixie. He looked down at Digby darting between our feet. 'Nice dog. Pedigree, is he? A terrier?'

'Yes, he's a Border,' I said, moving round the man on the path, my tummy a bit squiffy as I tried not to look down at the fierce sea lashing the rocks that were like giant's stairs below.

His arm shot out and grabbed mine, his anorak crackling with the sudden movement.

'Saved your life,' he joked.

I looked at him uncertainly and fear gripped my stomach as I shook him off before heading away, a little quicker than before; my heart pounding a little faster. I realised how deserted it was up here, how stupid I had been. I should have stayed on the beaches. I should have stayed in sight of people.

335

'Dig,' I commanded over one shoulder, 'come on. *Now*, Digby.'

'Sorry,' the man was calling forlornly as I slid through the sludge. 'I was only messing around.'

'Hilarious,' I muttered, and tried not to actually run.

By the time I got to the car I was sweating despite the chill. I locked all the doors and then laughed tremulously to myself again as Digby gazed at me curiously from the passenger seat. Perhaps I was going insane. Some poor hill-walker trying to be friendly and I think he's a stalker. I started the engine before scrabbling through the glove compartment in hope of a cigarette, but I remembered I'd binned them all last night.

And then I looked up and the man was at the farm gate. He must have practically run to catch up with me and he was shouting something and he was climbing over the gate towards me and that was it – I pulled off, except I revved the engine too much, so much that my tyres stuck in the mud for a second and I wasn't moving, I was just spinning up dirt, and the white-eyed farm dog was barking frantically and the man was getting nearer, he was waving something at me, something shiny, oh my God was it a knife: and then eventually we shot off. I kept my foot pressed to the floor until I reached Polzeath, where I sat for a minute until my heart stopped racing, and I saw how normal everything around me was: the winter surfers lolloping up the beach, boards under their arms, wetsuited like sleek black seals, laughing, flicking tangled curls from their squinting eyes, and for a minute I thought of Sam.

Then I took a deep breath and started the car again, heading home to safety. Only when I reached Pendarlin and went to unlock the front door, shopping bag in hand, that cold fear gripped me again, irrevocably this time. Someone was inside, inside my house. The front door was unlocked, and someone was inside. Someone who was playing my piano.

# Chapter Forty

No one had a key to Pendarlin except Val in St Kew, and my father up in London. Frantically I searched for my phone, but my phone wasn't in any of my pockets, or my bag. My phone wasn't here at all, I realised with a sinking heart. The man running down the farm path with the shiny thing in his hand. Not a knife at all. My bloody phone.

The pub would be open now – there were vehicles in the car park, I could see them through the trees, but I knew I wasn't in shouting distance. Should I go into the cottage, or should I jump in the car and find help?

I pushed the door tentatively; it was ajar. 'Hello?' I called gingerly. 'Who's here?'

I recognised the melody. The allegretto of the Rondo was perfectly judged, the movement flowing seamlessly. But who the bloody hell played that well?

'Hello?' I called again, more vehemently this time. I took a deep breath and stepped inside.

Of course he wasn't actually playing it. The piano stood untouched in the corner of the room, the muslin I'd draped over it last year still unruffled. He'd just helped himself to the stereo in his usual arrogance, choosing a CD of Beethoven's piano sonatas as he lounged on the sofa waiting for me.

As I crossed the room, heart still thumping painfully, I was gratified to hear Digby actually manage a growl for once. 'Good boy,' I murmured to the dog, who was stuck steadfast at my heels. 'How the hell did you get in?' I asked, reaching the stereo and snapping it off.

He smiled his oily smile, his deep-set eyes inscrutable. 'You left the door unlocked, my dear Maggie.'

'I'm sure I didn't.'

'Well, someone did, I'm afraid.'

'I didn't see your car. How did you get here?'

'It's over at the pub. I walked the last fifty metres. I'm exhausted, darling.'

I sat on the arm of the old squashy chair that had been my mother's favourite. 'Why are you here, Charlie? I've said my good-byes.'

'I missed you, darling. And I fancied a little spin in the country.'

I sniffed. 'I thought Dubai was more your thing?'

'It is, darling, to be honest. So bloody parochial around here. All the cottagers' curtains twitching the minute I pulled up at the pub, and everyone knowing exactly who you were when I asked for directions. Talking of which –' he stood up and stretched, 'let me buy you a drink. I may loathe the West Country, but they had a damn fine-looking steak and Guinness pie on the menu over there and I'm bloody starving. Thrashing the Alfa down the motorway has given me an appetite.'

For a moment I just glared at him. 'So you haven't come to kill me?'

'No, darling. 'Fraid not.' He studied his perfectly shaped nails. 'If anything, actually,' he didn't look up, 'I've come to apologise.'

'Blimey,' I said, whistling for Digby. 'Wonders will never cease.'

The fire danced in the old metal grate as an overly jovial Charlie ordered at the bar, debating the best pub red with the melancholy landlord as if he drank here every day. Longing for a cigarette, I tapped my foot impatiently against the antique settle, waiting for an explanation.

It took Charlie a good half an hour of blowing his own trumpet and talking about new ideas and an LA office that he thought I might *just* be interested in running, while I said nothing much and ate my chicken pie, every morsel, because I was so hungry. And then he said it.

'I'm sorry, Maggie. I dealt with the whole affair very badly.'

The final pea eluded me, rolling round the plate. 'What affair?' I murmured, concentrating on its capture. 'The awards ceremony, you mean?'

'The whole thing really.' Charlie folded his napkin and placed it on the table.

I waited.

'Sam, your accident, your – your breakdown. I should have realised you needed help,' he said eventually, and topped up his glass. 'That it wasn't really you.'

'What wasn't?'

'All that business with Alex and Sam. The drugs and the drinking. Your fall from grace. I should have been more –'

'Understanding?' I suggested.

He laughed. 'Darling, I don't do understanding. No, *tolerant* was the word I was looking for. Sometimes, you know, I get caught up in –' He paused again.

'What?'

'My own ambition. And frustration. I couldn't believe it of you, Maggie. I was shocked you fell so far.' He regarded me for a moment; I thought I read regret in his look. 'I'd expected such great things of you. I just needed you back on your feet.'

'I thought it was more my knees you wanted me on.'

'Well, that too, darling.' He grinned, and with a shudder I remembered that night in his flat. 'That would have been nice. You're an extremely attractive girl –'

'Fuck off, Charlie.' I choked on my cider. 'Quit while you're ahead, why don't you?'

'Look,' he poured himself more claret, 'suffice to say, contrition is not my thing, Maggie. But,' he concentrated on the dark liquid in his glass, 'I do regret the way I dealt with the whole affair. I had Lyons breathing down my neck; I was terrified Crosswell was going to the press. I was trying to redeem myself.' Finally he looked me in the eye. 'I should have realised the whole trauma show was one step too far. And I should have warned you about inviting Fay on first.'

'Yes, you should.'

He shrugged elegantly, the firelight flickering in the gold of his signet ring. 'I'll try better next time, Miss Warren. I promise.'

I gazed into the flames. 'There won't be a next time for me, Charlie. I'm all done.'

'Don't be stupid, Maggie,' he snapped as I stood up. 'Sit down.'

I called Digby to heel. 'I'm not stupid, actually, Charlie,' I said pleasantly. 'Thanks for lunch anyway. I guess you can claim it on expenses, so I'll let you get it. For old time's sake, shall we say?'

'Maggie, you –'

'I what?' I stood over him and last night's fury welled up again. 'You expect me to forgive you for the way you blackmailed me? I was at my weakest, most vulnerable ever, and you used that absolutely to your advantage.'

With a huge shudder, I remembered his visits to my father's house, my dad grateful for Charlie's apparent concern while he'd actually muttered in my ear about drugs and prostitutes and millionaires' sons – but mostly about how I'd let him down.

'You knew I was delirious from shock and painkillers, and you made me feel so cheap, so worthless I wanted to practically kill myself.' I winced as I saw myself in that hospital bed; in my old bedroom at my father's when I would wake sweating, convinced I was trapped in that coach again. Winced as I remembered praying Alex would come and make it all all right again, only he never did.

'You twisted things so I was terrified my dad would find out

340

– and that's the only reason I agreed to your stupid deal. I hadn't really done anything wrong. I was just in a mess.' I slammed the chair under the table angrily. 'So I lost myself for a bit, so what? I'm better now.' I stared down at him. 'And d'you know what else?'

The pub held its collective breath. Charlie smoothed his bouffant hair back nervously.

'You can take your stupid show and stick it up Renee's arse, that's what.' The barmaid's eyes were round with astonishment. 'You'll forgive me if I don't invite you back for coffee.'

Peter Trevenna from the farm across the lane nearly fell off his stool with excitement as I crossed the snug, Digby skittering on the flagstones behind me. Slamming out into the crisp December air, I muttered all the way home, crunching up the drive to Pendarlin, and when I was inside I locked all the doors behind me.

'Good riddance to bad rubbish,' I said, shooting the final bolt home. 'Hey, Dig?' For once I knew I'd done the right thing.

# Chapter Forty-One

But, right or wrong, I hardly slept that night. For the first time since I'd been coming to Pendarlin alone, I felt nervous in the cottage. I could hardly bear to admit this new fear to myself, so I didn't. After my showdown with Charlie I rattled round the kitchen noisily, baking a cake. I didn't need to weigh the flour or sugar because I knew it all instinctively – only this time something went wrong and I burnt the top. Sadly I chucked the charred sponge away and went to bed with a cup of camomile tea, leaving the radio on quietly beside me, flicking through Nigel Slater's new book until eventually I drifted off with the light on. But I never fell into that sleep so deep you wake refreshed. Instead I skated on the surface of a host of nightmares that kept me waking in the shadows, wishing fervently it was dawn.

The phone rang in the kitchen as I was boiling the kettle the next morning, and I failed to stifle my yawn as I answered.

'Malvolio's broken his bloody leg. He got a bit carried away in the yellow stocking scene and forgot the stage is only about six-foot bloody long. I think he thought it was the National, not a two-bit pub platform.'

I couldn't help laughing at the image.

'It's not funny, babe.' Seb's tone was plaintive. 'He hasn't walked since, and we've got to cancel the first night. We're going to have to cancel the whole bloody run if Jonah can't learn his lines over

342

the weekend. The good news is, I can come down and look after you.'

Was it good news? Pouring the steaming water onto the teabag, I watched it turn a murky brown. 'Oh,' I said. 'I see.' The teabag sank.

'I'll get the train, I think. It'll be quicker. Can you collect me from –'

'Seb,' I interrupted softly, 'I don't want to be rude. I'd love to see you, I really would. It's just –' I watched a spider outside the window wrapping a ladybird in a silken shroud.

'What?'

I said it very fast before I changed my mind. 'I think I need to be on my own this weekend.'

There was a long pause. 'Seb?' I said eventually, and I was on the verge of pretending I had been joking.

'Yeah, sorry, Maggie. I'm still here.'

'It's not that I don't want to see you,' I said quickly, and that was true, it was very tempting, especially after my haunted sleep. But I was running away from the truth, I knew that now. Running from the terrible void that splitting with Alex had caused in me; the emptiness I hadn't really dealt with yet.

'I'd love to. It's just – I've been in a really bad place, and I need to sort it out before I rush into anything. Do you understand?' I asked hopefully. Why should he, after all.

'Yes, Maggie, I do actually. I do understand. You've been so on edge, I'm not surprised.'

I felt a rush of relief. 'Oh God, Seb, I'm so glad. It's just – it wouldn't be fair to get you all the way down here when I feel like this. I need to clear my head first.'

'It's fine, honestly.'

'Really?'

'Listen, babe, relax. I'll still be here when you get back.'

He was such a nice man. I needed a nice man, but I needed him in about a year's time. I sat heavily on a kitchen chair. 'Thank you, Seb. You're lovely, really. I'm just a bit of a headcase right now. I'll cook you dinner when I'm back in London, next week. Is that okay?'

'Course it is,' he said cheerily. 'I'll look forward to it. And Maggie –' He paused.

'Yes?'

'Here's looking at you, kid.'

There was one thing left to do before I could lay all the spectres to rest, but I wasn't exactly sure how to go about it. I cleaned the cottage windows vigorously with vinegar and newspaper like Gar used to, prevaricating until eventually I summoned the courage to ring DI Fox. His colleague at the station told me Fox was out of town on 'business', and that Alex had been cautioned but was no longer in custody. I took a deep breath and rang Alex: he didn't answer. I left him a short message saying I'd like to speak to him and then I bundled Digby into the back of the car and drove to Port Isaac to buy some fish for supper.

It was a glorious winter's day, the kind that makes your cheeks go cold but your heart feel glad, and Digby and I tramped round the headland to Port Gaverne, over the green-black rocks that looked deceptively soft, like fuzzy-felt. In the pub by the tiny beach I had a crab sandwich and half a cider, sitting in the window in the showy December sun that gave out no heat. The sea was so still and blue I might have draped it round me like a length of silk.

Feeling almost revived, we tramped back again to pick up my turbot from Dennis Knight's fish shop on the quay, and Digby got very excited at the lobsters waving their mournful tentacles at him through the glass and barked until I grabbed him by the collar and drove us home.

I was startled to see a patrol car outside Pendarlin. A smiling policewoman got out of the driver's side and said she'd just left me a note to call her: was this the phone I'd reported lost? And she had my mobile phone in her hand, a little muddy but none the worse for wear. She popped it into my hand and I thanked her very much. And then she got back in her car and slid her window down as I was retrieving the fish from the back seat.

'Take care, my love, won't you?' She started the ignition. 'Nice flowers, by the way,' she said, pulling off.

And I looked at the front of the house where she'd jerked her thumb, and there, on the doorstep, was a bunch of flowers. A bunch of my worst nightmare: lilies.

As I staggered through into the kitchen with my bags of shopping the phone rang again.

'You wanted to talk?' His voice was so quiet I could hardly hear him.

'Alex.' My mind went blank. 'Where are you?'

'In Bristol. Looking at the old theatre. They want a refurb and –'

'Why did you do it?' I gathered my thoughts. 'You swore it wasn't –'

'It *wasn't* me, Maggie,' Alex said vehemently. 'I don't care what you say, or what that Fox bloke says, I haven't been stalking you, I swear.'

'Did you just send me more flowers?' I demanded. 'Down here, today? Horrible lilies that you know I hate.'

'Never, Maggie. I've never sent you lilies. I did –' He cleared his throat. 'I did send you some flowers at your dad's the other day.'

'Really?' I could hardly believe that. 'So why did you have that mobile then? If it wasn't you, why did you have the phone that I got those bloody texts from?'

'I found it,' he muttered.

'You must know how utterly lame that sounds.' I was scathing.

I almost felt his shrug down the phone. 'Maybe it does, but it's true. It wasn't me, you have to believe me. Someone must have planted it.'

'What do you mean, planted? This isn't *Starsky and Hutch*,

you know, Alex. It's real life.' Though I wasn't sure about that either.

'It was in that box of stuff I picked up from the flat, Maggie, I swear. Fully charged and working. I thought it was yours. I mean, for all I know –' He paused.

'What?'

'*You* put it there.'

'Are you joking?'

'Are you? If it wasn't you, Mag, then someone means you no good.'

'Well, I know that much, thanks, Alex. Of course it wasn't bloody me.'

'I thought you might –'

'What?'

'Be trying to, you know, punish me. Set me up.'

'Why would I do that?' To my dismay I found I was crying, silent tears slipping down my face, emotions buzzing round my head like angry hornets. I breathed a long, juddery sigh.

'Why would I set you up? I love you, Alex.'

'Loved.'

'Love, loved, whatever. I'm not going to set you up. I'm more worried about what *you're* trying to do to me.'

'For Christ's sake, Maggie,' he howled, 'I can't come anywhere near you anyway. They're talking about restraining orders now.'

There was a long silence broken only by Digby worrying at the lamb bone I'd chucked him earlier. 'Alex,' I whispered eventually, 'I'm frightened. I don't know what's going on.'

'Well, go home then,' he said roughly. 'Or are you with that bloke? He'll look after you, won't he?'

'No.' I stared out of the window at the darkening afternoon. Digby's ears suddenly pricked up; he growled at a ghost. 'Ssh, silly. No, I'm on my own.'

'That's a bit stupid, isn't it?'

'I just need some headspace. Headspace for a headcase.' I was glad to hear Alex insisting it wasn't him; but I was confused and scared, desperate to know who was after me – and underlying it all there was a terrible yearning sadness. Then I had a thought that hurled me out of my nostalgia.

'Talking of headcases, how come you were wining and dining Fay the other day?'

He snorted. 'Wining and dining? Hardly. I had a coffee with her. She said she had something to tell me.'

'What?'

'I don't know. She banged on about being famous and friendship, what a good friend you've been to her, and then halfway through her cappuccino her phone rang and she had to go. And that was that.'

I bit my lip. 'Did you fancy her?'

'You do sound a bit mad, actually, Mag. You want to –'

I jumped as someone tapped on the back door. 'God, who's that?' I couldn't see anyone through the frosted glass.

'Who *is* that?' Alex sounded worried.

'I don't know. Val, maybe. I'd better go. I'll –' *I'll what? Run screaming back into your arms?* 'I'll talk to you sometime.'

'Mag –'

This time I was sure the knock was at the front door. There was nothing left to say anyway, so I put the phone down and strode up the hall, plucking the door back to find no one there. Naked wisteria twigs tapped the glass like fossilised antennae; a breeze shivered through the trees and the few tenacious leaves left trembled gently. Digby shot out between my feet but I called him back uneasily, locking the doors before drawing every set of curtains in the cottage. I struggled with the broken blind in the kitchen for a bit, peering out into the gloom, wishing now that I'd had it fixed when I'd meant to. Tomorrow I'd go back to Greenwich, safely home to my father.

\*   \*   \*

I tried to ring Bel, but God alone knew what time it was in Australia and she didn't answer. I had a long bath and then lit the fire, and made some potato puree to go with the turbot, though I really wasn't hungry. I took the plate into the sitting room and pushed the food around in front of a rerun of *Parkinson* until he introduced a simpering Renee to join the indomitable Billy Connolly. I pulled a face and put some Bach on instead, opening the bottle of wine I'd been trying to resist. I lay on the sofa nursing my glass, pondering my strange new life, until the final movement jogged to a close.

As I went to change the CD the muslin cloth caught on the belt of my jeans and slithered down from the piano. I untangled myself, and then, on a whim, I pulled the whole thing off, the swirling dust cloud making me cough. I ran a finger across the polished oak of the lid and then tentatively I opened it and, still standing there, played a note, and then one more. The wisteria tapped against the windowpane again as, slowly, very slowly, I sat down on the stool, and my fingers were cold and stiff but I slid up a scale and down again, and then I started to play. Instinctively I played Debussy's *Clair de Lune*, and at first I was rusty, hitting the wrong notes as my fingers slowly unfurled after all these years, like they'd been clamped in tight cat claws – but after a while I began to feel like I'd never stopped.

The lights went off. My right hand shot out inadvertently in shock and hit the high keys as my gasp reverberated round the room – a gasp that sounded like the sea being sucked over shingle. And then it was silent and utterly dark as the piano notes died slowly.

I jumped up and rushed to the light-switch, kicking the wine bottle over and standing on Digby's paw in the process so that he yelped piteously. The switch clicked back and forth ineffectually and I was trying to think, to think calmly about where the bloody fusebox was, when the lights flickered and came back on. I laughed shakily.

'I think I'm losing it,' I informed Digby weakly, but he just stared up at me with reproving eyes, before licking his sore paw sorrowfully. I thought for a second and then I rushed down the hall to the kitchen, grabbing the phone to see if Val had had a power-cut – I'd ask if I could go over there anyway. There was no dial tone. I shook the receiver a few times in growing disbelief – but there was no sign of life at all. The phone line was dead.

Frantically I looked around for my mobile: I'd plugged it in to charge, only I couldn't for the life of me remember where, and then all the lights flickered, flickered and went out again. It was entirely dark now. A sob of terror pushed its way out of me a bit like in that crashing coach. I called Digby in a hoarse kind of whisper because I was suddenly quite sure we weren't alone; and then I thought I heard a car door slam. It was probably over by the pub: I should go there too, I needed to get to people. Groping along the worktop, finally I found the drawer where the torch should be and actually there it was, the torch. My fingers were so clammy they kept sliding off the switch, but eventually I slid it on and for once it was working, thank God. And then there was a noise outside and I peered out of the kitchen window – and my heart stood still as if it might never beat again.

Silhouetted in the silvery moonlight but shrouded by the bowing trees, a tall figure was walking across the drive. Then the moon slid behind a cloud again and the shape was lost.

I dove back into the kitchen's darkness, although the man had been walking away from me. I waited for a second until I could breathe a little more calmly. Flicking the feeble beam around the room, I finally spied my mobile on the breadbin. Snatching it from its socket, I grabbed my car-keys from the hook.

I opened the back door cautiously but by now there were only shadows dancing under the moon, which was full and squat over the far hill. Inching towards my car, Digby suddenly hurtled between my feet and disappeared across the lawn, barking ecstatically at the stars.

'Come back! Oh, stupid dog,' I swore softly. I'd call him again when I reached the car: now I could see the door-handle glinting in the torch-light –it was only about twenty feet away – and then, behind it, I suddenly made out another vehicle, parked over by the barn. Alex's old Land Rover.

There was no time to think any more, I just needed to escape before he returned.

# Chapter Forty-Two

I heard Digby bark and I hesitated. No doubt he'd disappeared into the undergrowth beside the stream to sniff out the mice and pointy-snouted voles who lived there still. Wherever the dog was, though, he was oblivious to my increasingly anxious shouts. Clambering down the bank, I could hear him now – and then through the hedge I saw a police car come down the drive. Thank God! I began to scramble up again but my cardigan got caught on the barbed wire that edged the stream. I was actually trapped in the ditch.

The police car was already at the house. 'Hey,' I yelled fruit-lessly, my voice snatched up by the wind that was beginning to bluster busily through the garden. I struggled frantically, holding the torch under my chin as the wire clawed into my arm.

'I'm here!' I couldn't see the car any more but I heard it stop and a door open and slam. 'Hey, I'm down here!' I was shrieking now, finally pulling my arm free, leaving half a skein of wool behind me on the wire as the torch went spinning out of my grasp into the water. I scrambled up the bank as the policeman got back in his vehicle and the car pulled straight off: straight out of the bottom gate.

'Come back!' I started to run down the lawn but it was too late: they were truly gone. 'For fuck's sake,' I swore now, panting and sweaty and furious, and then I heard Digby's happy bark as a new set of headlights swept round the corner of the road, past the front gates, before the night fell like soot again, leaving only blackness behind.

And then I heard that car stop suddenly on the other side of the huge hedge and begin to reverse. I hurried toward the road.

Digby suddenly appeared now, bounding up towards the gate to check out this visitor, to greet them in his guileless way, and I heard his bark – and then he too disappeared from sight.

I started to sprint toward the car, hidden from view still by the hedge, the car that suddenly seemed like my salvation – when a shape swooped down through the night. I almost threw myself prostrate on the lawn. It flapped on up into the sky and I laughed shakily when I saw it was only the barn owl diving for his dinner.

A low whistle and a voice, an indistinguishable greeting as Digby barked again, his friendly kind of hello bark, the stupid mutt, and I was running now but I heard a car-door slam. I ran faster, I shouted 'Wait for me', but the car pulled off, and as I rounded the corner and saw the empty road, glimmering in the moonlight, I realised with a stony heart my dog had gone too.

An engine choked into life behind me. I turned to see Alex's Land Rover pulling out of the far end of the drive, onto the village road. Hidden from his view on this side of the house, I fumbled now to switch my mobile on, sprinting to reach my own car, my bad foot really starting to throb. As I ran I felt the icy sweat of fear despite the cold night – but I could see my own car now and the phone was on, bleeping frantically with messages it had collected since it had died in the police's keep.

I tried to phone 999 but the signal was so bad here I couldn't get through, and then I dropped the phone. I stumbled as I bent to pick it up and nearly hit the floor, grazing my hand on the gravel, but I didn't care. I reached the car and the door was unlocked – I always left the doors unlocked down here because I felt so safe, only now I felt the very opposite, quite terrified in

fact, and my hand was shaking as I thrust the key into the ignition. I kept missing the slot because of the shake, and then finally
it went in and I turned the key and –

Nothing. The engine made a half-hearted stutter and died
completely. I turned the key again; my worst nightmare was
coming true.

The cottage was still in darkness, but through the trees I could
see the pub's twinkling lights. I tried 999 again but there was
still no reception. A single text envelope had popped up on the
screen.

**DID YOU GET MESSAGES? PLEASE TAKE CARE. LOVE
YOUR FRIEND FAY XX**

Oh Christ. Even Fay knew Alex was a nutter. I took a deep
breath and slid back out of the car. My only option was to run
to the pub for help.

My ears craned for sound as I walked as fast as I could
towards the orchard, towards the small bridge that would lead
me to the pub. All seemed quiet now: just my ragged breath
and the old owl hooting all melancholy into the night, having
devoured his prey. A sliver of laughter carried from the pub as
the wind dropped again – the pub that seemed suddenly so
very far away. Silence surrounded me here, though – so perhaps,
please God –

Light arced across the garden, a greedy spoon of white catching
me in its harsh beam. Bewildered by it, I crashed into a great
naked rosebush, the bare branches snatching at me like Hansel's
bony fingers. I'd long celebrated my lack of neighbours, the soli-
tude – but, God, I cursed it now.

The car was on the drive, heading straight for me: I'd finally
been hunted down. I heard a noise – and then I realised it was
me; I was actually whimpering with terror. The light swung back
across the garden, holding me hard, the gap between me and
my persecutor closing fast as the engine was gunned. I couldn't
outrun a car. I'd run back home. Turning, I went the other way.

I could see the door. I pounded the ground – my bad foot was so sore now as I panted with fear, and then, behind me, the car churned up the gravel, skidding to a halt, pinioning me between it and the house. Alex was going to get me. It was too late to flee.

I turned again quickly. I had to face my hunter; I couldn't stand unseeing, exposed. The car door swung open as the moon slid out from the fingers of cloud, an oily disc of moonshine that lit up everything.

'Oh God,' I laughed with relief, though I felt more like crying. 'It's you. Oh God, I'm so pleased to see you. I was so scared. Have you got Digby with you?' I lifted my hand to my chest as if to still my beating heart and my hand was trembling, properly shaking, and I took a step towards him.

'I've never been so glad to see anyone,' I started to say, and then I caught his eye and my smile died. I stared at him and his smile met mine – a traitor's smile. And now he took a measured step towards me as I reeled in shock like I'd been punched, gut-punched where it most hurt. Mortally punched.

'Why are you looking at me like that?' I said numbly. 'It *can't* be you.'

'But it is me, Maggie.' And that smile, it was a flat smile, a smile of utter malice. 'Weren't you expecting me?'

# Chapter Forty-Three

In retrospect, perhaps it was all my own fault. I shouldn't have rushed so; I should have stuck to my instincts, should have let my sore heart heal; let sleeping dogs snore and not enticed them to tell lies.

But of course I wasn't thinking any of that right now. I was simply panicking as he marched me into my own house, grasping my upper arm as if he'd like to sink his fingertips right through it.

'You're hurting me,' I pleaded. 'What are you doing? You're scaring me. Let me go.'

'Just shut up and walk,' he commanded, as I stumbled across the woven rug on the old slate floor.

'But I can't see properly, it's so dark,' I mumbled, scared now – really wholeheartedly terrified. His response was to push me forwards so I tripped again and went hurtling into the wall, banging my forehead on the corner of a picture-frame that swung wildly before me.

'Ow.' I clutched my head as I was propelled into the sitting room, still dark except for the fire now dying in the grate.

'Light the candles,' he ordered, gesturing to the old brass sticks on the mantelpiece. He pulled back the curtains to let in the moonlight and turned, his teeth bared in a triumphant kind of grin. 'It's dark because I cut the electric, babe. Clever, aren't I?'

And it was now I realised the severity of the situation; that he really wasn't messing around.

I took a deep breath and crossed the room, picking up the squashed box of cook's matches. The first three all fizzled out as I tried desperately to steady my hand, to hide this palpable fear. The only thing I knew with any clarity was that I must stay calm. I had to stay calm or he would win.

'What's wrong, Seb?' I asked quietly as the first wick finally took, glancing back at him. 'Why are you so very upset?'

'You said you didn't want to see me,' Sebastian muttered, and his twisted grin died then, the grin I'd thought was charming. His voice was very strained, and his face was very pale in the moonlight that tumbled through the window now, two spots of high colour on his cheeks. 'No one says that to me. Not when I – I love them.' He clenched his fists. 'I said I loved you, Maggie. That should have been enough.'

A small figure of Sebastian, an image from an edit all sped up, flitted through my head. What did this remind me of?

'Enough?' I repeated slowly, wracking my brain.

'I would have stopped then.'

'Stopped what?' I asked, shaking my head in confusion. I had to handle him right . . .

'I just needed some time,' I implored, risking a tiny step towards him. 'It wasn't an insult to you, honestly. It's just about where I am at the moment. A bit all over the place, you know. I didn't want to mess it up. That's all. Please, Seb . . .' I reached out a hand to him.

'Shut up,' Seb snapped, and my thudding heart plummeted. 'Just shut up and let me think.' He turned his back on me and leaned his forehead against the window, staring blindly out into the dark garden.

'I –' I forced myself to say it, 'I love you too.'

'Not enough,' he intoned. 'It's never enough. I thought – after a while, I thought you were going to be different.'

'Different?'

'I mean, I only chose you in the first place to punish you. And because I thought you'd be useful for my career. So it's not your place to end it, is it, babe?'

'Chose me?' My stomach rolled over again. 'To punish me? For what?'

'Yes, punish you, you stupid cow. For interfering.' He turned round again, staring at me like I was a stranger in his home.

'What are you talking about?' I whispered urgently. 'Interfering with what?'

'And then – then there was just something about you.' He was lost in his own reverie now. In the candlelight his dark eyes looked demonic. 'But in the end you're all the same. You tricked me, Maggie.'

'You've lost me now, Sebastian,' I pleaded, suppressing my terror almost physically, trying to shove it down. 'I thought things were good between us, honestly. I never meant to – to trick you in any way, I swear.'

'Didn't you?' he sneered. 'My mother warned me about women like you. If things were so good, why didn't you want to see me this weekend?'

I cast around frantically for something to bring him down a little, to bring him back to now.

'Digby'll be so pleased to see you,' I said stupidly, and God I tried so hard to smile. 'We both are, honestly. I'm really glad you're here now. I was missing you.'

He stared at me blankly. 'He wasn't pleased. He wasn't pleased at all, the little shit.'

His tone was utterly unnerving. I stared at him. 'What do you mean?' I whispered, my voice cracking in the darkness.

He smiled and it was a mad smile; a truly mad and malicious smile. My phone chirped then, and my fingers almost went to my pocket – but I just stopped myself in time.

'Give me that,' he demanded, holding out his hand.

357

I played dumb. 'Sorry – what?'

'The phone, you stupid bitch. I heard it beep. Give it to me.'

How could I have got it so terribly wrong? How could I have considered actually falling in love with this monster that stood before me? The candles flickered and danced above us on the ceiling as I pointed into the dark depths of the room.

'It's over there.' I indicated the table piled up with cookbooks and photos and old folders of recipes my mother and Gar had collected. 'I put it on to charge.'

Frowning, he went to check. I made a lunge for the poker lying discarded against the fireguard and I thought about whacking him then but I chose escape instead. I ran for it like a woman possessed. Down the hall, into the kitchen – the back door was open still – out into the night again. Seb was behind me already; I could sense him closing on me although I pushed myself fast, but he was taller, fitter, stronger, and he brought me down in a rugby tackle that knocked every bit of wind from my lungs. The poker went skidding across the grass.

'Oh God,' I moaned in anguish, 'my ankle.'

And before I could even try to move he was over me now, grinning under the white haze of the moon, and I lashed out at him, catching his lip with my fingernails so that he slapped me across the face so hard I thought he'd broken my nose.

'You ungrateful bitch. Didn't you like all the attention? I thought you were enjoying it.' He wiped the blood from his mouth with the back of his hand and sat astride me, pinning my arms to the ground. 'You liked being on that TV programme, didn't you? I saw your smug little face. That's why I sent you the flowers; to congratulate you for fucking everything up. You liked telling everyone what to do, didn't you? Messing with our lives.'

With a massive surge of adrenaline, I realised I had to fight or die here, here on the lawn of my grandmother's cottage, here where I'd played so happily as a child. I remembered the lilies, the graffiti, the text messages, the sheer petrifying fear, and I summoned every ounce of hatred I'd felt for the mysterious person trying to terrify me so and I propelled it into the knee that I brought up with all my might into Seb's groin.

'Oh Christ,' he bellowed, toppling off me in surprised agony. 'You fucking whore.'

Up and running now, I didn't hang around to commiserate – only this time my ankle was throbbing like it had in the hospital after the crash and I knew I didn't have long before it gave way for good.

I'd head back towards the pub; it was the only place I'd definitely find help. Seb was still grunting in pain somewhere behind me on the lawn and I ran like I used to run when I loved life; when I was twelve and really good; when both my parents were still on the side of the school track. 'Run, Mag,' I heard a whispering sigh through the tall dark trees. 'Run for your life, Maggie. Don't stop now.'

I was panting, gasping for breath as I came beside Seb's car. He'd left the door open in his haste to get to me, and as I passed I glanced in and oh my God the keys were actually in the ignition. I didn't look back, I climbed inside and I turned the key and the engine fired –

Feet crunched on the gravel, nearer, nearer . . .

'Oh come *on*, Mag –' I fumbled with the unfamiliar gearstick, slamming it into reverse by mistake. I heard his curse and I prayed I'd run him over. And then the car was moving forward and I was trying to slam the door, but he'd wrenched it open again, and then I heard a muffled yelp and Seb was leaning over me grappling with the steering wheel, but we were still moving, faster now, and I realised it was my heroic dog on the back seat, sinking his teeth into Sebastian's arm.

'You little fucker,' Seb spat, and I almost laughed but Digby's head was wet and shiny as I looked down, and I realised it was blood, my little dog's blood, and then Seb swung him out of the car in one smooth action, and before I could move, before I could stop him, he twisted Digby around, and the brave dog snarled with all his broken might but he was badly hurt already, he didn't stand a chance. Before I could stop him, Seb threw the dog against the tree right there with all his force. With a sigh and a small whimper, my scruffy little dog slumped down the trunk into the undergrowth.

'No,' I screamed, too late. 'Noooo!' I looked up at Seb, still looming over me. 'You fucking nutter,' I hissed. 'What did he ever do to you?'

'I should have done it ages ago,' Seb grinned, and, reaching down into the bushes, he retrieved Digby's limp form and flung him callously onto the drive.

For a second I'd been frozen with horror, but now I came to. 'You're mad,' I yelled, tears of fury flooding down my face, 'absolutely fucking mad', and I revved the engine, backed the car up. I would get him now, the crazy bastard. I put my foot down and I drove at Seb fast; I floored the car and I couldn't see anything any more, just red, just anger at this man who had ruined my life for a reason I didn't understand. And I nearly got him, I nearly did, but he threw himself out of the way just in time, and then there was the old chestnut tree right in front of me and that was it; it was too late to brake – and then it all went black.

# *Chapter Forty-Four*

Stevie Nicks was singing mournfully about players only loving you when they're playing as I came round. My head felt like it might actually split in two, and I was lying half in, half out of Seb's car, my own blood running into my mouth, and Seb was pulling me onto the ground, grunting with exertion. And I knew I'd blown it; I'd had my last chance to escape.

'What are you going to do?' I mumbled, and I was in real pain; my lips were cracked and my voice was tiny. Seb didn't answer, just stared at me like he couldn't focus and switched the radio off before stepping away to retrieve something.

And then I saw he had a can of petrol from the boot, and he reached forward and delved in my jeans pocket and I flinched from his touch.

'Dirty habit, smoking,' he said, eventually finding a lighter in my cardigan pocket. 'You should've known it'd kill you in the end.'

I watched horrified and literally unable to move as he splashed petrol around the car.

'They'll think it was a terrible accident,' he said. 'Poor Maggie. Such a tragedy. So much promise, blah, blah, blah. Such a manipulative bitch, blah, blah, blah. You really were the original gilded lily, weren't you?' He smiled at his own wit.

'Please, Seb,' I implored desperately. '*Please* don't do this.'

'Shut up,' he snapped, concentrating on the task in hand. 'It's too late, Maggie. Too late for you, anyway.'

'Please don't,' I pleaded piteously. 'What did I ever do to you, Seb? I don't understand, I really don't.'

'You should have left us alone. We were happy, you know. Until you came along.'

'Who?' I croaked. 'Who's we, for God's sake?'

'The only positive thing I can say about you is', he glanced at me, pushing his unruly hair out of his eyes with his forearm, 'at least you weren't a bad shag. When you weren't too pissed, that is, Maggie-may-I, Maggie-yes-you-may, Maggie-I'll-just-roll-over-and-let-you-do-whatever-you-want.' He threw the empty petrol can aside and lit the lighter. I stared transfixed at the flame. 'Nice knowing you, bitch,' he said. 'Ta-ta for now.'

And then someone blew that flame right out.

'That's not very original now, is it, mate,' a familiar voice scolded from the gloom. 'I think Hannibal Lecter might have said it first.' The next moment a bewildered Seb lay crumpled on the ground as Alex emerged from the shadows, looking a little surprised himself, the poker in his hand.

'Blimey. That packs a punch.' He shoved Seb with a mud-flecked boot. 'I hope the bastard's still breathing. I don't fancy doing time for him, you know.'

'What are you doing here?' I gazed up at him in bemusement. 'Have you come to punish me too?' I croaked, before passing out.

They landed the air ambulance in Peter Trevenna's field to take me to Truro hospital. I remembered very little about the whole thing except feeling terribly sick, which was, they later told me, the concussion I'd sustained when the car hit the tree. I vaguely recalled Alex being in the helicopter too – I thought he might have even stroked my hair, but when I woke up the next morning in the hospital, it was my father and Jenny beside my bed.

'Maggie –' my dad leaned forward to kiss my bandaged fore-head, 'thank God!'

362

'Hello, darling,' said a beaming Jenny, her usually immaculate hair hidden under a scarf. 'I'll go and get some coffee, shall I?' She vanished down the ward with a tactful swoop of her poncho-type affair.

'We must stop meeting like this,' I joked feebly, and my father gave my hand a little squeeze. He looked grey and exhausted and old, and I felt the eternal twinge of guilt.

'I really would like to know what's been going on,' he said weakly, and I thought he was trying not to cry.

I remembered the utter hatred in Seb's eyes the previous night and the venom with which he spat my name out. With a huge shudder, I thought of being in bed with him the first time we'd been to Pendarlin – the other time. And then I saw Digby's small body as Seb flung him at the tree, and my eyes began to fill.

'I don't suppose –' I gulped hard. 'Digby, he –'

My father squeezed my hand again. 'I'm so sorry, Mag. He's – well, Alex found him when he went back last night, poor little chap. Alex has, you know, taken care of things.'

'Oh God.' I stared at my father, tears brimming now. 'I don't understand any of it, Dad. I don't know what I did to Seb, I really, really don't. He was just so – so bloody mad last night.'

A dough-faced nurse plodded up to the bed. 'Morning there, my lover.' She popped a digital thermometer into my ear cheerily. 'And how are you doing this lovely day? Bit sore, my sweet?' Turning to read the display, the morning sunlight caught the fine hairs of her bleached moustache. I smiled feebly at her and wiped my eyes.

My father cleared his throat tentatively. 'There's someone here who's very keen to see you, Mag.'

'Alex?' I asked, brightening.

My father eyed me warily. 'Not Alex, no. He's had to get back to Bristol. He sent his love, though.'

'Oh,' I mumbled. 'Of course.'

'No, a policeman called Fox has been here since first thing.

363

He wants to take a statement as soon as possible, apparently.'

My father must have noticed my shiver.

'Don't worry, love.' He patted my arm, and I noticed how speckled with white his remaining hair was these days. 'The police will deal with Sebastian, I'm sure. You just concentrate on getting well, all right?'

# Chapter Forty-Five

As it turned out, though, what I had to concentrate on immediately were all the finer details from the previous night – again. A bedraggled-looking DI Fox was most apologetic about making me go through it all so soon; he even brought me a tepid hot chocolate from the vending machine in the corridor as a sign of goodwill.

When it came to talking about Alex hitting Seb with the poker, Fox wouldn't quite meet my eyes, and I understood it was because he hadn't believed my instinct about Alex. '*Told you so*'s' seemed pointless, though.

'He's not saying much, your mate Seb.'

I scowled at the policeman. 'He's hardly my mate, is he?' I replied tersely. My head was pounding now.

'Granted.' Fox adjusted his shiny blue tie nervously. Like most of his clothes, it had seen better days. 'You know what I mean. He's not very forthcoming, anyway. He's a very accomplished liar, I'll give him that.'

'He would be, I suppose,' I said slowly, 'he's an actor, after all.'

'He's certainly got a few identities going on, and Seb Rae ain't the real one, that much we do know. But we need to get clearer on his motive, and he's not playing ball, the bastard.' Fox looked at me, his nose twitching rather like his namesake's would. 'That's where I really need your help, Maggie.'

'I'm not clear myself.' I shook my head morosely. 'I keep

thinking of how Seb ranted about the TV show I work on. He always seemed to hate it, actually, the show – even when he was being nice to me. Before he tried to – you know.' I found I was plucking the bedclothes anxiously with my good hand; I forced myself to stop. 'It doesn't make any sense to me.'

I looked away from Fox, stared out the window for a moment to contain my misery. The hills rolled gently away from the hospital and there was a glimpse of blue between the December clouds. I remembered something my mother used to say about enough blue for a sailor's trousers, and for a moment I imagined her there, patting my shoulder comfortingly as the night in the Porto-bello Hotel came back to me – thrashing in the bath, terrified.

'I don't think it was the first time, you know,' I said quietly.

'The first time what?'

'The first time he'd wanted to –' I found it very hard to say the words. 'To – um, you know. To kill me.'

A yawning Fox left with assurances to get to the bottom of it all. The hospital said they'd probably discharge me the next day, all being well, and my father and Jenny talked about a nice hotel on the coast near St Ives that they'd heard was lovely. 'Unless you want to go straight back to Pendarlin?' my father mumbled with some trepidation.

I thought miserably of Digby chasing his tail round the lawn. Of Seb glowering at me with such hatred by the fire; of me running for my life out of the back door. 'In a few days, perhaps,' I said quietly.

The moustached nurse arrived back at my bedside. 'You look wiped out, my sweet, and I need to change the dressing on your head. Come on, Mum and Dad. Our patient needs some rest.'

I caught the look Jenny shot my father at the nurse's words, anxious but happy at the same time – the hand she slipped into his. I didn't bother to correct the mistake.

*   *   *

My dreams were full of barks and screams and a crying Gar sitting in her wicker chair on the lawn of Pendarlin behind a piano that played itself, Debussy's music soaring into the sky. I woke just after five, sweating and disorientated. Moustache Face had gone off duty, apparently, and in her place was a neat little nurse with cropped hair and a mole like a Jelly Tot on her neck. She smoothed the rumpled bedclothes and poured me a glass of water, helping me to drink it like she would a child.

'You've had an awful shock, Maggie,' she said, as I mumbled about being pathetic. 'It's going to take a while. You have to give yourself time. The morphine will make you feel odd too.' She moved the roses beside the bed so she could put the water down. 'They're beautiful, aren't they, you lucky thing. Who are they from?'

I shook my head as a hundred bunches of unwelcome lilies pirouetted over the bedspread like the hippos in *Fantasia*. I felt my eyes well up.

'All right there, lovie. Don't upset yourself.' She produced a clean white tissue from a box. 'Is there someone you'd like me to call for you?'

'Not really, thanks.' I shook my head again, feeling utterly alone. The tears came then, a deluge I thought might never stop.

I must have dozed off again for a while. I woke with a start; I could hear the inane chirrup of a game-show from the television down the corridor, and then a door closed and all was quiet. I was slipping off to sleep again when footsteps approached down the hall – two sets of them, slightly out of rhythm. I expected them to keep going, but outside my door, they stopped. My heart skipped a beat. What if Seb had convinced Fox he was innocent? He'd obviously mastered the art of persuasion . . .

I hoiked myself up in my bed and reached for a weapon, but all that came to hand was the water-jug. My tummy felt like it was being squeezed through an old-fashioned mangle. Then I heard whispering outside, and before I could grab the jug, a little face popped round the door.

'What the hell are you doing here?' I croaked, and in response she smiled, rather timidly for her, I thought afterwards.

'Just come to see if you're okay, Maggie.'

And then, from behind Fay, another taller figure appeared. Alex. He stood there with a hand on her shoulder, and he too was smiling rather oddly. Grimacing was a better word, in fact.

'Come in,' I said rather hysterically, 'come in and join the party, why don't you? I can show you my war-wounds if you like.'

They stepped nervously into the room. They. Fay and Alex – my stalker and my ex. A perfect combination – a veritable match made in heaven.

'So,' I mumbled, feeling rather peculiar again, 'what can I do for you? Other than thank you, Alex, obviously.'

'We were worried about you. Thank goodness you're all right,' Fay murmured, blinking a lot.

'Have you come to break the news?' I tried to pull myself up on the pillows. God, my arm hurt.

'News?' Alex shook his head in confusion as Fay looked up at him, bewilderment in those great violet eyes. 'What news?'

I decided I should get up now; I felt like a trussed-up chicken ready for the oven lying there while they both gaped at me. Slowly I swung my legs out and stood – pain shot up my ankle like a surge of electricity so that I stumbled onto a chair, Fay and Alex both rushing forwards to support me. I gazed up at them.

'You make a lovely couple, actually,' I mumbled, and promptly collapsed again.

# Chapter Forty-Six

However hard you try, sometimes you can't escape yourself. I sat in the room on the hill by the sea and I tried to hide from the horrors that haunted me; I tried to remember the person I'd been before all this began. But I lived in the midst of flashbacks and a perpetual ache in my injured ankle, waking from night-sweats terrified that Seb had come for me again, my ears constantly straining for the faithful patter of Digby's feet.

The sea rolled in and the sea rolled out again. I gazed at the water that changed colour every day, its unbroken surface belying the treacherous rocks beneath it. When I couldn't sleep I watched the fishing boats bobbing out before dawn past the harbour wall on a good day; the craggy hillside opposite like some pagan god had whacked out his fury there. I watched the locals off for a pint at the pink-painted pub on Fore Street, the few holiday-makers in cagoules and wellies tramping down to get their fresh fish, or struggling with flapping ordnance survey maps that were welded to their bodies in the wind.

When my father had to get back to work in London, Jenny took some time off and stayed with me – and for that I was truly grateful. I didn't want to see anyone else now; I wanted to hide. But when Bel rang from Australia, I was happy to hear her voice.

'I knew he was no good, the bloody bastard. The handsome ones never are. I did say that, Mag, I'm sure I did.'

'Did you?' I asked wearily. 'I must have missed that bit.' I caught sight of my colourless face, the cut on my forehead stitched and covered still with a large plaster. 'I could use some of your magic, Bel, I must say. I look like the living dead.'

'You need some sun, my girl. Look, Maggie, I know it's awful, what you've been through, but you've got to forget Sebastian now. Come out here – we'll look after you.'

'I'd love to, Bel, if it wasn't so bloody far away.'

'Sydney's amazing,' she ignored me, 'we've got a huge apartment right on the bay, and there's loads of work for bods like you. The TV's atrocious here. They're crying out for your experience.'

Beneath the window a young couple tugged a sturdy black Labrador behind them, their little girl in a pink sou'wester fighting to keep her hat on in the December wind.

'How's Hannah?' I changed the subject, doodling on the pad by the phone. 'I really miss her, you know.' I drew a bucket and spade.

'She misses you too, darling, but I have to say, she's loving it. There's just so much outdoor life here, Mag. The food's amazing; I'm getting really fat. Actually,' she went all coy, 'that's not the only reason.'

'You – fat! Pull the other –' I stopped drawing. 'Oh my God! Bel – you're not! Already?'

'I am! I mean, it's early days, but please, think about coming.'

'You need a babysitter, you mean. Oh that's great news, Bel, congratulations! How fantastic.' I was delighted for her, really – but I couldn't deny the tiny acorn of envy deep in my gut, envy for the stability I'd craved for so long. I shoved it down.

'I can get you loads of meetings if you do come.' Bel was oblivious, thank God. 'You know, with all the right people.'

'I'm not sure I want to make TV any more, you know, Bel.' I drew a small box. 'I'm thinking about retraining.'

In what, though? A diploma in choosing the wrong men?

'Mag, just because things went wrong at Double-decker, it

doesn't mean all television's bad. It doesn't mean everything you've done is worthless. You know that, right?'

'Right now, I don't know much, Bel.' I flopped back on the bed. 'I don't trust my own instincts any more.'

'You've had a bad year, that's all. That's why you need to get away. At least say you'll think about it, hey?'

'God, you're even starting to sound like an Aussie.' I managed a laugh as I gazed up at the ceiling, picturing the sun and golden beaches, barbeques and opera houses. For a moment my heart lifted. 'Okay, I'll think about it, I promise.'

'That's my girl,' said Bel cheerfully. 'Right, well, gotta go, darling. It's well past my bedtime now. You get on that Internet and check out some flights, okay? You've got to grab the bull by the horns now, Mag.'

But I'd done that already, hadn't I? And the bull turned out to be quite mad and savage. I didn't think I was going anywhere for a while. Not till Seb's trial came up.


The day after I'd moved to the Port Isaac Hotel, a rather muted Fay came to see me.

'Do you want me to stay?' my father asked discreetly. Frankly, I was just relieved that she'd come alone. I shook my head and he disappeared into the afternoon drizzle for a walk with Jenny.

Fay and I sat in uncomfortable silence as the matronly owner set out tea and mince pies in my small suite, recently festooned with flowers from Charlie 'and the gang'. Over the steaming teapot I watched the moss-green *Hope of Port Isaac* chug back into harbour as I waited for Fay to explain her presence.

'I feel so guilty,' she said eventually, and I poured the tea so I could keep busy while she spoke, shoving away images of her and Alex together. She didn't look quite as glossy as usual; she looked young and rather swamped in a long gypsy-style dress, her hair a mass of short curls now it had started to grow out, back to its natural dark colour.

'These things happen, Fay. It takes two.'

I winced as a spot of boiling liquid splashed my hand.

'Maggie –' She looked away. I waited patiently. I had all the time in the world these days.

'I led him to you, I think.' Her voice was small, her hands clasped tight in her lap.

'Alex?' I stared at her until the teapot's handle began to burn my palm. 'I don't understand.' I relinquished it onto the table.

'Not Alex,' she muttered. 'Troy.'

'Troy? I still don't –' And then we gazed at each other. I felt my eyes go wide. 'Troy? You don't mean Troy is – is Seb? They're the same – the same person?'

'Yes.' Her voice was little more than a whisper.

'Seb is your – your ex-boyfriend Troy? God.' I felt like I'd just been punched in the head. 'Does – have you told the police?'

'Yes, of course.' She stood up and walked to the window, her hem swishing on the carpet. 'I'm so sorry, Maggie. I mean, I knew he was unstable. I just had no idea to what extent.'

'*When* did you realise?' I was trying frantically to piece things together. My head felt like a child had set his spinning top off inside it. 'Why didn't you warn me if you knew it was him?'

'I didn't know until the afternoon he came to – to get you, I swear,' Fay pouted prettily. 'He'd fairly much disappeared when we split up. I only rang him to get a forwarding address for his post. And then on the phone that day he started ranting about how much you'd hurt him.' She sat down again, perching like a bird on the edge of the sofa. 'I was truly shocked, Maggie, to be honest. That you'd been together, I mean.'

I looked down at my stripy pyjama knees, at my bandaged foot. I refused to feel guilt now for Fay as well.

'I mean,' she went on, 'the previous time Troy had mentioned you, when we split up, he said he hated you. He blamed you, you see, after he saw us together on the show. It took me a while to get my head around it to be honest. You and him, I mean.'

Those great violet headlamps searched my face. 'But you have to believe me, Maggie. I didn't know he was after you. *Of course* if I'd known what he intended I would have tried even harder to let you know. I thought at the worst he might smash a few things up, or, I don't know, lock you in a cupboard. You know – to punish you.'

'To punish me,' I echoed numbly. Seb's words from the other night rattled like a spectre in the room.

'That was the expression he always used. If you hurt him, he'd have to "punish" you. He felt things very deeply.'

'Obviously,' I said dryly.

'But I can't believe', she could hardly look at me now, 'that he actually tried to kill you. He'd never been violent before. Not to me, anyway.'

'No, well,' I said flatly, 'I obviously have that effect on men.' I had the sense of a great pressure bearing down on me; of everything I'd known shifting shape again. I wanted to stand and scream; to burst out through the roof into oblivion. I picked at the bandage on my hand instead.

'So I asked DI Fox to let me tell you myself,' she quickly pointed out. 'I thought I should. That's why I'm here.'

'Thank you,' I said stiffly, still trying to grasp this new reality. The text message I'd received from Fay that night at Pendarlin finally made sense. 'So – you were trying to warn me about Seb then? I thought you meant Alex when I got your text.'

'I'd been ringing your phone all afternoon, since I'd spoken to Troy, but I just kept getting your voicemail. I assumed you'd have got the messages, but in the end I rang Alex because I was worried by how mad Troy sounded. Alex was in Bristol, so he drove down. I don't think he really believed me, but he rang the local police.'

I remembered the slowly cruising police car; my voice snatched up by the wind as I shouted desperately at its tail-lights, trapped by that bloody wire.

'I didn't get your messages in time,' I said slowly, my mind somersaulting wildly as I started to compute it all. I felt sick. 'Fay, sorry. Would you mind just giving me a minute?' I staggered to my feet, my leg stiff from sitting for so long.

'No, of course not.' She stood quickly as if to help me – but I was all right on my own. 'I need to ring my agent anyway.'

I pulled open the balcony door as Fay left the room, and stepped out into the cold.

Below me the grey-green sea swelled gently like a giant sigh. The afternoon was colourless, the sky a huge merging of cloud and colour into grey. Into nothingness.

Tiny pins of moisture pricked my face as I leaned against the damp rail watching a single gull wheel and surf the sky. For a moment the smooth-breasted white figure battled against the wind, and then he gracefully pivoted above me to let the slipstream take him where it chose. And I knew that I must succumb to the fate that had brought me here, that there was no point fighting it; that to recover from Seb's campaign of terror I needed to somehow accept it – accept it and get on.

When Fay came back I attempted a smile as I sloshed out the last of the Earl Grey with an almost steady hand. The tea was stewed.

'My agent's got me an audition for *I'm a Celebrity*, can you believe it?' She looked shell-shocked.

'I can, actually,' I said politely, passing her a cup, strangely reminded of Gwendolen and Cecily's tea party in *The Importance of Being Earnest*. This was the version on acid.

'I'm not sure about the jungle.' She was genuinely worried. 'All those horrid beasties. Snakes and things. Ugh!'

I ignored her. 'But I don't understand why Seb bothered to actually go out with me.' I thought uncomfortably of everyone who'd said Fay and I looked alike. 'To get at you, I guess?'

'I don't think it was that simple.' Fay wrenched herself back from the jungle. 'He blamed you for splitting us up, so it probably started out of revenge. After what you said on the show, you know.' She added a dainty spoon of sugar to her tea.

'What did I say?' I racked my brain.

'That being overprotective wasn't necessarily right, that wanting to know where I was at every moment might just mean he liked control, not love. In a way, you know,' Fay gave me that intense look I remembered from that first show, 'he was right, you did split us up.'

'Oh, great,' I muttered. 'So you blame me too?' A moment on the lips, a lifetime running away from madmen you'd inadvertently offended.

'No, no.' She was quick to refute it. 'I mean, I never would have left him if you hadn't pointed out a few home truths. I wasn't strong enough. But it was absolutely the best thing I ever did, splitting up with Troy.' She reached out and grasped my hand in her little one. 'I'm really grateful to you, Maggie, honestly.'

'Oh,' I said. I didn't dare remove my hand. 'You know, Fay, the funny thing is, for a while there I thought it was you out to get me.'

She looked aghast. 'God, no.' Her fingers slid off mine. 'I just wanted to be your friend. It took me a while', she looked down, 'to realise you didn't want to be mine.'

I felt a pang. 'It wasn't that simple, Fay. I – I've been in quite a bad place for a lot of this year. Dealing with a lot of trauma that I – I maybe haven't handled very well.'

'Shock's a very hard thing *to* deal with,' she said sagely. 'That's why I wanted you to join my Survivors' group so badly.'

'Yeah, well, maybe I should have done. At least I mightn't have been alone so much.' I thought about that first bunch of lilies arriving at my house, the same day she'd turned up. The fact I must have somehow shown I hated them on TV. He'd been watching hard. 'How did Seb get my address? You know he sent me loads of funeral flowers?'

'That nice policeman told me.' She shook her head sorrow-fully. 'Seb was so angry after I'd appeared on telly that day, kept ranting about people out to get him, and you sticking your nose in – but I didn't take him seriously.' She fiddled with a tassel on her dress. 'He insisted on giving me a lift when I brought you the crash photos. I'd given him the address so he could look it up beforehand. Oh God –' She caught her bottom lip with two pearly top teeth. 'I'm so sorry, Maggie.'

'It's not your fault, Fay.' I abandoned my foul tea. 'I guess he loved you very much.'

She toyed with her mince pie. 'I think he loved you too. He just had such a distorted view of it all. Poor Troy.'

'Why, though?' I felt the anger rise again. '*Why* was he so messed up?'

'He had a very odd image of women generally. I was so in love with him, it took me a long time to realise it,' she said sadly. 'He invited us both to the film premiere, you know, though I didn't realise it was him then. Perhaps he was hoping I'd see you with him and be insanely jealous.'

I looked at her. 'Would you have been?'

She walked to the table in the window, flicked nervously through a *Country Life* magazine. 'Probably. I knew he was wrong for me, but I loved him so much.' Her eyes filled with tears and I thought of my love for Alex despite all the pain we'd been through, and I felt an enormous bolt of sorrow for the mess we were all in. 'So much, Maggie. That's why I put up with it for so long.'

'I understand that, Fay,' I said quietly. 'I do, really.'

'But I do think Troy really fell for you, Maggie.' She was trying to be generous. 'The only other time I spoke to him he told me he'd met someone really special, and I believed him. I was kind of relieved, but it still hurt.' She looked at me now. 'I just didn't realise it was you.'

And this was where my mind hit a wall. The sheer intimacy I'd shared with Seb, the sex, the eventual protestation of love.

The fact that all those terrible things he'd done, he'd done after we'd been to bed together. He'd crept downstairs and painted abuse on the wall, he'd crept out and slashed his own tyres. He'd texted me even when we were at dinner together; he'd smashed up my flat and then casually joined me at Heathrow for a weekend in Cornwall. And he must have planted the phone in the box of stuff I'd returned to Alex, trying to frame him.

His malice had wrapped its insidious tendrils around almost every bit of my life, crept into everything and pulled at it until my very stability was shaken to its foundations. And the worst thing was, I couldn't help but feel it was all my own stupid fault.

I'd known better than to get involved again when I was so down, so precariously near rock-bottom. I'd ignored my instincts, just refilled my glass time and time again and grasped onto Seb in a drunken haze as a welcome distraction. And I – and this is what I struggled with most – I'd found him very attractive and utterly convincing.

'How could he have loved me?' I mumbled. 'He hated me so much.'

Fay looked out at the darkening sky. A flurry of raindrops hit the window in a sudden squall. 'You know, right at the end I managed to get him to counselling. The therapist warned me he might be suffering from some kind of disorder – that he had a mother fixation – and she thought he needed proper help. But he refused to go back. I wish now – I should have insisted.'

'It was his responsibility, Fay,' I said quietly. 'Not yours.'

We sat in silence for a while, both of us caught up in our own thoughts of this man who'd gone so mad. Eventually there was a gentle knock and a pink-cheeked Jenny popped her damp head round the door.

'We're back,' she said cheerfully. 'I could eat a horse! All those hills. Need anything, girls?'

'I'd better go, actually,' Fay said, standing. 'I've got to get back to London tonight.'

For a moment we gazed at each other. I stuck my hand out to shake hers, and then she bent to kiss my cheek, and on impulse I threw my arms around her neck.

'Thanks so much, Fay,' I muttered into the side of her head, my mouth muffled by her curls – and I meant it with sincerity. 'I owe you – well, I just owe you, don't I?'

'Don't be silly. You'd have done the same.'

Would I?

Fay stepped out of my embrace with a beatific smile, and buttoned her coat. 'That's what friends are for. Keep in touch, okay?'

I think we both knew I wouldn't. She moved toward the door.

'Fay –' My voice sounded like it was stretched over cheese-wire, but I had to know.

She turned, her hand poised to open the door.

'So in the end,' I said as diffidently as I could manage, 'there's a strange symmetry to it all, isn't there?'

'What do you mean?' Her brow wrinkled delicately under her dark fringe.

'Well, me and mad Seb. You and – you and Alex.'

Fay stared at me. 'What do you mean, me and Alex? You've got it all wrong, Maggie. Honestly, you really are quite silly. It's you he wants, not me.'

# Chapter Forty-Seven

'Narcissistic Personality Disorder,' Sally said neatly, popping another of my grapes into her generous mouth, before offering me the bunch rather belatedly.

I shook my head. 'Sorry, what?'

'We did a show on it, don't you remember? *Narcissists – men who love themselves too much.* That very good-looking surfer type was on it. We paid him five hundred pounds to appear – I remember because Charlie went mad. He had anger management issues too, I seem to recall.' She ate another grape. 'The surfer, not Charlie.'

'He wasn't a surfer, though, was he?' I said mournfully. 'He was a window-cleaner from Dagenham. Called Keith.'

'No, that's true. But he looked like a surfer. And he had delusions of grandeur too.'

I thought of Seb's driver, the Armani, the restaurant and the expensive hotel. I'd never questioned any of it; it went hand in hand with what I believed he was. But I realised now I'd never even seen where he lived. I thought I had recognised him from a TV drama; it was only now I realised it was from the hospital, after the crash. He'd come to see Fay – the young bloke in the beanie, dropping his phone at my feet.

I thought miserably of all the shows I'd produced brimful of cod-psychology and people who weren't entirely what they seemed. Of how someone like Seb, already hovering on the edge, might easily have been pushed over by a power-hungry presenter like Renee Owens.

'Seb needed help,' I said quietly. 'Not to get involved with a pisshead on the rebound. He had a terrible relationship with his mother, apparently. I think she – there was some kind of abuse, Fay said. It all stemmed from there, I guess.' I contemplated the shrivelled grape-stalks Sally had left. I thought about that final phone call, telling him not to come down to Pendarlin. 'Perhaps – perhaps if I hadn't rejected him, it would have been okay.' Then I thought about the texts, the flowers, the smashed-up flat, the way he'd tried to convince me that I was mad. I looked at Sally. 'It wouldn't, though, would it?'

'No, Maggie.' She shook her head sorrowfully and chucked the remains of the grapes in the bin. 'I don't think it would.'

The day I had my stitches removed, I returned to Pendarlin with my father. He hurried inside the cottage to fetch some things I needed, and I averted my gaze from the scarred tree Seb's car had hit. Then I gritted my teeth and walked to the end of the orchard to see Digby's grave. Alex had planted a small pink azalea on the mound, which amazed me. He'd scratched out an epitaph on an old piece of slate and stuck it in the ground behind the just-flowering shrub.

*Dearest Digby, 2001–2007*
*Died in heroic action saving his beloved mistress.*
*Much missed by all those who loved him,*
*especially Maggie and Alex.*
*May you burrow down many holes in heaven.*

Hot tears sprang sharply to my eyes. I stood and gazed until my father appeared behind me and put an arm round my shoulders. 'Come on, old thing. Let's get you home,' he said, and for once I was happy to leave. Deep down I think I knew it would be all right one day, that I would come back to Pendarlin in the end, the good history would win out. My mother and Gar and a hundred happy childhood memories would emerge from beneath the thunder clouds again. But right now I needed distance from the place.

In London I went back to the flat above the cake-shop, but I couldn't settle. Alex had apparently taken it off the market, and until I decided what to do next, I was glad – although I knew I wouldn't stay there for long. I visited Gar every day and she was as quiet and lost in her own world as ever, if a little more frail. She'd developed a bad cough and I sensed Susan was trying to warn me that it might not be long before my grandmother gave up the fight.

Bel kept ringing me, harassing me about Australia. Charlie kept ringing me, offering me work. I hid away again, alone, trying to decide what to do with the rest of my life. I'd have to decide soon because my small savings account was almost empty. I attended my appointments at Guy's Hospital religiously and walked by the high grey Thames in the mornings before the banks got busy with tourists, down to Shakespeare's old Globe and the Tate and back again, missing Digby desperately. I found myself yearning to take up running again, enviously watching the sweating joggers pounding past me into the distance while I was still grounded. 'When you're fit,' said the fresh-faced young physio, manipulating my damaged leg, 'don't rush. It won't help.'

I arrived back from Gar's one evening just before Christmas to be intercepted in front of the flat by a fur-swathed Mrs Forlani, emerging dramatically from the festive crowd.

'*Bellissima*, your lovely boyfriend, he left this for you.' She nudged me playfully. 'He is so tall, no? I think that is so handsome in a man. Correct, you know. Me, I never like the short men. I say to Matteo when we marry, you must grow a few inches.' Her parcels nearly went flying as she gave a theatrical shrug. 'But he never do.'

'Right.' I took the packages she was brandishing at me, lost for words. 'Goodness. Thank you.'

'I put a small Panettone for you.' She tapped the shiny pink box on top. 'For Christmas. Come and have a glass of Spumante with us, please, before we fly home, *si, bella*?'

'I will. I promise.'

Upstairs in the flat I sat alone in the gloom, the lights from the busy street flickering across the freshly painted whiteness of the walls, the jolly sound of carol singers outside the pub making my heart ache. I opened the box tied with red satin ribbon. Inside was a stack of new sheet music, a postcard of Mozart's piano and a small carved wooden dog. And a hand-drawn Christmas card of a snow-covered cottage with a big tree outside: Pendarlin. It made my tummy hurt.

*Dearest Mag,*

*I hope you are okay. I wanted to come and deliver this in person, but you looked so appalled to see me in the hospital that I don't want to add to your trauma.*

*I just want to apologise for being so generally rubbish. And as a token of my enormous esteem for you, here is some music you might like. That night at Pendarlin when I was outside, I heard you playing the piano for the first time and I was really glad (and impressed, despite a few duff notes!). Don't give up again, please. I'm just sorry I didn't come in to see you right then. I went over to the pub because I thought you were fine and I didn't want to inter-rupt your creative flow. And because I thought Fay was bonkers, and making it all up. I feel pretty terrible about that now.*

*When you are ready, I'd really like to get you a new puppy. I know Digby wouldn't like you to be on your own.*

*Sorry I let you down, dearest Maggie.*
*Your useless friend,*
*Alex xx*

*PS 15 days, 4 hours and 10 minutes sober.*

I spent a quiet Christmas with Dad and Jenny, Gar nodding off in an armchair with a glass of sherry beside her that she never touched. I felt out of place, missing Cornwall, out of sorts and unfortunately no longer out of my head since I'd curbed my drinking.

Usually I cooked the Christmas dinner but this year Jenny did it because she was so keen, though we all lived to regret it. The sprouts were bullet-like and the turkey resembled a piece of old carpet, the bread sauce was inedible and the roast potatoes burned to a crisp. When I nearly cracked my tooth on the salt spoon in the plum pudding and Jenny looked aghast, I laughed.

'Oh dear. I wondered where that had got to! Still, you've got the pound as well.' She slipped a coin onto my plate. 'That's lucky, eh, Maggie?' She didn't say I needed it, but I imagined that's what we all thought.

In the evening my dad and Jenny played Scrabble while I curled up in front of the fire, wishing Digby was here to keep my feet warm. *Dangerous Liaisons* was on BBC2, Michelle Pfeiffer being all winsome and chaste under the dastardly Vicomte Sébastien de Valmont's scrutiny. Listlessly I reached for the Quality Street.

'It's beyond my control,' Valmont said, his lips very red against his pale powdered face. A shiver went down my spine. Where had I heard that recently? Valmont said it again. 'It's beyond my control.'

I changed the channel before Sébastien killed Michelle by breaking her heart in two.

# Chapter Forty-Eight

'You're late.' The woman with complicated highlights tapped something into her computer. 'And you've changed your hair,' she noted accusingly, handing back my passport. Her voice was rather whiny and nasal.

'Er, yes.' Self-conscious now, I pushed my mop behind my ears. 'A few times since that photo, actually. I needed a – a change, you know.'

Streaky looked entirely disinterested. 'As I said, you're late. There's not –' dramatic pause, 'no, not a single seat left.'

I stared at her aghast. She was so orange, she reminded me of Charlie. 'The traffic was terrible. We got stuck on the M25. There must be one seat, surely. I –'

'Always allow plenty of time, we do say.' The crown of her head was like a map of spaghetti junction in different blondes as she looked down at her screen.

'So what does that mean, then – no seats?' I asked nervously. She didn't answer, her cerise talons tapping again. I watched the glamorous young couple at the First Class desk kissing, her fluffy cream jumper leaving hairs over his black T-shirted chest as she gazed at him adoringly. I couldn't bear it if I fell at this last hurdle. Escape was on the horizon; they couldn't stop me now.

'It means,' Streaky sniffed with disapproval, 'it means, fortunately for you, you'll be seated in Business.'

'Business?' I repeated foolishly. Oh, the joy. 'It must be a sign.'

She eyed me suspiciously.

'You know, like a good omen. I'm due a bit of luck.'

Streaky sniffed again as I gathered up my bits. 'You're lucky to get on this flight, that's all I know. Gate fifty-eight. Closes in ten minutes.'

The girl at First Class played coquettishly with her gold earring as her man shouldered the heavy Vuitton bags. I tried not to notice that I was practically the only person in the whole airport alone.

The traffic-jam had made us so late that I'd insisted my father drop me outside.

'I'm not going forever,' I assured myself as much as him. I thought about the last time I was at Heathrow, sad about Bel but expectant about Seb, waiting in the car park with a growing sense of excitement. Seb, who'd based most of his love-making on film quotes he'd stolen; who'd named himself after John Malkovich's ruthless lover from *Dangerous Liaisons*, I'd finally realised on Christmas night. With a shiver I remembered the '*lick every inch of you*' line – it had turned out to be from *The Long Good Friday*. I suppose Seb had warned me he was a film buff.

Stamping my feet against the cold and the memories, waiting for my dad to open the boot and immersed in banishing Seb's ghost, I missed the florist's van pulling off a few cars in front.

'I'll be back in a month or two for the trial.' I hugged my bereft father tight. 'As soon as the date comes through.'

'You take care out there, Maggie.' He kissed my forehead. 'Be sensible, all right?'

'Dad, I'm thirty, not thirteen.'

'You'll always be thirteen to me, lovie.'

I refused to cry; I'd never stop. I kissed his cheek; he smelled like my childhood and I savoured it for the last time in a while. 'I love you, Dad,' I muttered. 'And you'll let me know about Gar, won't you?'

'Of course I will. Here, let me.' He swung the suitcase onto the trolley. 'Try not to worry about her. She's at peace at last, I think.'

The New Year had dawned truly freezing, a throwback to the winters of my childhood. I hated January with a vengeance; it spoke of bare cold earth and no hope, the festivities over and no colour in the sky. The wind whisking round the eaves whispered of my mother's depression, always at its worst during this bleak point of the year.

I had enrolled on a music therapy course – I'd truly finished with TV – and then Gar had slipped into a coma, and they couldn't say how long she might have left. I held her soft, frail hand and watched her sleeping; imagined her dreaming of my twinkly-eyed grandfather, of my mother and her brother Harry running on the Cornish beaches as children, kite-flying at Daymer Bay, scrabbling down to mussel-gather at Epphaven. Of Pendarlin at dusk, the smoke from the chimney curling up to the sky like a child's painting. Of baking fruitcake and whipping up lemon meringue pie for Sunday lunch, and letting me scrape the bowl clean.

I kissed Gar's soft face and I cried and cried. I said goodbye forever, for she was gone now, and then I booked my ticket to Australia.

By the time I got to the gate it was almost deserted, the tunnel empty apart from a flash of a little pink wheelie-case whisking round the corner to the plane. I had to wait while the greasy girl at the barrier laboriously checked my boarding-card, and by the time I turned left on the plane, I felt hot and self-conscious; like the whole crew were waiting for me.

But once I was ensconced in the enormous seat, I started to relax, though I did look rather nervously for the kissing couple from check-in – I wasn't sure I could endure twenty-four hours of snogging. Thankfully they were out of sight.

A sudden squall of rain hit the window. It was dark now, the lights of the airport orange and glaring as we began to taxi for take-off. The runway gleamed slick and wet as I looked down from my lofty height, and then the rather gorgeous air-steward called Dylan arrived back with a glass of champagne.

'The only way to take off, my lovely.' He smiled and plonked it into my hand. 'See you in the air!'

I didn't have time to say I didn't drink. I clutched the glass as we got up speed, feeling a rush of adrenaline as the great plane thundered down the runway. The bubbles in the champagne shot up to the surface and I thought about the past six months, about Seb, and Alex, who hadn't been in touch since Christmas. I stretched my bad ankle out and contemplated the fact that however well I healed, I'd always be scarred, inside and out. I'd never be quite the same again.

With a rattle and a sigh we were airborne. I watched England fall away behind us, butterflies in my tummy as the lights faded to blackness. Soon I'd sleep – but right now, I needed the loo.

Walking back down the aisle, I got confused and went the wrong way into Economy. And then –

My heart banged.

She was leaning down in her seat changing her shoes, a small pink suitcase on wheels on the chair beside her. I couldn't believe it; she couldn't be here. I took a small step towards her; and then I stopped. My heart was hammering like it hadn't in months, the adrenaline rising until I had a sour taste in my mouth.

'Fay?' I said tremulously.

She looked up, holding one baby-blue cashmere sock.

It wasn't Fay. The woman was older, more haggard, smaller even than Fay. Half-Chinese, perhaps. They just had the same hair.

I smiled a shaky smile. 'Sorry. I was – I thought you were someone else.'

The woman smiled back. I turned and hurried down the aisle

in the right direction. My palms had gone clammy the minute I'd spotted her; I wiped them on my jeans. Over the seat-backs I realised someone was now reaching down into my place.

'Excuse me,' I huffed, reaching my row, 'that's my seat.'

The steward turned from placing an enormous bunch of pink flowers on my chair. 'This is for you too, you lucky thing,' he winked, handing me an envelope. 'I do love an intrigue – and I adore wild roses! *So* romantic.'

I recognised the handwriting, and my heart sped up again. As I read the letter slowly, I half-smiled.

*It doesn't have to mean anything, Mag, if I do come out, and I certainly won't if you don't want me to, though I do genuinely have business in Australia. (If Bel doesn't have me assassinated first.) But I just want to see you, badly, away from everything back home. I want to tell you that I'm so sorry. That you're the best thing that ever happened to me and I'm so incredibly sorry for messing it up; I'll regret it forever if it's the end. Plus I've always fancied a bit of yoga in Byron Bay. I'm discovering my inner child, you see. He's about ten and a right pain. But I expect you knew that already.*

Alex doing yoga? I laughed despite myself.

The plane bumped through some turbulence and the engines went into full throttle and pushed us on, thrusting us forward until we passed through the cloud, until we emerged on the other side and continued our smooth path again.

I looked out of the window, and it was absolutely dark now, only the lights of a tiny far-off plane visible from here, and, as we turned, one solitary distant star.

For the first time in many months, I felt calm, sealed safe inside. Finally I was mistress of my own destiny, finally I felt serene. I closed my eyes and saw Bel and Hannah hand in hand, standing in the Arrivals Hall in Sydney, tanned and happy, waiting for me. I saw myself smiling, dashing towards the arms of my oldest friends – my good friends, my very good friends.

I looked at that small star again, and then I slid down into my seat, pulling the shutter closed against the darkness of the night.

For the first time in such a very long time, I was ready to begin again.

# A CONVERSATION WITH CLAIRE SEEBER

Q: *Your books are deeply rooted in a sense of place, from your debut novel* Lullaby, *in which the action largely took place in London's Blackheath, to the Cornish and London settings of* Bad Friends. *How important is it to you to have the location in mind when you are creating your novels?*

A: They say write what you know – and whilst I don't necessarily always agree with this (I've never had a baby stolen, or been stalked, thank goodness), I think it helps to use locations you can write about convincingly to create atmosphere. South-East London where I grew up appears in both my books – it's a rich area for a writer – pockets of refinement beside deprivation. I always knew BF would be split between London – the hub of TV-land – and Cornwall, one of my favourite places in the world. It was important for the story that Maggie had somewhere to run to – somewhere she felt safe; and my own enforced separation from the sea means I can write about Cornwall nostalgically.

Q: *Did you have anyone in mind as inspiration when you created Maggie, Alex and Seb? Who do you think could play them in a movie?*

A: Maggie is mainly fictitious, but I guess there are elements of me in her. Seb I have never met (please draw your own conclusions!), whilst Alex is inspired not by an ex-boyfriend but partly by someone I once knew, a long long time ago! How about Sally Hawkins to play Maggie? Sienna Miller could play Bel, I think – or skinny Serena! Seb – James McAvoy or Dominic Cooper? And Alex – well, my favourite film-star of the moment is Casey Affleck – he may be a little on the short side, and he's American of course, but I'm sure he'd be happy to practise his British accent! Or what about Andrew Buchan from *The Fixer*?

Q:  *Do you draw upon your own experiences with family and friends as you create characters and plots?*

A:  I think any writer would be lying if they said they never drew on personal experience, but I certainly don't start with family or friends as the basis for characters, although sometimes little bits of people I've met might creep in somewhere. A trigger for *Lullaby* was a real-life incident when I got separated from my baby son, but it was only a trigger. In BF, obviously my career as a TV director meant I understood the workings of that world, and I wanted to write about the responsibility we have towards the people we rely on to be in our programmes. Fortunately the rest of the book is definitely invented!

Q:  *Which writers do you particularly admire? What kinds of books have inspired you?*

A:  I'm a voracious reader and love all sorts of books from Miss Marple to psychological thrillers such as Nicci French's through to classic love stories like *Wuthering Heights* or Jean Rhys's *Wide Sargasso Sea* – the solution to Charlotte Bronte's mysterious and mad Mrs Rochester in *Jane Eyre*. As a teenager I vividly remember staying up all night reading Daphne du Maurier's *Rebecca*, driven to discover the secret of the missing character Rebecca and what Maxim de Winter really felt for her. I also like writers who have something to say about society without making it too obvious – like Jane Austen or Justin Cartwright.

Q:  *What is your daily writing routine?*

A:  With two small kids, I write when I can – it's as simple as that! A free hour and I'll be scribbling away in a café or at my computer if the house is empty . . .

Q:    *What are you working on next?*
A:    My third book! It features a heroine called Rose whose life might appear perfect but underneath it all, perhaps things are rather different. I'm fascinated by things not being what they seem . . .